THE
HAPPY
COUPLE

ALSO BY SAMANTHA HAYES

The Reunion
Tell Me a Secret
The Liar's Wife
Date Night

SAMANTHA HAYES

THE
HAPPY
COUPLE

bookouture

Published by Bookouture in 2020

An imprint of StoryFire Ltd.
Carmelite House
50 Victoria Embankment
London EC4Y 0DZ

www.bookouture.com

ISBN: 978-1-78681-747-6
eBook ISBN: 978-1-78681-746-9

For Simon… and TTTNAT

CHAPTER ONE

Now

Jo whips out her phone, quite used to her heart racing every time she hears it ring or ping.

It could be news.

She's also used to the rush of adrenaline burning through her body, dissipating in disappointment as soon as she sees her screen.

It's not Will. Not her missing husband.

Afterwards, she's left feeling frustrated, drained and useless, each false alarm a mini-trauma, though no one would know this to look at her. Barely a flicker of her eyes these days, and her palms hardly sweat any more. She wonders if her friends and family know what they do to her with their well-meaning calls and texts.

But each time, she thinks as she fumbles with her phone, *each time is one call closer to getting news. To knowing where he is.*

Jo remembers her counsellor telling her to look on the bright side, to stay positive. *What are you taking about?* she'd thought, mentally shaking her head, almost wanting to lash out as tears welled through a forced smile. *Not helpful. Not even close.* The woman clearly had no idea how she was feeling. But, a year later, she can see that maybe it *was* helpful, albeit in the simplest of ways.

Fake it till you make it, the counsellor had said, making Jo wonder if she's not doing as well as she thought – that she still needs to fake it because, even now, she's still not making it.

But what is it she is supposed to fake – Will's return, as if nothing has happened? She could do that, she supposes. Pretend he's there when he's not. In fact, she often does, although she can't help it. Has no say in when he comes. She sees him lying beside her in bed, hears him singing in the shower, smells the deliciousness of his Friday-night classic – jerk chicken with rice and peas, the thick, sweet smell seeping through the house. Happiness seems so long ago. As if it belonged to someone else.

No. She's sick of faking life.

'Easier said than done,' Jo mumbles as she answers her phone. She trips on a raised paving slab, almost running into a man wheeling his bike along.

'What is?' comes the voice down the line.

'Oh… oh, nothing,' Jo says, regaining her footing. 'Just me thinking out loud.' She glances back at the man with an apologetic look. She's relieved it's just Louise calling. She doesn't think she can cope with do-gooders as *that day* approaches. She doesn't want to use the word anniversary. Ever. That implies something to celebrate, to share, to mark another milestone. She hates it even *has* a date – a date she has no choice but to remember, live through for the rest of her life. It's tattooed on her soul.

Wednesday 20 May.

Sometimes she wishes Will had never existed, that they'd never met, and she hates herself for that.

'Well, don't,' Louise says. 'Thinking is dangerous, especially out loud.' She laughs. 'What are you doing?'

Louise. Her best friend. Straight to the point.

Jo slows her brisk walk – more in tune with how she's feeling, finally stopping and leaning on the railings of a park. Should she reveal that she's retracing the steps of the last walk she and Will took together the day before he vanished, that she's wondering if she might catch a trace of his aftershave on the breeze, spot a tissue or receipt from his pocket blowing along the pavement?

Should she mention that she's got a bagel in a paper bag, clutched in her right hand – salmon and cream cheese, the same as they'd had that day – most likely destined to end up in the park bin because she's not had an appetite in nearly a year?

Should she let on that, if she's honest with herself, she's hoping to catch a glimpse of Will amongst the lunchtime crowd, that even if it's not really him and just a figment of her exhausted mind, or someone who vaguely resembles him, simply imagining he's there would be enough?

'Getting lunch,' Jo replies, gripping the paper bag. It's a ritual she feels she must perform each day, even if food rarely passes her lips. Maybe a bite or two if she's in the mood. She hates how thin she's become, how she's taken to wearing baggy clothes to hide the jut of her collarbones, the sharp blades of her shoulders, the lack of tone to her once-fit legs. Her chestnut hair falls in straggly layers around her shoulders.

'Well, don't fill up too much,' Louise goes on. 'You're coming round for dinner tonight.'

'I am?'

'At seven,' she says. 'No need to bring anything except your cheery self. Archie's inviting a work colleague. He's new at the hospital but they've played squash a few times and—'

'No, Louise,' Jo replies as firmly as she can manage. What she really wants to say is *Christ, Lou, what are you trying to do – destroy me? Not only are you playing matchmaker with some innocent guy who would run a mile if he knew the truth about me, but you have just informed me, unwittingly or not, that Archie has a new squash partner. A squash partner who's not Will.*

'No?'

'No.'

'So, what, you're going to sob into your pillow with a bottle of cheap wine, maybe trawling the missing persons websites if your tears stop long enough for you to actually see straight?'

Jo waits a beat, a technique she's learnt to employ these last few months. *Fake it until you make it...*

'Yes.'

'Jo, when are you going to—'

'Sorry, Lou, got to go.'

Jo hangs up, not with any kind of angry flourish or jab of her screen. Louise will know from the tone of her voice that the boundary is set, that she is not furious with the world like she used to be (she has little energy left for that) but having dinner as part of a cosy foursome during the anniversary month is not something she can cope with. And yes, she'd rather sob into her pillow with a bottle of Echo Falls on the bedside table while scrolling through the faces of missing persons. One of them might, just *might*, be Will.

'Hey,' comes a voice beside her. A hand on her back. Jo freezes. 'Fancy some company?'

'Oh... sure,' she replies, turning to see Beth. Part of her wonders if she's followed her from the workshop, tailed her to the bakery and stalked her to the park. It happens too often – bumping into people she knows, well-meaning phone calls, friends 'popping in'. Jo also wonders if Louise has had words with everyone in her life, organising some kind of rota for keeping watch. She imagines they have a WhatsApp group to coordinate whose turn it is.

She was fine at lunchtime. Spotted by the park. Didn't eat her bagel though. Who's on night duty?

She loves Louise for caring, for always being there for her.

'There's some real warmth in that sun today,' Beth says, holding up a brown paper bag with the same bakery logo on as Jo's. 'Shall we go and sit down over there?'

'Why not?' Jo says, really wanting to be alone. But Beth is a harmless girl, quite new to the workshop and good at what she does. She wonders how much she knows – what, if anything, Margot has told her about her situation.

'You know, Jo, I really admire your...' Beth stops, prawn sandwich against her lips. She stares at the sky for a second. 'How you—'

'You don't have to say it,' Jo interrupts. She doesn't want the pity. 'It won't make any difference, but thanks for your concern.' She smiles.

Beth raises her eyebrows as she nibbles at the sandwich, staring at Jo. 'I was just going to say that I really admire your flair for making something amazing on a budget,' she continues, unfazed.

'Oh.' Jo shrugs and swallows, even though there's nothing but the taste of guilt in her mouth. 'Thank you.'

'Where did you train?'

'London,' Jo says. 'It's where Margot and I met. After our course, we moved up to the Midlands and started Sew Perfect.'

'That's cool,' Beth says, chewing. She stretches out in the sun – her legs clad in cream flares, feet in scuffed brown ankle boots. 'Respect to you both.'

Jo unwraps her bagel, taking a bite. Eating, she has decided is easier than talking.

'And look, I know I haven't known you that long, Jo, but Margot told me about... about *you know*, and I just wanted t say—'

'You don't have to say anything, Beth,' Jo says with her mouth full, knowing it was coming. She holds up her hand in a sto sign, smiling. 'Really.'

She's just being nice, Jo. Give the girl a break. It's hardly her fau your husband didn't come home from work. And not her fault almost a year since the first prickles of concern that afternoon h swollen into a full-blown fever by the next morning. When are going to accept that he's not coming back, that he didn't want you shakes her head, trying to silence the voice.

'So, remind me again where you worked before you joined Jo asks, quite used to changing the subject. It was Margot v

interviewed Beth a couple of months ago, saying she was just what they needed to move their little business forward.

'I was at college,' Beth says. 'And before that, I was a teaching assistant.'

Teaching, Jo thinks, feeling the pang in her heart. *Will was a teacher*, she wants to say but doesn't. Somehow, everything always comes back to Will. *A teacher and an actor. When he wasn't 'resting'*, she thinks with a smile. *How he hated people saying that. Will never rested. He had one of those minds that never stopped, audible even when he was sleeping.*

'Ah yes, that's right,' Jo replies, recalling what Margot had told her about their new employee. 'Local, wasn't it?' Jo asks, thinking the bagel actually tastes good.

'Just south of here,' Beth goes on. 'At a little village school. My daughter is a pupil there and it was easy for childcare, you know, to be able to work school hours. Hardly my dream job, but when she was old enough to do after-school clubs, I did a dressmaking course at college, and here I am. Working my way up stitch by stitch. Oh, and now that her dad's not being an idiot, he helps out more with childcare.' Beth accidentally spills some Marie Rose sauce on her pale jeans. She wipes it but makes it worse.

'I've got some Vanish back at the workshop,' Jo says with a wink. 'It removes everything.' *Even blood*, she thinks, just as her phone rings again, making her jump as she answers it.

'You're coming,' Louise says. 'Seven o'clock at mine, or else.' And she hangs up. Disappearing as if she was never there.

CHAPTER TWO

'You know what you need?'

Jo stands there, her hand outstretched to Louise, the fabric of her vintage velvet kimono quivering in time with her shaking arm. Little flutters of pale pink and black. *Me and Will*, she'd thought when she'd seen it at the flea market a couple of years ago. She'd had to buy it and Will loved her in it, especially with skinny jeans, her high boots. He couldn't keep his hands off her.

'Earth to Jo…'

'Sorry,' Jo says, taking the glass of wine.

'Fucking hell. Drink up. Stay over. Bed's made up.' Louise clatters the bottle back into the fridge.

'I—'

'What you need is a holiday. And random sex while *on* holiday.' She stands squarely in front of Jo, hands on her lower back, the way pregnant women do. Behind her, Jo sees Archie stirring something at the stove, hunched over the pan, meticulously adding a measure of this, a pinch of that as if he's performing an operation. The extractor hood hums noisily. Jo's eyes flick to him for help, but he's not looking. Likely not even listening.

So Jo sips her drink, silently squaring up to Louise with the briefest of smiles, knowing that she won't hear her when she says that no, she doesn't want a holiday without Will and she certainly doesn't want sex with a stranger. No holiday is right for her without

Will. What she needs is a holiday from her thoughts. What she needs is her husband back.

'Can't afford one,' Jo says, perching on a bar stool. Managing alone is tough, but her nose is still just above the waterline, though none of the work they'd started on the house is completed, and the car still needs new tyres. *And the bodywork needs sorting*, she thinks, a chill running through her. Despite her best efforts, the balance on the credit card she's had to take out gets worse each month.

In contrast, Louise and Archie's trendy warehouse apartment is all aluminium and rusty iron girders. High ceilings with exposed pipework and doors with trendy, waxed paintwork add to the designer look. Original parquet floors are littered with huge patterned rugs, and expanses of wall are painted in the darkest grey with empty, chunky white frames hanging in clusters, almost as if she and Archie have no history to display in them, no fond memories to share. Just the grey showing through.

Will and I have history to display, Jo thinks. *Oh, how much history we have! We could fill those frames with laughter and memories...*

Louise is particular about her apartment, doesn't put just anything on show. 'Statement pieces only,' she once said. 'My interior designer said the space can take maximum impact so we shouldn't clutter it with, well, clutter.'

The apartment ('flat' seems inappropriate, Jo has always thought) cost them a fortune but Louise had said it was 'future-proofing', explaining, with a hand on her belly, that they could be there for many years without the need to move.

'Space for several kids and top schools close by,' she'd said, as if she'd had the foresight to map out her future with only good things in it, whereas Jo had not. 'Plenty of room for when Speck is born,' she'd said after finding out she was pregnant. Her bump was hardly a speck any more, but the name had stuck. Unlike her and Will, when the time had come Louise and Archie had had no trouble conceiving.

Though Jo, as she glances through the full-height Crittall glass walls making up one side of the kitchen, can't imagine a child frolicking in the courtyard garden. Can't even imagine a baby in a pram out there, let alone felt-pen walls or ice-cream sofas.

'Garden's looking good,' she says, wanting to divert from the subject of holidays. *Though it's more Amazonian jungle than kid-safe haven,* Jo thinks. *And no room to kick a ball.* It's all philodendron and firepit. Painted wrought iron and Aperol spritz. Jo imagines a snake winding its way down the glass, its tongue flicking in and out.

'Even just a caravan for a week? By the sea. You like the sea, Jo.' Louise pulls out a stool beside her, leaning on the wooden top of the kitchen island as she balances herself. She's not letting up on the holiday. 'I'd offer you Mum and Dad's little cottage, but they're renting it out now. Airbnb.'

Jo whips back to the moment, smiling at Louise. 'Yes, yes I like caravans,' she says, knowing she would have refused the cottage even if it had been an option. She could never go back there – not after… She shudders, hoping Louise doesn't notice. 'They're so cosy, aren't they? The pitter-patter of the virtually guaranteed rain on the roof.' Her voice quivers, sounding almost delirious as it transforms into a laugh. She's trying, really she is, and ever grateful to Louise for trying to inspire her.

'Will and I stayed in a caravan at Harlyn Bay a few years ago. An autumn break to miss the crowds.' *Miss the higher prices,* she thinks but doesn't say, even though she knows Louise and Archie aren't like that, not in the least bit snobby. They like nice things, earn good money, but they like *real*, too. And they like – *liked* – her and Will. Part-time drama teacher and seamstress meet obstetrician and solicitor. But now they only have *her* to like, because Will is gone. Somehow Jo feels as if she's failed their best friends, let the side down. Last man standing, playing with only half a team.

'Oh, that'll be Ted,' Louise says at the sound of the buzzer, sliding off her stool and wriggling down her stretchy work skirt. Her tight top hugs her belly, her protruding navel the cherry on top.

You look beautiful pregnant, Jo thinks, watching her go to the intercom and buzz their guest in… *You're everything I hoped you'd be and more, everything* I *wanted to be.* Louise and Jo had been friends since high school, then lost touch in their twenties. But fate had brought them together again years later. *A woman, a wife, a lover, a professional… and soon to be a mother.* Jo smiles. *I'm so happy for you, Louise.*

'I'm so happy for you,' Jo says as she shakes hands with Ted. *Christ, did I actually say that?* 'Pleased… I mean, I'm so pleased to meet you,' she adds, forcing a smile, seeing Ted's confused expression.

'You too, Jo,' Ted says, his hand lingering around hers. Jo notices his easy manner, his kind eyes, and can see why Louise and Archie have befriended him. A replacement for their depleted portfolio.

Friends for all occasions, that's what Will once said, lying in bed, Jo's head resting on his shoulder, breathing in the scent of him after they'd tried yet again. And it's true – Louise matches her guests to the occasion like she matches her shoes to her handbags. Will reckoned they were their go-to 'guests for all occasions'. Solid. Dependable. And always good company. The reliable old-timers. Jo had laughed, trailing her fingers through the tight black fuzz of Will's chest. 'We're an awesome team,' she'd said, kissing him, feeling so happy.

And now we are not, Jo thinks as Ted finally relinquishes her hand. *Will and I are not awesome any more. Not a team. And neither am I happy.* Ted goes over to Archie at the stove, taking the glass of wine Louise offers as he's passing. Louise glances over at Jo, giving her one of those *it'll be OK* winks while touching her belly.

Several weeks ago, she asked Jo to be Speck's godmother. Jo said yes, even though she didn't want to be. Didn't want to be any kind of 'mother' if it wasn't a part of Will. They'd been trying to conceive naturally for the best part of two years and had finally succumbed to getting help, with their first round of IVF scheduled. And then Will disappeared.

'So you two met at work?' Jo says when they're eating. She lays down her knife and fork, glancing between the two men. She doesn't want to appear uninterested.

'On the squash court, to be precise,' Archie says, raising his eyebrows. 'But yes, Ted's in the department.'

Jo looks at Ted's hands, seeing they're equally as clean and smooth as Archie's. Big, capable hands, and she wonders how many babies they've delivered. Archie quoted her his stats once – it was in the thousands. Jo would only like one baby and now, at thirty-nine, falling in love with someone as deeply as she loved Will is not going to happen before her time is up. She can't betray Will's memory, even though she hates him for disappearing, pretty much wants to kill him for leaving her – if he isn't already dead.

'So go on, fess up. Who beat who?' Jo asks, forcing a smile.

'He's good,' Ted says. 'But not yet good enough.' His confidence doesn't just show in the tone of his voice but in the way his shoulders sit broadly in his fitted pale blue shirt, his strong forearms, his purposeful laugh and those kind eyes. *He's nice*, Jo thinks. *But not nice enough. Not Will.* She knows Louise has arranged tonight on purpose. Thinks it's time for her to move on.

'There's a casual ongoing competition between staff,' Archie explains. 'I was hands-down winner until Dr Mason muscled in.' He laughs.

'Everyone needs a good shake-up from time to time,' Ted bats back, eyeing Jo over the rim of his glass. Jo feels a sweat break out.

'Excuse me,' she says, retreating to the toilet, leaning her head back against the door when she's alone, sighing out. *Will, Will, Will...* she thinks. *You'd like it here tonight, your cool wit quite able to take on Dr Mason and Archie. Your smooth voice out-smoothing the pair of them, me watching you, loving you, appreciating you. Maybe I didn't do that enough. Appreciate you.*

She flushes, washes her hands and returns to the table, steadier now she's had a moment. She has to go with them, the 'moments'. Succumb to time out, reset herself, however long it takes. Sometimes it's days of shutting herself away.

'Louise tells me you're planning a holiday,' Ted says as Jo picks up her knife and fork again.

Jo flashes her a look. 'She did?'

'Can't you tell she needs one?' Louise says, getting away with it only because of the caring undertones.

'I'm fine,' Jo says by way of defence. 'It's just the cost of it. You know…' She smiles again, a brief glance up from her plate. 'Holidays are expensive and every penny counts right now.'

'Have you ever thought of house-sitting?' Ted says. 'It's free and there are some beautiful places to be had. A pal of mine does it. You know, one of those drifter types who gets off feeding other people's dogs and living their dreams by proxy. He's a writer. Well, he wants to be a writer, hence the "no fixed abode" all being part of his bohemian image.' Ted laughs. 'But seriously, it could be an option for you.'

'That's a great idea, Ted,' Jo hears Louise say as she tries to imagine herself in someone else's home. She can't.

'Well, I…'

'You should investigate,' Archie chimes in. 'I bet there are websites.'

'Indeed there are,' Ted says. 'Sitters and owners are all rated and have feedback so you know what you're getting into. You could pick somewhere by the coast or the Lakes. Even overseas.'

Three against one, Jo thinks as she listens to the well-meaning chit-chat, zoning out, their voices fading as she imagines going on holiday – just her and Will. They'd been planning a break on the South Coast but hadn't managed it, other commitments getting in the way. She catches her breath as she sees him standing over by the fireplace, elbow leaning on the mantelpiece, watching her with smiling eyes. Proud eyes.

Jo shakes her head, taking a sip of her drink. And, when she looks up again, Will is gone.

Later, at home, having declined Louise's offer to stay, Jo's phone pings. Her hand reaches out to the bedside table, clattering her glasses and watch onto the floor as she frantically hoists herself up onto her elbow, fumbling for the lamp switch. Her heart thumps. It's late. That's a good sign... someone texting her late.

Will...

But it's not.

I've signed you up. Have a look.

And then Louise sends login details for a website.

For what seems like the entire night, Jo lies awake, staring at the ceiling. When she's certain sleep won't come, she fetches her laptop, balancing it on her crossed legs as she sits on the bed. After she's proved to herself once and for all that it's a silly idea, that she really doesn't want to be feeding pets and cutting lawns for other people, she'll go on the missing persons websites. It's been twelve hours since she last looked. A lot can happen in twelve hours – it took a lot less than that for Will to disappear, after all.

But then she wonders if Louise is right, if time away from home would help her recharge, help her heal. Even a single hour that isn't filled with wondering where he is – either hating him for leaving his life, for leaving *her*, or grieving for him because he's dead – would be a respite. And a respite, if she's honest with herself, is what she needs more than anything.

Just, for the briefest of moments, not to have to think about Will.

CHAPTER THREE

Did you look at the website?

Jo glances at her phone screen. She can't reply to Louise's text right now. The alterations need finishing by lunchtime and delivering back to the theatre straight after. The tech rehearsal is scheduled for this afternoon and the last-minute adjustments are key to the entire production.

Well?

Jo wants to put her phone on silent but knows she can't, never will. Just in case. If she'd had time to reply, she thinks as she changes the spool on her machine, then she'd have said Yes. House-sitting is not for me though but thanks x. Jo glides the fabric of the seam through the machine, removing the pins as she goes, each stitch taking her closer to the end of the day when she can go home and shut the front door on the world. She imagines Will is waiting for her, having made that amazing sticky pork dish of his (his mother's recipe), the smell of it announcing his return even before she sees him. She talks to him every night. And he always answers.

Louise says I should do a house-sit, of all things, she'll say later. *Instead of a holiday. Doesn't sound great, does it, cleaning up someone else's cat mess?*

Will would laugh then, she knows that. *What, you're going away* without *me?* he'd reply before rolling his eyes, flashing her that smile of his. Jo would laugh for a moment, too, watch him standing there, wooden spoon in hand, twinkle in his eye. But then she'd start shaking her head, slowly at first as her eyes filled with tears, crinkling up as the sobs came.

Well, you went away without me… she'd scream, before hurling the pan across the room.

And when she opened her eyes, he'd be gone. Just as gone as he is now.

'Oww!' she cries, sucking on the bead of blood on her forefinger. Beth tosses the box of plasters her way, three pins held between her lips. There are many such boxes dotted about. No actor wants *real* blood on their costume.

What about South Wales? Didn't you and Will go there once?

It's clear Louise isn't going to let up.

Can't chat now. Crazy busy here, Jo messages back, but it's too late. There are two drops of scarlet on the cream silk skirt.

When she gets home, the house is quiet. Of course. Jo closes the front door behind her, turning the key, putting the chain on then taking it off again, removing the key from the lock. If he were to return in the middle of the night, she wants him to be able to get in.

No cooking smells. No aroma of sticky pork in the air. No Radio 4 on for Will to turn down to a simmering background noise when she comes in, dumping her bag on the table as he gives her a kiss. Will usually got in before her – unless he was in a play, rehearsing or performing. Then it would be much later, sometimes the early hours. *I couldn't get out of the after-show party, Jo-jo, you know what it's like…* But when he was teaching, he was home by five. He would have turned the heating up if it was cold outside, or lit the coal fire in their small, square living room, plumping up the cushions on their saggy sofa, the one from Gumtree that was going cheap.

'Hi,' Jo says out of habit. She flicks on the kitchen light. It might be early May but it's gloomy and wet outside. 'How was your day?'

Year Seven were little shits, as ever, she imagines him replying. *But there's that one kid, reminds me so much of me at that age. Something stuck inside him, as though he needs to express himself through acting. I'll bring him out of himself, you watch.*

Jo smiles, remembering the school play. 'The show must go on,' someone had said, even though Will, drama teacher at Wroxdown High School, had been missing a month and a half by then.

She'd watched the performance through blurry vision, tears rolling down her cheeks, and sitting at the back so she could duck out as soon as the curtain dropped in the school theatre. And the kid certainly did Will proud. The kid who had something stuck inside him. In fact, it was parts of Will she saw coming out on the stage that night, little flourishes of her husband who had clearly taught him well. The intonation, the motivation, his presence as he lost himself entirely in the character. And now Will is the one who's lost.

Jo opens the fridge and stares inside. Half a packet of spinach, slimy at the edges. A small piece of mouldering pecorino, a dish of chickpeas with condensation on the cling film, two tomatoes and three slices of bacon. And a bottle of wine. Well, the remains of a bottle of wine. She clatters it out, sloshing some into a tumbler. The *European way*, Will had once said, and she'd liked that. Still did it now.

Jo sits down at the small kitchen table, glass in one hand, fingernails of the other gouging into the woodgrain. Her phone pings in her bag, making her jump.

So? Did you look yet? Get on with it then I can get you and
Ted together again to discuss it. He likes you.

Jo sighs at the winking emoji and fetches her laptop, knowing
she'll get no peace until she checks out the house-sitting site properly. She got as far as the home page last night but then diverted
to the missing persons forum. There were no new responses to
her pleas for help.

Double-checking the details Louise sent last night, Jo logs into
the already created account on the House Angels website, rolling
her eyes at the password Louise chose – T3d&joj0. After a few
minutes, she's familiarised herself with how it works and clicks
randomly on some featured properties at the top of the main page.

Two weeks in a lighthouse in beautiful Mull?
Hillwalker's delight… three Dalmatians in Snowdonia need you!
Reliable horse lover wanted for month in Dorset – allowance paid.

'Wow, people actually do this,' Jo says, sipping her wine. 'Well,
I have no idea how to look after horses,' she says to herself, eyes
fixed on the screen as she clicks on another property.

Jo taps in more detailed search criteria. Dogs, check. Cats,
check. Small pets, check. Light cleaning duties, check. General
house security, check. Lawn care and weeding… she hovers over
this one, checking the box and unchecking it. Since Will went,
she's struggled to keep up with their garden. It's only a small patch
at the back of their terraced house, but the grass always seems to
need cutting and the weeds somehow multiply faster than she can
pull them out. For now, she leaves it ticked. Then she clicks a few
other boxes: general errands, taking deliveries, and suchlike. But
when it comes to location, she's stumped.

She doesn't really want to go anywhere. What if Will comes
back while she's away?

'Brighton is nice,' Jo says, pretending she's talking to herself
but really it's to Will. It's the kind of vibrant place she could get

lost in. Better to have the buzz of people around her so she doesn't drown in her own thoughts, plus she knows Will liked it there. And he loved – *loves* – the coast. *But then it'll just be full of happy couples*, she thinks, deciding that, if she's really considering doing this, rural might be better. No one at all around apart from cows, sheep and whatever animals she'd be in charge of. The solitude might be good for her.

She clicks on a few counties on the interactive map: Yorkshire, Derbyshire, Norfolk, Suffolk, Cornwall, Devon, Somerset… all beautiful places. But she can't think of a single reason to go to any of them. Jo idly clicks on a few of the properties that come up on her search list. Some are requesting house-sitters with a review count of at least ten. Some are for a month or more. Some look like properties she couldn't possibly cope with and one or two frankly look as though they want pulling down.

'Not much of a holiday to be had there,' she says, wide-eyed at the pictures of the shack-like place. 'And what about the owner's personal stuff?' she says to herself, sipping her wine and scrolling other properties. 'I wouldn't want a stranger rooting through *my* belongings,' she adds, shaking her head and glancing up as if Will is there.

'Oh,' she says, clicking on an image of a thatched cottage. 'This looks nice…' She imagines Will already there when she arrives, standing at the stove, apron on, candles lit, music playing, the spicy scent of his Caribbean cooking in the air.

She whips round, grabbing the back of the chair, tears in her eyes. 'Where the hell did you *go*?' she says, almost shouting as she stares around the empty kitchen. 'How could you just *leave* me?' she yells. She wants to cry, but can't any more. In the early days, the tears came hot and fast, burning her cheeks, streaking her eye make-up down her cheeks.

Now, she's just plain angry.

Found anywhere?

I'm looking, Jo texts back.

The nightly cry used to release the chemical build-up of the day, helping her stay asleep – albeit a fitful sleep. Now, if she does drop off before midnight, she's usually awake again at 2 a.m. Then at three, four, five. Staring at the ceiling, wondering, thinking. The alarm is set for seven but she never needs it.

'Must like reptiles,' Jo says, unable to help the smile. 'That's no holiday.' She winces at the photos of the two snakes that would be her charges. She shudders, returning to the main list.

What about Hastings?

Jo looks up at the sound of his voice. In her mind, Will is standing there, the tea towel wrapped around his big dark hands. *We were thinking of going to that B & B there, do you remember?* he says.

Jo stares at him, not wanting to speak, not wanting to destroy the magic of him, have him dissolve again. *Yes, yes I remember,* she thinks. *The rooms looked so cosy, the open fires, the views, the beach walks. But we never made it…*

Go on, have a look, Will says as Jo takes another sip of her wine. When she looks up again, he's gone.

'Hastings,' she types in the search box, not even remembering which county it's in. They'd wanted an escape, needed a long weekend away, with Will suggesting the area, telling her that someone had given him the idea. Even though Will hadn't got the part he'd recently auditioned for and money would be tight for a couple of months, the voucher website had a deal they could just afford. But when they'd finally got round to planning it, the only dates they could manage had been booked up. Instead, they'd made do with a lock-in weekend by their own fire at home. Phones switched off, their favourite food in the fridge, a stack of movies with the wine bottle beside them. They spent most of it on the sofa or in bed… just *being*.

Now neither of them was being. One gone, one barely existing. 'Ten sixty-six and all that,' Jo mutters, remembering, as the search list pops up. 'Good place for a seamstress, you said,' she reminds Will, glancing up to where she'd imagined him standing. 'OK… what have we got here?' She turns back to the screen, scanning the results. 'This one's not bad. Two Labradors need long daily walks,' Jo reads. 'And because our house is isolated, we don't like to leave it empty.' Jo quickly clicks off the property, perturbed by the bars on the windows, and that it's set in the middle of nowhere.

A few other properties look vaguely interesting, with one in a village not far from where she and Will had planned to go. 'This one's really nice,' Jo says, clicking on the property.

She reads out the description. 'Someone caring and kind needed to look after my elderly cat and crazy spaniel. Ten days mid-May. Light housekeeping and some gardening, but feel free to use my home as yours. I travel a lot so I'm quite used to house-sitters. Non-smokers only and a love of houseplants essential!'

Promising, Jo thinks, clicking through the photographs. Fifteen in total. Everything from a close-up of the sleeping cat to the bouncy dog… the kitchen, the garden, the bedrooms, the living room, the garden. The local area.

The living room.

Jo clicks back, freezing. Staring at the picture.

Then she looks up slowly, looking for Will, waiting for her mind to play tricks on her.

When he doesn't appear, she stares down at her laptop screen again. Blinking.

Her eyes drifting in and out of focus.

The living room.

She looks up again, hardly daring to breathe. Will is back briefly, smiling. Making that silly face of his. *What are you waiting for?*

Jo turns back to her laptop, her shaking finger accidentally clicking on another photograph – the bedroom with its painted wooden floor and pretty white bed linen.

'Oh my God…' she says, panting, breathless, her finger suddenly useless on the mouse as she tries to go back. She shakes her head, knowing she must be seeing things again, that it can't possibly be real.

'Living room, living room…' she mutters, fumbling, clicking back one more picture, then another and another. She leans in closer, zooming in on the mantelpiece.

Photographs. Right there. Three of them. Clear as day.

She clutches her face, pressing her fingers into her cheeks.

She squints. Rubs her eyes in case she's imagining it.

'Oh my *God*…'

Jo turns round, scans her now-empty kitchen. Gets up. Presses her forehead against the wall, hands splayed on the plaster, then pulls at her hair.

She sits down again. Focuses on the screen.

Blinking hard.

On the mantelpiece, in the photograph of the house-sit living room, Jo clearly sees three pictures of Will. She refreshes the image over and over and over, and each time they are still there.

Will. In someone else's home.

CHAPTER FOUR

Three adult bridesmaids, three young bridesmaids – one of whom is very young and won't stand still for more than fifteen seconds as Jo tries to pin her hem. 'Hey, sweetie,' she says, her lips pursed from the pin stuck between them. 'Hold still a few more minutes, then you can see what I've got in the cookie jar over there.' She takes the pin, sliding it into the hem which she'll hand-stitch later. She's not been able to concentrate all day.

The kid swings round, grizzling. 'Don't, Charlotte darling,' her mother says. 'Let the nice lady sort your dress. You want to be a special girl at Aunty Sarah's wedding, don't you?' The kid grizzles again. Jo ignores the ache in her lower back from stooping to the hem, even though little Charlotte is standing on a platform.

'Nearly there,' she says, knowing that at least the ten-year-old twins will stay still as she works. Finally, she stands back, asking the mum to slowly turn her daughter around as she inspects the length. 'Good, I think that's it.' Jo checks the fit of the waist, the give on the shoulders of the pink, puff-sleeved dress. The wedding isn't for another month yet but a three-year-old can grow a lot in that time.

'There,' she says fifteen minutes later after she's pinned up the twins' hems. 'If you all slip out of the gowns now, I'll have them done by the end of the day. Now we know you're in silk pumps, there won't be any more alterations necessary.' Jo smiles and stands up, watching as the three women and the children retreat into the changing area. 'Just watch you don't knock the pins out when you undress,' she calls out. 'I'll put the kettle on.'

Jo knows their bridal clients like to make a thing out of the fittings – it's a social event for them as much as anything. 'You happy?' she asks Sarah, the bride-to-be as she watches on from the armchair, her fitting already taken care of. Her hands are resting on her burgeoning belly and Jo is happy she's allowed enough room in her dress for an extra month's baby growth. She stares at it for a beat too long – long enough for Sarah to look uncomfortable.

'Very,' Sarah smiles warmly. 'I just love what you've done with my dress. I was so worried I was going to look like a tent. Or, you know, one of those floaty summer gazebo things. But I don't. Gary's going to pass out when he sees me.'

'Good, that's good,' Jo says, filling the kettle in the kitchen area of the bridal room. She and Margot redid the interior themselves a year ago, painting the walls a soft and calming shade of grey with swathes of white brocade and voile at the French doors for privacy, even though they look out over a private courtyard. For summer fittings, they open it up, serve Prosecco if the bride wants.

'Here, help yourself to cupcakes,' Jo says, checking the dresses are all hung up and well out of the way. The little girl dives in, her mother rescuing the cake from the grip of her eager fingers, sitting her on her knee and popping pieces into her mouth.

'Do you have children, Jo?' Sarah asks, adjusting her stretchy top over her belly.

'Nooo,' Jo laughs too loudly, too self-consciously. 'No, no I don't,' she adds. 'None at all.' She smiles, checking everyone has a cup of tea. 'No.'

And then Will is on her mind again – more than on her mind. She swears she sees him standing in the corner, watching her, grinning, arms folded in that way of his with one foot crossed over the other, head tilted.

You shouldn't be in here, she thinks. *There are women changing.*

Don't worry, I waited until everyone was decent, he replies in her head.

'Decent,' Jo says wistfully, holding the plate of cakes.

'Totally,' Sarah says. 'Such a nice idea to have afternoon tea as well. It's so exciting that…' But Sarah's voice fades away as Jo stands there, staring at the pale grey wall that just a moment ago was the backdrop to Will.

And then the house-sitting website is on her mind again. It's barely left her thoughts all day.

When the clients have drained the tea and eaten the cakes, and arrangements have been made for delivery of the dresses, Jo flops down into the armchair, still warm from Sarah and her bump.

'Hi Lou,' Jo says a moment later, answering her phone. Her mouth is dry. She can't explain to Louise, to *anyone*, what she saw on that website. Doesn't want to explain it to *herself*, even.

Will. Photos of him. In someone else's house.

'So?' Louise says. 'And?'

'And what?'

'Did you apply for a house-sit? For a holiday? I'm worried about you.'

Jo makes a face. 'Why are you so keen for me to get away?'

'Do I even need to answer that, Jo-jo?'

Jo winces a little. Only Will's ever called her that. But she knows Louise is only trying to make her feel OK, to keep the familiar alive. And she's right, she does need a holiday. But what she saw has changed everything.

'There was… there was one property that looked interesting.'

'Good. Where?'

'Near the South Coast.'

'Nice,' Louise says. 'Much of a menagerie, or house care only? What made you choose the south?'

'Cat and dog. And… and…' She pauses, thinking.

If she and Will hadn't planned that romantic weekend near Hastings, had she not wanted to somehow feel close to him, imagining what it would have been like for the pair of them if they actually *had* gone away, then she'd never have thought to search for a house-sit in East Sussex. She can't fully remember where the idea of Hastings came from, though she thinks Will mentioned a colleague at work recommended it, but she's not sure if it was at the school or the theatre. *Maybe another teacher*, she thinks. And then she'd spotted the B & B doing a special deal on the voucher website.

'I was wondering,' Louise says. 'Maybe we could go together. You know, a girls' break. It would do us both good.'

'Oh. No,' Jo says back too quickly. Her heart thumps. She doesn't even know if she's going herself yet, hasn't applied, may not even get accepted. The thought of reaching out to a stranger who has photos of her missing husband on the mantelpiece makes her feel nauseous. Especially as she should really be getting in touch with the police, telling them what she saw. But she can't. She *absolutely* can't. Just in case... And certainly not until she's found out more for herself.

Besides, she hasn't absorbed it properly yet. Still wonders if it's her imagination playing tricks. She keeps checking the screenshots she took of the website on her phone, zooming in, looking at them in different lights. There's no mistaking it's Will – especially on the close-up photo of the cosy log burner, flames burning bright, the fat oak beam above it bedecked with fairy lights and candles. And the three large photographs of Will, leaning against the bare brickwork of the chimney as if he were part of a shrine.

'You can't come, Lou,' Jo says, not meaning to sound abrupt. 'It's too close to your due date. You need to stay near the hospital. Near Archie. Near everything familiar.'

'Guess you're right,' Louise says flatly, instinctively knowing not to crow too much about Speck's imminent arrival. Jo is happy for her friends, of course – knows they are ecstatic about their baby, too – but she also knows that Louise has played down her pregnancy, almost been reserved about it, despite Jo insisting she should just act normally, that if she and Will were meant to have conceived then... *he wouldn't have disappeared, would he?*

'Anyway, it's probably best I take the time to be alone. You know. To reflect. On stuff.'

'I understand,' Louise says, pausing for a moment. 'Have you applied?'

'No, no, I haven't yet,' Jo says, suddenly feeling light-headed at the thought. 'I'm still thinking about it. Anyway, I've got to go, Lou.' And the two women say their goodbyes.

Oh, Christ... she thinks. *What the hell am I supposed to do?*

Jo opens up the screenshots on her phone again, shaking her head slowly, biting her lip. 'I'm sure I've seen these photos before,' she whispers to herself. 'I think I probably *took* them.' She stares at them a moment longer before pulling up the contact number of the family liaison officer she was assigned at Warwickshire Police. PC Janine Daniels. A pleasant woman, Jo thinks, remembering her visits in the early days. But they soon fell away as the police enquiries scaled down after several months.

'People go missing,' the officer in charge of the case had told her when they'd run out of leads and, most likely, resources to keep the search going. 'And what you have to remember is that sometimes they don't want to be found.'

Jo tucks her phone back in her bag, staring out of the window, not knowing what to do.

CHAPTER FIVE

Then

The first time I met Will Carter, I was down on bended knee.

'Shouldn't it be the other way around?' were his first words to me as I stooped beneath him.

And 'Oh Christ, I'm *so* sorry!' were my first words to him. I'd managed to stick myself in the cheek with the same pin that I'd just jabbed into Will's thigh, unable to help the squeak.

'Blood brothers now,' Will said from above. I looked up. My smile matched his.

'I'm so, *so* sorry. I… I'm not usually this chaotic.' My hand shook as I reached for another pin from the pot on the floor. 'Well, actually,' I said, pausing. 'Some would argue with that.' I laughed nervously.

'I wouldn't argue with you about anything,' Will said calmly in that deep voice of his that I would come to love so much.

I glanced up again, my left hand folding in the brocade fabric of his split breeches while the fingers of my right hand carefully slid the pin in place so I knew where to stitch it to prevent the same thing happening again – a large split seam where there really shouldn't have been one. Apparently there had been complaints. There were schoolchildren in the audience.

'I didn't see a problem with it, actually,' Will added, a wry smile breaking. 'I was wearing full hose beneath.'

I kept my eyes firmly focused on the fabric, trying to stop the smile, choking back the nervous laughs. 'I don't think it's your hose that was the problem,' I said, daring a quick glance up. 'Right, that should do it. Keeps the feel of the costume without being too—'

'Revealing?'

'Exactly.'

'Well, nice work, Mrs...?' Will raised one eyebrow, another little trait I'd come to love over the following months. The following years.

'Oh, it's not Mrs,' I said immediately. 'It's Miss. Miss Langham, and pleased to meet you... Mr Carter.' I stood up, trying to be graceful except I lost my balance and my foot caught the pot of pins as I staggered, upending them everywhere. I froze, my shoulders dropping briefly, my head shaking, as I bent down to pick them up. Before I could protest, Will was down on his hands and knees helping me.

Cast and crew members were bustling around as some of the actors were called to rehearse a specific scene. Aside from breeches splitting and a few other costume glitches, there had been some technical issues that needed ironing out. The play had only been running a week and had garnered some pleasing national reviews.

''Scuse me there,' a prop hand said, wheeling part of the set past, ushering Will and me aside. He ran over the remaining pins.

'I'm not needed for a while,' Will said, standing up and squeezing close to me as the backstage bustle took hold. 'I shall change out of my breeches in order that you may stitch them up before it is time, once again, for me to tread the boards.'

I laughed at his silly, overstated voice and hand flourishes, giving a quick salute in return. 'I'll be right here, with my needle and thread awaiting said breeches.' My eyes locked onto his for a second. Then I shook my head. 'It won't take me long,' I added. 'To... to stitch them up. I'll have you put back together in no time.'

Will walked off, his gaze lingering on mine as he glanced back before heading down to his dressing room.

Meantime, I busied myself with tweaks and tidy-ups on other costumes that had already suffered the ravages of the first week after opening. Margot and I worked tirelessly keeping the garments pristine, organising both the laundering and dry-cleaning as well as general repairs. There were always buttons to be sewn back, rips to stitch up, embellishments to replace and alterations if a cast member either felt uncomfortable or had put on or lost a few pounds.

Having been through college together, Margot and I were a dedicated team with big plans. One day, we swore, we'd have our own business premises – we'd already chosen the name. Sew Perfect was going to be the go-to place in the county for unique designs and professional alterations, with an emphasis on bridal. We'd been trained by the best in London, but had moved back to the Midlands when we couldn't afford the rent in the south. But for now, what we were doing – ducking and diving from one job to another – sufficed. We were still young – in our mid-twenties – and, compared to many our age, already living the dream. Albeit in a shared studio flat with piecemeal dressmaking work, stints waitressing or working behind a bar, and a few weeks here and there signing on when necessary. But mainly, we were loving life.

'I saw him looking at you,' Margot said, her prominent jaw jutting, her eyes twinkling. 'Othello.' She swung her legs back and forth, perched on a couple of stacked crates backstage.

'Oh, stop it,' I said, glancing towards the door that led down to the dressing rooms. 'He's hot, though,' I admitted. 'And I *really* didn't mind pinning up his breeches.'

'Need more room, did he?'

I took a playful swipe at Margot just as Will re-emerged wearing jeans and a T-shirt that clung to his broad chest. He approached us as we sat side by side sipping from cans of Coke.

'I wouldn't trust anyone else with my breeches, Miss Langham,' Will said, holding them out to me.

'Just so you know, it wasn't me who made them in the first place. Had I sewn these beauties from scratch, you would have had no embarrassing splits onstage.'

Margot made a noise, almost choking on her Coke.

'I am perfectly sure that would be the case,' he replied, sitting down next to me as Margot slipped away. 'So, what got you into all this?' he asked. His voice was treacle, his black skin equally as tantalising. With his kind eyes and broad shoulders, Will's proximity seemed to take away my ability to speak. Normally I prided myself on quick wit and banter when it came to guys. But I'd not had a proper relationship since finishing college in London several years ago, and I was suddenly wondering if I'd left my confidence back there, too.

'Oh, you know. I always just made things. Dresses for my Barbie dolls. Clothes for me when I was a teenager and had no money. I'd buy jumble sale bargains and cut them up, make something new. That kind of thing. And then I ended up training professionally. So how about you? Why an actor?'

'Why not?' Will replied cryptically. 'I can be anyone I want, which, more often than not, is better than being me.'

I thought about this, inwardly agreeing and disagreeing with him. Everyone needed to escape themselves occasionally but the way he said it sounded almost… ominous, as though there was something wrong with him that even he needed to avoid. But I brushed it off. I barely knew the guy and wasn't about to judge him on a throwaway comment.

'But acting isn't my full-time job, sadly. Since I left college, I've also been working as a drama teacher. Bit of a baptism of fire at the school I'm at, but hopefully my wit and charm will win the little buggers round.'

'Wow,' I said, impressed, thinking that must be a tough job, especially as I guessed Will was only in his mid- to late twenties himself. While I'd had huge respect for the staff at my school, whatever their age, I remembered how some of the kids gave the younger teachers a hard time.

'Meantime, I'm hoping my semi-pro acting will get me spotted. My agent has high hopes.'

'You have an agent?' I was even more impressed.

'Yeah, and I've had a couple of small TV parts. *Holby, East-Enders*, a couple of period dramas. But theatre is my main love.'

I smiled, looking at him sideways, not knowing what to say. There was something between us – a spark, perhaps – I felt sure of it, but it wouldn't be the first time I'd had a leading-man crush and that had never ended well. I may as well have not existed with the last one – he'd barely noticed my shaking fingers as I stitched up the braiding on his jacket at close quarters, let alone the rest of me. I should listen to my gut this time, I decided. Listen to what sensible-and-together Louise would tell me now that we were back in touch. I'd always admired my oldest friend's wisdom, boundaries and sense of self. And I should definitely not listen to Margot, who was hovering nearby, giggling and making gestures to me from behind the wing curtains. I forced myself not to look, suppressing the laughter.

'Do you fancy getting a bite to eat after we're done here, Miss Langham? Maybe at that new pizza place around the corner? I'm starving.'

I thought for a moment. It was Monday and there was no performance tonight. Usually, I'd go home, get an early night, or perhaps work on some new patterns. Margot and I had been designing and making bridesmaids' dresses to sell at bridal fairs. Everything we'd made so far had sold instantly.

'You know what?' I said, sliding off the crate and building up to the *I'm going to get an early night* excuse. But I paused. Looked into Will's large, deeply dark eyes and swallowed. Well, I *tried* to swallow but it was hard, as if every automatic function in my body now needed forcing or overthinking. 'That would, well I'm, um… that, actually that would be lovely,' I said, going against what the voices in my head – mainly Louise's – were screaming at me. I knew my closest friend only had my best interests at heart, remembering how I'd been hurt and messed about one too many times, even at the age of twenty-six, but right now I was simply listening to myself. What *I* wanted. 'I'd love that. I'd really love to have pizza with you after I've stitched up your breeches, Mr Othello.'

And that was that.

CHAPTER SIX

Now

On Monday nights, Jo used to do Pilates. Often Will would have a script run-through or, if it was term time, he would sometimes schedule a school play rehearsal if there was one in production, and Jo would let herself into an empty house after work. She knew Will liked to go out for a drink either with work colleagues or other cast members. 'Helps our onstage chemistry,' he explained. 'If we know what makes each other tick.'

'Will,' she'd replied with a grin, holding onto his arm. 'You don't have to justify going out for a beer with your mates. It's fine. If anyone at Pilates was under the age of sixty and up for it, I'd probably do the same.' She'd kissed him then, grabbed her mat and headed out.

'Another normal Monday night, then,' Jo says to herself now, dumping her bag and keys on the kitchen table, knowing things are far from normal. 'Alone.' Automatically, she heads to the fridge, pulls out the remains of a bottle of wine, pours a glass, wondering why she's even bothering with the glass. She hasn't turned on the light in the kitchen and the peachy dusk casts an eerie glow in the room.

Shivering, though not cold, Jo heads to the little sitting room, taking her laptop with her, and curls her feet under her legs on the sofa. She opens it up, hardly daring to look at the website again.

If she hadn't taken the screenshots on her phone, looked at them disbelievingly several times throughout the day, she'd have gone the last twenty-four hours thinking that she'd dreamt it or had perhaps taken one too many sleeping pills or antidepressants, and that her mind was playing tricks. She was still struggling to come to terms with what she'd seen – photos of Will in someone else's house. How could it even be possible?

She picks up her phone, turns it round and round in her hands. Goes into her contacts and pulls up PC Daniels' number again. *Should I call? Should I tell the police what I've seen?* She takes a large sip of wine, shaking her head, sighing heavily. *It's the right thing to do, but how can I?* Her thoughts knot into a tangle. *What if it's to do with…* She shudders again, dropping her phone onto the cushions. She can't do it. Not yet. Not until she knows more. *Will would not be happy…*

Jo logs onto the House Angels website, her fingers trembling as she types the silly password Louise cooked up. Which reminds her – she hasn't replied to Louise's earlier text.

Ted wants your number. You OK with that?

No, no I am not OK with that, Jo thinks, tapping out a quick reply to the same effect, grateful at least that Louise has asked first. While she knows her best friend's attempts at getting her back 'out there' and dating are well intentioned, they're unwanted. Jo does not want to date. She does not want to meet another man. She just wants Will back. And now she has a lead. The most solid lead since he disappeared.

'Can you think of any reason at all why your husband may have had to take off and leave? However insignificant it may seem,' the officer, PC Logan, had said at that first meeting nearly a year ago, after she'd made the call to the police. Will had been missing twenty-four hours by the time they came out. The officer had cleared his throat. 'Including personal reasons.'

Jo had sat silent, thinking, tearing her mind apart in search of anything helpful she could tell the police. She shook her head. 'I mean, we're not up to our eyeballs in debt or anything like that,' she said softly. 'There's the mortgage, but it's just about manageable. The car's bought on tick but we really need it, and again, it's budgeted for, though… there are a few repairs that need doing. But we have the emergency fund for that.' Jo dug her nails into her palms, not wanting to discuss the car. 'Will refuses to have credit cards or personal loans, and we don't owe any family members money. There's not a lot left over at the end of the month, but we're OK. Will is not running away because of debt.' Jo was sure about that.

'What about gambling, or drinking? Is it possible your husband has run up a secret debt and has taken off because he's scared?'

Jo was already shaking her head before he finished the sentence. 'No, no, that's ludicrous. Will doesn't gamble. He won't even buy a lottery ticket. Sometimes we'll have some wine, and he likes a few beers, but he's not an alcoholic. Far from it.' She was uneasy that the two officers were sitting in her living room, laboriously handwriting notes, taking her statement, wasting time. *You should be out there looking for him!*

'I'm afraid the next couple of questions might seem intrusive, but they could help us with the inquiry. How was your husband's mental health, Mrs Carter? Did he suffer from low mood at all, or depression? Has he ever self-harmed or taken drugs – prescription or otherwise?'

'Will?' Jo said, sounding almost surprised, as if she'd never considered the possibility. 'What, you mean you think he might have…?' She bowed her head and sighed. She couldn't bear the thought… Will alone at the edge of a cliff or on a high bridge.

Sitting in his car with a hosepipe inserted through the window from the exhaust – it was unthinkable. Except the car was left at his work car park, and his keys, wallet and phone were found on his desk in the small office he shared with the other drama department staff.

'It's something we have to consider,' PC Logan replied. He was a big man, probably only late twenties, and his thick upper arms bulged out of his short-sleeved shirt. Jo thought he looked trussed up in his police garb, things attached to him everywhere, his radio crackling intermittently until he turned it down.

'Well, I... I...' Jo had stared out of the window then, praying for Will to walk down the street and up their short garden path. If nothing else, it would end this grilling. 'He was fine, as far as I know.' Jo swallowed. *Should I tell them?* she'd thought. *Should I tell him he'd been distracted and nervous ever since...* But then they'd ask her 'ever since *what*', and that she couldn't possibly answer. 'He seemed absolutely fine. He wasn't depressed as far as I know. Everything was just... normal.'

'OK, thank you,' the officer said, tapping his pen on his pad. 'And what about the possibility that he's taken off with...' PC Logan glanced at his colleague as she gave Jo a sympathetic look. 'Well, someone else? Do you think there's another woman in your husband's life?'

'No!' Jo said, feeling even more indignant about that than the thought of Will committing suicide or having a gambling debt. 'Absolutely not. No more than I would run off with anyone else.' It was unthinkable. They'd been together twelve years, married for eight. Will would not do anything like that. He was a talker, a sharer, a caring, kind and decent man. And they trusted each other implicitly. 'Why did you even have to ask me that?' Jo said, whispering, on the verge of tears.

'I'm so sorry, Mrs Carter. It wasn't my intention to upset you, but we do have to cover all bases.'

'Yes, yes… I understand. It's just… I just can't take the not *knowing*. It's been twenty-four hours now, and it's so out of character.'

Twenty-four fucking hours, Jo thinks now, swigging her wine, reminded of the debt racking up on her credit card – the one she's had to take out to keep her head above water now she's surviving on just her salary. It's getting harder each month. *What I wouldn't do for the sheer hope that a mere twenty-four hours brought back then*, she thinks, staring at the house-sitting home page absent-mindedly.

Back then, it was still plausible that he'd perhaps suffered a bump to the head and had forgotten his way home – yes, she could have convinced herself of that. Or maybe he'd had a bit of a session with his mates down the pub and felt guilty for staying out all night, intending on slinking home the next evening to face the music. Or perhaps he'd had one too many after rehearsals and got behind the wheel, been pulled over by the police and arrested. He could have been making his way home from twenty-four hours in custody just as she was speaking to the police in their sitting room. *But not now. Not nearly a whole year in custody*, Jo thinks, mustering the courage to click on the house with Will in it again. *Not a whole bloody year of wandering the streets lost or feeling sheepish and sofa-surfing between mates.*

Jo breathes out a sigh she didn't realise she'd been holding. Will is still there. On photos five, seven and eight of the house-sit page.

Strangely, it's somehow comforting, seeing him there. Knowing where he is, even if it is just the internet. She imagines it might feel the same if she'd spotted his face on one of the many missing persons sites she's signed up to. Or glimpsed him on a bus, or getting on a train, the doors closing before she could follow. There, but not there.

After touching Will's face on the screen, Jo browses through the other photos of the house looking for clues, for remnants of

Will. The kitchen looks nice – homely in a muddled, eclectic kind of way, as if someone artistic lives there. The cat is in many of the photos, with a couple including the dog, one outside of him charging for a stick, his silky ears flapping. Then the bedroom (she pauses on that one, wondering if Will has slept in the bed, and if so, who with), the bathroom, a few exterior photos and pictures of the village, the little tea room nearby, the coast… as well as a list of chores to be done and the local facilities. But there's nothing else to suggest Will's presence, apart from the three pictures on the mantelpiece.

Jo sighs, knowing she has no choice.

I have to apply for the house-sit, she thinks, her voice clear inside her head. 'Someone's got three pictures of my missing husband on their mantelpiece,' she adds in a whisper when she looks at the owner's profile – which has a 99.8 per cent approval rating from other site users. Jo wonders what the lost 0.2 per cent was for. 'Stealing other people's husbands, perhaps?' She glares at the generic grey outline of a head. She's not uploaded a profile picture – not all members have.

Jo's fingers hover over the keys, the mouse pointer positioned on the 'Begin Application' button. *Should I?* she thinks. *Should I make contact with this woman – SusiQ19? Should I ask her why she has pictures of Will in her living room? I'm going to sound mad, deranged, like a stalker, and perhaps she'll even report me, have me thrown off the site before I've begun.*

'Or perhaps I should anonymously report her to the police,' Jo says to herself, setting down her glass. 'But for what?' She needs to keep a clear head. Her hand reaches out for her phone again. *PC Daniels would be all over this*, she thinks. But she quickly puts it down again. She needs to deal with this the right way. The only way. The way Will would want.

Jo is familiar with the website now – knows where her profile is located, how much information Louise has filled in on her behalf – which is not much. *Louise*, she thinks, picking up her phone again just as it pings. Always trying to help.

Why not? You can't hide away forever, Jo.

Jo thinks about this; wonders, for a second, if Louise is right. But then she shakes her head and puts her phone down again, turning back to her laptop. *Because there are more important things to worry about right now than giving Ted my number*, she thinks. *Like filling in the blanks on my profile.* She knows that the site is reviews-based, that many homeowners are looking for verified house-sitters only, with positive feedback. And of course, she has none. The phrase '0 per cent New Angel' is displayed beneath her own greyed-out profile head. She needs to add substance to her application.

'Upload your passport or driving licence to help us identify you. The blue tick gives confidence to property owners… all information remains confidential and real names are never revealed until you're ready…' she reads, scanning the small print.

Half an hour later and her profile is complete, including identification checks and a brief bio about herself, who she is, what her interests are, why she is trustworthy, responsible, good in a crisis and *far and away the best person ever to look after your house*. But she isn't ready to put up a photograph of herself yet. She ends with, *And if you need any mending doing while I'm looking after your home, then I'm your woman! I'm a professional seamstress.* She hopes it will help, go some way to securing her ten days at Hawthorn Lodge, East Wincombe as she hits the 'apply' button. She prays SusiQ19 finds her appealing.

'Right,' Jo says, stretching back her neck and closing her laptop, suddenly feeling nervous. Her eyes track across the room. Will is standing there, leaning against the chimney breast, shirtsleeves rolled up, an appreciative look on his face.

So, he says in that drawn-out way of his, wearing his suggestive, lopsided smile that always meant he wanted to take her to bed. *Are you done on your laptop for the night?*

Hi… Jo replies softly, so grateful he's there. *Yes, yes… I'm done, and yes, I'm—*

Done interfering, you mean?

Jo turns cold.

She stands up, walks a couple of steps towards him, her hand outstretched, her heart on fire, just wanting to make everything OK again. She loves him in those jeans, that shirt… She can even smell him – his musky aftershave. But when she reaches out for him, when she takes hold of his hand, he's gone.

CHAPTER SEVEN

Jo wakes early: 4.24 a.m. She knows she won't sleep again before it's time to get up for work. Rolling onto her side, she clicks on her bedside lamp and opens the drawer in the little painted cabinet beside her, her hand fumbling as she pulls out her notebook and pen. Sometimes, in the early hours, she reads back through her jottings and notes and sometimes she adds to them. It's not really a diary; rather a place for random thoughts and feelings to be held captive. To get them out of her head.

'If you write your feelings down,' her counsellor had said, 'then it's almost as if they've been taken prisoner. Isolated. The negative thoughts, anyway. Feel free to keep the positive ones flowing outwardly.'

That'll keep me busy writing forever, then, Jo had thought, trying to engage with the idea. *I simply have no positive thoughts.* This was in the first six months after Will went missing, over twelve sessions of therapy through her local GP's counselling service. But that had ended now, and she couldn't afford to pay for private sessions, not with having to manage the bills and the mortgage alone. The car would probably have to go in the next few months and she hated the thought that she might have to ask her parents for help. She couldn't stand the I-told-you-so's… Would rather get a second job or sell the house, rent a small flat, though she couldn't stand the thought of Will coming home and her not being there. As though she'd been the one to desert *him*.

She opens the notebook, flipping to the page she'd last written on a couple of weeks ago. *FUCK!!!* is scrawled in huge capital letters. Angry sketches fill the pages preceding that – horrific faces with bared teeth and butchered bodies beneath them. Childlike drawings, but with a bloody intent. The contents of her tortured mind. The anger coming out. The pages before that, though, have notes about her feelings, her hopes and fears surrounding what happened. What *might* have happened.

First Christmas alone, she'd written five months ago. *How many more will there be? I can't even stand one. How do I get through all the anniversaries, the birthdays, the various celebrations? How do I do all that alone? I can't. I just fucking can't...*

Best things about Will not being here, Jo had written on 13 February, nearly three months ago. An attempt to make herself feel better. To take back control.

1. Don't have to worry about Valentine's wars tomorrow. She'd jotted a laughing face then, as if it was funny. But it's what they'd called it. Valentine's wars. *No more wondering if he'll outdo me again. Spa break for me versus my vintage vinyl for him. He won hands down. Though it was an original Pink Floyd album I got him. And he did love it.*

'As if it was actually funny,' she whispers, scribbling out the stupid emoji thing.

2. No snoring. 'I'd give anything to hear your night-time wheeze now,' she whispers, hating herself for being so shallow. But that's how it was with Will. Nothing to complain about. She was scratching about for upsides.

3. No worrying if we'll get pregnant or not. That was true. The stress of conceiving had taken its toll on both of them. Every time her period came, she had to think how to tell him, how not to feel like a failure, less of a woman. But without Will here, failure was guaranteed. She didn't want anyone else's baby – now or ever. But similarly, she couldn't come to terms with the cancellation of their

IVF treatment, or the hormone therapy she'd not long started being curtailed shortly after D-Day. As if she was even more of an empty husk without him. Her ovaries had needed a jump-start and the treatment had been going well. And then suddenly Will wasn't there. She couldn't do it alone. Didn't *want* to do it alone. She needed him.

'That's the thing,' Jo says into the night. 'With you here, there was always hope. Whatever happened, good or bad. Always something to travel towards. Someone's hand to hold along the way. I'm not sure I can do it on my own.'

Jo's phone pings an alert.

'Oh… what?' she says, her eyes bleary from lack of sleep, her brain unable to switch off. She reaches for it, sees the unfamiliar House Angels app alert on her phone.

One new reply to your House Angels application.

Jo reaches for her glasses. She can just about see OK without them, but everything becomes crystal clear when she slips them on. She opens up the app.

A new message alert sits in her inbox. It can only be from SusiQ19. She hasn't applied for any other house-sits. Doesn't *want* to. None of the others has pictures of Will in their living rooms. Her heart races. What if she's been turned down? She's new to the site, after all. Has no feedback or references, only her ID checks via the site.

'What – what the *hell* am I doing?' She drops her phone down onto the duvet beside her, unable to look at it, knocking her notebook and pen onto the floor. 'He's not coming back, *OK*?' she tells herself, covering her face. 'He left you, and that's that. He doesn't *want* you. He's done with you. He was just too cowardly to tell you that he's moved in with another woman.'

Jo leans forward, bringing her knees up to her chest, hugging them, sighing into the duvet cover. *Even if you* are *out there,* she

thinks, *I'm not sure I'd even want you back now.* 'Not after everything you've put me through,' she says, lifting her head.

Jo takes a deep breath, refusing to pity herself, refusing to let
Will's choices bring her down any more. Then, unable to resist,
she grabs her phone and opens up the message. For a moment, her
eyes are blurry. But then, as she focuses, she sees it perfectly clearly.

> We're sorry. This homeowner only accepts House Angels
> with three reviews or more over 80 per cent. But please
> do keep your angelic applications coming…

'Great. Just *great*,' Jo yells, hurling her phone onto the bed
and her head onto the pillow. Somehow, she needs to get into
that house.

CHAPTER EIGHT

Jo cups her hands around her mug, watching as Louise bites into her sandwich.

'Not sure just the one is going to be enough,' she says, grinning. 'This is delicious.'

Jo smiles. 'You can have mine, if you like. I don't really have an appetite today.' She'd been quiet since they'd met up on the corner of Regent Street and the Parade, their usual weekly meeting spot if they each had time to grab lunch together. Given her mood, Jo had been reluctant to go, but then figured that what she needed most was time with her best friend. Even just being in her company lifted her, took her head away from the dark place in which it was permanently fixed.

'Go on then, what's up?' Louise dabbed at her mouth with a paper napkin, brushing crumbs off the shelf of her pregnant belly.

'Oh, no. Nothing. It's fine.'

'I've only got half an hour left, so if you want advice, you'd better hurry.' She glances at her watch.

Jo rolls her eyes, flashes a brief smile. 'I applied for a house-sit,' she says.

Louise's face lights up. 'Good for you,' she says, nodding, smiling. 'You really deserve a break. I hope it's somewhere lovely?'

The photos of Will on the mantelpiece flash through her mind. *Do I say anything? Do I tell Louise? She'll insist I go to the police...*

'Well, it *was* somewhere lovely. But I didn't get it.'

'What?'

'The house owner turned me down because I don't have any reviews or feedback.'

'Oh, how ridiculous,' Louise says, laying down her sandwich. 'How are you even supposed to start, in that case? If you need a reference, I'm happy to provide one. Surely a few glowing words from a solicitor would count for something. Anyway, that particular owner was clearly a moron. Forget that one and apply for another.'

I don't want to apply for another, Jo thinks. *I want* that *one*.

'Doesn't matter. I should probably stay around here anyway. You know, in case.'

'Oh Jo, just leave a note on the door or something. You can't never go away again. He's got your number, hasn't he? It's not exactly like he's gone out of his way to call it this last year, so he's hardly likely to arrive back...' Louise trails off, reaches her hand out to Jo's. 'Shit, I'm sorry, Jo-jo. That was harsh. But I hate to see you suffering and putting your life on hold.'

Jo sniffs, refusing to cry. She's done enough of that, and it's not helped any. It doesn't bring Will back. 'If only I *knew*, you know? Just if he was dead or alive, that would be a start. And if he's alive, then if I had just a single fragment of a reason why he left me, I might be able to come to terms with it. In time. Can you understand that?'

'Of course, and—'

'If he'd gone off me because... because we were having trouble conceiving and he was desperate to have kids, you know, I could eventually get my head around that. Maybe. Or even if it was because he didn't like the colour I'd dyed my hair, or he hated the way I dressed or thought I'd put on weight or looked frumpy, or he wanted someone with bigger breasts, longer legs... you know, I'd eventually buy that shit. I'd hate him, of course, but at least there would be a cause for my anger, my grief. Some kind of closure. Right now, right now I don't even know what I'm grieving. Don't even know if it's Will's death, or simply his selfishness. That's all I've got. Which is a big fat nothing. It's killing me.'

Louise hangs her head. 'Oh, Jo...'

'No, I'm sorry. It's fine. Absolutely fine. No need to pity me. You know that's not what I want or need.'

'I know. Really, I do. As much as anyone can. Christ, we've known each other since forever, feels like we're sisters. I hate what you're going through, and if there was anything I could do to take away your pain, make it better for you, then I would.'

Jo nods, smiling. 'Thanks, Lou. That means the world. I honestly don't know how I'd have got through this without you. And Archie, of course. He's been a rock, too, mainly because he's indulged you in indulging me.'

Both women laugh then and Jo picks up her sandwich, waving it at Louise. 'Last chance before I comfort-eat, and order a slice of that chocolate cake too?'

'Eat,' she says, flapping her hand. 'Look, Jo, I don't want this to come across wrong, but... but can I help you out with a holiday? You need a break so badly, and we can call it a loan but without any pressure. You could take a week in the sun or bugger off to a cottage somewhere in the UK if you preferred. Anything to take your mind off... off the interminable waiting.'

Jo thinks about this. It's tempting. Of course it's tempting, and she knows Louise can afford it. She doesn't begrudge her her good job and career. Far from it, in fact. She knows that money isn't particularly important to her and Archie, rather a thing that they just have through circumstance, through their passions. Louise, a family solicitor, specialising in representing women in abusive relationships; Archie, an obstetrician, dedicated to his charity work. Every year he takes leave to donate his time to hospital maternity wards in Africa, helping raise awareness, raise money, raise standards. And giving his expertise to the local doctors.

'Oh, Lou, that's so kind of you. But that's not what it's about.' Jo thinks, trying to put into words what it *is* about. 'Since the moment Will went, left, disappeared or died – call it what you want – I've kind of made a pact with myself. That I will survive. Sounds silly, perhaps, but it's my chance to prove, if only to myself, that I'll be OK. Will and I met quite young and I'd only had a short time on my own, really. It's important to me to know that I can do this by myself. Does that make sense? I hate that I might have to ask my parents for help, and I'm praying I won't need to.' *I'll be buggered if I need to*, she thinks. 'But if I have to sell the house and get somewhere cheaper, or take on more work or another job, then so be it. I just want to know that whatever happens to me is *because* of me, and not someone else. Enough of that has happened already. Do you understand?'

'Perfectly,' Louise says quietly, her eyes flickering warmth. 'And you're amazing,' she adds. 'You're awesome with knobs on.'

'So if I'm going to go on holiday, it will be because of me, and all my doing – even if it is clearing up someone else's dog mess and guarding their house against burglars.' Jo laughs, trying to lighten the mood. She's brought it down for too long when the focus should be on Louise and her baby.

'Show me that place you were hoping to house-sit and we can search for something similar that doesn't have such strict criteria. I'll help you. Norfolk is beautiful, as is Somerset. Have you thought about there, or Dorset?'

Jo hesitates before pulling her phone from her bag. She doesn't want Louise to see the pictures of Will on the mantelpiece. 'Thanks, Lou,' she says, smiling. It doesn't take long with Louise to make her feel better, for her positivity to rub off. They've done it enough times for each other over the years, and even after stints apart when Louise went off to study law and she went to art college to study fashion, the gap of time apart wasn't enough to break their friendship.

'Oh,' Jo says, glancing through her notifications. The usual text and WhatsApp messages, plus a couple of alerts from Facebook. But at the top of the list is a message from House Angels.

SusiQ19 has sent you a message.

Without saying anything, Jo unlocks her phone and opens the app.

Hi, this might seem odd and thanks so much for your application. I have my criteria set to certain specifications, including automatically ruling out those with no feedback. (Been there and paid the price!) The app sends an auto-response for me. But I read your profile and it chimed with me. And, well, if I'm honest, I'm a bit desperate. I have a regular sitter but they've just let me down. I can't leave my animals. Is there any chance you could house-sit for me at the end of the week for ten days? I know it's short notice but thought I'd ask. All the best, Suzanne.

'Oh,' Jo says again, a puzzled look on her face which gradually turns into a smile, even though her heart is thumping.

Suzanne… so that's what you're called.

'Looks like I got me a little holiday after all,' she says, waving her phone in the air. 'That house-sit came good.'

'Wow, that's marvellous,' Louise says, pushing the last of her sandwich into her mouth. 'Show me where you're off to, then.' She leans in.

Jo freezes. 'Oh, there aren't many photos,' she says, shielding her phone before pulling up a shot of the front of the house, then one of the nearby beach, flashing a quick look to Louise. She's careful not to show her any of the inside. 'It's near Hastings,' she adds. 'There are some lovely walks and pretty places to see nearby.' Then she tucks her phone back inside her bag, asking Louise about her due date, her recent scan, if she's all ready for her impending bundle of joy. Not mentioning the photos of Will at all.

CHAPTER NINE

The weekends are worst, Jo thinks as she walks slowly back to work after lunch. *So perhaps taking off for the coast would be a good thing.* Often she goes Friday afternoon to Monday morning without seeing or speaking to anyone. She fishes around in the bottom of her shopper for her umbrella as she feels the first specks of rain on her face, hoping Louise doesn't get soaked heading back to the office. She rushed off in such a hurry – as much of a hurry as her size allowed – after receiving a text, making Jo wonder if there'd been an emergency.

'Oh *no…*' Louise had said, tucking her phone away again, her cheeks aglow. They'd been that way since she'd first found out she was pregnant. She'd looked radiant throughout.

'Everything OK?'

'There's a work crisis. I'm so sorry, but I have to go.' She'd reached out and touched Jo's hand, a pitying expression sweeping over her. 'I feel terrible, but there's an important court case tomorrow and I need to liaise with counsel before he hits the golf course in an hour.' Louise had rolled her eyes then.

'Don't worry, I understand. You've told me enough times what the barristers are like.'

'A lot of them seem to think they're part-timers. Don't realise we're not just at their beck and call. This one in particular,' she'd said, draping her patterned scarf around her neck and gathering her jacket. 'He's good, one of the best, but along with that, he's very…' She glanced at the ceiling a moment. 'Very demanding, shall we say.'

'Go,' Jo had said, completely understanding. 'I'll settle the bill. It's my turn anyway.'

'Rubbish,' Louise had said, pulling a twenty-pound note from her purse without hesitation. 'If I can't buy my bestie a sandwich, then what's the world coming to?' She leant down and kissed Jo on the head, giving her a squeeze round the shoulders. 'I'll call you later. You can tell me more about the house-sit. And make sure you reply to the owner. It looks absolutely lovely.'

Jo had nodded, watching as Louise left, gathering up her own stuff as soon as she was out of sight after paying the bill at the counter. It was only a ten-minute walk back to work, down towards Jephson Gardens where Sew Perfect was tucked away in a pretty mews courtyard development, all brick and cobbles and once the stables to one of the big Regency town houses. There was an artisan bakery, a little art gallery and picture framer's as well as an upmarket shoe shop in the out-of-the-way cluster of businesses.

Walking in the door, Jo smells the tantalising aroma of fresh sourdough. Margot or Beth must have been to the bakery across the way for their lunch. She shakes off her umbrella, leaving it in the stand, and shrugs out of her jacket. Once she's settled back at her work table, she logs into the House Angels app, pulling up the message from Suzanne again.

Thanks for getting back to me, she writes in reply. **I'd be happy to house-sit for you. If you send me your address and any other details, I can be there by 9 p.m. on Friday evening. Let me know any special instructions.** And she hits send before going back over the house photos for the hundredth time, just to make sure Will is still there. He is. Of *course* he is. Making her feel as if he's almost back in her life.

*

'Boo!' Beth says an hour or so later. 'Penny for them.' She puts a cup of tea down on Jo's sewing table.

'Oh, thanks, Beth.'

'You were miles away.'

'I was?'

Beth reaches for the garment spread out on the table, holds it up. 'This is stunning,' she says. 'So different.'

'I love working on pieces like this,' Jo replies. 'Far more interesting than the usual frilly white things.'

'Oh yes, I totally agree,' Beth says, running her fingers over the burgundy, gold and jade brocade on the bodice. Long blousy sleeves in dusky rose-coloured chiffon end with vintage lace cuffs.

'The bride has collected antique fabrics for years, and her grandmother gave her some interesting samples, too. She wants all the bridesmaids' dresses made from them, a kind of patchwork of memories of her family's life.'

'That's lovely,' Beth replies. 'And so unique.'

'She's having a peasant-style wedding,' Jo explains, pulling up some pictures on her phone of the mood board the bride sent through for inspiration. 'She's going to arrive at the village church on the back of a horse-drawn hay wagon. All the flowers are going to be collected from the hedgerows – cow parsley mainly – and there's going to be a hog roast and a folk band in an old barn afterwards. Firepits and all.'

'Nice,' Beth says, nodding her approval. 'Reckon I'd like that when I get married. *If* I get married,' she adds with a laugh and a wink. 'No man ever seems to stick around long enough to ask me. They all piss off for one reason or another. The last idiot ghosted me and— Oh God… I'm *so* sorry,' she says, checking herself and blushing. 'That was utterly insensitive of me, Jo.' Beth carefully lays the little dress back down on the table. She's new, but Margot had filled her in on what had happened to Jo when she first started.

'It's fine,' Jo replies in a voice she hopes will ease Beth's guilt. 'I don't want people treading on eggshells. Not any more.' She looks up at her, feeling her faux pas pain.

'Tell me to mind my own business, but are you OK?' Beth says, touching her shoulder. 'I mean… you know, as OK as you can be? It's just that before, when I brought your tea, you seemed miles away. You didn't really seem present.'

'Oh,' Jo says, laughing it off, 'don't mind me. Daydreaming, most likely.'

'About him?'

'Yeah…' she replies with a shrug and a half-laugh. She can hardly tell Beth it's because of the photos of Will on another woman's mantelpiece.

'Hi, Mum,' Jo says, pinning her phone to her ear with her shoulder as she riffles through her wardrobe. Everything reminds her of Will. *This is the dress I wore on our last meal out… this is the top I made from the fabric he bought me as a surprise, remembering how much I'd loved it.* She was gathering a few items together to take away. 'Everything OK?' Her mum only usually called if something was wrong. Or to check if she'd met someone else yet.

'Yes, darling. And don't say it in that tone of voice.'

'What tone of voice?'

'*Your* tone of voice.'

'You mean, just my voice?' Jo steps back from the wardrobe, sitting down on the bed, repressing the heavy sigh she wants to let out. She holds the phone against her ear with one hand, rubbing at her neck with the other.

'Now, now,' Elizabeth Langham says. 'That's just what I mean, darling. Sarcastic and, well, a bit bitchy, if I'm honest. It's upsetting.'

'Bitchy?' Jo says, closing her eyes and counting to ten. 'Mum, you know I'm the least bitchy person around. Is that what you called to tell me?'

'No, no, of course not. Can't a mother call her daughter once in a while without an ulterior motive?'

'Of course, Mum. I'm sorry.' In another life, with another mother, Jo would pour her heart out – how she's been upset, *deeply* upset, since she saw Will's photos online; how she may, in a couple of days, discover what happened to him – that he's living a perfectly happy life with another woman and not giving her a thought. About how she would have to go to the police if she found him – how she *should* go to the police right *now*. But she can't – she can't tell her mother, or the police, any of that. Not without discovering more first herself.

'In another life what?'

'Sorry?'

'You just said "in another life".'

'Oh, I—'

'Now, the reason I'm calling…'

Here we go, Jo thinks. *Disaster or demand. Which will it be?*

'The Cresswells are having a party at the weekend. An engagement celebration for Phoebe. Everyone will be there. And so will you. You might meet someone, Joanna. It's the right set.'

'What?' Jo's head thrums. *Demand, then*, she thinks. 'I can't come, Mum. I'm sorry.' *And I don't want to meet anyone. I'd quite like to have my husband back, thank you. Not have so-called suitors thrust in my face, Mother.*

Jo claps her hand over her mouth. *Please don't let me have said all that…*

'Why can't you come?'

'Because I'm going away.'

'Where?'

'Just a little holiday, on the South Coast.'

'Well, how can you afford that? You say you can't afford anything any more.'

'Mum, can I call you back later? Someone's... someone's just rung the doorbell.'

'Well, I didn't hear it.'

'I'm upstairs. Mum, I'll call you back, OK? Bye.'

Jo taps the red button to hang up, flopping back onto her pillow. She can't stand a grilling, can't take the questions, the disapproval that would inevitably follow. She knows exactly how the conversation would play out.

If that stupid man hadn't abandoned you, then you wouldn't need to be cleaning up dog mess, pretending it was a holiday. You should be sunning yourself in the Caribbean, darling, not being a skivvy. If you'd married someone decent, like your father and I told you to, then none of this would have happened, would it?

No... no, Mum, it wouldn't, Jo thinks in response. *Because if I hadn't met and married Will, I'd still be searching for the love of my life, just like I am now anyway.*

CHAPTER TEN

It's raining – driving columns that come at Jo from every angle as she walks briskly home from the bus stop. She is taking the bus more and more now, the fare cheaper than petrol and parking. She knows the car will soon have to go, but not before she's made the long drive down to Hastings to find out about…

'Oh, just get *in*!' she says, frustration taking hold as she fumbles with the key in her front door, struggling with her bag as it falls off her shoulder, her umbrella straining in her hand as the wind whips up. She's trying to keep her hair dry as there's no time to shower now before she leaves for Hastings, and she doesn't want to turn up looking like a drowned rat.

What if she's faced with Suzanne and Will when she gets there? This Suzanne woman looking glamorous and groomed, holding onto Will as he slips his arm around her waist, pulling his beloved new woman away from the wet, dishevelled, sobbing creature at their door? Jo imagines Will whispering to Suzanne that he has no idea who the crazy woman is, that they should lock her out, call the police.

'Christ,' Jo says once she's inside, catching sight of herself in the hall mirror. She leaves the umbrella on the mat and kicks off her soaking shoes. 'If only I'd left work five minutes earlier,' she says to herself.

But then she'd never have encountered the panicked bride – a young woman getting married tomorrow, rushing back into the shop with her gown for a last-minute alteration. Jo had told her that it looked fine at the fitting earlier in the week, that she didn't feel it warranted any adjustments, but the girl had been insistent.

'It's just that… just that…' She glanced around the workshop, trying to make eye contact with someone – *anyone* – who might understand her. But it was only Jo who was listening. 'It's just that my mum sent me, said that if I don't get the waist nipped in a bit, I'm going to look like a…' She'd hesitated before letting out a little sob. 'A *doughnut*,' she whispered to Jo, her face contorted with worry.

The young woman was beautiful, Jo thought, looking her up and down, and very far from a doughnut. But she could hear her own mother saying something similar, delivering a crushing and personal blow that was supposedly 'just a joke' and that Jo always knew was anything but. She knew just how the bride felt – that cutting comments were hard, if not impossible, to unhear. And Jo didn't want her walking down the aisle in a gown she'd made feeling like a doughnut.

'Right, come on,' Jo said, touching her arm and glancing at the clock. 'Let's go out the back and see if we can't make you believe you're the beautiful woman I'm seeing, eh? You show me where you want it altering and I'll see what I can do.'

Jo had left Sew Perfect an hour after everyone else, sending a very happy bride on her way as she wished her well for her big day tomorrow. She'd gone round locking up, putting on the alarm and just missing the bus home. She'd had to wait twenty minutes for another and then, while the bus stop-started through the Friday traffic, the heavens had opened.

Jo stares at the empty suitcase, then at her wardrobe. She shivers, though it's not from being soaked through. *What does one wear to face the woman your husband has run off with?*

Jo opens the wardrobe door and grabs a few hangers, whipping the clothes off and roughly folding them into the small suitcase. A couple of pairs of jeans, two sweaters, a few tops, underwear… then she gathers up some toiletries and make-up from the bathroom, dropping the items into her cosmetics bag. *None of this matters*, she thinks. *And none of it* will *matter when I'm faced with the unbearable truth.*

Jo glances at the bedside clock. Twenty past six. She should have left nearly an hour and a half ago to get there by nine. She pulls up the House Angels app on her phone, knowing she'll have to send a message, warn Suzanne she's going to be late.

'A great start,' she whispers to herself. 'Letting the woman down before I've even arrived.' Because, of course, a part of her hopes that Suzanne is entirely innocent and has nothing to do with Will in a romantic sense, that the only reason she has his photos on her mantelpiece is because he's a passing acquaintance, or the mate of a distant cousin of hers, or… or…

'Or perhaps she saw him in a play, or when he was on TV a while back,' Jo says, mulling over the possibility. 'And maybe she developed a crush and sent off for some signed photos or printed them off the internet herself.'

That'll be it, Jo tells herself unconvincingly, shaking her head as she zips up her case with one hand, her phone in the other. *Suzanne is just an innocent fan and me seeing his photos is a crazy coincidence.* Though Jo knows as well as anyone that Will's acting career hadn't exactly been at the dizzying heights of garnering fans. *He was hardly a household name*, Jo thinks as she opens up the House Angels messages.

But Suzanne has beaten her to it.

A quick heads-up. Can't be there tonight to greet you so Simon, my neighbour, is going to let you in and show you the ropes. He's got keys and will sort the animals this evening so no rush on your part. I forgot to send my number last time. Any problems then contact me on 077…

Jo breathes in and out heavily, adding the number to her contacts. *Suzanne will not be there*, she thinks, not sure whether to feel relieved or not. *And if the neighbour is letting me in, then it doesn't sound like anyone else will be there either – including Will. So it's unlikely they're living together, unless he's away with Suzanne too…*

'For heaven's sake, stop overthinking this,' Jo tells herself, lugging the suitcase downstairs. 'Just get there, find out what you can – which may be nothing – do your job then come home and get on with your life. And who knows, maybe you'll even have a nice time.

'And stop bloody talking to yourself,' she says as she pulls the front door closed, locks up and heads out to her car.

CHAPTER ELEVEN

Jo has never minded long drives. *Thinking time, talking time,* she and Will always used to say. Their holidays together had never been lavish – far from it, with a teacher and a dressmaker's salaries not stretching to the glamorous and expensive getaways her mother envisaged them having. But they'd always had the best time together, whether it was in a little caravan by the sea, a budget B & B in Wales or a last-minute deal on a city break. They'd always returned home refreshed and more in love, if that was even possible.

Jo grips the steering wheel. The rain is still coming down hard and her wipers are on full pelt, squeaking with every stroke. She's been meaning to get the blades replaced, plus a couple of other things that need fixing, but she's not wanted to put the car in the garage, have questions asked. Besides, every penny has counted lately, and she doesn't drive far these days anyway. Except tonight. The three-and-a-half-hour journey south suddenly seems as if she's set off to cross a continent, especially without Will by her side. She glances across at the empty passenger seat. Usually she'd be the one sitting in it, with Will behind the wheel. She'd take her turn, of course, but Will enjoyed driving. Said it made him feel free. *Free and in control,* Jo remembers, wondering what he meant.

And then she shudders, remembering *that* night…

'Christ!' she cries, jamming on the brakes, lurching forward. She nearly ran a red light. 'Focus, woman. You've barely even left home yet,' she mutters, turning on the fan as the windscreen fogs up. She puts on the radio to distract herself from her own thoughts, to try and shove thoughts of *that* night back in the box. In the days and weeks afterwards, she and Will had barely mentioned it – each of them believing that if they didn't speak about it, then maybe it hadn't even happened. *Correction*, Jo thinks. *I did try to speak about it, but Will was having none of it.* 'He was just scared,' she says, turning the radio up even louder to drown out her thoughts.

But the music suddenly cuts out as the Bluetooth takes over and her phone rings. She presses the button on the wheel to answer.

'Jo-jo…' comes Louise's voice. 'What's occurring?'

Jo smiles at Louise's silly accent, grateful for the distraction. She doesn't think she'll make it through the drive if her thoughts are left to themselves. 'We're all going on a summer holiday…' she sings in reply, forcing herself to sound bright. 'Except, of course, it's not really summer yet and there's no *all* about it. And it's pissing down. Just me on my way to the house-sit. So not even really a proper holiday. How's you, Lou?'

Silence, and Jo isn't sure if it's bad reception or if Louise just isn't saying anything.

'How did it go with Bertie Barrister the other day?' she says to break the silence. It was the last time she'd seen her.

'Sorry, what?' Louise replies.

'You know, after we'd had lunch and—'

'Oh, yes. That seems ages ago now. It went fine.'

But Jo doesn't think Louise herself sounds fine. She knows her well enough to read beneath the cheery veneer.

'Spill,' Jo says, glancing in her mirror before changing lanes. She's relieved that so far, the traffic is light.

There's a barely perceptible sigh. 'I had a hospital appointment today.'

'OK…' Jo says in a way that indicates she's listening, that she's here for her friend. 'How did it go?' If Louise needs support, she'll turn right round and go back to help.

'My blood pressure's up a bit.'

'Really?' Jo says, not knowing what the implications are. 'Can they do anything for it? Is it dangerous?'

'They're worried about pre-eclampsia. If it keeps going up, they'll maybe have to take action and deliver early.'

'You mean as in—'

'A Caesarean, yes.'

Jo knows Louise has been set on a natural birth from the start. Has had her birth plan signed, sealed and delivered almost as watertight as a legal document approved by the courts for months now. Woe betide any midwife or obstetrician who goes against it. Archie was in two minds whether to deliver the baby himself, but as well as considering the ethics, he decided that he'd rather have the father's role in the birth of his child, rather than that of the professional. And of course, if needed, he'd step in. He was top in his field.

'Lou, I'm so sorry to hear that, though you know they'll look after you and do what's best for the baby and you.'

'I know, I know…' Louise replies. 'But it hardly seems like a minute since I got pregnant, and to have him or her whipped out because of…' She trails off.

And what a day that *was*, Jo thinks, reminded of when Louise had told her the news – two bombs dropped. She'd just been informed of a lead on Will's whereabouts, a possible sighting after she'd done a leaflet drop in the area of Birmingham where his parents had lived before they died. She wondered if he'd gone home, somehow dissolved back into Solihull, where he'd grown up.

And then the call came – a woman who thought she recognised him from the hundreds of printed flyers Jo had distributed.

'I swear I saw him on the bus yesterday,' she told Jo, breathy with excitement at being able to help. 'The one going between Solihull and Hall Green on the way to the city centre. I only remember because he got quite shirty with the driver, arguing about change. He was a tall man, a good-looking man. And a dead ringer for the chap in your flyer.'

That doesn't sound like Will, though, Jo had thought, suddenly deflated, although she thanked the woman after taking her details. The Will she knew was kind and laid-back, rarely getting angry. In fact, the only time she'd ever seen him properly lose it was when… She'd had to pull her thoughts back from the brink then, not associate Will's disappearance with *that*. Though she couldn't deny it; it concerned her. That what had happened that night and Will going missing were somehow linked. But there was no way she could tell the police. She and Will had made a pact.

And shortly after the woman had hung up, Jo's phone had immediately rung again. It was Louise.

'I've got something to tell you,' she'd said, after ten minutes of preamble. Ten minutes of idle conversation that Jo saw straight through, even though her mind was still reeling from the previous call. Louise never phoned without reason. Louise didn't waste words or time. Even her personal life, it seemed, was on a billing cycle, costing everything out. 'It's not time well spent,' she'd once told Jo when she was going off on what seemed like wild goose chases in her search for Will. *But it's time well spent for me*, Jo thought though didn't say. But she'd sounded nervous on that call. And that wasn't like Louise.

'Spit it out, then,' she'd replied, wanting to get on with following up on the lead, desperate to drive back out to Solihull, perhaps take a journey on the same bus at the same time of day. Hand out some more flyers. Pace the streets, calling out his name as she went.

'I'm pregnant.'

Jo hated herself for pausing, for feeling smacked in the face, for almost wanting to hang up on her best friend at what was the happiest time of her life. And she hated herself for not immediately finding the right words, for not congratulating her without delay, for not squealing with excitement. *A baby! Oh Lou, I'm so pleased for you and Archie!* And finally, she hated herself for the bitter taste in her mouth, the ache in her heart, the ache in her empty belly. The two gaping holes in her life.

'*Pregnant?*' she'd said after what seemed like an eternity. 'I...'

The tears had filled her eyes then, flooding her vision with regret as she struggled to speak. *Say anything, dammit... Just make her know you're OK with this.*

'Lou... that's...'

She loathed that she was making Louise's happiness her own misery.

'That's just fabulous news, Lou. Oh, I'm so *very* pleased for you both.'

There. She'd managed it. Said the right thing.

*

'Jo, are you still there?'

What did I do wrong to make him leave?

It is a question Jo has asked herself a thousand times over the last eleven months. And now she is asking it a thousand times more on what is turning into an interminable journey. The M25 is at a complete standstill.

'What did I do *wrong*?' she whispers, drumming her fingers on the wheel, glancing across at a young couple in the car next to her, laughing and joking together. Behind them, she sees a baby fastened in its seat, staring out of the window, transfixed by the orange lights above. Jo turns away, tears in her eyes.

'Jo, are you there...?'

She'd never wanted to believe Will had left because they'd not been able to conceive, that her body wouldn't fuse with his, making her worry they weren't compatible. Nature's way of telling them they shouldn't have got together in the first place. But Will wasn't shallow and accusing. He was completely the opposite, in fact, embracing her flaws – *loving* her flaws – knowing that if Jo felt good about herself, then he did too.

'Hello, Jo… Are you there? Can you hear me?'

The first time she'd taken a test, they'd done it together, setting an alarm down to the exact second when to check the stick. After doing what she'd needed to do in the bathroom, Jo had set it on the shelf and Will had come in. They'd both stood there watching, waiting for the lines – or line – to appear. Each second had seemed like a year and, as the wetness seeped up the results window, Jo's heart beat hard inside her chest.

'Are you *sure?*' she'd said afterwards as Will had held the stick under the window, examining it, trying to catch sight of a faint second line.

Will turned to her, taking her by the shoulders. His dark eyes bored into hers. 'I'm sure, Jo-jo,' he'd said in that rich and soothing voice of his. 'Not this time… but maybe next.'

Jo had rested her head on his shoulder then and they'd stood there together, taking in the news that this month at least, Jo wasn't carrying his baby.

'Yeah, we'll get lucky soon, eh?' she'd said when the disappointment had sunk in. It was only their first try, after all. She knew it could take a few attempts.

A few attempts… Jo thinks now, ramming the car into first gear as the vehicles in front creep forward.

'Jo, are you OK? Say something…'

She jumps at the sound of Louise's voice. 'Yes, Lou, I'm so sorry. Traffic's horrendous. I was just concentrating. Do you want me to come back, to look after you?'

'Oh goodness, no. Definitely no need for that. You go and enjoy yourself. I've got Archie by my side, don't forget.'

Then she apologised profusely.

'It's fine, it's fine,' Jo replied. Somehow mustering a laugh. She was getting better at brushing off the thoughtless remarks, making people feel less awkward about saying the wrong thing. 'You're allowed to have a husband that's not disappeared,' she added, gripping the wheel even tighter.

CHAPTER TWELVE

Then

During that first shared pizza with Will after rehearsals (the first of many we had over the next few months), I managed to knock over two drinks, spill the contents of my handbag on the floor, lose my glasses so I struggled to see what I was eating, get stringy cheese stuck in my hair and fall off the banquette. Will was suddenly up out of his chair and beside me, hoisting me up as gracefully as he could before I'd even realised what had happened. But the shock still jolted through me, still made me see stars.

Made me fall in love.

'Is that all it takes?' Will said smoothly, shielding me from the other diners with his broad body. My hands were still wrapped in his as I regained my balance. 'Just one beer?' He'd given me a squeeze then, making sure I was steady, barely batting an eyelid at my latest misfortune on top of everything else.

I slid back onto the shiny plastic bench seat, abandoning my visit to the toilet for now as my cheeks burned scarlet. 'Yeah, I'm a cheap date,' I said, clearing my throat, rolling my eyes, laughing, coughing – anything to hide my embarrassment. 'I thought… I thought the seat was continuous and joined in with the next one,' I whispered, pointing to the gap between my bench and the one at the table beside us. 'I was just sliding along to get out and bang, no bench. I'm not drunk,' I said loudly enough for those nearby to hear. Some other diners glanced over, one looking concerned, a couple of others still laughing. I shook my head, blushing.

'I like it,' Will said, reaching over and removing my hands from my face. 'You're real. You're honest. You're you. But I don't like that you may have hurt yourself. Are you OK?'

'Yes, yes, I'm fine. Only my pride dented,' I said with a laugh, finding a little humour in the situation. Though I could already feel the thrum of a bruise blooming on my thigh. 'I can be so clumsy. It's amazing I manage to make such intricate clothing without more mishaps. My passion is making bridal wear – so much lace, fine fabrics and detailed stitching. I guess I'm just a little...' I trailed off, deciding I oughtn't to say it.

'I get clumsy when I'm nervous, too. But it mainly happens when I'm in the company of someone I *really* like. Someone very special.' Will raised his right hand slowly in a grand gesture and purposefully knocked over his bottle of beer in a slow-motion way. The neck hung over the table, the contents spilling out and spattering his feet as he made a fake shocked face. 'See? Totally clumsy right this minute. I must be in the company of someone *very* special indeed.'

I stared at him, almost disbelieving. *Who is this man? Why does he seem to just* get *me? We seem so similar...* I couldn't help my eyes widening, the grin forming.

Before I knew it, I was laughing. Then belly-laughing, picking up a piece of pizza and shoving it into my mouth virtually whole, struggling to get it in because of its size and also because I was spitting crumbs and cheese back onto my plate, getting tomato sauce on my chin. 'Me...' I said through a doughy mouthful. 'I comfort eat when I'm with someone I really, *really* like. As though I just can't get enough.'

The days turned into weeks, which then turned into months. Loose summer dresses and floppy hats transformed into sweaters and

boots right through to thick coats and scarves wrapped around our
necks when we met up. Will and I spent time with each other in
and out of the theatre, winding our way through the seasons in a
blur of happiness. I was at the rep fairly often those few weeks, as
and when alterations or repairs were needed for the costumes. It was
just Margot and me, as we couldn't afford to employ a runner to
do the laborious and seemingly unending trips to the dry-cleaner's
and laundry but, between us, we managed to get the job done.
With the theatre having been let down by their last seamstresses,
Margot and I had stepped in with our bid for the contract at just
the right moment, which had a knock-on effect for our dressmaking
services, especially bridal. In exchange for good rates, the theatre
included an advertisement for Sew Perfect in each programme.
It was just what we needed to take our business to the next level.

'You're the first woman I've ever thought I could…' Will had
said just before that first Christmas, a week before the end of
term. But he'd trailed off, distracted by the cast of fifteen-year-olds
buzzing around him. It was the opening night of *A Christmas Carol*
at Wroxdown High, where he taught, and I'd offered my services
with the costumes.

'Could what?' I glanced up at him from the hem I was restitch-
ing, fighting the smile. I knew what I wanted to hear but he'd not
actually said it. We'd been seeing each other for a few months now,
and things had quickly got serious between us.

'The first woman I've ever thought I could live with,' he'd
whispered in my ear, bending down to the low stool on which I
was perched.

The inner smile bloomed slightly ahead of the one forming
on my face. No one had ever said anything quite so life-affirming
to me before. It was far more of a compliment than the usual
'Your hair looks amazing', or 'I love your lips/face/legs/laugh' I'd
had from men before. But I instantly found myself fighting the
automatic pang of fear that made my heart race: my mother and

father – or rather, my mother. They'd only met Will once (once was enough, and I'd promised Will I'd never put him through it again, though he was unfazed, said it had gone over his head). But I knew my mother, how gradually and persistently she separated and isolated me from people she didn't approve of – usually boyfriends. And I'd immediately sensed she didn't approve of Will – with Dad not daring to disagree. As their only daughter, she'd made it her life's work to shape and mould me into the person she thought I should be. And failed. I'd fought hard for happiness, to become who I wanted to be, to know who I truly was. And I knew Mum was projecting onto me whatever she unconsciously sensed was lacking in her own life but didn't have the self-awareness to fix. I consoled myself with knowing that at nearly twenty-seven, I had plenty of time to make my own mistakes.

'Right,' Will boomed at the class in his teacher's voice, but similarly sounding as if he were making a grand entrance onstage. He was able to take command of a group of excitable teenagers, hold an audience captive for two hours or, at the opposite end of the scale, he could sink deep into his own mind and thoughts, as if he needed time to recharge. It was one of the things I loved most about him, that he knew when to take time for himself, to reset his mind.

'Overload,' he'd once said, not long after we'd met, almost as if it was a warning. 'It comes easy to me. Almost *too* easy, and it's a bit like a drug, as if I know it's bad for me but I can't help myself.' I never forgot the dramatic pause. 'If I'm not mindful of when to stop,' he'd whispered, glancing at the ceiling, 'sometimes I fear there'll be no way back.' His eyes had flashed to me then – waiting a beat before closing, as if the curtains were coming down.

For the remainder of the evening, I held onto what he'd said – that I was the one woman he felt he could live with – trying not to overlay it on the other comment. I shuffled into my seat, parents and grandparents standing up as I passed along the row, apologising as I went, and prepared to watch the first night of the play. Will had spent two terms casting, producing, directing and whatever else it took to get a group of teenagers to remember their lines, come in on time, sing in tune and, above all, enjoy themselves – but, while I admired what Will had done with the kids, clapping furiously after each scene or song, I couldn't get what he'd said out of my mind, as if the thought of us living together had blown up the things I'd chosen to overlook.

Sometimes I fear there'll be no way back...

And then I couldn't help wondering if my mother was right, her words tap, tap, tapping at my brain. Making me wonder if we *weren't* right for each other. Thing is, I couldn't think of a single reason why.

'If you ask me,' my mother had said on the phone the day after Will and I had gone to dinner at my parents' country home, 'he's acting. He's not who he says he is. I can smell it a mile off. You can do better.'

'Mum, you've met him once for a couple of hours. You grilled him to within an inch of his life. Why do you have to be so judgemental? Every single time I bring someone home it's the same. Please...' I'd felt the tears welling up – tears of frustration that my mother would never change. If only she would see my point of view, accept that I knew best what made me happy – even if she only managed it for a day – I'd feel validated in some small way at least. But my mother was unrelenting. And now, sitting watching the play, even though Will had just confided a *good* thing to me – that I was the only woman he'd yet felt he could live with – here I was, wondering if my mother was right. That he *was* somehow acting.

CHAPTER THIRTEEN

Now

The rain has stopped completely as Jo drives into East Wincombe, her eyes flashing to her satnav screen every few seconds. *In two hundred metres, your destination will be on the left.* Since leaving the main road to turn off towards the village, the countryside has taken on a deeper, darker shade of black, as if she is being swallowed up by the night, the trees closing in around her. And she can almost smell the sea, knowing it's only a few miles away. She and Will always loved walking along the beach together, or taking a clifftop stroll, allowing the gusts of wind to carry their excited chatter about the future out to sea... *children, a home in the country, dogs, everything perfect.* Jo loved nothing more than to discuss plans, hopes and dreams with her husband, but now she's wondering if he ever felt the same, if she was simply talking to herself – just as she does now to fill the lonely nights.

Jo suddenly steps hard on the brakes as she rounds a bend more sharply than she was anticipating, lurching forward as she immediately spots the house sign on a gate to the left – Hawthorn Lodge. She reverses back a few yards, wary of the blind corner behind her, and indicates, turning into the gravelled driveway. A thick hedge overhangs the gateway, making a black arch above as she enters, her eyes focusing on the old red-brick cottage set back from the road, the gravel crunching under the wheels as she pulls up near the front door. A dense copse of trees surrounds the house, making the already dark night even blacker. There are only a couple of street lights in the lane, and the coach lamp above the door isn't giving out much of a glow. Jo stares up at her new home for the next ten days – wondering if it is *Will's* home too. As she pulls on the handbrake and switches off the engine, she feels herself shaking. She's not sure if she can face whatever it is she's about to discover.

'For God's sake,' she mutters to herself, undoing her seat belt. 'You already know there's no one home. So stop worrying, OK? At least for tonight,' she adds in an attempt to comfort herself.

She glances at the car clock – 10.23 p.m. Not bad, considering the traffic, but she's still exhausted from the long drive. Wants nothing more than a cup of tea and bed. *But what if it's* Will's *bed?* she suddenly thinks. *How will I ever get to sleep, knowing he's been in it with another woman all this time, while I've been worrying and grieving and putting my life on hold?* Any hint that that's the case and she resolves she'll sleep on the sofa, if not leave immediately.

Trying to put the thought from her mind, Jo gets out of the car and goes to the boot to fetch her bag. She stops, hand on her case, glancing around as though she's being watched.

Did she hear something? A twig cracking… something rustling in the bushes? She shakes her head. She's being stupid. All she can hear now is a car cruising past on the lane and a dog barking.

Now that the car headlights are off and her eyes have grown accustomed to the dark, she thinks she sees a flash of light coming from the neighbouring property. She freezes for a moment, hearing a noise – a door opening, perhaps, or a window closing. When everything is silent again, she heads up to the front door to find the keys. Suzanne messaged earlier to say she'd leave them underneath a flowerpot.

Jo fumbles in her pocket for her phone and puts on the torch. 'Well, there's the pot,' she says, upturning it then looking around to see if there's another. 'But there are no keys.' She moves it aside completely, patting the ground underneath again, seeing that her hand is rummaging amongst woodlice and worms in the torchlight. She recoils, making a disgusted noise. 'Great,' she says, straightening up and wiping her hand on her jeans. She tips back her head, staring up at the sky, amazed by the number of stars as she wonders if she should phone Suzanne.

'Is that you, Jo? Hello?'

A man's voice. Coming from behind. Footsteps crunching the gravel.

Jo freezes. Feels herself wobbling, thinking she may topple over completely.

Will…?

She forces herself to turn round but it's as though she's sunk up to her neck in the gravel. *Say something, for heaven's sake…*

'Jo?' the voice says again. 'Is that you?'

'Will… *Will*…' Slowly, she turns, her vision blurry, her entire body trembling. She wants to swallow but her mouth is so dry. She's imagined this moment a thousand times during the last year, how it will play out, when and where he'll come back to her. She never imagined in a million years it would be on another woman's driveway near the South Coast.

In her mind, she'd envisaged them staring at each other for the briefest of moments, their eyes drawing them back to how things were that morning before he left for work, before falling into each other's arms, the air thick with innocent explanations of what had happened. None of which she can remember at this exact moment.

'Hi,' he says when she finally manages to turn, setting eyes on him. 'Will…? I… Sorry, will I what?' he adds with a laugh, approaching her with an outstretched hand. 'Will I let you in, I should imagine you were going to say,' he says with a broad grin. 'Have you been here long? I'm Simon. So sorry I haven't put the keys under the pot yet. I meant to come round earlier, but things ran on down at the Crown and, well…' He trails off when he sees Jo's face. 'Are you OK?'

'Sorry,' she whispers. 'You must think I'm an idiot.' Jo quickly gathers herself, clearing her throat. 'Yes, I'm fine. A bit tired, that's all. I just got here.' She lets out an unconvincing laugh.

She takes his outstretched hand, giving it a light shake in return. Mainly, she wants to yank his arm off because he's *not* Will, scuff gravel at him for making her think he was. She hates him already for not being her husband. In her head, his voice sounded exactly like Will's. But now, in reality, she can hear it's not. And neither is he anything like Will to look at, standing within the dim cone of light from the lamp above the door. 'Oh, and yes, I was just saying "Will you let me in?"' She clears her throat again.

The man, tall (about the same height as Will at least, she supposes), stares at Jo for a moment before rubbing his hand nervously through his sandy hair. 'Oh, sorry… of course.' He fumbles in his coat pocket, finally pulling out a set of keys. He immediately drops them. When he bends down, he staggers sideways. 'Not drunk,' he says, laughing and peering up, his hands patting the gravel. Jo flicks at her phone and illuminates the area with her torch.

'Thank you,' he says, glancing up again. 'I only had three. Well, maybe four pints,' he adds. 'Pool match,' he explains, standing up and waving the keys in front of Jo. 'But I've got a couple of days off, so I'm allowed.'

He needs to stop talking and just open the door, Jo thinks, seeing something familiar in him. *Herself.*

'And did you win?'

'Of course,' he replies with a smile, pushing the key into the lock. It won't turn. 'Damn,' he mutters, wiggling it, trying to get it out. 'Actually, we lost. Comprehensively.' He makes a face. Rolls his eyes.

'Shall I try?' Jo offers after a while.

Simon stands aside and Jo turns the key gently one way, then the other, lightly lifting it a little as she slides it out. 'There,' she says softly, blinking through watery eyes. *Not Will… This man is not Will.* 'Shall I try this one?' she says, holding up another key. Without waiting for an answer, she puts it in the lock and turns it easily, pushing the door open. Immediately, something is on her – something warm and furry bouncing about at her feet, half jumping up at her, knocking her off balance while letting out excited whines and half-barks.

'Spangle, get down,' the man says, lunging at the dog, making an apologetic face.

'It's fine, he's fine,' Jo says, grateful for the distraction. She bends down, cupping the dog's face in her hands, feeling his long silky ears. His eyes are wide and glistening, looking directly into hers as his entire body wags along with his tail.

Has Will petted you, boy? Has he taken you for walks, groomed you, fed you?

'Well, you're a beauty, aren't you?' she says, meaning it. He's a fine-looking dog – his tan and white coat soft and shiny, his teeth gleaming and his lolling tongue bright pink.

'By contrast, you'll find old Bonnie rather aloof,' Simon says, pointing to the end of the hallway. A black and white cat presses up against the door frame, slowly winding its way closer, its tail twitching vertically.

'Hey, puss,' Jo says, thinking both animals seem harmless enough. She's sure she can do a good job looking after them while she's here. In fact, they'll be good company. Since Will went, she's wondered whether to get a small dog. It would get her out and about more, take the focus off herself and her own misery.

'Do you have much stuff to bring in?' Simon asks. 'I can help.'

'Oh, that's fine. Don't worry. Just one small suitcase.'

'Honestly, allow me,' he says, slipping her car keys from her hand. 'It's no trouble,' he adds, going back outside. A moment later, he returns with Jo's case. 'Tell me you didn't prang your car on the way here?' he says, winking.

Jo freezes, eventually giving a little shake of her head. 'No,' she says quietly. 'It's… it's an old dent.'

'Relax, I was joking,' he says. 'I'll take your bag upstairs in a moment. Suzie asked me to show you around, give you the lie of the land and all the house's quirks.'

'Great, thank you,' Jo says, her eyes flicking around, wondering why the owner doesn't just ask Simon to tend to the animals while she's away. He seems very familiar with them, and the house.

'Right, living room is in here,' he says, signalling the door to the left, opening it only a few inches. 'It's cosy when the fire gets going.'

Living room. Fireplace. Mantelpiece… Will.

Jo feels nauseous.

But Simon closes the door again. 'Suzie doesn't allow Spangle in there unless he's really dry. He can get on the sofas if he's clean. And Bonnie just goes where she wants. You know what cats are like.'

Jo smiles, looking back towards the living room as Simon leads the way to the rear of the house. She doesn't care about the other rooms. She only wants to go in there, see the photos of Will on the mantelpiece, forensically analyse everything about them – the size of them, the angle at which they're set, the other things around them, if there's any dust on them, when they were taken. She will glean what she can from them and then she'll set to on the rest of the house. Picking it apart for signs of Will. All the while terrified of what she will find.

CHAPTER FOURTEEN

'You shouldn't need to touch the cooking range,' Simon explains.
'It stays on all the time and kind of looks after itself. The central
heating controls are in the utility room if you need to adjust the
temperature. It's going to cool off in the next week or two, so you
might need a boost. Especially if you've taken Spangle out for some
bracing walks. And trust me, to wear him out, you'll need to.' He
strides around the kitchen, gesturing to various things faster than
Jo can absorb, especially when her mind is on him leaving so she
can venture, alone, into the living room.

To see Will…

'Suzie likes her sitters to feel very much at home, so do help
yourself to anything you find in the cupboards. Her *casa* is your
casa, as they say. Oh, and the stopcock is under the sink in case
of emergency. There's a little handbook here that Suzie has put
together over the years to help, with her number, my number,
other local services you might need – trusted tradesmen and the
like.' He points to a folder lying on the counter.

'So how come Suzanne doesn't ask you to feed her animals
when she's away?' Jo pulls out a chair at the small round kitchen
table and sits down. 'You're right next door. It would make sense.'

Jo watches as Simon fills the kettle. 'Tea,' he says, more a
statement than a question, avoiding hers entirely.

'Thanks,' she says, deciding the living room can wait a little longer.
This man may know things. 'Just what I need after my long drive.'

She looks around the kitchen – cluttered, yet purposeful and stylish in a rambling country way. There are open shelves on the walls, adorned with a multitude of glass Kilner jars, each filled with different ingredients: pasta, rice, various grains, dried fruit. And several jars of apricots, which she stares at for far too long.

My mother's secret ingredient, Will had said, tearing open the packet. *Dried apricots...* He'd added a large handful along with a bunch of fresh thyme before sliding the huge pot of chicken into the oven. It was a Sunday tradition in winter.

'Here,' Simon says, placing two cups of tea on the table. 'Milk and sugar. Help yourself.'

Spangle twists and wags between them, his tail whacking one or the other of their legs. 'Lively chap, isn't he? Does he ever sleep?'

'For a few minutes,' Simon says with a grin. 'But he's a good boy. Useless guard dog, though.'

'Oh... will I be needing one of those then?' Jo asks, steering the conversation. 'I'd have thought what with Suzanne living out here all alone, she'd have chosen a German Shepherd or similar.'

Simon's face breaks into a smile, tiny lines fanning out from each of his grey-hued eyes. *Warm, kind eyes*, Jo thinks. And, if he knew her story, why she was really here, they'd probably turn into pitying eyes.

'Suzie is rarely alone,' he says with a laugh. 'Though she's hardly here these days. She already had the animals when her career took off and she couldn't bear to part with them. She inherited this place from her mother a few years ago and couldn't bear to part with that either. She grew up here. The place has history for her.' He pauses briefly. 'And she's had other... issues to deal with lately.'

'I see,' Jo says, wondering what he means by 'issues'. 'Is she married?'

Simon tips back his head, another laugh. 'Suze? Nah... She's far too, let's say, independent for that. Though...' He trails off, thinking better of it.

'Any men on the scene?'

What am I doing? she thinks. *I'm sitting in the kitchen of the woman who may have stolen my husband, grilling her slightly drunk neighbour.*

'They come and go,' he says with a laugh.

'I see,' Jo says again. Then she remains silent, remembering how her counsellor would sit there, patiently, waiting for her to speak. The fragile silence between them worth more than a thousand words. At first it was uncomfortable, but after a while she grew used to it. Somehow it drew things out of her. The *painful* things.

Simon sips his tea. Looking at her over the rim of the mug. 'Trust me, I'm an actor' is printed on the side. There are two arrows pointing up at him. Jo freezes, her own mug halfway to her lips.

Quickly, she looks away, down at Spangle who licks her hand.

'Suzanne has a kind of bohemian lifestyle. Taking off wherever and whenever she wants. Filming, theatre, living her best life and all that kind of stuff. She's a good woman.'

Jo doesn't know whether to like her or hate her.

'But everything's different now,' he adds.

'She's an actress?' Jo asks, almost choking. *An actress who has ripped my life apart...* 'Sounds like she has a great life.'

'Yeah, she is,' Simon says, tapping the side of his mug. 'Though she'd say otherwise. An artist in turmoil. Living for her art, yet suffering for her talent.' He laughs.

'Sounds like you know her quite well.'

'We've been friends forever,' Simon says, adding more sugar to his tea and stirring it vigorously. 'I grew up in the village too. I've known Suze since way back.'

Jo wonders what it would feel like to move back to her old village. The village where her parents still live. The only word she can think of is *stifling*. 'Does she have a partner? Someone special?' She's pushing it, she realises, but she's not sure if she will see Simon again during her stay here. Needs to find out what she can while she can.

'To be honest, I'm not sure,' Simon replies. 'I think there may be someone new on the scene after...' He trails off. 'If there is, I just hope he makes her happy this time.'

'That's all anyone wants,' Jo says, feeling annoyed at how vague he's being. 'Anyway, she has a lovely home and I shall enjoy looking after it for the next ten days. She's very brave, inviting a stranger in. Not sure I could do that.'

'Me neither,' Simon replies. 'But Suzie always seems to get good people in. As though she attracts the right things in her life. The last chap she had to house-sit was great but he had to let her down at the last minute. I know he felt awful about it, but a family issue took him away. He was a good bloke. I met him a few times.'

Jo's heart clenches. *Will. Is he talking about Will? Is that how they met?* 'It's not something I'd even considered doing until lately,' she says, trying to keep the conversation going. 'A friend of a friend suggested it as a... well, as a kind of cheap holiday.' Jo looks away, suddenly feeling embarrassed. 'It sounds a bit sad, really, but I love animals and I love the sea,' she adds, justifying her presence. 'And I can't afford anything else right now.' That's as close as she's going to touch on her situation.

'Then you're in the right place,' Simons says. 'Beautiful walks nearby, coastal and countryside. I'm sure Spangle here will guide you. Let him follow his nose and he'll show you the sights.'

Jo smiles. Spangle is a good dog, she can already sense that. He's picked up on something, his nose working overtime around her, never still, his claws clacking on the terracotta tiles as he scoots over to his water bowl, returning for a pat, his mouth dripping.

'Sounds great. So...' Jo says, her mind in overdrive. If the last house-sitter was Will, surely he wouldn't have put photographs of himself on the mantelpiece? That sounds more like something Suzanne would do if she was... arranging pictures of her latest love. Jo shudders. 'What do you do for work?' She wants to know why Simon hasn't been asked to look after Hawthorn Lodge and the animals.

'Oh God, don't ask,' he says. Bonnie suddenly jumps up on Simon's lap, digging her claws into his thighs. He yelps, gently lifting the creature and unhooking her from his jeans. 'Oww, that hurt, puss,' he says, wincing as he lowers the cat to the floor. 'So what is it you do?'

'Oh,' Jo says, wondering if it was the cat distracting him or if he's being evasive. 'I sew. I'm a dressmaker.'

'That's really cool.' He sips more tea. 'Creative, then.'

Jo shrugs. 'It's mainly bridal now. Still some theatre work.' *It's how I met Will*, she wants to say but doesn't. 'I love helping people make their big day special.' *Even if it kills me inside…*

Theatre, Jo thinks, wondering if that's a more likely scenario for Will and Suzanne meeting. They might live in different parts of the country, but Suzanne clearly travels for her work. She could have been in the Midlands.

'Creative *and* practical, then,' Simon says, seeming impressed, giving her a look. A look she's not had from a man in a long while. 'When Suze messages me, asking what her new sitter is like, I shall tell her she is…' He clears his throat. 'I shall tell her she's picked a good 'un again.' Simon looks at her. 'Right,' he says, standing up. 'I should be going. Let you settle in. Honestly, call me if you need anything. I'm around the next few days. Any problems, give me a shout.'

'Sure, thanks,' she says, itching to get into the living room.

'Maybe I'll see you tomorrow?'

'Perhaps. I'm sure Spangle here will have me up and out early,' Jo says, smiling. 'I might even take him for a quick walk now, to help him settle for the night.'

Simon nods, heads for the door. 'Goodnight, then,' he says in the hallway, hand outstretched.

'Goodnight, Simon,' she replies. 'See you around.'

He nods and heads off into the darkness, crunching across the gravel. Jo shuts the door, locks it and leans back against it. Spangle bounds down the corridor, giving a tentative jump up at her.

'Hey, boy,' she says, bending down and fussing him. 'It's OK. We'll be OK.' The cat lurks near the kitchen doorway again, sizing up her new carer from a distance. Jo makes a chirping sound at her, making the cat's eyes narrow briefly, as if she's understood. Then Jo steps towards the living room doorway. She glances back at the front door, knowing it's locked although still feeling as though she's being watched. Simon may have another set of keys.

Slowly, she pushes the living room door open, going inside. The first thing that hits her is the smell. No, *scent*. Orange blossom and lilies... *Lovely*, Jo thinks. Evocative and sensual. But she doesn't like it – doesn't like her senses being stimulated when she's bracing herself for heartache.

A big comfy sofa and two armchairs. All of them upholstered in cream fabric with thick sheepskin throws draped over them. A dog's bed in the corner... lamps, a bookshelf crammed with an assortment of titles, a small side table brimming with bottles – Jack Daniel's, gins, vermouths, brandy... The glinting colours pale against the vibrant sea-turquoise walls, from which the giant gilt mirrors hang, the drapes heavy at the window. The scene takes Jo's breath away. It's beautiful. It's someone's home.

Her husband's lover's home...

Then she turns to the fireplace.

The stone surround with the black log burner in the middle.

The large rug on the bare boards.

Just like in the House Angels photographs.

Jo dares to cast her eyes up to the mantelpiece.

Candles. Many unlit candles.

Strings of fairy lights, also unlit. True to the website pictures.

Shells, plus a tiny stuffed hummingbird perched on a small branch as if it's been there all its life, are arranged on the mantelpiece. A small piece of bleached driftwood sits on the hearth, an incense burner beside it. She walks closer to the fireplace.

Something isn't right.

She takes her phone from her back pocket, opening her photo stream, opening the screenshots she'd taken.

Will.

She looks between the two. Perhaps a dozen times. Comparing them.

Spangle weaves between her legs, sniffing, licking, semi-barking, half whining, bouncing and almost lying down, his front legs splayed to get Jo's attention.

Jo turns – right round one way, then right round the other, scanning the rest of the room. She pushes her hand through her hair, zooming in on the photos on her phone.

'Oh no, oh no… dear God, *no*…' She can't bear to be wrong. For it not to be true. For everything to be a waste of time. What has she *done*?

She goes right up to the fireplace, in case she's missing something, inspecting it at close quarters. Everything is as it should be. Just as advertised. Exactly as the website showed.

Except there are no photographs of Will.

CHAPTER FIFTEEN

Jo wraps her dressing gown around her, tying it at the waist. She didn't sleep well. As she approaches the kitchen, she hears Spangle's claws clacking on the tiles, scraping at the door with an eager whine as she goes in. 'Hey, down boy,' she says, catching him by the shoulders as he jumps up for a lick. 'Steady... ooh, yes, and a good morning to you too.' She manages to hold him still long enough to press her face into his neck, breathe in his scent. Even though he's Suzanne's dog, he's some kind of comfort.

'Maybe I'm wrong,' she says, grateful to have two animals to justify talking to herself as she fills the kettle. 'Maybe Will was never even here and I was just seeing what I wanted to see.' Then, for the hundredth time, she pulls up the screenshots and examines them. He might have been missing for a year, but she hasn't forgotten his face – his bright eyes, strong jaw, his perfect-shaped head that he always kept clean-shaven. There's no mistaking him.

'Have you seen this man?' she says to Spangle and then Bonnie, as the cat sits on the windowsill staring out into the back garden. Spangle wipes his nose on the screen, almost as if he's picking up a scent, but Bonnie just turns away, uninterested, a faint purr at the back of her throat.

'It's crazy, but you two probably know the answers to all the questions I need to ask. You've probably witnessed everything that would fill in the blanks in my life,' she adds, spooning some instant coffee granules into a mug. The 'actor' mug still sits by the sink. Jo twists it round so she can't read the words.

Last night, she discovered three bedrooms upstairs, deciding to sleep in the smallest one at the back of the house. It only has a single bed, but she couldn't face sleeping in the double bed in Suzanne's room. She only managed a few minutes in there, gazing round at the belongings – few and far between, and none looking as though they belonged to a man. Suzanne had laid out fresh towels on the clean duvet with a note saying 'Welcome to my home'. Jo had left it undisturbed and headed for the landing, wanting somewhere else to sleep.

'Odd,' she'd said, discovering one of the other bedroom doors was locked. But then she realised it was likely where Suzanne kept her valuables. She would do the same with strangers coming and going. So that only left the rear bedroom. And a fitful night of sleep after she'd given Spangle a quick run down the lane.

*

'Right, you two,' Jo says, 'let's get you sorted.' In the utility room, she mixes up a large stainless steel bowl of dog meat and biscuits, following the quantities written out on a chart taped to the cupboard. Then she empties a sachet of food for Bonnie. 'Feed separately', the note states, and Jo can see why when Spangle gulps his breakfast down in only a few snaps of his mouth, while the cat pecks at hers.

After they've finished, she lets the cat outside and puts on her coat and boots before hooking the extending lead onto an overexcited Spangle's collar. She grabs her phone and keys and heads out of the front door, squinting into the bright morning light. Then she stops, turns and leads Spangle back inside – the dog dragging his feet when he thinks the walk is aborted. 'Just a minute, boy,' Jo says, pushing the living room door open slightly, enough for her to see the mantelpiece. She just needs to check one more time.

Her shoulders drop. *Still no Will.*

She heads off down the lane with Spangle on a shortish lead while on the road, doing exactly what Simon suggested – allowing the dog to follow its nose. They pass through the village – almost picture-postcard perfect with a mix of black-and-white timbered houses as well as stone and red-brick places, some with dark-stained timber cladding, traditional in the area. As they approach the centre of the village, Jo sees the church – more austere than the other buildings and clearly very ancient. Opposite is the pub, the place that Simon mentioned yesterday. Mainly stone with a red pantile roof, a gnarled wisteria winds its way along the front of the building, half obscuring the sign.

'The Crown,' Jo says to herself, slowing. *Perhaps I'll go in for an early supper one evening,* she thinks, seeing they allow dogs. Right on cue, Spangle gives an excited bark, looking across at the place and wagging his tail excitedly.

'Do you go in there, boy?' she asks, imagining Suzanne and Will strolling down here arm in arm on a Sunday lunchtime, having a lazy roast dinner with Spangle at their feet before heading back to Suzanne's cosy place. She shudders, seeing the blackboard menu outside – 'Roast beef with all the trimmings' – and a sign advertising the pool match that Simon also mentioned. 'Quiz night Sunday 8 p.m.,' Jo reads from another board. She shakes her head and walks on. Things like that aren't for her. Not any more.

After a few more houses and a couple of lanes – Church Hill, Battle Lane – Jo finds herself out in open countryside. For the first time in what seems like an age, she feels warmth in the sun, even though it's not yet 8 a.m. The hedgerows are greening up and the last of the cherry blossoms are still out, with rabbits darting across the fields as well as in front of them on the lane, making Spangle strain on his lead. His tongue lolls out of this mouth as he eagerly pushes on.

'You want to go up there?' Jo says, noticing how he has veered into a gateway. There's a public footpath sign, so Jo follows him, deciding the dog knows best. She sees the steep incline beyond, the path winding up around the side of a grassy field before disappearing into a wooded copse. She reckons the views from up there will be worth it as she squeezes through the kissing gate, allowing Spangle to weave through first.

By the time they reach the top, Jo is puffing and her thighs are aching. Her cheeks smart from the breeze. She's not let Spangle off the lead yet, partly in case there are still lambs in nearby fields but also because she's not certain the dog won't simply run off. She's not his owner, after all. But she allows him plenty of freedom to run on a long lead. At the top of the hill, before the path disappears into the thicket of trees, Jo stops to catch her breath, turning round to take in the scenery.

'Wow,' she says, just able to see the coast in the distance. A patchwork of fields spreads out before her in varying shades of green and brown, with hamlets, villages and farms scattered across the quilt of the land. She wonders if Will is somewhere down there, within sight, yet out of sight too.

She feels tears stinging her eyes, but manages to blink them back as Spangle bounds up to her, letting out a whine as she drops to a squat. He presses up against her and Jo puts a hand on his back, pulling him closer – anything to feel the warmth of another living thing.

'You know what, dog?' she says, wiping her fingers under her eyes, determined not to cry. 'I feel less alone up here with you than I have the entire last year surrounded by people.' *Even caring people*, she thinks, mainly about Louise. Her friend has done everything to help her – from cooking and shopping, offering money without the need to repay, a bed for the night, a social life and now, it seems, matchmaking. She's done everything except move in with her. But, as well intentioned as Louise is, none of these things really helps. None of these things has brought Will back.

She drops down onto the grass, not minding if the wet soaks through her jeans. Spangle makes another deep whine and rests his chin on her bent knees, looking into her eyes as if he understands everything behind them. Jo laughs through a sniff, giving his silky ears a good stroke.

'That day…' she says, her words carried away on the wind. 'If only I'd known back then that almost a year later I'd still be looking for him.' She shakes her head in disbelief, hoping the view will ground her. 'I'd only ever tell you this, Spangle, but there was a point a few weeks before Will disappeared when I thought things couldn't get any worse. But they did. *Oh* how they did. And I'm the one left wondering what to do with that information, not knowing if the two things are connected, if I should tell anyone… And if I do, then what?'

She fusses Spangle again, taking deep breaths to calm the welling anxiety. She stares into the dog's huge, eager eyes. 'I'm not sure I can keep it in any longer,' she whispers. 'The size of it… it's like a tumour growing inside me, eating me up. But how can I tell anyone, let alone the police?' She shakes her head.

She made a pact with Will that night. She can't go back on her word.

'Maybe we were both in shock,' she tells Spangle. 'Acted in panic. Hindsight is a great thing. But then time goes on and it becomes too late to change things, becomes a way of life, something you learn to live with. But how I'd have done things differently if I'd known Will was going to vanish into thin air.'

Jo stands then, brushing mud and grass off her legs. 'Right, come on, Spangle. We can't sit around here all day moping. Let's get you worn out so I can get on with…'

Jo trails off, imagining herself rifling through Suzanne's possessions, desperate for clues, desperate to find those photographs, desperate to prove that she isn't going mad. That Will has been in Suzanne's house. That he is still alive.

CHAPTER SIXTEEN

As she heads back to Hawthorn Lodge, Jo can't help her mind wandering, switching from one painful memory to another as if her brain is torturing her. Thoughts of *that* night mixed up with the day Will disappeared, when the gravity of the situation was only just becoming apparent. Of course, she'd had to call her parents.

'Oh, *Mum*,' Jo had said, wanting nothing more than to fall into her mother's arms as she opened the door. Usually her mother's arrival, which was extremely rare, if not unheard of, sent knots of anxiety through her, but not now. She'd never needed her mum more and prayed she could rely on her, prayed she would put aside her judgements about Will. Apart from Will himself standing there when she answered the door (he'd left without his keys, after all), her mother was, sort of, the next best thing. Yet, deep down, she wasn't comfortable with relying on her for anything, let alone emotional support. Their relationship had turned into something more businesslike over the years, rather than mother and daughter.

'Darling,' Elizabeth said, stepping inside, a pained expression set on her face as she gave her a cursory embrace. But that was nothing new. Jo's father, Dennis, followed, giving his daughter a longer and tighter hug as he came inside, making a comforting grumbling sound in his throat.

'Simply wretched of him, that's what it is,' her mother said, going into the small living room, hesitating before sitting down.

'Where are the police? I thought they'd be here. Don't they want to question us?'

'Why on earth would they question you, Mum? You've chosen not to see Will since last summer.' Jo couldn't help the bitterness in her voice, which her mother would no doubt interpret as bitchy. But Will wasn't there to defend himself. 'I don't think there's anything you could say that would help find him. I'd rather the police were out looking than sitting here chatting to us.'

'We could perhaps give them another angle to his character. It might help with all their profiling stuff. It's amazing what they can work out these days, you know.'

'What, you mean maligning him just because you hoped your daughter would marry a bank manager or stockbroker instead of an actor?'

'He's a schoolteacher, darling, let's be real. At a comprehensive.'

'Elizabeth…' Dennis had said then, giving his wife a look. 'We're here to support Joanna, not dish out I-told-you-so's.' He sat down, sinking deep into the saggy sofa next to his wife.

'Thanks, Dad,' Jo had said then, preparing herself for more of the same as she explained what she knew so far, which was pretty much nothing. Her mother's vitriol was the least of her worries back then.

Thanks, Dad… Jo thinks now as she walks up the driveway of Hawthorn Lodge, remembering how old she thought he'd looked that day. She'd never noticed it before. And back then, she also had no idea how *she* would age as the days turned into weeks and then months. As things stood, she had no idea how many years would go by before there was news.

Lack of sleep, the wrong food (or no food), too much wine to take away the pain, and cortisol levels through the roof from anxiety had all taken their toll. She can't help the smile as she remembers the emergency hamper Louise brought round several months on from D-Day.

'For you. Use them,' she'd said in that Louise way of hers, tossing out the boxes and bottles and tubes onto Jo's bed. 'This is for your eye bags. This is for the eczema flare-ups. This will make your hair shine, guaranteed, and this is the ultimate night cream. Oh, and use this on your hands. It's expensive. There's a chance your skin will...' She'd grabbed one of Jo's hands then, studying the crepey texture. 'Well, there's a chance it might regenerate in time.'

Jo hadn't had the energy to protest or defend herself, to say that really, until she knew what had happened to Will, her beauty regime (not that there was much of one in the first place) was not a priority. 'Thanks, Lou, that's so thoughtful.'

And she'd meant it.

'Oh,' Jo says, seeing the package on the doorstep, glancing back out onto the lane in case the delivery driver is still about, wondering if she should have signed for it. She hasn't fully read through Suzanne's email of instructions yet, but she thinks there was something mentioning a couple of deliveries over the next few days. She picks up the large, sealed plastic bag and takes it inside.

'No, no, Spangle, *no*!' She lunges at the living room door to close it but is too late – Spangle charges inside, tracking muddy paw marks over the rug. 'Get down!' Jo shrieks, making the dog freeze then bow his head. He gives a little whine before lying down on the white sofa, his wet tail thumping against the cream upholstery, leaving feathery lines of dirt on the fabric. 'Oh, Spangle, you're going to get me into trouble,' Jo says, approaching him calmly. When she's next to him, she scoops him up in her arms. It seems he's quite happy to be held, even though he's heavy and a little too big to be picked up.

Jo takes him to the utility room and gives him a good rub down, making sure he can't get out of the kitchen. Then she stares at the grey package on the kitchen table. The wrapping has several large barcode stickers on it, with Suzanne's address and a return address, plus some dirty scuff marks. She pokes it. There's something soft yet substantial inside. Clothing, she suspects.

Open it, a voice says.

Jo glances up. *Will*, she says, feeling the relief wash through her.

You know you want to. His deep voice resonates through the kitchen as he leans against the worktop, head tilted, a mischievous look in his eyes.

'I can't,' Jo says out loud. Spangle gives a quiet little bark, bouncing about at Jo's feet, as if to say, *Who are you talking to?* 'It's not addressed to me.' She picks up the package again and googles the website name on her phone. 'Men's clothing,' she says, her heart suddenly thumping. She looks to Will for encouragement, for one last *Open it,* but he's gone.

It only takes a moment to carefully peel back the sealed flap of the plastic bag, though some of it tears in the process. But it looks as though it will seal up again OK with some tape, and Jo can always blame Spangle, say he'd had a quick chew before she could stop him. She slides out the contents.

Two men's shirts.

Her mouth goes dry as she reads the collar size – 16½ inches. Will's size.

Coincidence, that's all, she thinks, hardly able to look at them. She can't lie to herself – they're exactly the type of shirt Will liked to wear to work. Not too formal, one striped grey and white, the other a deep blue. Both fitted and semi-casual.

'Get a grip,' she tells herself. 'Simon mentioned Suzanne might have a new man in her life. They must be for him. It's probably his birthday or something and she's ordered him a gift, that's all.' She slides the plastic-wrapped shirts back into the bag and presses down the seal again.

But what if her new man is Will?

*

Jo opens every drawer and every cupboard in the living room. It doesn't take long. There's a sideboard – painted in a faded antique white. The bottom cupboard is filled with all sorts of things, from magazines and old pamphlets, to board games, tablecloths and mats, some dusty old dried flowers with their stalks tied together, an old camcorder and a few DVDs and video cassettes. Nothing unusual, particularly, and no photographs or anything indicative of Will.

Then she goes through the wooden chest that sits between the two sofas as a table. More of the same – the type of bric-a-brac that wouldn't look out of place at a car boot sale. She opens a couple of drawers in a small cabinet on the far wall and scans the tall bookshelf in case the photos have been tucked between some books. Nothing.

Where would I hide photos from the mantelpiece if I wanted them out of sight but not got rid of?

Jo peels back the rug in front of the fireplace, on every side so that the wooden boards beneath are exposed. No photographs. She removes a couple of prints from the wall in case Suzanne has tucked something behind, but there's nothing. She looks underneath the sofas, behind the furniture, inside the curtain linings and even in the log burner to look for remnants in case Suzanne has burned them. Nothing. Anywhere.

'OK, I need to either give up or find some other kind of proof that Will has been here or is linked to Suzanne. Or think completely differently,' she whispers to herself, dropping down onto the sofa. Then she hears a noise followed by claws on the hallway tiles. 'Spangle, how on earth did you open the kitchen door?'

The dog trots into the living room and slumps down at Jo's feet. She can't help grinning.

'Before I do anything, though, I need to clean up that mess.' She points to the muddy marks on the sofa beside her as Spangle thumps his tail on the floor. *Guilty.*

Finding what she needs in the utility room cupboard, Jo gently rubs at the mud with a damp cloth. She uses a fabric-cleaning spray she found but, to her horror, the stain gets even worse, spreading out in a muddy blot. 'Oh, dog. Did you have to?' she says, pulling out the seat cushion, hoping the cover is removable. It looks like it would wash OK in the machine. 'Thank goodness,' she says, unzipping the cover, relieved it comes off.

It's just as she's extricating the cushion from its tight covering that she notices – freezes, catching her breath. Several pieces of A4-size card have been tucked underneath the sofa cushion, slightly crumpled and indented from being sat on.

Jo lets the seat cushion drop to the floor, making Spangle dart out of the way. She reaches down to retrieve them, her hand shaking. They feel thick, slightly glossy. And when she turns them over, she sees that they are photographs. Three in all.

Three photographs of Will. The same ones that were propped on the mantelpiece.

'Oh… my… *God*…' she whispers, feeling light-headed.

She stares at them, one after the other, seeing her husband's familiar expression. One picture shows him looking over the photographer's shoulder, as if he's gazing at something in the distance. He's outside, with countryside behind him, a moody grey sky. Another picture is a head-and-shoulders shot of him in a café making a silly face, and the last one is of him in a car, sunglasses forked on his head – a selfie taken just before driving off.

Jo recognises them all. At one time or another, he's used them as his Facebook profile picture. And not only that, but she took two of them herself.

'These two have been enlarged and cropped,' Jo says to herself, thinking back. 'And I was actually *in* this one myself,' she says, studying the countryside photo again. 'And this one, I took it but I'd included our lunch. Someone – *Suzanne?* – has zoomed in on Will and removed everything else.'

Jo flops down onto the sofa again, staring at the pictures for what seems like hours, as if somehow, by doing that, it might bring Will back. Or, at the very least, he might speak out from within the images, telling her where he is.

CHAPTER SEVENTEEN

Jo wakes. There's something wet on her hand. And a noise. Ringing… knocking.

'Oh…' She sits up, rubbing her eyes, pushing her hair off her face. 'Spangle,' she says as he licks her, trying to wake her. There's someone at the door. She gets up off the sofa to answer it. Something falls off her lap.

The photographs.

She looks down at them, seeing Will staring up at her. Then she quickly scoops them up and shoves them back under the sofa cushion, smoothing down her top and running her fingers through her dark hair as she glances in the hall mirror. She was staring at the pictures so long, she'd fallen into a deep sleep – almost as if having Will there with her had made her feel secure and safe, giving her permission to drift off with him beside her. Just like they used to. She glances at her watch. *Three hours*, she thinks, shocked.

'Hello, Simon,' she says, putting on her best smile as she opens the door.

'Thought I'd just stop by, you know, see how you're getting on.' His hands are in the front pockets of his jeans, as if he doesn't know what else to do with them. He shuffles from one foot to the other. 'All OK with the animals?'

'Oh, yes, yes. All fine,' Jo replies, not knowing if she should invite him in. Perhaps Suzanne has sent him to check up on her. 'Hey, Spangle, come back inside,' Jo suddenly says, lunging down for the dog's collar as he bounces around Simon's legs. 'Would you like to come in?' she says, surprising herself, glancing up at him as she realises she doesn't want to be alone. That company – any kind of company – is preferable to sitting staring at photos of her missing husband and rooting through Suzanne's house, driving herself crazy.

'Sure,' he says, stepping inside, trying to hide the smile. 'I never turn down the offer of a coffee.'

'I'll put the kettle on, then,' she says, bringing Spangle back inside, switching to idle chit-chat mode as she fills the kettle, listening to Simon describing the best local walks in detail, how Spangle loves nothing more than a run along the beach, suggesting a couple of cafés that don't mind dogs… She *thinks* that's what he's saying anyway, as she nods and *mmm*s in what she hopes are the right places.

But her mind keeps veering back to the pictures.

'It's like I just zone out of everything now,' she'd said to Louise, about two months post-D-Day. 'As if I don't exist in the real world any more. I'm… I'm somewhere else and I think it's the same place Will has gone, except I don't know where that is. Does that make sense?'

'No,' Louise had replied. Despite having not long been back from work, and after a day in court, her face was still perfectly made up and her hair still styled in its purposefully messy updo. It looked as though she'd had time to visit the nail salon recently, too – her long nails glinting a subtle moonstone shade at the end of slim fingers. Jo had scrunched up her hands then. Sat on them on the bar stool in Louise's kitchen. Archie was on nights and Lou had invited her over. Somehow knowing she needed it.

'I keep seeing him. Everywhere, when I'm least expecting it. I talk to him. And… and the crazy thing is, he replies. Does that mean I'm going mad?'

'Probably,' Louise had said, making two gin and tonics. She wasn't pregnant then, or, if she was, she didn't know. 'Drink.'

'So what do I do? How do I come back to *my* life? How do I carry on with work, with my friends, my family…?' She'd let out a big sigh then. 'My period didn't come just after he went missing, you know. I was convinced that I was pregnant, that even though Will had gone, he'd left something of himself behind. But then I came on and that was that. It must have been the stress that made me late.'

'Oh, *Jo*,' Louise had said, putting her arms around her. 'Just be kind to yourself. None of this is your fault. You might be married to him, but you're not responsible for his actions. I know the not knowing is unbearable and I can't even begin to imagine how you must feel, though believe me, I do try. What I do know is that you're here, you still have your life and, however long this goes on for, I want you to live it. And I will help you do that.'

'I don't know what I'd do without you,' she'd said then, giving her a squeeze back. 'Thanks, Lou.'

*

'Sorry?' Simon says with a smile. 'Lou?'

Jo hands him his coffee. 'What?'

'You just said "Thanks, Lou". You seemed miles away.'

'Oh… sorry, yes. My mind's a bit all over the place at the moment,' she says, sitting down a little too carelessly and sloshing her coffee on her jeans. 'Oh God,' she says, rolling her eyes. 'I mean, I'm totally responsible, so don't worry. I mean, don't worry on Suzanne's part. The dogs and house will be cared for perfectly. And I'm not always this clumsy,' she adds, sponging her leg with the dishcloth. She tosses it back in the sink but it lands on the floor.

'I can tell,' Simon says with a laugh. 'And don't worry. Obviously Suzanne checks in with me about any new house-sitters, but I'm not here to keep tabs on you. I called by because… well, I…'

Jo clears her throat and sips her coffee, not knowing where to look.

'I'd like to get to know you more.'

'Oh…' Jo feels the blush burning up from her chest, rising up her throat and neck, sweeping over her cheeks and forehead.

'You seem… interesting.'

'I'm not,' Jo replies quickly, wondering why, after knowing this man a very short time, she feels she could tell him everything. *Wants* to tell him everything. 'I mean, not really,' she adds, forcing a laugh. She wishes she hadn't invited him in now, though she admits there's something intriguing about him. If circumstances were different, she might even go so far as to say she liked him. But for now, he's a welcome distraction. And besides, he might know things.

'There's a quiz on at the Crown tomorrow night. I wondered if you and Spangle might like to join me. I usually meet up with a couple of friends from the village and we make up a team. We'd be delighted to have you along, and Spangle is very good at getting the answers right.'

Jo feels her blush returning. *Is he asking me on a date?* She feels something inside her curl up, retreat, shrivel. 'Oh, I…'

'You have other plans?'

'Well, no,' she says. 'Though I might have had. But you wouldn't know either way. Of course you wouldn't. Sorry. What I meant was, because I'd just arrived. No time to make any.' She sips her coffee, her hand shaking. 'Plans, that is.'

Simon just sits there, smiling at her, an amused expression in his eyes.

'I'm gabbling. Sorry.'

'I'd like to say it's endearing,' he says, about to continue.

'But it's not. I know that.'

'No, it is. I just thought perhaps I shouldn't say it, seeing as we don't know each other. You seem… real. Honest. But also… vulnerable?'

'Making a lot of assumptions there,' Jo says, raising her eyebrows but also smiling in what seems like a— *Jo, you're* flirting. *Stop it!* She hopes it will be enough to make him quit the analysis.

'Well?' he continues, unruffled, ignoring her. 'Quiz night. You up for it?'

'Sure, why not?' she says in an attempt to portray herself as vaguely normal. She needs to maintain her cover.

*

After Simon has left, after she's fed and watered the animals, tidied up the kitchen, Jo takes a deep breath and heads up to Suzanne's bedroom. *It's not snooping as such*, she tries to convince herself. *She obviously intended for me to use the room.*

She tries to imagine what Suzanne looks like. So far, she's a faceless woman on the House Angels site, though she's not entirely sure she wants to fill in the blanks. But it could help, could join a dot or two – is she Will's type, for a start? Tall, short, blonde, dark... more attractive than her? She doesn't even know how old she is – her profile didn't give away much. In hindsight, she's taken a risk coming to a stranger's house. But at least Suzanne had over twenty reviews, all positive. *But what if they're fake?* she thinks, her mind working overtime as she goes into the bedroom. *What if Suzanne has lured me here, to get rid of me so she can have Will all to herself?*

'Stop being so stupid,' she mutters. '*You* contacted *her*, for a start, and it was you who saw the photos of Will on her mantelpiece, which was purely a coincidence.' Jo halts. 'Oh, hello puss. Are you allowed to be in here?'

The cat is curled up on the end of the bed, her face tucked under her tail. Jo strokes her gently and she briefly looks up, giving a little chirp in the back of her throat.

'I'll let you off this once,' she says, not knowing where to begin. Then she flops down on the end of the bed next to Bonnie. 'To be honest, cat, I feel a bit like an intruder. This isn't something I'd normally do or be proud of.'

And then she spots the picture on the dressing table – just a small framed photograph of a woman. She gets up off the bed, going over and picking it up, somehow instinctively knowing that it's of Suzanne. Her heart thumps as she stares at it, focusing on the close-up portrait, the sea in the background. Jo can't deny that she's beautiful – wavy blonde hair blowing in the breeze, set around a symmetrical face, her teeth white and straight in her broad smile. *And she looks happy*, Jo thinks, wondering why. 'Is it because of Will?' she whispers, placing the picture back on the dressing table.

Jo turns, gazing around the room, seeing the cat has gone back to sleep as she takes everything in, wondering where to start. Wondering where to find even a tiny trace of Will in another woman's house.

CHAPTER EIGHTEEN

Jo stares at herself in the mirror as she brushes her hair, rolling her lips inwards to lessen the effect of the rust-coloured lipstick she's decided, on a whim, to wear.

Lipstick, Jo – really?

She pulls a wipe from her make-up bag and rubs at her lips. 'Ridiculous,' she says, cross with herself, staring at the dark circles under her eyes. *Will loved my eyes*, she thinks. *Always complimented them, said they were the darkest brown he'd ever seen.* She does up her blouse one button higher, making sure the back of it hangs down low enough to cover her skinny jeans as much as possible. She was going to wear her long boots with a heel but decides against them, shoving her feet into flat ankle boots instead. 'That will have to do. I am *not* sending out signals.'

Oh but you are, someone says.

She swings round. '*Will…?*' She catches her breath, her heart melting at the sight of him. 'No, no, really I'm not. I don't even want to go to the pub quiz, but it might be a way… well, a way to find out if Simon – he's the neighbour – knows anything. I saw your photos online, you see. Then I actually found them. Which is good, because it means I'm not going mad. But bad because it means… well, I don't know what it means. Even though I didn't find anything in Suzanne's room, and I know I'm crazy for even looking, I sense you're close, Will. Really I do. I just want to find you. Know what's happened to you. Do you understand that?' Jo reaches out to put her hands flat on his chest, to feel him beneath her touch. But as soon as she moves towards him, he's gone.

The doorbell rings.

'Christ,' Jo says, glancing in the mirror one last time. She grabs her coat and bag and dashes downstairs.

'Simon,' she says, breathless as she opens the door. 'Shall we head straight off?'

'Aren't you forgetting something? Or rather some*one*?'

'Oh, of course… Spangle!' she calls out, taking the lead down from the coat hook beside the door.

'Craig, Dawn, this is Jo. She's house-sitting Suzie's place for a bit. Spangle's really taken to her, as you can see.' Simon bends down to Spangle, who's nestled himself between Jo's feet. He ruffles the dog's fur.

'Very pleased to meet you,' Jo says, shaking each of Simon's friends' hands. 'But I should warn you, my general knowledge isn't exactly top-notch.' She grins, forgetting herself for a moment as Simon heads off to the bar to fetch drinks for them all. The pub seems like a pleasant enough place – the usual heavily patterned carpet, dark wooden tables, a cluster of locals at the bar, the beams of the low ceiling bedecked with hundreds of horse brasses. And first impressions are that Craig and Dawn seem pleasant, too. Normal people doing normal things.

Surely you can enjoy yourself for a couple of hours, Jo? Pretend you're not twisted up in knots?

As they settle down at the little table, Jo finds herself scanning around the pub. Wondering if Will is here, or has *ever* been here – not in the ethereal sense, but rather really here. If he's somehow connected to Suzanne, it may follow that this is the area he's chosen to move to. To *run away* to. She catches Simon's eye as he comes back from the bar, four drinks precariously grasped in his hands.

'Hey, let me help you,' she says, leaping up and relieving him of a couple of pint glasses. She puts them on the table, sitting down on the stool again with Spangle still at her feet.

'Got us some snacks, too,' he says, unloading several packets of crisps from his jacket pockets. 'Brain food,' he says with a wink.

'I signed us up already,' Craig says, sliding the sheets of paper and four pens into the middle of the table, avoiding the drips. 'Competition's likely to be tough tonight, though,' he says with a sweep around the bar, eyeing up the other teams.

'It's just lucky Suzie and her lot aren't here,' Dawn adds. 'They all seem to know everything, especially that tall chap she's brought a couple of times lately. I can't remember his name.'

Tall chap...

Jo stares at her, waiting for her to say more, to describe him in detail. But she doesn't.

Just ask her, for heaven's sake... ask her who the tall chap is...

'Bill, you mean?' Craig says, glancing at the quiz sheet for the picture round. 'Yeah, he was one smart dude. Oh wait, look – I know a couple of these answers. Jo, how about you? Any ideas on number one? Name the year and the movie from the actor's photo.'

Bill... Bill... Will... He never called himself Bill. It was always William or Will. But what if he's changed his name slightly? It's what someone in hiding or reinventing themselves would do, after all.

'Hmm, I'm not sure,' Jo replies, pretending to ponder the picture round as she sips her drink. The gin is warming her brain, soothing her breaking heart.

'You'll get a taste for that, if you're not careful,' Louise had said that night back at her place when Archie was on a late shift. 'Don't let alcohol take away your pain, Jo-jo. I mean, a drink here and there is fine, but... but try to cope with this in other ways, too.'

'Mother's ruin,' was all Jo could think of to say, shrugging and knocking back more. And, for her, motherhood had well and truly been ruined. 'It's not just Will I've lost, you know,' Jo had gone on, staring out into the jungle-like courtyard at the rear of the apartment. 'I've lost his baby, too. Not in the literal sense, but in the *potential* sense. I've lost *all* his babies.'

'You don't know that he won't come back,' Louise had said, thinking she was helping. 'He could, you know. Perhaps when you least expect it.'

Jo looked at her, wondering if Louise was even hearing her. 'Do you actually understand what I mean, Lou? How much I feel I've lost – apart from my best friend, my lover, my soulmate? Worse than all that, Lou, *way* worse, is that I've lost my future, too. All our hopes and dreams and plans for the rest of our lives. Gone.' She'd made an exploding gesture with her hands then, knocking over her drink, scrabbling to set it upright before the glass rolled onto the floor.

'*Back to the Future*,' Jo says, surprising herself as she stares at the quiz sheet, not even really studying it. 'Number five. That's Michael J. Fox.'

'Do you know the year, too, smarty-pants?' Simon says, nudging her, nodding approval at Craig and Dawn. 'See? I knew it was a good idea to invite her along.'

'Now you're really testing me,' she says. *I only know the film because it was one of Will's favourites*, she wants to say. *We'd curl up on the sofa on a Sunday afternoon and binge on old eighties movies.* 'He loved Charlie Chaplin, too,' she says with a faraway smile, staring out of the pub window. Rain pelts at the window, winding its way down the small panes.

'Michael J. Fox was a Chaplin fan?' Craig says. 'You're certainly full of random trivia,' he laughs.

Jo jumps, like she sometimes does when she's on the brink of sleep and something pulls her back to wakefulness. 'Oh, no. No, sorry. I didn't mean that. I was just thinking out loud. It was someone... someone I used to know who liked old classics.'

'I think it must have been about 1984 or 5-ish,' Dawn says. 'Put down '84, I'd say.' She takes the pen from Craig and fills in the details as the three of them huddle around the quiz sheet, waiting for proceedings to begin.

*

'Righto,' the quizmaster says into his microphone. He's a large man with a thick beard and bruise-coloured tattoos running the length of each arm. His jeans hang down low, leaving a gap front and back between the denim and his T-shirt, a roll of fat hanging over his belt. After every few words, he draws a large swig of his pint. 'Final round,' he booms, a white-toothed grin showing through his beer-foamed facial hair. 'You've had your sport. You've had your geography. You've had your celebrities and entertainment. And now it's time for my mixed-up bag of random questions to get your brain cells sizzling.'

There's a rumble of approval and oohs and ahhs from the locals. Jo is sipping on her fourth drink now – one for each round. 'A tradition,' Simon had told her earlier. 'Somehow makes the questions easier,' he'd said, leaning close and winking. She'd smiled but didn't say anything, was simply enjoying the relative numbness the alcohol gave her. And so far she'd not had to buy a single drink.

'Round four, question number one…' The quizmaster takes a flamboyant swig then ruffles his hand through his dishevelled hair. '"Love one another" were the final words of which Beatle?'

There's a ripple of low chatter amongst the teams as they huddle close to debate. Jo hears hissed whispers: *John Lennon… George Harrison…*

'Definitely George,' Simon whispers in her ear, slipping his arm around Jo's back and drawing her closer. 'Do you agree?'

Jo freezes for a moment.

'Ex-excuse me, I just need to…' She stands up, praying that she doesn't topple the stool or trip on Spangle's lead. 'Here, can you hold him?' she says to Simon. He takes the lead but ends up grasping her hand for a moment too. 'And I think you're right, it's definitely George,' she says, bending down to whisper back. Her hair brushes his face.

There are two other women in the toilets – one washing her hands, the other applying lipstick. Jo goes into a cubicle, her shoulder bumping on the door frame, and leans back against the wall, closing her eyes.

Sober up, woman, for goodness' sake. What are you thinking?

She yanks down her jeans, her thigh muscles as tense as her thoughts.

Love one another, she thinks, remembering the question, tears collecting in her eyes. *Oh, how I thought we did.* 'How *much* I thought we loved one another, Will,' she says, buttoning up her jeans again, flushing the toilet.

And then there's Simon. How it's been tonight.

He put his arm around your back. And whispered in your ear.

'Fuck, fuck, *fuck*…'

'You OK in there, love?' comes a voice outside the cubicle.

'Oh, yes. So sorry for the bad language. All good here.' Jo composes herself before coming out, washing her hands, pushing her fingers through her hair to bring back some of the waves before applying a slick of lip gloss.

'We needed you just now,' Simon whispers as she sits back down again, Spangle's tail thumping the floor. 'Got stuck on a few.'

'OK, you lot,' the quizmaster booms into his mic before Jo can reply. 'Final question, so now's your chance to pip the competition. I have a feeling it's going to be close tonight.'

Spangle lets out a whimper and Jo puts a hand on his head.

'What is the collective noun for a group of crows?' he says, pausing a moment, his eyes scanning round the room as he draws on his pint. 'The collective noun for a group of crows… Ooh, I'm seeing lots of blank faces out there.'

Jo glances at the others on her team, each of them pulling a puzzled expression.

'Group of crows, group of crows…' Dawn says thoughtfully.

'A flock?' Craig whispers, glancing at Simon.

'It's not going to be that obvious,' Simon adds, rubbing his chin. 'You know what Smithy's like with his quizzes. He's a tricksy bugger.'

'I know,' Jo says suddenly, clapping her hand over her mouth when she realises she's talking too loudly. The others lean in close to her as she flicks her eyes around the group, hardly able to say it. 'It's a *murder*,' she whispers, her eyes meeting Will's as she spots him standing at the end of the bar.

CHAPTER NINETEEN

Then

The first time Will went missing was only a year after we were married. In the space of an hour, I went from mildly concerned to increasingly worried to angry and downright fuming when, finally, six hours later, he phoned me.

'What the *hell* were you thinking?' I said after he'd arrived home. I'd waited ages outside the school as we'd planned, finally going inside only to be told he'd already left. We were meant to be going to my parents for dinner. 'You could have told me if you didn't want to go and that would have been fine. But oh no, instead you had to…' I trailed off, seeing he looked done in, exhausted, emotional and not quite there.

'I'm sorry,' he said, standing in the hallway, water dripping off his shoulders. It had been raining all evening and he was soaking.

'Let's get you out of this, then,' I said, reaching up to slide off his mac. He shrugged out of my way, taking the coat off himself. 'I was worried about you, Will.'

When he didn't reply, I sighed and went into the kitchen to make some tea. 'Here,' I said when he came in. 'Drink this.'

We sat together at the tiny kitchen table, our knees touching. 'I couldn't do it,' Will finally said, staring into his mug. 'Not tonight. I know they hate me. And I can't change that.'

I hung my head. 'They don't hate *you*,' I said. 'They hate everyone. Everyone I've ever introduced to them, anyway.'

'Last time I saw your mother, she looked as though… as though she wanted to kill me. There was loathing in her eyes, Jo. I can't be dealing with that.'

'She doesn't want to kill you. She—'

'I know, I know. She wants to kill *everyone*…' Will took a deep breath. 'I'd had a shit day at work and I chickened out, that's all. I'm sorry. I should have let you know.'

I stared at his big hands as they cupped his mug. 'What else, Will? What else is wrong? I know you. And you've been in the company of my parents enough times to know how to deal with them, how to ignore Mum's snipes.' My voice was soft, caring. Will looked up, his eyes heavy.

'You're right.' He took a breath. 'Look, I didn't get the part, OK? They've cast someone else.'

'Oh, *love*…' I said, taking his hand in both of mine. 'Why didn't you call me when you found out? I'm *so* sorry. I know your heart was set on it. We could have cancelled my parents.'

'Yeah, well,' he said. 'Now it's *not* set on it. I couldn't take a battering from your mother tonight too, so I went… I went to a bar in town and got pissed instead.'

I shook my head slowly. 'Oh Will, you should have told me. I'm your wife. I love you. I *understand*.' I pulled him close then, hugging him tightly, breathing him in. It was then that I smelt the alcohol. 'Jack Daniel's, right?' I said through a half-laugh. I felt him nod. 'You hide it well. I'd have had no idea.'

'I'm an actor,' he said, kissing my neck. 'But I'm not acting when I say that I love you too, Jo. Deeply.'

'I know. I know. And there'll be other parts, right? Better parts. Keep auditioning, keep getting yourself out there.'

Will nodded again, pulling away, wiping his big hands down his tired face. 'I'm going to have a shower,' he said, and when he got up, pushed the chair out, he only staggered a tiny bit. Barely noticeable and, if I hadn't smelt the whiskey, I wouldn't have known any different.

*

'Do you think I'm finally in their good books now?' Will said one Sunday evening a few months later. Since landing a part at the local rep theatre with a professional company, I'd noticed a real change in his mood. He was brighter, more focused and positive, more caring and attentive towards me, and he'd started running again, out for several hours at a time. And, as if good fortune were infectious, Margot and I had been inundated with bridal enquiries after the daughter of a lord wore one of our designs at her wedding. Our luck had changed, but quality time together was getting scarcer.

'What, because you basically saved Dad's life?' I dropped my head back on the sofa, laughing. 'Definitely. You're golden boy now, for sure.'

'Yeah, right,' Will replied, changing the channel.

'I *was* joking, you know.'

'I know. Anyway, I'm just glad I spotted it, that I recognised what it was.'

The melanoma had been on the back of Dad's head so he'd not noticed the change himself, and Mum had told him it was just a mole and not to worry, brushing it off in her usual way. But Will's own father had had something similar and so he knew the signs, even though it looked slightly different on white skin.

'Thank God you did,' I said, snuggling up to him. We were both full of Sunday roast. 'And it was such early days, so the prognosis is good. He's going to be fine.'

'He might be an arsehole sometimes, but he's still your dad. Anyway, I don't actually believe he *is* an arsehole, not deep down. I think your mother does something to him, almost as if he's her… I dunno, puppet. It's not healthy, the way he just does everything she says.'

'You're absolutely right,' I said. 'I do know this. But arseholes or not, they are grateful to you for flagging it. I know she should have said it to you, but Mum did say as much to me. In her own kind of arseholey way.'

Will pulled me close, brought me in for a kiss. 'Heaven knows how you turned out so perfect, growing up as an only child with them. But you did.'

'I know,' I replied, laughing and shrugging, cupping his face. *Or maybe I'm just a good actor too*, came the voice in my head.

CHAPTER TWENTY

Now

'Steady, steady,' Simon says, taking hold of Jo's elbow as they leave the pub.

She glances behind her one last time, her eyes flicking along the length of the bar. There's no sign of Will.

As Jo had struggled into her coat, getting tangled up in the dog's lead and knocking her bag onto the floor, the contents spilling out, Simon had gone over to a couple of his mates at the bar to say goodnight. When he returned, he'd found Jo on her knees scraping together spilt coins, a hairbrush, lipstick, hand cream, her phone, a few screwed-up tissues and various other items that had fallen out of her bag, including, to her mortification, a tampon.

'I'm… I'm fine,' she says now as the cold air hits her. She breathes it in deeply. 'See? I'm all good.' She stumbles sideways, laughing as Simon catches hold of her arm.

'You're slurring,' he says.

'I so am so not,' Jo says, frowning. 'I didn't even finish that last gin. It's nice to have a drink, though. It… it makes everything go away.'

'Hey, it's this way,' Simon tells her, guiding her in the opposite direction.

'I knew that,' Jo says, giggling again, bumping into him. 'Just testing.'

'So you have stuff that you want to go away?' he says, still guiding her.

'Doesn't everyone?' she says, clearing her throat.

Hold yourself together, woman. And no blurting…

'Maybe,' he says. 'But not everyone finds escape at the bottom of a gin glass.'

'Oh no, now you're going to think…' Jo can't help the hiccup. 'Now you're going to think… think that I'm… I'm a drunk. A drunk with issues, yeah, that's me.' She pushes her hair off her face, the usual brown waves having mostly flattened in the damp air. A fine drizzle falls around them.

'I don't think that,' he replies.

'Thing is…' Jo says. 'Thing is… I feel good,' she adds, trying to be serious. 'For the first time in ages, so thank you. Thank you very much for that.' She hiccups again.

'Oh, well… you're most welcome.' He laughs then and Jo senses he's far from sober himself. 'Sounds to me like you've had some things going on.'

'You're very… very perceptive. That was hard to say,' she adds. 'Actually, I don't know why I'm laughing. It's not funny. Not funny at all.'

'Nearly home now,' Simon says. 'How about you come in to mine for a coffee? Then I'll know you're OK.'

'You think I can't cope?' Jo says. *It doesn't take a detective to see that…*

'Not at all,' Simon says, stopping at his gateway. Spangle winds between both their legs, binding them up with the lead. 'I just thought it would be nice to, you know, have a coffee. Maybe a nightcap. A chat.'

'Actually, that would be lovely,' Jo says, turning to face him. *Not quite as tall as Will, but you're good-looking, I'll give you that.* She smiles, praying her thoughts aren't audible.

'Come on, Spangle,' Simon says, reaching the lead around behind Jo's back to untangle them. 'You'll have us both on our backs if you're not careful.'

And Jo bursts out laughing again, covering her mouth as she follows Simon up the path to his front door.

'Right, drink this,' Simon says, handing her a strong coffee. 'And I made us some cheese and biscuits,' he adds. 'Thought it might help...'

'Soak up the booze?'

He smiles, sits down.

'Despite what you may think, I'm very responsible and not a total mess, even though I might seem like it now.'

'You can't be that drunk. We wouldn't have come third in the quiz if it wasn't for you knowing that final answer.'

'Murder,' Jo says, sipping on her coffee. *Murder, murder, murder...*

'I honestly never knew that. I quite like it. It's sinister, and I find crows quite sinister, don't you? Harbingers of doom.'

'I didn't even know I knew it myself, to be honest. But it must have been lurking somewhere in the back of my mind...'

Keep it to yourself, Jo. Whatever you do, keep your mouth shut.

She takes a big bite of a cracker, hoping it will stop her speaking, shoving it in. She looks around Simon's living room as he slices some more cheese. It's simply furnished but pleasant.

'You live alone?' she says, spraying out crumbs. She didn't need to ask. It reeks of man living alone, but his furniture is tasteful, his possessions minimal and tidy. Everything in calming shades of grey or bare wood. She likes the unassuming style, as if anyone could live here with ease, slide right into his life. There's a stack of classic car magazines on the coffee table, two black T-shirts hanging to dry on the radiator, a spider plant trailing down off the top of a bookshelf, though she can't read any of the titles. They're too far away for her alcohol-blurred eyes.

'Is it that obvious?' he says, offering her more cheese.

'Yeah,' she says with a full mouth. 'But it's... it's nice.' She looks at him for a beat longer than is comfortable, holds his gaze.

Is that your tactic, Jo? You don't trust yourself not to blurt everything out, so you're flirting with him instead?

'I guess it could do with a few more... you know, feminine touches. But it does me fine,' he adds.

'What, you mean like, pink fluffy things dotted about?'

'Sorry,' Simon says. 'You're right. I'm not into stereotypes, just so you know.' He brushes her knee.

See what you've done now? He's flirting back. Talk nonsense with him... anything!

'Nonsense?' he says, an amused look on his face. 'I'm going to have a whiskey to go with this cheese. Ever get the feeling that...' He hesitates then, his left arm hooked up on the back of the sofa, his fingers just touching Jo's shoulder.

If you stay still, it means you don't mind. If you pull away, it's a signal for him to back off.

Jo stays perfectly still.

'Ever get the feeling that the night isn't quite over?'

'Yes,' she replies quickly, wishing she'd paused a moment. 'I've had far too much already, but you're right. This cheese is definitely lacking something, and I'm also convinced it's whiskey.' She grins.

New plan. Get so pissed you are incapable of speaking.

'Good,' he says, getting up and going to the kitchen. He returns with two glasses and a bottle, setting them down on the table.

'Looks serious,' Jo says, suddenly feeling more sober.

Then Simon taps his phone a few times and music comes on and the lights are dimmed. Will is standing over by the bookcase, the spider plant trailing down over his shoulders.

'How did you actually *do* that?' she says. 'With your phone? Is there an app for that?' *To make missing husbands reappear?* Then she's giggling again.

'Yeah, I can pretty much control my entire house with this,' he says, tossing his phone on the sofa beside him.

'No, I meant *that*,' she says, pointing. 'I don't seem to have any control over when he comes. He turns up whenever he bloody likes, just appearing and messing with my head.' She knows she's slurring, can't help it.

'Sorry, what?' Simon says, a curious smile forming. He pours two shots, hands Jo the smaller of them and gets back into the same position as before. Only closer.

His leg is definitely touching yours now. Don't move. And don't blurt.

'I blurt a lot,' Jo says, swallowing, rolling her eyes at herself. She needs to be serious for a moment.

Don't be serious. If you're serious, it'll come out. And then you'll cry. And he'll think you're a messed-up crazy criminal and… and then he'll call the police!

'Blurting can be good,' he says in just the right tone of voice to stop her feeling silly. 'Nothing wrong with a cathartic blurt if it makes you feel better. And I'm a good listener, if it helps. It's a big part of my job. I couldn't do it if I wasn't.'

'You're a therapist?'

'Yeah, you could say that,' Simon replies. 'So go on, who just turns up and messes with your head?'

'Will…' Jo whispers, staring at him over by the bookshelf. He's watching them both as they sit there on the sofa, his face deadpan rather than having the usual appreciative look he has in his eyes.

What the hell are you doing? Will says to her, his voice matching his disapproving expression.

'I know you're cross,' Jo says across the room. 'I'm sorry… honestly, nothing's going to happen here, and…'

'Firstly, I'm not in the least cross,' Simon says, looking slightly puzzled at whatever Jo is saying. 'And as for the other bit, well no, that's fine. *I'm* sorry now. I'm probably coming on a bit strong and—'

'What? No, wait… I didn't mean you…' Jo says to Simon and, without thinking, she takes his drink from him, leans forward and kisses him full on the mouth. It's the only thing she can think of to make herself keep quiet.

CHAPTER TWENTY-ONE

'God, I'm *so* sorry…' Jo pulls back. Simon stares at her.

'Don't be. If you hadn't done it, I would have.' He touches her cheek, wiping away a stray tear. 'But not if I'd known it was going to make you cry.'

Jo touches her face, drops her gaze and sighs. 'Sorry… I didn't mean—'

'It was a lovely kiss,' he says softly. 'Can't deny I haven't wanted to do that since I first saw you.' His eyes smile along with his mouth as she stares into them.

Then she looks over at Will.

Simon looks over his shoulder, towards the bookcase. He frowns. 'So are you going to tell me who Will is?' He runs his finger along Jo's forearm, gently stroking it.

She shudders. 'I'm not crazy, just so you know.'

'I never said—'

'He's just someone I used to know,' she replies, looking at his finger on her arm.

'Boyfriend?'

'Husband, actually.'

Simon thinks a moment. 'Ah,' he says, taking his finger away. 'I didn't realise you were married. You're not wearing a ring.'

'I'm not. I mean, I am, but… I'm… I'm kind of separated.'

I only took it off because I didn't want people asking questions – why are you house-sitting alone? Where's your husband?

'It's complicated.' She shrugs.

'And now it's more so?'

Jo laughs, reaches for her drink and knocks half of it back in one go. 'It couldn't be more complicated whatever happens now, so no worries there.'

'People... people escape for all sorts of reasons, you know. There's no shame in wanting time out, time away.'

'Escape?' Jo's heart thumps. 'No, no. I'm just here for a break.' She swallows.

'Depends what you're having a break from, I suppose,' he says. 'And if that makes it escaping or not.' He leans forward, kissing her – so softly, Jo isn't even sure he's doing it. And when she opens her eyes, looks over his shoulder, Will is still standing there, hands on hips – watching, slowly shaking his head.

*

'Oh God, oh God, oh *God*,' Jo whispers after Simon has gone to the bathroom. She pushes her fingers through her hair – partly to make it look more presentable but also because she feels like tearing it out. Really, she wants to slap herself round the face. *How much more complicated do you want your life to be? And* do not *have any more to drink...*

She stares around the room. No Will now. She breathes out a heavy sigh.

She's about to stand up to fetch some water from the kitchen when her hand catches on something cold, half submerged between the sofa cushions. 'Oh...' she says, pulling out a small bunch of keys. *They must have fallen out of his pocket*, she thinks, about to place them on the table. But then she sees the label. Hawthorn Lodge... the same handwriting as on the set of keys she's been given. Except there are four keys on this ring, whereas there are only two on hers – one for the front door, one for the back.

'So what are the other two for?' she whispers, looking at them, seeing one is for a mortice lock, the other for a Yale lock. The same type as would fit the locked bedroom door in Suzanne's house. Hearing Simon coming back downstairs, and without thinking of the consequences, Jo quickly shoves the keys in her bag.

'So,' Simon says, sitting down close to her. He takes one of her hands, pressing his mouth against hers again before she can speak. Jo feels her insides melting, trying to convince herself she doesn't like it. But it's not true. She does. 'Tell me about Will, then,' he says, pulling away a little. 'Has he upset you in some way?'

Simon's face swims in and out of focus and the room spins behind him.

I've just stolen your keys… and whether the keys fit or not, I'm going to break into that spare room. I think Suzanne knows where my missing husband is… I think she's having an affair with him.

Jo hiccups.

'Did I… did I just say anything?' She reaches for her glass. Drains it. Sears the back of her throat as if in punishment. Simon pours more, even though she puts up a mini-protest with her hand. The coffee and cheese have helped sober her up, but now she's feeling woozy again.

'No,' he says gently, the soft lines on his face showing concern within a small smile, a quizzical frown. 'But I'm here to listen if you need.'

'Oh, thank… thank goodness,' Jo goes on, briefly turning away. 'OK.' She takes a breath. 'I guess, given your job, I can explain a little. But…' She pauses, waiting for the hiccup. 'It's just between us, OK? But then you'd know all about that anyway. Heaven knows, I've had enough counselling over the last few months to know it has to stay confidential.'

Just get it off your chest, Jo. You're never going to see him again after this week. It might help…

Simon raises his eyebrows, his expression filled with compassion. 'Jo, firstly, I can't be your therapist. Though you can completely trust me, OK?'

She nods, hiccuping, again knowing the rules they have to adhere to. Soon after Will went missing, she'd approached Margot's sister, also a counsellor, to arrange some sessions. She'd popped into Sew Perfect to see Margot, and Jo had taken the opportunity to ask her, hoping she might get a good rate. But she was told that their connection through Margot, however tenuous, went against her professional code of ethics. That's when she'd gone to her GP and taken her turn in the NHS queue.

'Have you ever had a secret so big it feels as though there's this... this *thing* living and growing inside you?' Jo says quietly. 'And the longer you keep it in, the harder it is to contain until one day, you realise it's taking all of your willpower, all of your functioning capabilities just to hold onto it? But all you can do is keep the secret, grip onto it for dear life as it gets heavier and heavier, dragging you down until you can barely even breathe or eat?'

Simon waits a moment, nods his head slightly. 'So there's something you want to get out, but can't?' He pauses. 'I understand. I can hear it in your voice, see it written on your face.' He shifts one leg up underneath him. 'And look, I don't know what's going on here...' He points back and forth between the pair of them. 'Apart from a very nice kiss, of course.' A grin. And Jo returns it. 'I don't want to make things more complicated for you, but if you've got stuff you need to get off your chest, I can be your emergency friend, if you like.'

Oh, Christ, Jo thinks, trying to focus on what he's saying. *He's backing off, thinks I'm a terrible person because I told him I'm married...*

She bows her head, letting out something between a laugh and a groan.

'What?' Simon says, stopping. 'I don't think you're a terrible person at all. I've seen and heard some bad things in my job, I can tell you, so not much shocks me these days. And of course, while I can't be your therapist, we can pretend, right?' He takes her hand again, gives it a squeeze, a stroke.

'Thanks,' she says, her mind exploding with fireworks. *Would it help? Would it alleviate the pressure if I kept it vague? They say a problem shared...*

'A problem halved,' Simon adds.

Jo stares at him, wide-eyed, taking another sip of her whiskey, her head thrumming and spinning.

Finally, she takes a breath. 'What if... what if you know someone – *knew* someone – who'd done something so bad you couldn't even stand to give it space in your own mind, let alone talk about it?' Jo hears her own voice, but it doesn't sound like her. Doesn't seem to be coming from her, as though she's detached from it. 'And what if you were a part of what had happened, without knowing at first, and that same person then swore you to secrecy? Forever. And you couldn't tell a single soul because if you did, that would... that would...' Jo shakes her head. 'That would mean the end of everything you held dear? I'm asking for a friend, of course,' she adds with a croak, clearing her throat.

'Sure, I understand,' Simon says, narrowing his eyes as he looks at her. His voice is deep and thoughtful as he rubs his chin, raises his eyebrows. 'Sounds like a conundrum indeed,' he adds. 'So someone you know is in this predicament?'

'Yes. A... a good friend of mine.' Jo looks away. 'She doesn't know what to do. Something else bad has happened since and, in light of this other thing, well... hindsight is great, of course. But only in hindsight.' She shrugs.

'I understand. I think,' Simon says, looking confused. 'You mentioned counselling. Has your friend had any?'

'Yes. Lots, though she never spoke about *this*. She was conscious that some things – the really *bad* things – aren't actually confidential.' Jo feels her cheeks colour and it's not from the whiskey.

'True enough. But usually only where there's something like a child protection issue, or a terrorism risk, or... or...' Simon watches her, his eyes flicking about her face. 'Or murder.'

Slowly, Jo's hand comes up to cover her mouth when she catches sight of Will standing on the other side of the room, giving her a look, shaking his head, his eyes filled with something she doesn't recognise.

CHAPTER TWENTY-TWO

The dog is walked. The cat is fed and asleep. A delivery of logs has been taken and Jo has cleaned the bathroom and watered all Suzanne's houseplants. As she carries out the duties she's been set, she forces herself to detach from what it is she's likely doing: looking after the home of her husband's lover.

She puts down the voile curtain she removed from the kitchen window, the needle half way through a stitch. The hem had come down and she'd spotted a sewing basket in a cupboard, thought she'd procrastinate more by doing a few extra jobs around the house. Easier than facing what she'd really come here to do.

What are you expecting to find in the locked bedroom, exactly? Will? His body? And what if the key doesn't even fit? What if Simon notices you stole his keys and catches you red-handed? And no more blurting!

Jo shakes her head, exhausted from the constant chatter in her mind. She lays down the curtain and heads upstairs, the stolen keys in her pocket. Her head thrums from last night's alcohol and her heart is bruised from what she and Simon did.

Will is now not the last man you kissed…

She'd repeated the words over and over as she lay in bed after getting back last night until, finally, she fell into a fitful sleep. But it was a restless, sweaty sleep filled with dreams of Will and Simon playing golf together, having a drink together, driving home drunk together – Will at the wheel.

She'd sat bolt upright then, drenched and gasping for air as she wondered where she was. Her mouth was dry, her lips almost stuck together she was so parched.

My lips are sealed...

Jo removes the keys from her back pocket. She looks at them, jangling them between her fingers. 'I don't feel good about this,' she says, glancing back down the stairs, seeing Spangle in the hallway. He lets out a little whine as if to say *Don't do it...*

'What if Suzanne has nothing to do with Will?' she says to herself. 'Then I'm prying into the private space of a woman who has put her trust in me. Not only have I kissed a man, technically cheating on my missing husband, but I'm about to become nothing more than a low-down snoop, too.'

Spangle barks from the hallway, his claws clacking on the stone floor as he paces back and forth, half jumping up at the front door a couple of times.

'What is it, boy?' Jo says, frozen on the landing. 'Is someone there?'

Spangle lets out two more barks, causing Jo to head to the front bedroom window. She looks out to the drive below, her breath fogging a small patch of glass. Apart from hers, there are no other cars parked there and, although she can't quite see the front door fully, all seems quiet.

Perhaps Spangle is warning you...

Before she loses all her courage, convinced there's no one there, Jo pushes the key into the bedroom door's mortice lock. It's stiff at first but then, as she forces it to turn, she feels the lock bite and the mechanism move. Then she puts in the Yale key and, with one hand on the knob, she slowly pushes the door open, screwing up her eyes.

She jumps as her phone vibrates, ringing in her back pocket.

Quickly, she pulls the door almost closed, grabbing her phone from her pocket, glancing at the screen before answering. 'Lou, hi.

I'm *so* glad you called.' And she means it, letting out a big sigh. Another warning. *Don't do it...*

'Thought I'd just check how are things going,' Louise asks. 'Are you having a lovely time?'

'Yes, yes I am, thanks,' she replies slowly. In spite of everything, a tiny part of that is true. Though a *different* time is perhaps more accurate. The quiz was fun, walking Spangle is enjoyable, the house is comfortable and Simon is... Jo shudders. She can hardly tell Louise that she's kissed another man. 'The countryside is lovely around here.'

'Lots of bracing beach walks, I hope?' Lou replies. Jo can hear the drone of the car in the background, the echo of the hands-free speaker.

'Oh... yes, of course.' Jo hasn't taken Spangle to the beach yet, not set eyes on the sea since she arrived. She might as well still be in the Midlands.

'How are the animals?'

'They're great, actually. I'm tempted to get a pet when I come home.' Jo stares at the bedroom door, the half-inch gap. She can't see much inside, doesn't trust herself not to say something if she opens it while on the phone to Louise. By the tone of her voice – slightly flat – Jo senses she's called for a reason.

'So you're definitely staying down there for the duration?'

'Of course. I have to. Why?' Jo tries not to feel too affronted, but everyone asks her if she's OK, if she'll cope, if she'll manage, if she'll see it through and go the distance.

Maybe I'm finally toughening up, becoming more accepting of Will's disappearance. Thing is, I don't ever want to be at the point of... of not caring, of not looking for him in a crowd, or hearing his voice when I least expect it...

'Archie and I have had the biggest argument.' The line crackles but Jo hears Louise choke back a sob.

'Oh no, *Lou*... I'm so sorry. Do you want to tell me why?'

Silence. Just the hum of the engine.

'You don't have to, obviously, but... but a problem shared,' she says, feeling her cheeks colour as she's reminded of last night again.

'It was about money,' Louise says, sighing heavily. The engine noise quietens, as if she's pulled over, and then it cuts out completely. 'I've just arrived home but honestly, I'm dreading going in and seeing him. I'm in no fit state for it all to kick off again.'

Jo doesn't understand. Archie is a surgeon. Louise is a solicitor. Their incomes are reflected in their lifestyle. Money is the last thing Jo would have expected them to come to blows about. A birth plan disagreement, perhaps, or what colour to paint the nursery, or which caterer to use for the christening – she could understand those.

'I'm so sorry to hear that, Lou. I mean, is everything OK? Are you...?' She doesn't want to say 'in trouble' when referring to either of them. It seems ridiculous.

'No, no, it's nothing like that.'

'OK...' Jo says, not wanting to pry. 'You know I'll listen if you want to talk.'

'Last night, we were going over some finances. Looking at starting a savings plan for Speck, putting aside some money each month for private school, university – that kind of thing. But we've also been thinking about buying a bolthole by the sea, perhaps a place in Cornwall. You know we've had that on our "list of wants" for ages, and we can't use Mum and Dad's cottage now they're letting it out. Anyway, it's hardly luxurious and not a beach in sight.'

There are only two things on my list of wants... Jo thinks, touching her belly and thinking of Will.

'Yes, I know you've been hankering after a seaside place for ages. Sounds lovely, Lou, go for it,' Jo says.

'Thing is, and it's not like we're hard up or anything, but... but, well, Archie started getting funny about my spending. And I kind of flew at him. Verbally, of course.'

'Ah,' Jo says, sympathising. She and Will had had the same kind of conversation many times, but at the other end of the financial spectrum.

'I mean, we have our own finances, of course, and then the joint household stuff, which has always worked fine. So surely what I do with my hard-earned money is my bloody business, wouldn't you think? But oh no, Archie says I'm spending too much, that if I carry on like this we won't be able to afford to send Speck to private school and a holiday home will be off the cards.'

Don't say it. Think it, but don't say it, Jo. She's your friend…

'Jo, are you listening? Archie actually used the word "afford". Can you imagine how that made me feel?'

'I can,' Jo says, meaning it. She pictures a slow burn of rage brewing inside Louise's mind, with Speck the only thing preventing her from completely exploding in a fit of anger. Though it sounds like she did a pretty good job of that anyway. 'I don't imagine you liked it. And for what it's worth, I think what you do with your own money *is* your business. You're generous to a fault, Lou…' *That's true*, Jo thinks, remembering how she offered to pay for her to have a holiday. 'And I think it's a matter of deciding what *you* want. If you're actually set on the things on your list, or if you'd rather be a bit more frivolous with your spending and blow it on what you *really* want.'

Silence on the line for a moment. Jo hears Louise breathing, thinking. 'What I *really* want?' she says thoughtfully. 'Yes, yes, you're right, Jo, thank you. I need to focus on what I *really* want. And sometimes those are the things money can't buy.'

CHAPTER TWENTY-THREE

Jo hangs up, sliding down the wall and dropping onto the carpet. Out of nowhere, Bonnie appears, winding around her bent knees. She trails a hand over her soft back, the cat's tail rising further as her fingers reach the end of her spine. She sighs heavily, the cat making a little throaty noise in response, perhaps sensing what's on her mind. It's not talking to Louise that's made Jo feel guilty and remorseful about what she's going to do, that she's not there to support her pregnant friend – rather *herself*, by playing everything out in her mind. Last night with Simon… then the memories – the drive home *that* night, after the earlier talks about money, of never quite having enough even though, on paper, they should have. They *did* have. Didn't they? Is that what was wrong, why he left? Like Louise and Archie, it had also turned into a massive argument.

'Concentrate on the road,' Jo had said on the way to the party, not wanting to continue the discussion about money that had begun earlier. Will seemed intent on dragging it up again in the car, on causing an argument. All day, it had felt as though he didn't want her to be there with him.

She didn't let on that she hadn't been fussed about it in the first place, but had wanted to support Will. They were his friends, after all, and she knew she wouldn't know anyone there. But she was OK with that, would do it for him. For Will. To be by his side. Always for Will. But then he'd had a go at her again before they'd even left the house, almost as if he was trying to pick a fight. As if he didn't want her to come. She didn't understand. It was out of character.

'I can tell you're not keen, Jo-jo. No need to put yourself through it if you don't want, love. I won't be late, anyway. Just show my face.'

But she was already dressed, had put some make-up on. An above-the-knee dress she'd made from lightweight vintage velvet in aubergine. Long sleeves with deep cuffs for which she'd sourced antique shell buttons; a scooped neck, fitted bodice. Long black boots. She'd done her hair – chestnut feathery curls around her face, dark eyes and softly blushed cheeks. Definitely the wife of an actor. Definitely the woman she wanted to be. And she wanted to be it by Will's side.

'If you're not feeling great, Jo, then honestly, don't come.' Will had a nervous expression on his face, one cheek twitching just below his eye. *Apprehensive*, Jo had thought. *As though he's waiting for me to do the right thing and not come. But why?*

'I never said I wasn't feeling great. Don't be silly. I want to come. It'll be fun.'

He'd swallowed then. She'd noticed.

Jo had smiled – an attempt to allay whatever doubts he was having as she shrugged into her faux fur, keeping her eyes fixed on him, watching. After a moment, when she was standing there, waiting, eyebrows raised, clutch bag in hand, Will finally reanimated.

'Sure, that's great. You look stunning, by the way.' Then the familiar look in his eyes again – appreciation, love, warmth. Jo breathed out. She was imagining things, making too much of it. He'd given her a squeeze around the shoulders before they'd headed out to the car. 'I don't feel like drinking tonight, so I'll pilot,' he'd said, beeping it unlocked.

Annabel always hosted the best parties, according to Will. Though for some reason on the drive to Birmingham, he'd already decided that they wouldn't stay long, that there probably wouldn't be much of a turnout anyway, that it would most likely be a bit of a boring evening.

'She's chosen the wrong night for a do,' he'd commented, focusing on the road ahead. 'There's another after-show party at the Crescent. Everyone decent will be at that instead. We'll just show our faces and go.'

Jo knew Will had worked with Annabel a number of times – she was one of his favourite directors – and he'd often commented about the 'people she knew', how her contacts list was a rich vein, how there were people he was waiting to be introduced to. And Will was good at networking, even though it seemed to stress him out, drain him, force him into a recovery black hole for a few days. But she knew he was determined to one day quit his teaching job and act full-time.

'You look beautiful,' Will said to Jo again after they'd parked a couple of streets away from Annabel's city-centre apartment, his arm slung low around her back as they walked along. 'But really, we don't have to stay long. I know you find these things a chore.'

'So you keep saying,' she replied. 'And honestly, I don't. It's nice to be out with you.' She looked up at him, ponytailing her hair with one hand. It was windy. 'I want to share this with you, have you be as proud of me as I am of you.'

The Color Purple had been one of the most successful theatre performances Will had been involved in to date, even though he was lower down the cast list than he'd have liked. He didn't get the part he'd auditioned for so had settled for another character. Jo knew it had irked him. And now, looking to the year ahead, Will's acting calendar was far blanker than he'd like. He had a couple of day shoots for an advertisement booked for the Easter break but, apart from that, his main income was still his teaching.

She quickly touched up her lipstick, taking hold of Will's arm as they went up to the apartment, wondering if she'd know any faces.

Will hadn't mentioned anyone he was working with lately, whereas he was usually full of stories and tales and backstage gossip. She sensed his tension as they stepped out of the lift.

'Just enjoy tonight and celebrate the amazing run the company's had,' she'd said. 'It's such an achievement. It'll lead to other things, you'll see.'

Will had taken her by the shoulders then, looked into her eyes. 'Thank you,' he'd said earnestly. 'It means so much that... that you see something more inside me than I deserve.'

Jo shivers, hugging her legs as she sits on the carpet, thinking back.

She'd read between the lines. Or at least, tried to. Seen the frustration in the expression on his face. *He's an actor, for God's sake. An artist. A creator. This is what he's like...* He was also everything her mother had warned her about, since she was young, that she should avoid in a man. Yet, ironically, it was everything she desired. And how many times had she been woken by his night-time sleep-talking to know that he was scared, *terrified*, of feeling like a failure, of never quite being good enough and trying to live up to some blueprint of an idea he'd foolishly overlaid on his life? His sleep patterns had been affecting them both.

But despite the acting insecurities, Will had always brought in a steady income. He had day job security at least, and whenever Jo's mother made snide remarks, she was able to defend him on that score, especially as Sew Perfect was only as good as her and Margot's client list, which was up and down depending on the season. She barely made three quarters of what Will did each month.

'I see everything that's real in you,' Jo said, straightening Will's collar as he slid his hands down to her hips just before they went into the party. 'And it pains me that you don't. But I won't stop saying it until you believe me, Will. We're a team. And I want to show the world that we're a team. That we're invincible, OK?'

She'd taken his face in her hands then, pulling his mouth towards hers, destroying her lipstick. But she didn't care. She wanted to go in with a lopsided smile, with the same colour on her husband's mouth as hers. Now *that* was a team, she thought as they walked through the door together.

*

'We're going. Come with me,' Will had said barely an hour later. Jo hadn't spent any time with him, with Will disappearing off almost as soon as they'd arrived. But she'd met some interesting people, had a couple of drinks, some tasty food, laughed and listened to various stories. Then came Will's hand cuffing her upper arm, startling her – but not as much as the look in his eye as she turned to him. '*Now*,' he whispered sternly in her ear, his eyes cold and empty. Not the Will she knew.

'Why? What?'

'We're going. Now.'

'But… Did someone upset you? What happened?'

'Just do as I say.'

Jo had blinked a few times, watching the person she'd been chatting to drifting away, giving them an awkward glance. 'That was Gavin Mayfield, you know. I was telling him all about you, was going to introduce you. He's on the lookout for new talent.'

'Just get your coat and let's go.'

Loyalty drove her to do as Will had said, Jo remembers that much as she sits on the floor now, Bonnie winding around her legs. Smiling and uttering a few quick goodbyes to those she'd spoken to, someone catching her other arm as they left – virtually pulling her in two with Will attached to her other arm. 'Don't forget to watch that series I told you about,' the woman said. Jo had smiled, her heart thumping as she'd nodded a vague acknowledgement, trying not to appear rude.

'Will, what the *hell?*' she'd said as the cold night air hit her. She pulled on her coat as they went, racking her brains for what she'd done wrong to prompt his sudden departure.

'I'm sorry,' he'd said, striding back to the car. Jo wondered then if he'd staggered a little, if his gait wasn't quite as measured as it should be. But she put it down to an uneven paving slab, him tripping. She decided not to say anything when he nudged the back of the car parked behind them as he pulled away, or when he clipped the kerb as he turned a corner. But now she wishes she had. Wishes she'd insisted on driving.

*

'I can't do this,' Jo says to the cat, as she gets up off the floor. The cat, still a little wary of her, darts to the other side of the landing at her sudden movement. 'Hey, it's OK, puss,' she says, closing the bedroom door without peeking through the crack, relieved when she locks it again. She can't stand to look inside. Not yet. Maybe not ever.

And that's OK. You don't have to. Just pretend you never even saw the photos on Suzanne's mantelpiece. As if you never applied for the house-sit, as if Will never disappeared. Because he's safer inside your head.

'Hey, Spangle!' Jo calls out at the top of the stairs, trying to break her mood. She's not thought about Annabel's party in much detail since it happened, overshadowed by their journey home. But for some reason now, she wants to recall it, to remember the faces of everyone who was there, what they said to her, who Will was talking to, and why oh *why* they had to leave in such a hurry. She never did find out. Because soon afterwards, everything turned bad.

'Want some food, boy?' Jo says, as the dog yaps and wags his tail. She heads downstairs, calling the cat as she goes. Though Bonnie stays put on the landing, sitting elegantly, her back to the locked room as if guarding it.

And it's when Jo is mixing up dog biscuits that the doorbell rings.

CHAPTER TWENTY-FOUR

'Simon,' she says, gripping the door tightly as she opens it a little. After last night, she's not sure why she's surprised to see him, but she is. She glances down at the cake tin in his hands.

'For you,' he says, holding it out. Still the smile in his eyes, fine lines framing their depth. 'I sometimes… bake. I know, I *know*, before you say it.' He laughs then, almost embarrassed. 'Not a manly thing to do, but it helps me relax.'

'I wasn't going to say…' Jo trails off. 'That's really kind, thank you.' She opens the door a little wider, taking the tin.

'Chocolate brownies, in case you were wondering. Still warm.'

'Lovely,' she says, about to thank him again and close the door.

'If you've got the kettle on, we could do a taste check?'

Tell him you're about to go out. Tell him you're cleaning the floors or grooming the dog or… or about to meditate. Anything!

'Sure,' she says, pulling the door completely open. 'I was about to make a coffee.'

Jo screws up her eyes briefly, leading the way into the kitchen and ignoring the voice in her head. Simon follows. She's about to put the cake tin on the scrubbed pine table when she spots the keys. *Simon's* set of keys. And then she sees Will, standing by the sink. Somehow, as if in slow motion, the tin falls from her hands.

'Oops, I got it,' Simon says with lightning reactions as he catches it, managing to hold the lid on. She hadn't realised he was so close to her. As he takes the brownies over to the kettle,

Jo sweeps up the keys from the table, praying he doesn't notice the slight jangle they make as she tucks them in her pocket. Will stares at her, and then slowly turns to Simon, who is only about two feet from where he is standing.

Will... it's not my fault. I didn't know he was going to call round...

'You OK?' Simon asks as he fills the kettle. 'You look as though you've seen a ghost.'

'I'm... yes, I'm OK. I'm fine. Just a bit of a headache brewing. Nothing a brownie won't sort out, I'm sure.' She knows she's gabbling and glances at Will for reassurance, mouthing again that she's sorry. Simon follows her gaze, shrugging, looking puzzled as Spangle trots into the kitchen having just finished his food.

'Hey, boy,' he says, ruffling his fur. 'You had a good walk today?'

'Oh... well, we haven't managed to get out yet. I was just about to take him.'

'It's nice out,' Simon says. 'A good day for a beach walk. If you like, I can come with you, and then afterwards—'

Jo is holding her breath, thinking up an excuse, but breathes out heavily when Simon's phone interrupts with a shrill tone.

'Ah-ha...' he says, glancing at the screen, flashing it at Jo. 'This is good timing.' He swipes the screen and holds the phone out in front of him. 'Suzie... *Suzie*... how are you getting on? How's everything? You'll never guess where I am.'

Suzie... Suzanne...

Jo freezes before casting an eye around the kitchen. It's tidy enough. The animals are fine.

'I'm doing OK, Si,' the voice comes back. *Suzanne's* voice. 'As well as can be expected. You off work today?' she asks. 'And of course I know where you are. The background is a bit of a giveaway.' She laughs then – a laugh that Jo would instantly tune into if she'd heard it elsewhere, wondering who it belonged to, why they sounded so happy and carefree as if there was nothing weighing them down. The opposite of her.

The woman who has most likely stolen your husband sounds warm and kind, normal and friendly. Someone you'd get chatting to in a shop or a café...

'Ta-da...!' Simon says into his phone, flashing a quick pan around the kitchen. 'All good here, Suze, and I should probably introduce you to Jo, since you've likely just caught a glimpse of her and she *is* house-sitting for you, after all.' He laughs, twisting the phone round briefly towards Jo. 'Oh, and you know me, look – I made these...' He turns the camera on a close-up of the open tin of brownies.

'They look perfect as ever,' Jo hears Suzanne say. 'You're a good 'un, Si. And thanks for handing over the house for me. What a nightmare, the previous sitter letting me down. And hello, *Jo!*' comes a shrill voice directed at her. Simon comes up close, sidling in against her so she is also included in the video call. Their shoulders are touching. 'I'm so very pleased to meet you and utterly, utterly grateful to you for taking over at the last moment. Si has already told me you're a good egg, and—' Suzanne's face suddenly stills, her mouth open. Nothing moving.

'Damn, I think the connection's frozen,' Simon says, holding his phone closer to the router.

But Jo sees the flicker in Suzanne's eye, notices how her pupils widen and her jaw twitches slightly as if she's about to say something but doesn't. The connection isn't frozen at all. Suzanne is.

'Hi,' Jo forces herself to say to the unmoving image as she stares at the blonde-haired woman, slightly older than her, at her full lips, her blue eyes. Just like the photograph she saw, only prettier. *Is she Will's type?* 'Thank you so much for allowing me to look after your animals. I don't know if you can hear me, but they're a delight! And they're both fine, as is your lovely home. It's a beautiful place to live.' She can hardly believe these normal words are coming out of her mouth, but they are. She's a better actress than she thought.

Jo watches, waits as Simon tries to re-establish what he thinks is a lost connection. 'Typical,' he mutters, moving about the room.

'No, no, I'm… I'm here,' Suzanne says, touching her head, causing Simon to put the phone in front of them again.

Jo flicks her eyes towards the sink. Will is still standing there, his arms folded, watching as Simon pulls her in close, his arm around her waist so they can both fit in the screen. She notices a twitch under Will's eye, like the tic he'd get on his jaw if he'd had a bad day at work or something had upset him. Or that time after the party, when he'd virtually dragged her out, his hand clamped around her arm.

'We came third in the pub quiz last night,' Simon tells Suzanne. 'Jo kept the team on the leader board with her stellar knowledge of crows.' He laughs then, the phone shaking in his hand.

But Suzanne just stares at her, saying nothing. Fixated. After a moment, she looks away then looks back again, blinking. Her hair falls across one eye but she makes no move to sweep it out of the way.

'Hello?' Simon says, giving his phone a little shake as though that will help. He looks at Jo and rolls his eyes. 'Joys of living in the country,' he says. 'Terrible Wi-Fi speeds here.'

'That's… that's really great,' Suzanne says, finally moving again. 'Well done.' She stares straight out of the screen – her symmetrical face mesmerising Jo. 'I… I hope the kids are behaving.' She pushes her blonde hair back, no signs of a bad connection now as she slowly moves – deliberate, purposeful gestures while her eyes stay fixed on Jo.

Jo glances at Simon for clarification before realising what she means – the animals. Will is in her peripheral vision, shifting his balance from one foot to the other, arms folded.

Please don't hate me, Will… I have to find out. I have to understand. You'd have done the same…

'Sorry?' Simon says. 'Who'd have done the same?'

'Oh,' Jo says. 'I meant, *you'd* have done the same… in the quiz, I'm sure,' she says, forcing a smile at Suzanne, trying to appear normal and calm even though inside she's in turmoil. She glances over at Will.

What is it you see in her that you don't see in me?

Then she looks back at the phone, studying Suzanne – as much as she can see of her, anyway. She keeps moving away, as if in two minds about whether she wants to be on the screen or not – flashes of the ceiling, the floor. Jo braces herself in case Will appears in the room with Suzanne. He could be right next to her, listening to everything.

'We… we have this battle with other local teams,' Suzanne finally manages to say. She clears her throat as if she's struggling with the conversation as much as Jo. 'Pub quiz wars, eh, Simon?'

Simon is about to speak but Spangle suddenly yaps, jumping up and down at his feet, as if he wants to get to the phone. 'He can hear you, Suze,' Simon says, ruffling the dog's back.

'Hello, darling boy,' Suzanne sings out as Simon swivels the camera to show Spangle bouncing around, spinning in circles, his tail wagging furiously. 'Are you being a good boy for Jo-jo?'

Jo freezes, steadying herself with one hand on the back of a kitchen chair. *Jo-jo…* Will was the only person to ever call her that and subsequently – and annoyingly – Louise, as if she was filling the gap left by him, as though it was her duty, as best friend, to call her by her pet name.

But a complete stranger saying it? *It's not right,* Jo thinks. *It's too familiar.* Her heart thumps or slows, she's not sure which. Either way, it's not beating in its usual rhythm.

'By the way, there was a delivery for you,' Jo says, catching sight of the package on the side table. 'I'll keep it safe unless you need it forwarding on?'

Spangle yaps as Simon turns the camera towards them again.

'Oh…' Suzanne says, a frown forming. 'No, just keep it there. Thank you.' She pauses, thinking, the frown getting deeper, a strange look brewing in her eyes. 'Si, I'd... I'd better go. I've another call coming in.' She hesitates, looking at Jo – though it's hard to see exactly where her eyes are fixed now as they're glassy and staring. She turns away again, her hair falling over her face as though she wants to hide behind it.

And then the screen goes blank.

'Well,' Jo says, her mouth so dry she can hardly form words. 'Suzanne seems... lovely.' *It's true. You can't deny that. Would you expect Will to run off with someone who wasn't nice?*

'Suzanne's a brick. I've known her forever. We grew up together, and when her mum died, she decided to come back and live here in East Wincombe. It's funny how you eventually gravitate home. I was in London for many years but had to get out. I came back home for a week to think about my life and never left.' Simon says all that with a laugh in his voice, but Jo is pondering what he's said.

Her own childhood village is the last place she wants to gravitate back to. Venturing to London aged eighteen, applying for courses, for any kind of job going – from bar work to babysitting, waitressing and cleaning, scraping by with the rent each month for a tiny room in Camden – was the get-out she needed. And she never went back. Never *would* go back.

In her final year at college, she'd ended up sharing a bedsit with Margot, the seed of an idea forming as their degree came to an end, and Sew Perfect was born. The memory of her mother's crumpled face when she told her of her life plans was enough to keep her going, to know she was doing the right thing, following her dreams – however far removed they were from her mother's vision for her. And then she'd met Will. The last straw as far as Elizabeth was concerned, confirming that her only daughter had failed them.

And it turns out they were right, she thinks, fetching a couple of plates from the cupboard. 'Time for chocolate, I reckon,' she says, not caring if she's inadvertently voiced her inner thoughts to Simon.

'I'm with you on that one,' he says, gently touching her on the back. And, when she turns, seeing Will looming close by, it's as if he knocks the plates clean from her hands.

CHAPTER TWENTY-FIVE

'What you need to know about Suzanne,' Simon says after he's swept up the broken china, insisting that he do it, believing he'd startled her. 'What you need to know is that she's… well, she's been through a tough time.'

Jo freezes – a brownie half in her mouth. The dense chocolate suddenly tastes like gritty mud. She removes it, taking a sip of coffee instead and clearing her throat. 'I'm sorry to hear that.'

Don't say anything, Jo. He'll open up more if you just let him speak…

'Which is why she's gone away for a bit. This time, anyway.' Simon nods, as though he's done his duty, got it out.

'I see,' Jo says, a concerned frown forming. She forces the brownie in again, to prevent her from saying something she regrets. 'Mmm, you can certainly bake,' she says through a mouthful. 'This is delicious. Do I have chocolate everywhere?' She wipes her lips with her forefinger. Spangle hangs about under the table, waiting for crumbs.

'Not at all,' Simon says, that kind look in his eyes again, making Jo wonder how someone can actually *seem* kind without something sinister lurking beneath. Since Will disappeared, her calibration of people has changed. Been turned on its head. She doesn't trust her judgement any more.

'I just thought I ought to explain why she may have seemed a bit… well, a bit nervous or cautious on the call just now. That's not really Suzanne. I mean, she's an actress, for heaven's sake. She doesn't do nervous. Actually, that's not true. She *does* do nervous. Just not in the way you or I would. She does it with style. Purposeful nervous, shall we say. And she's usually much more… flamboyant.'

Jo watches as Simon stares out of the window, perhaps wondering how much he should reveal. 'I understand that sometimes… sometimes people need space to think if they've had a tough time. Or to heal. Or to take stock of life.'

Simon nods. 'Exactly,' he says, turning back again. 'Sounds like you're speaking from experience.'

Don't blurt again, Jo. Eat the brownie. Now!

'Oh, no… no, not really. I just wondered if…' Jo cups her hand under her mouth, looking at Simon with wide eyes, catching the falling crumbs as she stuffs the brownie in. 'So good…' she says.

'Probably needed more butter. Or milk. I kind of make it up each time, to be honest.'

Jo says nothing. She can't. Will is suddenly standing right behind Simon, his arms folded across his chest, taking a step closer.

'So where's she gone, then, Suzanne?' she finally forces herself to say when she's finished her mouthful, trying to ignore Will.

Simon thinks for a moment. 'I suppose you could call it a place to heal. To get better.'

Rehab? Jo wants to say. *An institution of some kind? A clinic? Maybe she has mental health issues… perhaps because of Will?*

'Fancy a beach walk?' Simon suddenly says. Jo senses it's a diversion.

'Why not?' she replies, standing up with almost military precision, knocking her coffee mug but catching it just in time. 'Spangle, come!' she calls, even though the dog is right by her feet. 'Where's your lead, boy?' she says, heading towards the back door but stopping suddenly because Will is in her way. 'Oh…' she says, going around him, realising Simon is watching, seeing her sidestep nothing. He must already wonder what's wrong with her, but how can she explain? Whenever Will appears to her, she's mostly alone or at home. Making excuses for his presence in front of others is quite foreign to her.

'Steady, there,' Simon says, appearing behind her just as quickly as Will has materialised in front. She feels hemmed in, sandwiched between the two men. Simon gently puts his hand on her back.

'It's fine, I'm fine,' she says, head down, sliding out from between the two of them.

'Wow,' Jo says, staring down the long stretch of sandy beach. The tide is right out – all the space Spangle needs to run and splash around in until he's worn out. The wind whips around Jo's face as they head across the small sandbanks dotted with marram grass clumps, making their way down onto the beach.

'Worth the half-hour drive, eh?' Simon says, raising his voice over the sound of the wind and waves.

'Totally,' Jo replies, stumbling a little down the uneven sandy track. She wants to throw her arms wide, run fast down to the shore… keep on running until she's swallowed up by the waves. 'It's incredible. Beautiful. I'd never have discovered it myself if you hadn't shown me.'

As they reach the firmer, wet sand – Jo thankfully having had the foresight to throw sensible boots in the car – they head west, the sea to their left. Jo unclicks Spangle from his lead – he's been straining on it since they left the car – and he immediately bounds down towards the shore, his long ears flapping behind him.

'So much energy,' Jo says, laughing.

'A bit pent-up,' Simon adds. 'Suzanne's not been able to walk him as often as she liked lately. He got frustrated. I helped when I could, but that wasn't often.'

'I see,' Jo says, seeing another opportunity without sounding as though she's prying. 'You say she's had a tough time. Was that physical… emotional?' She trails off, hoping Simon will fill in the blanks.

'Problems with her leg. She had to have an operation. But she's getting there.'

'Sounds rough,' Jo says, looking out to sea, shielding her eyes with her hand as the sun pierces through the clouds. Spangle is jumping about in the breakers, going into the water up to his belly then charging out again when a wave splashes down on him. They both laugh.

'Yeah, she's been through the mill a bit the last year or so. Her work has really been affected, though thankfully she still has a financial buffer. She's been doing a fair bit of voice-over stuff instead of her usual stage or screen roles. But even that's got a bit much for her lately. You know, emotionally.'

'Emotionally?' Jo says. 'As in…?' She's pushing it, she knows.

'The aftermath,' he says, turning to look at Jo, holding her eye longer than necessary.

Jo stumbles, lurching forward. Simon reaches out to grab her, catching hold of her coat as she regains her balance. 'Driftwood,' she says, looking back at what caught her foot. 'And me not being used to wearing these clumpy boots very often.' She tries to laugh it off but her face burns from embarrassment – and frustration for breaking the moment. Simon grabs the bent piece of wood, whistling for Spangle.

'Bit clumsy, aren't you?' he says with a wink before lobbing the wood as hard as he can down the beach.

'Yes,' Jo responds almost immediately, laughing. Spangle bounds across the sand in the direction of the stick and, as he runs back with it, she sees that his long fur is sticky with seawater and sand. And he has a piece of seaweed stuck on his tail. 'Oh no, look at the state of him. Your car's going to get filthy.'

'Not a problem.' Simon takes the driftwood from Spangle's slobbery mouth as he returns it, throwing it as close as he can to the shoreline. The pair keep on walking at a steady pace, the dog occasionally looking up to check where they are as he runs along carrying the stick. It's the perfect size for him.

'Tell me to butt out if I'm stepping over a line,' Jo begins.

'And likely tripping over said line,' Simon adds, gently nudging her with his shoulder as they walk along, the strips of seawater in the ridged sand splashing underfoot.

'But were, or are, you and Suzanne ever a… *thing*?' She hopes the information will help narrow down the men in Suzanne's life, work out if one of them is Will.

'As in the "R" word?' Simon looks sideways at her.

'"R" word?'

'Relationship. Romance…' He pauses a second, thinking. 'Rumpy-pumpy,' he adds with a laugh.

'Rumpy-pumpy?' Jo replies, rolling her eyes and shaking her head as she scuffs at the sand. 'But yes, yes. That.'

'Then no. No, we've never had a thing. Always just good mates, and that's the way I like it.' Simon calls out to Spangle, who's chasing after another dog. 'Come on, boy,' he yells, followed by a shrill whistle. 'You're asking because of last night?' Another nudge, gentler this time with a light touch on her back.

'Oh, heavens,' Jo says, staring out to sea briefly. 'I mean, not "Oh heavens" in a bad way. It was nice. Obviously. I mean, I was just as responsible. And it was a lovely evening. Probably too much alcohol on my part, but hey… and that wasn't what I meant, and yes, of course the kiss was nice, *very* nice, and—'

'Jo?'

'Yes?'

'Shut up.'

And before she knows what's happening, he's halted her, drawing her towards him with his hands gently around her wrists.

With the sound of the waves on the shoreline, the breeze whipping her hair around her face, he kisses her again. Warm and slow.

And for the first time in a long time, Jo feels a fraction more like herself. Something thawing inside.

CHAPTER TWENTY-SIX

Then

I couldn't help wondering if Will had disappeared again. Not in the physical sense this time – he was sitting right opposite me at the dinner table, after all – but rather in the emotional sense.

'You'll never get a straight answer from him about it, and his mood will be all over the place. You know what these thespian, arty types are like,' Mum had said earlier in the day when I'd called in to see her after leaving work early. Her face was pinched and taut, making it hard for her to sip her drink – her usual Friday afternoon gin and tonic – while I had a cup of tea. It was my weekly duty visit. Whenever I'd asked her to come to our place for a change, Mum always refused – or rather made up excuses. Since Will and I had been living together, she always had a reason why it was inconvenient to make the journey. She wasn't feeling well (but she was fine when I went to the family home instead), or she felt a migraine coming on (it never materialised), or she was expecting a delivery (which, of course, never arrived), or her most recent: 'Your father doesn't want to. He's not good with travelling.'

'But Mum, we're forty-five minutes away. It's not *that* far. And Dad might enjoy the change of scene. All he does these days is potter in the garden or read the paper.'

'I am here, you know,' Dad had said then, looking up from over the top of *The Times*. I made a sympathetic face at him – a face I knew he would recognise as *Sorry, Dad.*

'Well, anyway,' I continued. 'You know you're always welcome, both of you. Will and I would love to have you round for supper at ours, or for Sunday lunch. Show off our new place.' *Though it's not so new any more*, I'd thought.

'But as I was saying,' Mum went on. 'Someone like William is never going to give you the input you need about those paint colours, darling. You'll have to accept that.'

I almost saw my mother mouth the words, '*You've made your bed…*'

'You always seem to think I'm complaining about him, Mum. Just because you want to add your tuppence worth. But you know what? There's nothing to complain about.' I'd resigned myself to my mother never understanding.

'How much does he earn now?'

'Mum!' I gave a furtive glance at my watch. I'd only been there forty minutes. Less than an hour and my mother would get difficult about my curtailed visit if I left early. *More* difficult. And I'd barely spoken to Dad yet.

'A simple enough question, if the answer was enough, I suspect.'

I shook my head. 'He's a teacher and an actor. He's never going to live up to your expectations in that department. I know he's not the hedge fund manager or the surgeon you envisaged me marrying, but I love him. And he loves me. What he earns or what I earn… that doesn't mean much to us. Of course, we want a roof over our heads – and we have one, albeit a two-up, two-down, but it's home. And I'd love you to come and see it. We pay our bills and eat good food. We have friends and hobbies and adore each other. Why do you always have to criticise and pick my life apart? Just because it's not the same as yours. I'm not you, Mum.' I nodded a breathless full stop when I'd finally exhausted what I felt I had to say. There was so much more, but I knew I was pushing my mother close to her limits as it was. Mum had sat there, sipping tensely on her huge bowl glass of gin and tonic, trying to look as elegant as she could in her tweed skirt and high-necked blouse. But I saw her simmering inside; knew the signs well from when I was a child.

*

'Jo?' someone said. It was Will. His hand reached across the table. 'You OK, love? You were miles away.'

'Oh, gosh, sorry. How rude of me.' I snapped back to reality, glancing between Will, Archie and Louise. They'd come over for dinner. It was always a good night, the four of us unwinding, and I'd been asking their thoughts on colours to paint the living room and the little dining room we were squeezed into now.

'I think if we go too dark,' Will said, 'it's going to make it seem even smaller.' He laughed. 'I don't think Jo trusts me to go to the paint shop and not return with magnolia though, do you, love?'

'Magnolia would be fine, if you like it,' I said warmly, fuelled by the memory of my mother's pursed lips earlier. *Why couldn't she like Will? Why couldn't she accept him as her son-in-law?* I'd shuddered at the look on her face at her final comment – the comment that sent me reaching for my bag and keys only fifty minutes into the regulation hour's visit before I could escape. I had to get away before I said something I really regretted.

'Will and I are going to try for a baby,' I'd announced as Mum was making her second gin of the afternoon. Dad had instantly looked up, a delighted smile spreading across his face as he put down the paper and came over to congratulate me, arms encircling me. But he soon stopped once Mum virtually feigned fainting.

'You're trying for a *baby*?'

I heard the voice, quickly realising it wasn't my mother's, even though she'd said exactly the same thing. It was Louise speaking.

'Are we?' Will said in a shaky voice, looking embarrassed as he reached out for my hand again. He flashed me a look, his pupils constricting slightly, his lips tightening – imperceptible to the others, but I knew it was a gentle warning. We'd agreed it shouldn't be public knowledge yet.

I gave a little nod in return, glancing down. I hadn't meant to say it out loud. I really hadn't. It was private between me and Will, and yes, I'd told my mother earlier, but that was only to prove how much I loved my husband. So much that we wanted to create a new life together.

'That's simply wonderful news,' Louise had said, standing up and leaning over the table, her arms outstretched. I reciprocated, though I couldn't help feeling Louise's tone was a little flat, her hug rather light.

CHAPTER TWENTY-SEVEN

Now

She's ashamed of herself. So, so ashamed.

Back from the beach, Simon's kiss still burns fresh on her lips.

You're trying to recreate him as a whole person, aren't you? You see him everywhere, so now you're finding a physical connection so you have something resembling a whole Will. Accept it. Will is gone.

'Not until I have answers, I won't,' Jo whispers to herself, standing outside the locked upstairs room again. Her words come out through clenched teeth. 'Not until I *know*. I will die a crazy and tormented old woman if I don't find some kind of closure.' She turns away, leaning back against the door, breathing heavily, her chest rising and falling. She stares at the ceiling, clutching Simon's keys tightly in her fist, the other hand pawing at her head.

'What am I *doing…*' she says, refusing to cry. She feels Bonnie winding around her ankles, her soft purr vibrating through her jeans. 'Oh, cat,' she says, looking down at the black and white thing. *Probably hungry*, Jo thinks, as she hears Spangle stirring from his sleep downstairs, his claws clacking on the kitchen tiles. The beach walk wore him out. 'I just need to get on with it, don't I?' she says, bending down to Bonnie, giving her a stroke. 'And be prepared to face whatever's in there.'

And if there's nothing in there, then you're left with an empty space where your husband used to be and the mystery of why another woman had his photos on her mantelpiece.

The cat looks up, offering a shrill chirp of a meow.

'I'll take that as a yes, then, and blame you entirely if it all goes wrong.' She rubs the cat under her chin before fumbling with the keys, before inching the door open.

Then she stops. 'I could just ask Suzanne, of course,' she says, feeling the cat against her ankles again. 'But if there is something going on between her and Will, that's only going to make them smarter at covering their tracks. Make them go underground even more.'

Jo takes a deep breath and pushes the door open wide. And then she screams.

*

'Jo, darling, wake up, it's OK, it's OK.' The deep resonance of Will's voice gradually bringing her round, anchoring her to the reality she knew and loved. The *man* she knew and loved. 'You were screaming.'

'Christ,' she'd said, wiping her hands down her face and blowing out. 'Sorry.'

'Nightmare?'

Jo nodded. 'They're getting worse. More frequent.'

'Maybe it's time to see the doctor,' Will suggested, a hand on her shoulder.

Jo glared at him. 'You think I'm mad, don't you? That I must be unstable and that's why… that's why we can't…' She turned away, swung her legs onto the floor.

'Jo… of course I don't. I know what you're going through because I'm going through it too, don't forget.'

Jo whipped round. 'No, you're not. Not like me. It's not your body failing every month, is it? Every time I think there's hope,

I con myself into wondering if my breasts look bigger or I might be feeling sick in the morning. Then I have this dream and boom, we're not pregnant.'

Will bowed his head briefly. 'I know that. I *know*. But I'm here for you and will do anything to make you feel OK about this. Let's stop trying, let's just stop—'

'Let's stop analysing me might help,' she snapped, sighing out heavily. 'I'm sorry. I know you're trying to make me feel better, but the dreams, Will. They scare me. All these faces everywhere, closing in on me. People I know, people I don't know, all leering at me, getting right up to me so I can almost *smell* them. Taste them. Some smiling, some laughing or crying, some with evil expressions, some with blood and gore and cuts on them. But the worst thing of all is that these faces, whether I recognise them or not, are on the bodies of *babies*.' Jo shuddered, picking her dressing gown up off the floor. She stood up and slipped into it and, when she turned round to look at Will, he was staring at the bed where she'd been sitting. It was covered in blood.

*

Now, standing in the bedroom doorway, she covers her mouth as the scream burns up her throat. Her neck is tight, her eyes wide, her whole body juddering. Then the panting comes – quick, shallow and sharp breaths rasping in and out of her chest. Within seconds, she feels dizzy and nauseous, as though she's about to pass out or throw up. She grabs hold of the door frame, steadying herself, leaning against it, unable to take her eyes off what's in front of her.

'Will,' she says, barely audibly. 'I... I don't believe it. *Will...*'

Tentatively, Jo takes a step forward, as if she's venturing into a dangerous lair. She glances back at the door, fearful there might be someone there to somehow lock her in from the outside.

'What are you *doing* in here?' she whispers, staring at him, hardly able to believe he's been in here while she's been in the house. 'Will...' she whispers again.

But Will doesn't say a word. Rather he stares at her – his eyes tracking her as she cautiously approaches him from around the edge of the room, as if that might somehow be safer, her back against the wall. Jo's mouth is dry as she locks onto what she's seeing, unable to look away yet now knowing that she was right – Will *is* connected to Suzanne. But how? *Why?*

'Please, dear God, tell me why you're here,' she whispers again as she draws closer, reaching out to him with her hand. She jumps as Spangle barks downstairs, then she hears a clattering and the dog goes crazy yapping and making a fuss. Jo's heart rate rises even more, if that's possible, but then she realises it's just the mail coming through the door – always an afternoon delivery around here. 'Are you in love with her – is that it? Is she in love with you?' Jo's outstretched hand shakes.

Tell me no, Will. Tell me this is all a horrible nightmare and I'll wake up soon and we'll be back home in bed together, failing at making a baby but winning at making us.

But Will still doesn't say anything.

'OK, fine,' Jo says, trying to take back some control as he just stares at her, seemingly oblivious to her presence, all the trouble he's caused. She feels the stirring of something inside her. Something fizzing in her core. Something hot and painful, as if she needs to spew it out.

'She's beautiful – Suzanne,' Jo says to him. 'I've seen her, you know. Not the classic sort of beautiful, but she has something about her, I'll give her that.' Since the FaceTime call on Simon's phone, Jo has struggled to get Suzanne's image out of her mind – her doe eyes, her high cheekbones and full lips. Her blonde hair. From what she could see, she had a good figure, too. Slender yet

womanly. But it was how she *was* that was the attractive part –
the way she turned her head, perfectly timed with a look or a
slight parting of her lips. The way her words were aligned with
her expression, making her seem alluring, genuine, trustworthy.
Intriguing. Someone you'd want as your best friend. Your lover.

Jo lets out a noise – a cross between a growl, a stifled scream
and a frustrated sob. Still Will says nothing.

'Except *you're* not trustworthy, are you?' she spits out, echoing
her thoughts. Before she can stop herself, she takes a swipe at
him, her arm whipping through the air and connecting with his
head. He immediately falls to the floor, without a sound. Then
she swipes again, clawing at him, spitting on him, sweeping her
arm across the dressing table and sending everything else onto the
floor – perfume bottles, a hairbrush, toiletries. A couple of candles
in glass holders. Will lies amongst the mess, Jo sobbing above him.

'Oh, Christ, what have I *done?*' she says, falling to her knees,
clutching at him, stroking him, gathering up the dozen or more
photographs of Will in her shaking hands.

CHAPTER TWENTY-EIGHT

The phone answers on the fifth ring. Jo hears her own heavy breathing as she waits for Louise to answer, praying she'll pick up. She's sitting in the living room, still shaken.

'Hi, Jo, how's it going down there?' Louise says when she finally answers. Jo can't help noticing that she sounds a little... tense.

'Hi Lou... is it a bad time?' she asks, clutching one of the photos, not wanting to impose, especially if she's still got blood pressure issues. 'Do tell me if you're too busy to talk.' She knows it's the middle of the working day for Louise, that she could be waiting in court for a case to be heard, liaising with a nervous client or perhaps neck-deep in emails or partner meetings at the office.

'It's OK,' she says. Then a pause. 'I'm not actually in work at the moment.'

'Oh... is everything OK? How's your blood pressure now?'

'That's the reason I've taken a few days off, actually. The hospital said if I didn't take it easy, they'd have to admit me for bed rest. So here I am with...' She clears her throat. 'With my laptop on my knee going over a client's court bundle to hand over to a colleague.'

'Oh, Lou, I'm *so* sorry to hear that. I know you wanted to work up until the last minute. But things don't always go to plan and your health is so important. It doesn't sound as though you're resting, though. I'm worried about you.'

'I know, I know,' she says. 'But I have to sort it. It's an important case.'

'Is Archie there? Is he fussing over you lots?'

'He's been amazing. He's right here, bringing me food and tea every hour on the hour. I feel like some kind of fat, swollen incubator about to burst.'

'That's good of him,' Jo says. 'But not good that you feel you're about to burst, obviously.' She laughs, trying to add a little humour. While she'd never begrudge Lou and Archie their happiness, she hates how Will's disappearance has made her jealous of every happy couple she sees – every *un*happy-looking couple, too. She'd rather be one of those with Will than no couple at all. 'You make sure you lap up the attention.'

'Oh, believe me, I am.' A pause again. 'How's it going there?'

'It's…' Jo isn't sure whether to say anything now – if she should tell Louise that she's kissed the neighbour or that she's discovered a shrine-like display of photos of Will. 'It's all fine. It's… fun.'

''Course it is,' Louise replies drily. 'You'd have more joy in your voice if you told me you'd just cleaned the bathroom. Are you feeling a bit flat?'

'I guess it's just a bit… lonely.' Jo clears her throat, desperate to spill everything. But she doesn't want to stress Louise out, raise her blood pressure further.

She looks up, catches her breath as she sees Will standing by the fireplace, arms folded, one foot crossed over the other ankle. His head tilted and his face wearing an expression that says, *Didn't look like you were lonely from where I was standing…*

'Have you been on any walks? Visited the local towns?'

'I went on a nice beach walk,' Jo says. The photograph falls from her hand and Will looks down at it, shaking his head. 'With Simon,' she adds, as if it's more a confession to Will than to Louise.

'Oh, who's Simon? Mixing with the locals already, are we?'

'Yes. No… no, not really. Lou…'

'Jo, what *is* it? You sound upset.'

'He's here, Lou,' Jo whispers. 'Will is *here*. Or at least, I'm certain he… he has been.' She stares at him, watches as he walks over to the dropped photo, standing above it. 'He's so close,' she adds.

'*What?*' comes Louise's incredulous reply. 'Close? What do you mean? Are you *sure*? How do you know? Have you spoken to him? I mean, how is that even possible? Christ… you poor thing. No wonder you sound upset.'

Jo can almost see Louise's shocked face, her mind racing. 'Lou, don't get stressed, please. That's just what I didn't want to happen, in your condition.'

'Have you told the police?' she asks, sounding more composed.

'No, not yet.' Jo hadn't thought that far ahead. Being a solicitor, Louise was bound to advise telling them. 'I mean, I could be wrong. It was just…'

'Just what? For heaven's sake, woman, spit it out. Will's been missing for nearly a year and you think you've seen him, yet you're not telling me where or how and you haven't called the police?'

'Lou, please, don't get worked up on my behalf, or—'

'Of course I'm worked up, Jo. You've just told me that Will's been there. That's huge news.' Another pause. 'Though not as upset as you must be. I'm so sorry, Jo. Look, if it really is him that's a good thing, surely? Amazing, in fact. But you do realise it probably means he's been—'

'With someone else all this time. Yes, I know, Lou.' Jo sighs.

'But look, it might not be that. Maybe he had some early midlife crisis and needed time alone for a bit. Still shitty, but not quite as bad. And similarly, if it's not him, then you're just working yourself into a state.'

A pause, while Jo thinks about this.

'Jo, I hate to say this… and please don't take it the wrong way, but I remember you once confided to me that you *see* him. As in, you see him but it's not *really* him? Do you think this is the same—?'

'You think I'm going mad, don't you?' Jo says quite calmly, quite flatly.

'No, no, I didn't say that. But I do think you've been under a lot of stress. Maybe it's time to go back to your GP, Jo. Get some help. Some *professional* help. Medication, perhaps.'

'I had counselling. There's nothing wrong with me.'

'Maybe you need more than counsell—'

'You mean a psychiatrist?' Jo sighs. 'Trust me, there's nothing wrong with my mental health, Lou.'

Will bends down to pick up the photograph, his face only a foot or so away, his eyes boring into hers as he does so. But Jo lunges for it first, swiping it up, holding it close to her chest. Glaring at him.

'I found photographs of him, Lou. Lots of them. In a locked room and all laid out on a dressing table amongst perfume bottles and personal stuff. And there were candles and...' Jo stifles the sob. She's not going there. She's not going to turn into the crazy person Louise already thinks she is. 'I can send you a photograph of it all, if you like. It's... it's... like nothing I've ever seen. It's sickening. I mean, what the hell? *Why?*'

The line falls silent for a moment.

She's thinking how insane you sound. How messed-up, obsessed and deluded you are. And she's probably right...

'Hang on, you found photographs of Will?'

'Yes.'

'In the house you're looking after?'

'Yes.'

'Oh, *Jo...*'

She hears the pity in Louise's voice.

'But it's not like that. It's not what you're thinking.'

'What am I thinking, Jo?' Louise makes a noise then, as if she's shifting position and something is hurting.

'You think that… that I'm seeing things, hallucinating.' Jo takes a breath, knowing she has to get this off her chest. 'Look, I know how it sounds, but honestly, there was this locked room and I… well, I maybe sort of stole the keys off Simon, he's the neighbour I kissed – yes, I had to get that out there or I'll self-combust with guilt but to be honest now, it doesn't really matter because what Will has done, whatever the hell that is, is way worse than me getting drunk after winning the quiz with murder and then us drinking far too much whiskey, listening to nice music and eating cheese. But the keys were just there, they sort of fell into my pocket and may not even have fitted the lock, but it turns out they did. And I wasn't even going to go in. I chickened out and then we went for a lovely walk – albeit Spangle falling into this kind of quicksand stuff and needing a good hosing off – but then, then I just couldn't help myself.' Jo draws a deep breath, sucking in hard as if her life depended on that one inhalation. 'So I did. And I wish I hadn't.'

Don't cry. Don't cry. Definitely do not cry.

'Lou?' Jo says, concerned when there's silence.

'Oww,' Louise finally says, sucking in air and making a pained sound. 'Hang on, Jo… oh God, oww.' Then there's more noise, some kind of shuffling and banging.

'Lou? Are you OK? Please, say something.'

No reply. The line is dead. Nothing. Jo holds the phone away from her, staring at the screen. Call ended.

'Oh no, Lou,' she says, quickly calling back, wishing she hadn't gone on about herself so much.

Hi, this is Louise Ward… I can't take your call right now but please leave a message and—

Jo hits redial three more times and it still doesn't connect. 'Lou, please be OK. Please connect.'

What if she's gone into labour? What if the shock of what you just told her sent her blood pressure soaring and she's haemorrhaging – or worse?

'Landline,' Jo thinks, pulling up Louise's contact on her phone. 'Maybe her phone ran out of battery.'

It answers on the fourth ring. Relief.

'Hey, Archie, it's Jo here. How are you…? Yes, yes, I'm not too bad, thanks. I was just talking to Lou but we got cut off. I think her phone must have died. Can I have a quick word to finish up?'

Because I need to make her think I'm not mad. And I don't want her going to the police behind my back, thinking she's helping…

'Oh, I'm sorry, Jo, she's not here right now. She should be back soon though. Let me see, what time is it now?' A pause as Archie checks. Jo hears Radio 4 on in the background. She imagines him in the kitchen, chopping up vegetables for his famous pork meatball soup. 'She's a bit late home, actually. Probably got held up at work. I know there's a big case on at the moment.'

Jo is silent. Tries to swallow but her mouth is dry. Does she tell him that Louise has lied? That she told her she was with him right now, that wherever she is, she isn't feeling at all well? Does she betray her confidence – that she's clearly fibbing about her health to Archie, making out everything is fine, that she's working and feeling great, when she isn't? After all, as an obstetrician, Archie knows the dangers of pre-eclampsia, would insist on bed rest if he knew what she was doing. Perhaps even have her admitted to hospital. And yet, Louise is lying to Jo as well – telling her that she's resting, taking it easy. But she's not. She's still at work. Conning them both that everything is fine.

Christ, Louise could be lying on the floor in her office right now, writhing in pain, bleeding, her phone dead and no one hearing her call for help.

'She's not there?' Jo says, her voice wavering. She doesn't know what to say, especially since Louise told her about the argument they'd had. She hopes they've made up by now. 'Are you sure?'

'No, she's not, and I'm sure. But I'll tell her you called when she gets back. How's the house-sitting going, anyway? Lou has told me all about it.'

'Yes, fine, thanks,' Jo replies as the photograph slips from her grip again. And when she refocuses on the room, Will is gone.

CHAPTER TWENTY-NINE

You OK? Jo had texted again, before everything had gone black and she'd shut out the world.

Unintentionally.

It was as if something had swept over her – a thick, dark blanket hiding her. She wasn't even aware of it happening.

Sleep.

She was exhausted, and had woken on the sofa. But she hadn't rested well – she'd been agitated, sweaty and filled with dreams she didn't want to be a part of. She was concerned about Louise, of course – though not in a way that had her panicking or phoning hospitals or interfering by telling Archie what had happened. Besides, if Louise hadn't actually arrived home last night, Archie would have called her, asked her what she knew.

And while Louise might be heavily pregnant, and not without medical complications, she wasn't stupid. Far from it. She was a high-achieving woman who knew how to look after herself. If Jo had had to be concerned about either Louise or Archie, she'd have chosen Archie every time. He might bring new life into the world virtually every day, his big hands cradling tiny newborns, but he didn't come without his own Venn diagram of complicated emotions. Past hurt caught up with vulnerability, crossing the line with pride. He seemed to move from one intersection to another – and he'd often chatted it out with Will. Jo wondered if he confided as much in his other male friends, if he had anyone to talk to now – apart from Louise, of course.

Similarly, Louise had Archie for support. A good man in her life. Someone to notice if she wasn't back home from work or was upset or struggling or simply in need of a hug. Someone who could read the little signals, decipher the tiniest of expression changes or the way she moved, the lightest of sighs. Plus she had her colleagues to watch out for her while she was in the office. People who would notice if she was ill or in trouble or if she didn't show up when she was meant to. Louise was ensconced in life. Wrapped up in it. She will be fine. The baby will be fine.

'But will *I* be fine?' Jo whispers, stretching out, wishing she'd made it upstairs to bed.

And that's what hurts the most, she'd thought as she'd tossed and turned through the night. Jo didn't have that any more. She'd been stripped of her cheerleader. The one who understood her the best. Her go-to person when her feelings got the better of her. Happy or sad, or anything in between, the one person she'd always want to tell first about anything that happened to her was Will.

And he didn't even have the decency to take his bloody phone so I could call, keep sending him messages even if they weren't being read.

It would have been some kind of connection, at least, until perhaps, one day, he found the courage to reply. Part of her *wanted* the chance to make him annoyed and switch off his phone or let his battery run out on purpose. She *wanted* to be a nuisance. *Wanted* some kind of reaction from him. But she didn't even have that as an option. Will had made sure of it by leaving his phone behind.

Meantime, Jo had it permanently on charge in her bedroom, watching and waiting – random and expected messages coming in, of course, but getting fewer and further between as the weeks went by, as his contacts learnt what had happened. And there was certainly nothing received that gave any clue to his whereabouts or what had happened.

It had been left on his desk at work *that* day. D-Day. Along with his keys and his wallet. His jacket, too. And his car was in the car park.

'I saw him park in his usual spot this morning,' Dean, head of history and one of Will's favourite colleagues, had said as she'd ventured into the school tentatively that afternoon. As arranged earlier in the morning, she'd been waiting outside the school gates and they were going to go home together via the supermarket. But she'd been there ages and Jo had guessed Will had been caught up with a meeting that had run on, or perhaps had to cover an after-school activity at short notice. *He could have at least texted to let me know*, she'd thought, deciding to go inside, fed up of waiting.

Security was strict, but she managed to slip inside the passcoded door as a pupil was coming out. The woman at reception turned her back just as Jo walked past. Then Dean had found her, looking lost in a corridor, asking if he could help. He recognised her as Will's wife. Jo explained what had happened.

'Oh, well, I've not seen him at all this afternoon, I'm afraid, but that's not unusual. This place is huge. Let's check the staffroom and his other various haunts. You've tried calling him, I assume?'

Jo had nodded, following Dean as they briskly walked the corridors. No sign of him. Then, on the way to Will's office, they'd ducked out of a side door into the car park at the back of the main building to check if his car was there. The easiest indicator if he was still in the building, as it was much closer than trekking all the way to the staffroom to see if he'd logged out yet.

'He's probably forgotten our arrangement and gone home already,' Jo said, adding a laugh to indicate she wasn't bothered. Even though she was.

And they'd found it – Will's Renault sitting there, with Dean confirming that's where he always parked, only a couple of spots along from him. She knew Will got on with Dean, that he was one of the good guys who refused to be tied up in the red tape and policies the system enforced, treating the pupils as individuals rather than part of an anonymous whole. They often went to the pub together after work on a Friday, Will getting back late, the cobwebs from a stressful week having been blown away.

'I'm sure he'll turn up soon enough, Jo,' Dean had said as they stood in Will's empty office – a small space he shared with the other drama department staff. 'And if I run into him, I'll let him know you're waiting.' Dean had smiled then, Jo waving a breezy goodbye as he left her to it. She stood there, wondering if she should gather up Will's phone, keys and wallet that were left on his desk and keep them safe, or leave them where they were. The very fact that he'd left them there indicated he was coming back, that he'd be stranded without them, that he trusted his colleagues. So she decided against it.

And, as she'd headed out of Wroxdown High School that afternoon, she hadn't been particularly worried or concerned about Will, not in *that* way. More annoyed than anything. It had only been forty-five minutes since he wasn't where he should be at that point. But as the hours had gone on, as the afternoon had turned into evening, as the school had closed and Jo couldn't reach the office any more to see if they had news, as Will's phone repeatedly kept going to voicemail when she rang it and the WhatsApp messages she sent were left unread and unanswered, Jo was the only one overthinking Will's absence. No one else seemed to care. Everyone was just getting on with their lives.

Jo stretches again, her muscles aching and sore as she remembers last night, how Louise had lied to her and Archie, that she hadn't been resting at all. She hopes she's OK, wondering if Archie gave her a talking-to when she got home. She's known Louise long enough to figure that she'd have got caught up in an important case, was stringing them both along for the sake of a client. She knows how stubborn her friend is. Though she's hardly been Miss Squeaky Clean herself when it's come to divulging her deepest and darkest feelings. She'd *tried* not to spew certain things out last night, but now wishes she'd kept quiet about what she'd found upstairs. She must have sounded like a crazy woman.

Something warm and heavy weighs down on her hip as she sits up.

'Oh, Bonnie,' she says, stroking the cat. Jo fumbles around for her phone, wanting to check the time. But the battery is dead. She goes through to the kitchen, rubbing her stiff neck. 'Five twenty. Really?' She groans, glancing at the clock, knowing if she goes up to bed now, she won't sleep anyway.

She plugs in her phone just as Spangle heaves himself out of his bed, trotting across the room, letting out a cross between a yap and a whine, his tail wagging furiously. He gives the cat something between a nuzzle and a nudge with his nose as Bonnie slinks around her legs. They're both hungry.

'Hey, boy,' she says, reaching out a hand. Then she shudders, spotting the photograph of Will staring up at her from the kitchen table. One of many that she'd spread out and arranged from her findings upstairs.

'It's real then, Spangle,' she whispers, picking it up. 'I actually stole keys, went into a private room and snooped through someone's personal belongings. And I found what I didn't want to find. My missing husband. Many, many times over. But *why?*'

In the utility room, she opens up a sachet of cat food for Bonnie and mixes up some meat and biscuits for Spangle, putting the bowls down in their separate spots.

'There's more stuff up there,' Jo whispers as she washes her hands. 'Though I'm not sure I can bring myself to look. Surely I've seen enough...' she says, staring at her ghostly reflection in the window above the sink. Her eyes appear sunken, ringed with grey, her hair a ratty frizz around her shoulders, the darkness outside making her look even more wan. She's still in yesterday's sweat top, although she'd slipped off her uncomfortable jeans to sleep. 'Surely finding a shrine to my missing husband is all I need to know?'

Then PC Janine Daniels is on her mind. 'If you have any news or think of anything that could help us trace your husband, however seemingly trivial, then do pick up the phone, OK?' She'd placed a hand on her arm then, given a comforting smile – which was no comfort at all in reality. But Jo had appreciated the gesture.

So you think that discovering a dozen or more photographs of Will printed out from his social media found in an unknown woman's home isn't worth calling PC Daniels about?

Jo shakes her head, knowing she can't phone the police. Not yet. Not until she's worked things out, had time to think.

Her thoughts are interrupted by her phone lighting up and a text coming in.

'Louise,' she says, sighing out in relief as she opens the message.

All fine here. Feeling better today. It's you I'm more worried about, Jo. Call me when you can xx

CHAPTER THIRTY

After she's made coffee and the animals have eaten, Jo takes Spangle for an early walk around the village. She plans on taking him for a longer run later, perhaps down to the beach again, but for now her mind is preoccupied with other things. She lets the dog off the lead when they reach the edge of the village and they're safely surrounded by countryside. Spangle immediately pushes through a five-bar gate and bounds off through an empty field. Jo waits, leaning on the gate, letting him have ten minutes to burn off at least some of his energy and do what he needs to do. As soon as Jo calls him back, he obeys and runs towards her, tongue lolling, ears flapping – only a slight look of disappointment in his eyes as Jo clips on the lead.

Fifteen minutes later, Jo unlocks the front door, holding Spangle back as he's about to charge in. 'Wait, boy,' she says, reaching for the dog towel she left just inside the door. She's standing on the drive, rubbing him down, cleaning up his muddy paws, when she becomes aware of a noise coming from next door – a car – either Simon leaving or arriving home. Jo glances at her watch: 6.38 a.m.

'He's been out early,' she whispers to Spangle, allowing him inside now he's clean. A quick glance over her shoulder, and through the thicket of shrubs and trees separating the properties, the bang of the front door tells Jo that Simon has just arrived back from somewhere. She has no idea from where at this hour.

'Perhaps he went to get milk,' she says to herself, shrugging, closing the door.

Jo settles the dog and makes herself another hot drink, grabbing some toast and butter, even though she doesn't feel in the least hungry. Food has been low down her list lately, but she needs energy – mental energy more than physical, she thinks, as she spreads jam on her toast, knowing she has to put everything in the locked room back exactly as she found it.

She only manages to eat one of the two pieces of toast as she looks at the photographs of Will that she brought downstairs last night. She counts thirteen in total; most are fairly recent, from just before he disappeared, but one or two are from about eight years ago. Jo checks Will's Facebook page yet again. She virtually knows the order of his pictures and posts off by heart anyway, the various photos and cover pictures he has in his collection. She's on his friends list, naturally, and knows not all of his photos are visible publicly. As Jo checks them off, it turns out that all apart from three of the photographs on the table have come from Facebook, and all are available to view by anyone. Will has had most of them as profile pictures at one time or another. The others were from posts he was tagged in by someone else; several he'd shared widely about theatre productions he'd been in.

'Safe to say that whoever has printed these, presumably Suzanne, isn't his Facebook friend,' Jo says, looking at Spangle to make her feel a fraction less crazy for talking to herself.

Of course, since seeing the photos of him on the house-sitting website, Jo has already trawled through Will's friends list. Twelve hundred friends, and a search for one called Suzanne didn't yield likely results. There were five Susans, three Susis and one Susanne, but without the 'z'. And while Jo was familiar with a couple of the names, none of them seemed to come from the South Coast – or looked anything like *this* Suzanne. It was safe to say the owner of Hawthorn Lodge was not on Will's social media.

After she's snapped photos on her phone of all the pictures laid out on the table, Jo gathers them up and takes them back upstairs to the locked room – the room that's not locked any more. She stares at the mess she made, feeling guilty about the pretty perfume bottle that got broken – vintage-looking and made from pale green glass. The room now smells of sweet roses, reminding her of the scent her grandmother used to wear.

She's just tidying the final few things, eyeing up the couple of shoeboxes under the bed with various papers poking out from beneath the lids, when she freezes, holding one of the scented candles in her hand. She could swear she heard something – a bang from outside, perhaps. As she listens, she hears herself breathing, her pulse whooshing in her ears.

Another noise, but she can't tell if it's inside or out.

She goes onto the landing. 'Hello?' she calls downstairs. 'Is that you, Spangle?' She knows there was something but isn't yet familiar enough with the noises of the house or its surroundings to identify it – a neighbour's car, the dustbin lorry, nearby building works perhaps.

Spangle is in the hallway, suddenly letting out an excited bark, whining and jumping about just as Jo sees a figure approaching the other side of the old frosted-glass panels in the top half of the door.

A hand is raised and Jo hears the sound of metal on metal. A key being inserted.

Her eyes widen and her mouth drops open.

Christ…

Her heart thumps as she forces her body to work, to quickly get everything back in order as best she can and get out of the room. But she's frozen, can't seem to move as she watches the front door slowly open and a small red suitcase being pushed inside, propping it ajar.

Spangle goes wild with excitement now, pawing at the case, jumping up, whining and yapping with his tail barely visible it's wagging so fast.

'Yes, yes, *hello*, boy,' a female voice says. 'Just give me a chance to get my things in from the car...'

Christ again, Jo thinks, recognising the voice as she creeps back into the spare room, taking a panicked look around. She fumbles to prop all the photographs up or set them out in the right places, but she can't remember exactly how they were arranged, didn't expect to have to do it in a rush. All she can recall is swiping the whole lot on the floor in anger when she saw the makeshift shrine to her missing husband.

Suzanne, Suzanne, Suzanne... she thinks, her foot crunching in some broken glass on the carpet. She stifles a cry as the shard digs into her heel, and her hands are shaking as she puts the pictures back anywhere, picks up the candles and other items, arranging them as best she can. She quickly brushes the small glittery bits of glass towards the edge of the room, gathering up the bigger ones. In a panic, she shoves them under the bed and gives a quick glance in the mirror on the dressing table – three pictures of Will leaning against it, smiling up at her – as she ruffles her hair and wipes her fingers under her eyes. She's still got yesterday's make-up smudged on, the eyeliner looking more like extreme exhaustion and her mascara clumpy and flaking onto her cheeks.

'Hell-*ooo*...' she hears from downstairs, followed by the front door banging closed. 'Anyone home? It's just me, Suzanne, don't worry...'

Don't worry? Jo thinks, silently cursing, hearing Spangle's frenzy as he gets a big fuss from his owner. As softly as she can, barely able to control her shaking limbs, Jo creeps out of the spare bedroom and pulls the door closed, coughing to cover the sound as the Yale latch clicks into place.

It's as she's standing right at the top of the stairs, just as Suzanne looks up at her, that Jo realises the keys she stole from Simon are still on the spare bed, now locked inside the room. And she forgot to lock the second mortice lock.

'Oh…' Jo squeaks, stumbling at the top step. 'I – I…' She tries to smile, tries to look normal, but it's not happening. She takes a step down.

'*Jo*…' Suzanne says, warmly. 'Hel-*lo*… I'm so sorry to turn up like this, but…' She trails off, not explaining why she's back – rather just staring as Jo hobbles down the stairs, her heel still painful from the glass. She prays she's not leaving a trail of blood.

'Hi, yes, hello…' Jo takes another few steps down, gripping the bannister rail for all she's worth because without it, she knows she'll fall. 'Nice to meet you…'

You're even more beautiful in real life, I'll give you that. Will certainly chose someone striking to replace me with…

And as she approaches, faking that she's pleased to see her, Jo can't help the glance to the front door, half expecting Will to walk in at any moment. But he doesn't. Instead, Suzanne touches her head, turns white as a sheet and drops to the tiled floor.

CHAPTER THIRTY-ONE

Jo bolts down the remaining stairs, her legs feeling like jelly. She drops to her knees. 'Oh my God, *Suzanne*... can you hear me? Are you OK? Suzanne, wake up... oh, *please...*'

Suzanne's head rests on the cold Minton tiles of the hallway, her eyes closed, her mouth slightly open. Spangle paces anxiously around her, letting out subdued whining noises as he nuzzles her hands, then her face. If anyone can bring her round, it's likely to be him, Jo thinks, as she tries to roll Suzanne over into the recovery position. It was only the suitcase that stopped her head hitting the floor with full force.

Jo heaves her over onto her side, trying to remember what she needs to do – apart from call an ambulance.

Raise her legs above her head, a voice says. Jo glances up to see Will standing above them, his shaved head silhouetted by the light pouring through the stained glass in the door behind him, making him look almost biblical. *She's fainted. You need to get the blood back to her brain. Get her legs up.*

'Yes, yes, you're right,' Jo says, suddenly swamped with memories as if she's somehow living two lives.

The last time she'd seen anyone faint was years ago, at her and Will's wedding. They'd both heard the thud behind them as the vicar was reading out the vows, each of them looking into the other's eyes, lightly holding the other's hands as they carefully repeated what he was saying.

Then the *thunk*, gasps from the congregation and Jo was suddenly aware of the best man sliding behind them both in the narrow aisle as he acted quickly, getting Louise's feet up, holding the long skirt of her maid of honour's dress around her ankles to protect her modesty as he brought the blood back to her head. She and Will let go hands then and, when Will saw what had happened, he pulled off his jacket and bunched it up, placing it under Louise's head.

Jo had knelt down also, dropping her bouquet to check her friend was OK. 'Oh, Lou… Lou, are you OK?' And of course Archie had dashed from his seat on the front pew, started checking her out medically. Her eyes soon opened, blinking up at an experience she later described as like staring into heaven.

'I *do*…' were her first words when she came round properly, after Archie asked if she knew where she was. Louise's hand had reached out then and grabbed the bride's bouquet, clutching it to her chest.

Later, at the reception, the guests had chuckled at the impromptu addition to the best man's speech – about Louise pulling a stunt to be the first to catch the bouquet, that Archie had better step up and pop the question. But the main thing was that Louise was fine. She'd just been on her feet too long, and hadn't had a chance to eat much because of helping Jo prepare for her big day.

'Suzanne?' Jo says now, looking up to Will for guidance. He nods as she lifts her legs, propping them on top of the second, larger suitcase that she'd dragged into the hallway. 'Can you hear me? Please wake up… Suzanne?'

Suzanne stirs, her head moving from side to side as Jo sees the colour returning to her cheeks. She mumbles something.

'Oh, thank goodness,' she says, holding the woman's hand. 'It's OK, I'm here, you're not alone. I think you fainted.'

Another garbled noise comes out of the woman's mouth and, even though Jo can't make out the words exactly, she would later swear that Suzanne mumbled, 'Where's Will?'

*

'What an entrance I made, and how utterly embarrassing.' Suzanne is on the sofa – the same one that Jo spent most of last night on, clutching Will's photo. She's holding her head, shielding her eyes from the sunlight streaming in the window.

'Oh no, don't be silly. I'm just glad you feel a bit better. But I really wish you'd let me call an ambulance, or your GP at least. Get yourself checked out.'

'No, no really,' Suzanne says immediately. 'It's not necessary. I'm quite used to it.'

'Fainting?'

Suzanne nods as she sips her glass of water. 'Low blood pressure. And I haven't eaten all day and had a bit of a sho— a… a long drive.'

Jo stares at her, gives a little nod. 'If you're sure?'

'Totally. And I'm so sorry for surprising you like this, by coming home. You must think I'm a disaster, booking you in to house-sit for me at the last moment then arriving back early.'

'Not at all,' Jo says, though she doesn't mean it. All she can think about is that she'll now have to leave before she's had a chance to find out anything about Will, or why Suzanne has what seems to be a shrine set up to him in a locked room.

A room that you've gone and locked the stolen keys inside…

And then there's Simon.

'How have the kids been?' Suzanne says in a silly voice, all the while staring at Jo, her pupils dilating one minute and shrinking to tiny dots the next in the middle of her azure eyes.

She's very striking, Jo thinks, glancing at Will, who's standing beside the window, watching on – though not in his usual cocksure pose of arms folded across his chest, chin jutting upwards, legs spread in a confident stance. This time he's rather stooped. As though he's concerned, anxious… regretful, almost. *There's certainly something about her, Will…* He doesn't reply.

'Oh… yes, they've been great. Both got their own personalities, for sure.' On cue, Spangle nuzzles Jo as she sits in the armchair beside Suzanne. 'I'm going to feel awful leaving you alone like this, so I'll let Simon know you fainted before I leave, so he can come and check in on you.'

Suzanne sits upright, sloshing some of her water on her chest. 'No!' she says, almost sounding panicked. 'Please, you don't have to go. Stay. I insist.'

'But…' Jo is confused. Suzanne hasn't explained why she's come back early, not that she needs to – it's her house – but now she wants her to stay?

'I'll not hear of it. When you first got in touch, you told me you were looking for a break, a little holiday. And now I've gone and messed that up. You're obviously doing a great job around here, and I can see…' She trails off, watching as Bonnie winds between Jo's ankles. 'That the animals love you. Bon-bon is a tricky character. She either loves you or plans a vendetta, usually involving claws.' Suzanne laughs then, touching her head and wincing. 'I always get a migraine after fainting. It's only been happening since…' She stops then, almost as if she's forgotten what she was going to say. 'But look, *please* stay. Pretend I'm not even here.'

What, while I snoop through all your personal belongings to find out how you know my husband? Jo thinks, wishing she'd just got on with the job sooner. She'd not seen this coming. And she's not sure she can be civil or polite to her for much longer. But similarly, blurting everything out, grilling her, shaking her, screaming for answers, isn't going to get her anywhere either – apart from arrested.

'It's fine,' Jo replies, knowing she must head home. *It'll only take me ten minutes to pack and getting away from here is probably the best thing I can do. I'll call PC Daniels on the way, tell her what I've found and then leave it in the hands of the police.*

'But if you're sure,' she hears someone saying. *Her.* She glances behind Suzanne to see Will shaking his head, his eyes slowly rolling, his head dropping. 'Then it would be lovely to explore the area more and help you out with the animals. Thank you.'

There. It's done. You're going to see this through, find out what the hell she knows about Will.

'Perfect,' Suzanne says, staring at her from the sofa, where she lies supine. 'Something tells me we're going to get along… fine.' She sits up, slowly swinging her legs over the side. Jo has already noticed that one of her shoes is larger than the other – an odd platform shoe completely different to the expensive pony skin and patent leather designer flat she wears on her right foot. This one's big and black and laced up. When she stands and walks, Jo spots the limp. 'Let me get you something to drink. No guest of mine goes neglected, eh Spangie?' She ruffles the dog's neck as he follows her out of the living room.

Jo also follows, thinking she should stay close in case Suzanne faints again. She stood up rather quickly and is holding onto the walls as she walks.

'I left my stick in the car,' Suzanne says by way of excusing her slow progress, turning slightly, making a sound as if she's in pain. 'I hate having to use it.' Jo doesn't fail to notice the wince.

Jo, just go home, will you…? Accept that I'm not coming back, that I have a better life now. A different *life…*

Jo stops, turns, looks around. It wasn't Suzanne who spoke. And it certainly wasn't her.

Behind her, Will is following as Suzanne shuffles towards the kitchen. He glares at Jo, shaking his head slowly. And his face is sweaty, making his skin appear darker than ever.

Just like that night after Annabel's party, when they'd got home and Will had comprehensively messed up the front wing of the car. She'd thought he'd been about to hit her at one point as he'd inspected it, such was his… not *rage*, exactly, but something close. A cocktail of anger and fear, almost with a splash of relief. Perhaps because the night was over – he'd not wanted her there in the first place. But then she'd smelt the alcohol on his breath.

'You said you'd drive. That you wouldn't drink,' Jo whispered, flicking her eyes down to the damage. She was still shaking from the impact up the road. It could have been so much worse.

Will moved between her and the dent in the front right panel of the car, obliterating her view. 'Get inside,' he'd said, thrusting his hand out towards the house.

When Jo had stood her ground, Will had come even closer, his broad shoulders and puffed-up chest looming over her in the dark. She didn't want the neighbours to hear. She'd taken a step back then but stopped, seeing something in his eyes she'd never seen before; never wanted to see again. And the sweat on his face, each pore exuding something that looked a lot like guilt.

'*Now,*' he'd whispered, though he may as well have yelled it in her face. Jo turned and did as she was told, glancing back over her shoulder as she ran inside. Shortly after, she heard the front door open, then noises in the understairs cupboard. When she peeked through the curtains, she saw him outside at the car again, armed with rags and cleaning spray, watching as he tried to tap out the dents with a small wooden mallet they'd bought from a campsite last summer for hammering in the tent pegs when the ground was hard as concrete.

Just go home… Jo hears again, startling her as she follows Suzanne into the kitchen. Once inside, Jo swings round and firmly shuts the door in Will's face, screaming *No* a thousand times in her head.

CHAPTER THIRTY-TWO

Then

'The show must go on, eh?' Louise said.

I pulled on my coat. 'Man flu, if you ask me,' I replied, laughing. 'The pair of them.' I rolled my eyes.

Will had been at the theatre since just before lunch to get ready for the matinee. He'd called me not long after it had finished, asking me to bring in more medication when I came to watch the evening performance. He'd been coming down with something since about a week ago and it had finally taken hold.

'"I feed dike shit,"' I mimicked in a stuffed-up cold voice. 'Not great for performing, true, but he's dosed up on decongestant. I know he was putting it on for my benefit, anyway. Probably wants a massive pity lie-in tomorrow. He didn't seem too bad this morning, and I've not caught anything.'

'Archie's virtually *dying*,' Louise said, following me out to the car after I'd swiped up my bag and keys. 'I left him on the sofa with some chicken broth and a bottle of Night Nurse,' she said as she got in and buckled up. 'Though no doubt when I get back I'll find him several shots of whiskey down, a pizza delivery box on his chest and porn on his laptop.'

'Really?' I said, glancing across at Louise as I drove off in the direction of the theatre. 'Does he do that?'

'What, order pizza?' Louise nudged me gently, giving me a sideways wink.

'Watch porn.'

Louise laughed. 'Duh.'

Silence for a moment as I concentrated on the road, navigating a tricky junction.

'I'd hate that. Will watching that stuff. I think it's as bad as cheating.'

'Archie knows that he can look but can't touch.'

'Doesn't that make him *want* to touch, though?' I sighed, tapping my finger on the wheel as we waited at the lights. 'My mother says men always want to push one step further, take things they shouldn't to the next level. Hence me making my dislike of porn to Will quite clear from the get-go. His "one step further" would therefore be watching it. If he's already watching it, then one step further is what? Strip clubs? Private dances? Prostitutes? Anyway, apart from anything, I think it's degrading to women.'

'Jo, *Jo*… stop, my love. You're going to drive yourself crazy thinking like that.' Louise couldn't help the laugh. 'And you got this from your mum?' She paused, shaking her head, an incredulous smile on her face. Louise knew what my mother was like – not that my father had ever given Mum any need to worry. The poor man wouldn't dare put a foot wrong.

'Trust me,' Louise went on. 'Will has his eyes on two prizes in life and, from where I'm standing, neither of them is porn. One prize is called Joanne Carter and the other is called his acting career. And trust me again, as one of your oldest and bestest mates, I know when you're about to descend into one of your "overthinking" sessions, and tonight isn't the time. Let's have a wonderful evening watching Will dance about onstage in his Shakespearean tights, or whatever he's going to be wearing, and then enjoy the after-party. Deal?'

'Deal,' I said, suddenly feeling less anxious. Either way, I wished I could be as laid-back in my relationship as Louise and

Archie were. They'd only been married a year less than me and Will (Archie taking his cue at our wedding after Louise fainted, proposing to her that very evening at the reception during a slow dance), and their seven years, compared to our eight, somehow still seemed as if they were in the first throes of a relationship. Perhaps it was all the stress of trying to conceive getting in the way. Overshadowing everything. Of feeling like the biggest failure on earth.

*

The orchestra was tuning up when I came into the auditorium to find Louise. I'd been backstage to deliver Will's medication, take him a few extra things he liked – some energy drinks, some snacks, some cooling water spray for his face. I knew how hot the lights were. Plus I'd made him a little good luck card and slipped it in the bag, telling him to break a leg.

'I'm not going to understand a word, you realise,' Louise said, flipping through one of the programmes we'd bought in the foyer. 'I was rubbish at English at school and haven't read a word of Shakespeare since I was forced to for exams. And even then I didn't have a clue what was going on.'

We both stood up, allowing our seats to flip up behind us as a couple squeezed past to get to the seats further along the row.

'Don't worry,' I said, laughing. 'Take it from me, there'll be two guys who want to kill each other – usually because they're fighting over the same woman. Then someone's father will die, most likely at the hand of one of the jealous guys. A woman will dress up as a bloke and inadvertently save the day, there'll be feuding families, probably a war or a battle, characters falling on their swords, mistaken identities and a wardrobe full of amazing costumes. Of course.'

'You and Margot involved?'

'Did most of them,' I said proudly. Then I leant across to the person the other side of me who was reading through the programme, looking at the cast list and their photos and biographies. 'That's my husband,' I said, pointing at Will's picture.

The man paused, pushing his glasses on further. Then he looked up at me. 'Really?' he said, smiling, flicking his gaze between me and the programme. 'You must be so proud.'

But before I could say anything, how I was more proud than he could imagine, the house lights dimmed and the auto-announcement about mobile phones and recordings began. I nudged Louise as the audience fell silent.

'You don't think either of them would, do you, Lou?' I whispered in her ear. 'Will and Archie.'

'Will and Archie would what?' she whispered back.

'You know... *touch*?' I replied, wishing I'd kept quiet. Because, throughout the play – although I knew he was acting, that it wasn't real life – all I could see was the undeniable chemistry between Will and the beautiful woman playing opposite him.

*

'A-bloody-mazing,' Louise said when the curtain had come down and the applause was subsiding. 'I had absolutely no idea what was going on, of course, but to even remember all those lines – in that weird English – is a feat in itself. Respect to your good man.'

'Told you,' I said, beaming. My hands stung from clapping so much. 'Though I thought I'd lost you in the interval. Reckoned you'd got bored and gone down the pub instead.' I laughed.

'Sorry about that,' Louise replied. 'There was a massive queue in the ladies and I just *had* to go. By the time I got back, the second half had already started and they wouldn't let me in during the first scene, when it was all quiet. Some monologue or something, the chap at the door said. So he made me wait until a scene change and there was a bit of bustle.'

'That's the trouble with good seats like these. It's distracting to the cast if stragglers come in late.'

'Ha, stragglers indeed,' Louise joked as we stood and shuffled our way up the aisle towards the exit.

The after-party was to begin in the green room, and Louise and I made our way around the front of the theatre and down the side lane, weaving between the throng leaving the auditorium and dodging waiting taxis. After a few drinks in celebration of the company's best run yet, once the cast had stripped themselves of make-up and costumes, whoever was remaining would head round the corner to the Horse and Wagon, which served craft beers and did a cracking line in home-made pie and chips. Partners were welcome, and I had never missed one yet.

'Wait up a moment,' Louise said, rummaging in her clutch bag. She pulled out a cigarette and lighter, the glow illuminating her face.

'Ah, so this is where you really disappeared to in the interval,' I said, grinning. 'If you're trying to conceive as well, you'd better stop, you know. Doesn't help in the least, and you don't want to fall pregnant while smoking. Plus Archie wouldn't approve. He'll smell it on you.'

Louise shrugged. 'Not sure if we are trying for a baby or not, to be honest,' she said. 'So let me at least enjoy the last of this packet, Mrs Killjoy. There are only a couple left.' She took a drag. 'And don't tell Arch. It's my guilty little secret.'

I grinned again, plucking the lipstick-stained cigarette from between Louise's fingers and inhaling deeply. 'Takes me back,' I said, staring up at the austere brick wall of the back of the theatre while hugging myself with one arm against the chill. The lit-up stage door sign had several bulbs blown and so looked like 'age do'. 'Standing out the back, waiting for Will to finish, all pumped up from a performance. I love theatres – the smell of them, the anticipation, the cacophony of noises, everyone rushing about looking manic yet knowing exactly what they're doing, where they're going, whether they're cast or crew. The number of times I've literally had a needle and cotton attached to an actor's hem the second they're about to set foot onstage.' I smiled, handing the cigarette back to Louise.

'You're such a romantic,' Louise said, taking a last couple of draws before squashing out the butt in the gutter. She turned to head inside. 'Come on, let's go congratulate your man. He did good.'

'Lou, wait,' I said, taking hold of her wrist. 'Tell me I'm mad, but—'

Louise stopped. 'Yes. You're mad. Loopy as a box of frogs. Satisfied?' She laughed, heading towards the stage door, shivering, her coat only draped around her shoulders.

'No, listen to me. Did you see it too?'

'See what?'

'Onstage. Will.'

Louise rolled her eyes. 'No, I was asleep the whole time.'

'You know what I mean.' I looked away. It was going to kill me to say it, but if I didn't it would sit inside me all night, lodged in my gullet either ruining the rest of the evening or spewing out to Will in a way I couldn't stand. I'd never felt like this before, and Louise and I discussed everything anyway. This was no different.

'Will and that woman, the queen whatever her name was. The one with the white, made-up face and big crazy wig.'

'Yes, and?'

'Did you think they looked…?'

Louise tilted her head to the side while one hand reached into her bag for her packet of cigarettes.

'No,' I said, touching her wrist as she was about to take one out. 'No need for another. But did you think they looked, you know… as though they were into each other? Christ, this is going to sound crazy, but to me it seemed as if they had this *thing* going on between them. An unspoken thing. As if they knew each other *off*stage as well as on.'

'Of course they know each other offstage. How long have they all spent rehearsing together?'

'Lou, listen to me. I mean… *chemistry*. The way they looked at each other. The way he touched her. Held her. And then that kiss. Just the two of them onstage. I've seen Will perform dozens of stage kisses before and none has got to me like that before. There was this moment afterwards when… when it seemed as if they were the only two people in the world and we were just voyeurs. That they were completely oblivious to our presence.'

Louise put her cigarettes away and faced me squarely. She took me by the shoulders. 'That, my dear friend, is called good – no, *excellent* – acting. Now, come with me, let's find your poor oh-so-sick husband and get a drink.'

It was hot, crowded and noisy in the green room. I gripped Louise's hand as we walked in, trailing behind her. I went up on tiptoe, trying to spot Will and it didn't take long – he towered above the others across the far side of the room. I raised my hand to get his attention but he had a crowd of people around him – actors still in costume as well as cast and crew. He didn't notice me. Or if he did, he didn't show it.

'Drinks table's this way,' Louise called over her shoulder, weaving between the bodies. When we reached the other side of the room, Louise grabbed a ready-poured plastic beaker of Prosecco and handed it to me, taking another one for herself. 'Cheers, lovely,' she said, raising it and grinning, shouldering the bump she got from someone sidling past. 'Will's over there, look. Come on.'

Again, I followed, wondering why I felt about three inches tall. I'd had a hand in making or at least altering half the costumes in the room and knew most of the faces, smiling and nodding and congratulating people as we passed. But still, I felt as though I didn't belong, as if everyone else knew a secret apart from me.

'Oh, my liege,' Louise said in a silly voice as we approached Will and the group he was with. She gave a flamboyant bow, managing to hold her drink high and keep her coat and bag on her shoulders as she dipped down. 'What a mighty performance you gave. May I raise my drink in your honour?' And she did just that.

'Twit as ever, Lou,' Will said, leaning forward to dot a kiss on each of her cheeks. 'But thank you. Much appreciated and fandom noted.' Will's smile was broad, his white teeth glinting in the fluorescent light. 'Shame Archie couldn't be here.'

'Hey, love,' I said, attempting to get closer to Will, to edge in between him and the person next to him. 'Great performance.' It was only when we'd bumped shoulders several times that I realised it was the queen from the play preventing me getting near to my husband so he could hear me, or at least even acknowledge I was there. Which he'd not yet done.

Up close, the woman's white-painted face was stark and ugly, her wig a wiry mass of grey sitting precariously on her head. Her black-rimmed eyes looked like sinkholes, the false lashes on one eye peeling off at the corner, her lips smudged scarlet – presumably from kissing my husband.

'You were great, Will,' I said, looking hopefully at him. But the queen turned her back on me, talking to Will herself.

I tried to edge round the other side of the queen, squeezing behind her back. I wondered if the actress – whoever she was – could feel my breath on her bare shoulders. I noticed the pale nape of her neck, the very spot where Will's dark hand had reached around and drawn her in for the kiss, the contrast between them stark onstage. There was a mole on her neck and I wondered if Will had felt it as he'd touched her. Or if he was more focused on their lips meeting, was even aware of the little moan he let out, picked up by the sensitive radio mic taped to his cheek. It felt like a game of real-life chess – onstage as well as off as I tried to outmanoeuvre the queen.

Checkmate, I thought, relieved, finally sliding up to Will and giving him a long kiss.

CHAPTER THIRTY-THREE

Now

'You must be wondering why I'm back.'

'Oh…' Jo says as the pair of them watch Spangle charge around the empty beach. 'Well, that's none of my business. What I've learnt so far from the house-sitting website, other people's reviews and that kind of thing, is that you're there to do a job. Not stick your nose into other people's lives.' Jo clears her throat. Looks away. It's exactly the opposite of what she wants to do.

'And I'm sorry to hold you back if you fancied a long walk. I can possibly make it down to the shoreline, if you like?' Suzanne leans heavily on her stick.

'Don't be silly. Spangle's doing a fine job of taking himself for a walk, look.'

The dog zigzags across the sand, occasionally stopping to wrestle with a clump of seaweed.

'I'm happy to stay up here with you and watch. Plus we've got these.' Jo raises her paper cup of hot chocolate they'd picked up from a kiosk.

'To cut a long story short, the reason why I'm home early is that I checked in… somewhere. Then I checked myself out. It wasn't working for me.'

Don't say anything. Just let her speak. She'll open up to you and tell you all about Will, her affair, where he is now…

'Oh, OK,' Jo says immediately. 'I thought you'd gone away for work?' she adds, unable to stay quiet. She remembers Simon telling her about the theatre, what Suzanne does for a living. The coincidence with Will's profession is too great. But he also said she'd gone somewhere to 'recover'.

'Sadly, not work. Look, I know we've only just met, and after a very strange entrance by me, but I feel…' Suzanne looks at Jo a certain way, her eyes narrowing into thoughtful slits, as if she's trying to recall something. 'What I'm trying to say is that you have kind eyes. And I feel I can talk to you. That you're non-judgemental. Almost as if I know you already.'

All Jo hears is 'mental'. *Oh, you're mental all right, aren't you? Your best friend thinks you're crazy and your mother believes you're mad. Even Will thought you were obsessive, fixated… your only aim in life to be pregnant…*

Jo looks away again, pretending to look out for Spangle.

'I've had some… some emotional stresses lately,' Suzanne continues. 'Things were getting on top of me after… well, after a trauma I had a while ago. I've been diagnosed with PTSD and, despite all the medical help and support I've received, things haven't been improving as fast as I'd like. My life feels on hold.'

'That sounds rough,' Jo says, forgetting her own issues for a moment. 'I'm sorry to hear that.'

Jo balls one hand into a fist by her side, trying to stop herself blurting something out that she'll regret. All she wants to do is take Suzanne by the collar, pull her up close and demand answers.

'They stopped me driving. I have to take the train and taxis everywhere, though Simon's been great when he can. But his job is so demanding. And I find it almost impossible to work now. My memory is shot. It seems as though my symptoms are getting worse, not better.'

Jo sips her hot chocolate to stop herself talking.

What is it about her? You've known this woman all of a couple of hours, yet...

Jo shakes the thought from her head, silencing herself. She needs to keep her mind clear, listen to what Suzanne tells her, spot the signals she gives off, clues, anything. Not succumb to voices in her head rife with suspicion.

'Do you have a partner to help?' Jo says, rather more directly than she'd intended. She puts her cup on the top of a bollard for a moment, zipping up her padded jacket. She's not sure if it's against the wind or against what Suzanne might be about to tell her.

'Ahh,' Suzanne laughs, tipping back her head. Her long wavy blonde hair, lightly flecked with the first threads of silver, billows around her face, getting in her mouth. 'Men, men, men...' She pulls it back with long, elegant fingers.

Jo's heart thumps. Her mouth goes dry. When she sips more hot chocolate, it might as well be powder. 'That's a no, then?'

Suzanne turns away from the sea to face Jo, forcing one leg to move, leaning heavily on her stick. 'There was someone...' she says, one finger sliding a strand of hair away from her cheek. 'But he's no more. It's almost like...' Suzanne glances up at the sky for a second, making Jo do the same, as if all the answers are up there. But all Jo sees is a bank of swirling yellow-grey clouds rolling in, indicating rain. 'It's almost like he never existed. Do you know what I mean?'

Jo feels the heat of Suzanne's stare. 'Yes. Yes, I know exactly what you mean.' Jo's words are crisp and clear but the stiff breeze still manages to sweep them away.

'I loved him. He loved me. There's nothing else to say.'

'But that's like a story without a middle,' Jo says. 'Almost as if you've blocked it out because it's too painful.'

'Oh, it's too painful, all right. But the thing is, Jo, my mind doesn't work the same any more, so you'll have to forgive me. See, I can look at you and think, I know her. We've met before. My mind plays tricks and sends me down memory pathways that have nothing to do with you. It could be the same with anyone – a random stranger in the street. But then…'

Jo listens, failing to understand what this has got to do with the man she loved. Or Will.

'And it's not actually the middle of my story that's missing, you see. It's the end.' Suzanne laughs, whistling loudly to Spangle, who has run far down the beach. Instantly the dog turns and charges towards them, ears flapping, sand kicking up from behind his back legs. 'Anyway, turns out he was never mine to begin with. He's gone, and that's that. Not the ending I'd hoped for. Meantime, I'm left with this bastard brain of mine that lies to me more than he did.' She lets out a wild laugh then, probably to indicate that she doesn't care, Jo thinks, although she can see quite clearly that she does.

'Come on, I'll buy you lunch,' Suzanne says after a moment. 'There's a dog-friendly place nearby.'

'So what was he like?' Jo says when they're seated in the pub. A dry and rubbed-down Spangle is asleep at Suzanne's feet under the table, his head rested on her chunky boot. On the other foot, she wears a white trainer. 'And was he… was he something to do with your accident? Simon mentioned that.' She's pushing as far as she dare – already too much for a virtual stranger.

'Questions, questions,' Suzanne says, peering over the top of her red-rimmed glasses. 'I recommend the chowder. They make it here, along with the sourdough.' She's well spoken, but Jo notices something else in her voice – not a slur, exactly, but something close to not being able to form every word properly.

Jo puts down her menu. 'I'll have that, then,' she says. 'Sounds delicious. And sorry, I didn't mean to pry. It's just that you seem a bit upset and—'

'Strange? Is that what you mean?'

'No—'

'I am. I freely admit it.'

Jo feels the blush burn on her cheeks as the waitress approaches their table, notepad to hand. 'Ready to order?' the girl says, bending down to give Spangle a stroke.

'I'll have the—'

'I *do* know you, don't I?' Suzanne says suddenly, half whispering, one hand gripping the edge of the small round table between them, making the glasses wobble.

Jo looks uncomfortably from the waitress to Suzanne. 'Know me?'

Suzanne doesn't reply, rather she slowly removes her glasses with one hand, squints at Jo, then puts them back on again, tilting her head to the side. Her lips are slightly parted.

'I'll have the chowder and sourdough, please,' Jo says, turning back to the waitress. 'Actually, make that two. I think my… my friend wants the same.'

The girl nods and collects the menus, tucking her pad in her apron pocket and heading off to the kitchen.

'The same… the same… the same…' Suzanne chants. 'Now, does Suzanne want the same as Jo? Or does Jo want the same as Suzanne?' She cups her face in her hands, making her eyes go wide. Her green irises glow with confusion.

'Sorry?' Jo says, concerned by the sudden switch in Suzanne's demeanour. She's acting very strange, to the point where she thinks she should pack up and leave for home as soon as they get back to Hawthorn Lodge.

But you're not going to, are you? Because she knows something about Will…

'Christ… I'm so sorry,' Suzanne says, her tone of voice suddenly completely different. She bows her head, closing her eyes briefly. When she looks up, her expression has changed, too, as if a different person is occupying her now. She shakes her head, her shoulders shuddering – in fact, her whole body shivers.

'I get these *moments* from time to time,' she says. 'These weird shifts inside, almost as if I'm somewhere else. Some*one* else. "Episodes", my doctor calls them. There's a proper medical name but I can never remember it. Anyway, it's a fat lot of use them calling it anything if they can't cure me. They come from nowhere, triggered by something, apparently, but no one knows what. It could be a word, a smell, a colour, a loud noise, someone's expression. Someone's... someone's face. And seconds later, I don't even remember why they were familiar to me.'

'That must be terrifying,' Jo says genuinely. Whatever her connection to Will, it sounds awful.

'It's like, for a few moments of clarity, my brain sees all the things I've forgotten and blocked out. But it muddles them all up along with everyday things in my mind, confusing neural pathways or something. Whatever it is that's triggered a memory, rather than seeming clearer, it makes everything more confused and more lost than ever. It's scary.'

'That's tough,' Jo says. 'Will it ever go away?'

'No one knows. I've had so many scans, it's ridiculous. And there's nothing wrong with my brain on a physical level. But inside, it's prone to going a bit haywire. There's a treatment I want to try, EMDR. It's meant to help process traumatic memories. But if I can't recall them in the first place, processing them is going to be tricky.' Suzanne smiles but then her face falls serious again. 'The place I was just at was... was a residential clinic. I was hoping that some talking therapies, some group work, individual counselling would help, but...'

'But you came home,' Jo says. 'You said it wasn't for you?'

'Truth is, I can't properly remember why I had to come home. That's the weird thing. I remember talking to Simon on FaceTime – he's a good man, but I'm sure you know that by now – and then, as I was talking, I had one of the episodes. Afterwards, all I wanted to do was get home. It was a compulsion.'

'Do you remember speaking to me on FaceTime?' Jo asks.

Something flickers under one of Suzanne's eyes. 'We spoke?'

'Yes. Yes, we did.'

She shakes her head and Jo can see by her expression that she's forcing a memory, trying to wrest something out.

'Do you think *I* triggered one of your... episodes, Suzanne? You've just had another, after all. And you passed out as soon as you came home and saw me.'

Before Suzanne can answer, the waitress returns with two bowls of soup and crusty bread. Following behind her is Will. He sits down right next to Suzanne, glaring at Jo.

Watch yourself, Jo, he says. *You're treading on thin ice here. You have no idea what you're dealing with...*

But... But...

'But what?' Suzanne says.

'Sorry,' Jo says. 'The accident you mentioned – did you have a head injury?'

'An everything injury,' Suzanne says, rolling her eyes. 'But mainly my leg,' she says, rubbing her thigh. 'My femur was broken clean in two and my knee comprehensively smashed up. A fractured hip, too. There's a lot of metal in me.' She unfolds her napkin, talking as normally about it as if she was discussing the weather. A different person entirely to a moment ago. 'Which is why this leg is now a little shorter than the other. There's another operation I can have in a few months' time, but I've had so many, I'm not sure I can go through with it. I manage OK. The pain is bearable now. Once the episodes are under control, once the fainting stops, I'll hopefully be able to drive again. And work properly again.'

'You poor, *poor* thing. That's a lot to deal with. Do you mind me asking what kind of accident you had?' Jo asks, her spoon halfway to her mouth.

Suzanne stares at her, lets out a little sigh. 'It was a hit and run,' she says matter-of-factly, making Jo spill her soup down her front.

CHAPTER THIRTY-FOUR

'Oh, I…' Jo says, stopping in her tracks, shocked. It takes her a moment to realise what Suzanne is doing.

When they'd got back to Hawthorn Lodge after lunch, Jo's first thought was to pack up and leave. Everything had changed since Suzanne's return and she felt rattled, thrown by her presence.

'Are you looking for something?' Jo says, feeling almost guilty for questioning Suzanne, given that she is in her house. But then Suzanne is rummaging in *her* handbag. And apart from her fainting and the brief 'episode' at lunch, she's been nothing but pleasant, talking about her work – which seems to be more short films, TV and voice-overs, unlike Will's focus on theatre. It could well be that their paths have crossed. And at least the woman she's trying to find out about is now right here. It could make everything much easier. Earlier, she'd felt torn about what to do. Jo scoops up her bag and the spilt-out contents from the table, snatching it away.

Suzanne stares at her, that now-familiar flicker starting up under one eye. As if her conscious mind is using all its resources to dredge her brain. 'Yes,' she says. Then a little shake of her head. 'But stupidly, I don't know what. Probably just my keys.'

Keys…

She glances at the bag. 'I'm sorry, Jo. You must think I'm so nosy. I didn't even realise it wasn't my bag until you said.' Then that look in her eyes again, as if she was looking directly inside her rather than just at her. 'It's similar to mine.'

'It's… it's OK,' Jo says, putting the bag down on the table again. 'I do understand, you know. That you get confused.'

No, Jo. You've just caught a virtual stranger going through your personal belongings. What if she creeps into your room later… with a knife or something?

Jo shudders. Her imagination's running away with her.

'The knives are in the second drawer along,' Suzanne says.

'Sorry, what?' Jo's eyes widen.

'You just said something about a knife. There's some fresh bread over there. I got the taxi to stop at the bakery earlier. Feel free to have as much as you like.' Suzanne smiles.

'No, it's OK. I… I'm still full from lunch, thanks,' Jo says, wondering how she's going to get Simon's keys out of the locked bedroom and return them to him. Suzanne must have her own set somewhere. She needs to find them.

Then she spots the shadow in the hallway, a ghostly figure slipping past the door. *Will.*

Suzanne grips the back of the chair, making Jo wonder if she saw him too, whether she's somehow privy to her inner thoughts.

'There was another woman, you know,' Suzanne suddenly says, that look in her eyes again. 'So I got rid of him.'

Then it's Jo's turn to steady herself on a chair. 'Got rid of him? Do you mean… the man you mentioned earlier, the one you were seeing?'

'Yes. His name was Bill. Though it wasn't quite as straightforward as that. Turns out *I* was the other woman. I had no idea.'

'Oh…' Jo feels light-headed, wondering if she might also faint. She sits down, pulling her handbag towards her again. 'That's awful,' Jo says, meaning it for her own reasons.

'I never thought I'd be *that* woman, you know? So completely blindsided by love I didn't see the obvious. It all made sense after I found out, of course. How he wasn't available at weekends, going silent for days on end, locked down on social media and refusing to add me, saying he didn't want to rush things, that he wanted to savour our relationship slowly. Like a fine fucking wine, he told me.'

Suzanne drops down into the chair beside Jo. Lets out a strange sound, something like a deflated laugh.

'I'm so sorry, Jo, you must think I'm crazy. I have absolutely no idea why I'm telling you all this. It's weird, though, almost as if I feel I can. Like I said, it feels as if I *know* you.'

This is your chance, Jo. She's opening up. Find out what you can then get the hell out...

'Yeah, me too,' Jo says, smiling and sliding a hand on top of Suzanne's. 'If I lived closer, we could, you know, hang out and stuff. Support each other. Be good friends. Girl power and all that.'

Girl power? Hang out? Will glances around the kitchen door from the hallway, shaking his head.

'That's a mean stunt to pull on anyone, right? Men can be...' Jo glances at the door again, but Will has gone. 'Can be right arseholes.'

'It's weird, after the accident, it's left me with this feeling... like he existed but didn't exist. Which in some ways is sad, as we did have good times together – and I haven't completely forgotten everything – but then again, it's also a blessing. Means I don't have to go through more heartache. It's hard to grieve for a relationship you can't remember much about.'

'So what happened? Did you end it?'

'Oh yes,' Suzanne says, folding her arms. 'Absolutely. I made quite sure he was never coming back. Ever.'

*

'Wow,' Jo says an hour later. 'You've done so much in your career. I remember this series. I loved it. We watched it every Sunday evening.'

Suzanne rummages through the press cuttings, flyers, magazine clippings and photographs as they sit on the sofa, Bonnie perched up behind them and Spangle content at their feet. It's a whole career crammed into a cardboard box.

'We?' Suzanne asks, handing Jo another page from the *Radio Times*.

'Oh, me and my… my husband,' Jo says, not wanting to explain. 'You look amazing here. So glamorous.' Jo studies the photo, to see if there are any clues. Suzanne is sitting off set at a film shoot with cameras and lighting rigs around her, trailers and a big old house in the background. Someone is dabbing at her face with a make-up sponge, while her eyes are closed, her lips scarlet, her hair up in a period style, ringlets bobbing at her cheeks. 'I love watching historical dramas,' she says.

'Well, my part wasn't particularly big, and I was lucky to be included in this photo. The piece is actually about the female lead, as you can see. But it's a good credit to have. One of my last TV roles, actually. I did some theatre afterwards and then, *bam…* the accident. Since then, I've done some voice-overs, a couple of adverts. My mum died several years ago and left me this place, so I'm not penniless just yet. Even though I'm washed up when it comes to men.'

'Hardly washed up,' Jo says, suddenly feeling sorry for her, as though they have things in common. On that thought, she glances up, looking for Will but he's not there. Then her eyes are drawn back to the photo of Suzanne. There's something about it. Something familiar, though she's not sure what.

'And this was my last performance before…' Suzanne trails off, tapping her leg. 'Before it happened.' She's holding a theatre programme for a play. 'Look, God, I'm sorry. This is horribly self-indulgent and must be very boring for you.' She hands the programme to Jo and moves the box aside, getting up and reaching for her stick. 'I'll go and make us some tea and you can tell me all about your work, your life.' She goes off to the kitchen and Jo hears her putting the kettle on, leaving Jo holding the programme.

So are you going to tell her about Will? She'll send you packing when she realises he's the man who hurt her – Bill. So you need to find out what she did to him first…

Jo taps the programme against her leg, unsure what to do. Then the logo on the back of it catches her eye, makes her suck in a breath – *the rep theatre where Will played his last Shakespeare role.* She flips it over, her eyes wide when she sees a familiar photograph, the play's title displayed across the top. Her fingers fumble to get it open, flicking through the pages of local adverts, performance details, the cast list… until she gets to the key cast members' bios.

Will, she thinks, her eyes filling with tears when she sees his black and white headshot. She gently touches his face with her finger.

'I was *at* this performance,' she whispers to his photo. 'I was *there*. With Louise. I remember the night so well… how proud I was of you, the after-party on the last night – so proud to be by your side as your wife.' She glances at the ceiling, praying the tears will hold off. She doesn't want Suzanne to see her vulnerable, the weaker woman in the story that she is gradually piecing together. It's all becoming horrifyingly real.

But she can't help reliving the other feelings she'd had that night either – of being sidelined at the cast party, overlooked by Will, as if somehow she didn't belong. Louise had said she was being silly, that she was imagining it, that it was just what those theatre types were like.

'If you'd spent weeks and weeks rehearsing together, you'd have bonded, too. It's the last night of the show, Jo. Let him have his moment,' Louise had said later in the loos, her hands on Jo's shoulders.

But Jo wasn't convinced. She knew Will and he'd seemed different that night, yet she couldn't put her finger on why. In the end, Jo hadn't felt like going to the pub afterwards for pie, beer and the live band. So she and Louise had called it an early night, with Will getting a taxi back much, much later. Jo racks her brain, remembering him eventually arriving home, the sound of the front door opening waking her, glancing at the bedside clock: 4.23 a.m. She hadn't slept properly, waiting for him to come home, and he'd not been answering the texts she'd sent. What had he been doing all that time? She knew the pub closed its doors at midnight.

'I thought you were feeling ill?' she remembered saying to him as he crept into the bedroom. Well, he'd thought he was creeping but in actual fact, he'd staggered in reeking of alcohol.

And now, beneath Will's bio in the programme, Jo sees a head-shot of the character who played the queen – the character who had made her feel uncomfortable in the green room. The woman with the grey, wiry wig, the white face paint, the smudged, scarlet lips. Except in her headshot, she is just her normal self.

Suzanne McBride – graduate of Guildhall School of Music and Drama.

'Here,' Suzanne says, carrying two mugs of tea with one hand while the other leans on her stick.

Jo jumps. She tosses the programme aside, hardly able to look. *Suzanne* was the actress who played the queen. *Suzanne* was the woman she'd watched kiss her husband onstage, sensing that 'something' between them. *Suzanne* was the woman who'd prevented her getting close to Will at the party, and *Suzanne* was the woman who'd had a lover, who she'd made sure was 'never coming back. Ever'. And he was called Bill.

'I hope it's how you like it,' she says, holding a mug out to Jo. But, as she takes it, she's shaking so much it slips from Jo's grip and falls to the floor.

CHAPTER THIRTY-FIVE

Stay calm… Jo tells herself as she dashes for some cloths to mop up. Suzanne seems unfazed by the accident and continues chatting about her career, asking about Jo's work as she cleans up the spilt tea.

'I'm so very sorry. I'm completely clumsy. However careful I am, things just break or spill or fall over in my wake.' She presses down hard on the stain with several tea towels, absorbing the mess as best she can. 'Yes, yes, dressmaking… mainly bridal but some theat— other costumes, you know.'

'Should I blame you for my fainting earlier, then?' Suzanne says with a laugh. The two women look at each other – Jo on her knees on the rug staring up at Suzanne, her mouth slightly open, and Suzanne mid-sip. It's as if they each know there's something between them, a common denominator, yet neither of them can work out what.

Thing is, Jo, you know *what the link is, whereas Suzanne doesn't. Having lost memories from a crucial time, she has no idea that the man she was in love with is your husband.*

'I wouldn't be surprised,' Jo says, composing herself before she says something she shouldn't. She rolls her eyes, playing the part. And then she remembers her conversation with Simon, how she's told him far too much about her situation, how she opened up because he was so persuasive, so kind, so… understanding. Suzanne and Simon are friends, *good* friends. What if they talk?

'There, that should do it,' she says, dabbing at the rug. 'Again, I'm so—'

But Jo is interrupted by a knock at the door. Glad of the reprieve, she gets to her feet. 'I'll get it, you stay there,' she insists, gathering up the damp cloths. Spangle follows her excitedly into the hallway, yapping at her side, his tail wagging furiously. 'You're a useless guard dog,' she says to him, trying to sound normal, though her voice wavers. Her pace slows when she sees the shape of a man's silhouette behind the stained glass. A familiar figure.

She takes a breath. Pulls the door open. 'Simon…' she says, forcing a smile. *I was just thinking about you… Let's keep that I almost told you my darkest secret just between the two of us, eh?*

'Keep what between the two of us?' Simon says, grinning. He comes in, delivering a kiss to Jo's cheek but then changes his mind and adds one to her lips. Jo just stands there, stunned.

'Oh… oh,' Jo says, making a confused sound. 'You know me, scatty as ever. Don't know what I'm talking about half the time. I just spilt tea everywhere, see?' She holds up the wet cloths, laughing it off as best she can, feeling a sweat break out.

But Simon just looks at her, eyeing her up and down, an amused smile on his face. He puts his hand on her shoulder. 'I like scatty,' he whispers, leaning in.

Look, it's OK. They're not going to put two and two together before you leave, Jo, and, if they do, so what? They can't prove anything.

Jo is about to close the front door behind Simon, but Will is standing there, making her freeze.

'You OK?'

She feels Simon's hand on her back, hears the mild amusement in his voice as she stares at what must seem like empty space to him. 'Yes, yes, sorry. I'm fine.' She shuts the door in Will's face, a little piece of her shrivelling up inside.

When she goes into the living room, following Simon, Will is leaning against the fireplace, right next to where his photographs once stood.

'Confession to make, Suze,' Simon says, bending down to greet her – a kiss on each cheek.

Suzanne waves a hand through the air in a theatrical gesture. 'I knew it. You've been madly in love with me since the day we met in the playground, aged eight, right?' She laughs loudly, exposing perfect teeth.

'Yes, of course,' Simon replies drily, sitting down. 'But apart from *that*, I appear to have lost your spare keys. I've hunted high and low. I'm so sorry.'

Jo makes a noise – something between a squeak and a moan. Simon and Suzanne both look at her. Jo pretends to clear her throat. 'I'll just take these out...' She holds up the dirty cloths. But she hovers in the hallway, listening.

'So I'd suggest a locksmith and having the locks changed. Of course, I'll make arrangements and pay for it. I know someone good. My fault for being so careless. You know that's not like me.'

'Oh the irony,' Jo hears Suzanne say. 'That *you* have put my property at risk. But I'll forgive you and will take your advice.'

'Good,' Simon replies. 'Can't be too careful. If I lost them in the village, a savvy burglar might chance his luck on local houses at night.'

'Don't, you're scaring me,' Suzanne says. 'But at least you're next door. And I've got my own set, of course,' she adds. 'And Jo has the front and back door keys while she's here. I've invited her to stay on for the rest of the week. Poor woman wanted a relaxing break and I ruined it by coming back.'

Jo is about to creep away, to get rid of the cloths, when she hears whispering.

'Nice, isn't she?' It's Suzanne's voice. 'Though I swear I know her from somewhere, but you know me – I can't place her for the life of me. I had a couple of my episodes earlier. I'm sure it was because of her... that she triggered something. You know, like what happened with...'

Jo can't make out the rest of what she says.

There's silence for a moment. Then Simon coughing.

'Yes, yes, she is very nice,' he says in a normal voice. 'And I'm glad to hear she's staying on.'

'Lou?' Jo says, shivering in the night air. 'It's me. Can you hear me?'

'Hi, Jo. How's it going? Are you starting to relax a bit now?'

'I'm doing OK,' Jo replies, not wanting to burden Louise. The line isn't good so she presses the phone harder against her ear. 'I've just stepped outside for some fresh air,' she says. 'Firstly, how are you feeling now?'

There's a pause.

'I'm doing OK too, thanks. Keeping up with the bed rest,' she adds.

'Glad to hear you're finally taking advice,' Jo replies, her mind all over the place. Similarly, she desperately wants Louise's advice. 'She's come back, Lou. The owner. Suzanne.'

'Oh... what, why? Does that mean you're coming home now, then?'

'I should. I really, really should. But she's asked me to stay on. She knows something about Will, Lou. I've got a feeling she's seen him quite recently, and... and she said she's done something to make sure he'll never come back.' Jo fights to keep her voice even. 'To tell you the truth, I'm not even sure I *want* to know what she's done. It scares me. And then I went and had a few drinks and blurted stuff out to Simon, the neighbour, thinking it was in confidence, and you know, it most likely is given that he's a therapist and everything, and he'll be quite used to having crazy people spewing stuff out and probably forgetting what they even said a minute later, but I wish I hadn't. He seems really tight with Suzanne...

'Anyway, you'll never guess who *she* is. Suzanne – she's only the woman from the play we went to together. Will's play. The last one we saw him in. Suzanne McBride. The queen. Do you remember? The one with the wig. The one who kissed Will and it gave me the jitters because I sensed they had this chemistry together. She was the one in the green room who I thought was acting weirdly with me. I mean, what the hell am I supposed to do with that information, Lou? All the photos, and now this. I mean, she's in the same business as Will. It doesn't take a genius to work out what's going on. But I still have no idea where he is, and... and I don't think she recognises me, thank heavens, but—'

'Jo, for God's sake stop. Slow down. You're making me dizzy just listening to you.' Louise takes a breath, sounding tired.

'Lou, I'm sorry. You don't need this right now. I'll let you rest.'

'It's fine, Jo. Right, let's take this slowly. You think the woman you're house-sitting for has something to do with Will's disappearance?'

'Yes. One hundred per cent.'

'Then call the police! What are you even phoning me for?'

Because it's not that simple, Lou. I think she knows...

'I don't want to waste their time, I guess,' Jo says, hoping that's deflection enough.

'Look, do you want me to call them for you?' Louise's voice is kind and calm. 'You sound really upset.'

'No. No, please don't do that. Not yet. I just need to think.'

'I understand you're looking for closure, Jo, but I think you're adding up a couple of coincidences to get the result you *want* to see.'

'Maybe,' Jo says, steadying her breathing. She perches on the front garden wall, facing out into the street. The lane is quiet, but Suzanne's house is on such a sharp bend that whenever a car comes round the corner, it startles her.

'Just watch out when you pull out of the drive,' Simon had warned her when they'd walked down to the pub the other night. 'Cars come way too fast into the village. There have been loads of accidents over the years. Suzanne's had to have her front wall rebuilt about three times. It's a black spot.'

Jo glances down at the new brick section, different to the rest of the boundary wall further along. Feeling nervous, she gets up and moves.

'You really think it's all a coincidence, Lou?' Jo walks along the lane slowly, dragging her feet. 'Frankly, not knowing anything is better than finding out he had an affair with Suzanne and that she's somehow got *rid* of him. What if she—'

'Jo, stop it!' Louise speaks in her court voice. Jo always recognises it. 'How many house-sit houses were there on that website? I'm betting hundreds and hundreds. Probably thousands, right?'

'I expect so, yes.' Jo lowers her voice as someone walks past with a small dog on a lead.

'So why do you think that, out of all of them, you picked the one where the owner seems associated with Will?'

Jo pauses, thinking back, remembering what it was that drew her to Hawthorn Lodge – apart from the photos of Will.

'I chose this area because it reminded me of Will. We'd been planning a romantic weekend away here but it never happened. I suppose I wanted to recreate the magic we never got a chance to share. But instead, it's turned into a nightmare.'

'And whose idea was it to go for a weekend away near Hastings?'

'Will's.'

'Why? How come he chose there?'

Jo is silent a while, her mind whirring. 'Oh God, Lou. He said that someone from the theatre had mentioned how lovely it was down here. That we should come down and explore the area.' She sucks in a breath. 'Will only wanted to come down here because of *her*, didn't he? He was probably planning on slipping away for a few hours to go and see Suzanne.' Jo shudders at the thought.

Vaguely, she hears Louise's voice down the line, trying to make her see sense, trying to help her.

But Jo is distracted. Will is standing across the other side of the road, his padded jacket zipped up to the collar – the one she eventually retrieved from his office at school, along with his other discarded belongings when it was clear he wasn't coming back. He's watching her, his face devoid of expression.

Will… She reaches out a hand to him but he just stands there, on the other side of the road. It may as well be the other side of the world.

Jo turns and walks back towards Suzanne's house. Will follows her, still on the other side of the street.

'Jo, are you there?'

Louise's tone whips Jo back to the present.

'Yes, sorry. I'm listening.'

'I was just saying, if you were in court, your story would be thrown out by the judge. Even your own lawyer would be chuckling. Now, listen to me. Yes, Will probably chose Hastings because of a recommendation from someone at work. And perhaps that same woman, Suzanne, had a crush on him, hence the pictures. It's not so much of a coincidence that you looked at her house, if you think about it. How many houses are there in that area to house-sit anyway? You were bound to view hers online when you went through the search results and, when you saw the photographs of Will, it's entirely natural you were curious. But you have no proof she's done anything bad to Will or was even having an affair with him. Has she told you the name of the person she's ensured will "never come back"?' Louise sounds breathless.

'Yes,' Jo says, heading up the front drive, glancing back over her shoulder. 'She told me his name is Bill.' And it's just as a car comes screaming round the sharp corner that Will steps out into the road.

CHAPTER THIRTY-SIX

'If you can't beat 'em, join 'em, eh?'

'Beat who?' Jo says to Suzanne, standing in the doorway. Simon is crouching down by the wood burner, carefully placing more kindling on the fire he's lit. A text comes in from Louise but Jo doesn't read it, rather switches her phone to silent instead, putting it in her pocket. She can't take another dressing-down, even though she means well.

'Us. You can't beat *us*, Jo, so you may as well join in. Come and sit. Si will get you one of these.' She raises her drink – a measure of something rich and amber. 'You look as though you need it. We've just been talking about the past. It helps me, you see.' Suzanne taps the side of her head.

If you can't beat 'em, join 'em... One of Will's favourite expressions, Jo thinks as she edges towards the sofa. It was what he'd said when he'd had no choice but to increase his hours at the school to full-time. *Her* past. *Her* Will. *Her* missing future.

'Thanks,' she says, looking up at Simon as he hands her a drink.

'So who's your go-to rock in life, Jo?' Suzanne asks, glancing at Simon.

Jo can't help bristling inside, even though a part of her wants to warm to the woman, to see her as nothing more than an innocent party who's been kind enough to invite her into her home. Her manner is easy and unaffected. She's confident yet unassuming.

Brash but in an endearing way. And she's inquisitive and full of... *life*, despite her life-changing accident. Jo wants to admire her, but can't. She *knows* she's done something to Will.

'Oh, that would be Louise,' Jo says, knowing she's on safe ground there. She won't mention her husband, even though, of course, he was her rock. Her man. The love of her life. 'She's my best friend. We've known each other for years. Seems like forever.' Jo finds herself smiling, feels bad for shutting Lou down on the phone just now, refusing to take her advice. 'And we're completely different in every way, but utterly the same. We could be sisters.'

Suzanne smiles. 'The best of friends are always poles apart. You know what they say about opposites. How did you meet?'

Jo is aware of Simon clearing his throat, shifting on the arm-chair beside the sofa. 'We were best friends at school – inseparable. Then we ended up studying in different cities, but we always kept in touch. Then Louise came back to the area we grew up in. She needed some clothes altering, so came in for some fittings and I worked some magic with my machine.'

Jo remembers the day as if it were yesterday, how they'd fallen right back into their easy friendship, chatting as if no time at all had passed.

'It's funny, but people open up when they're stripped to their underwear and being measured. Sometimes it gets pretty intimate.' Jo laughs, feels the warmth of the drink trickle down her throat. 'She was telling me about her life, her work, her loves. Despite her profession – she's a solicitor – she seemed somehow vulnerable, softer than the Louise I remembered. And she'd just met a guy, who's now her husband. We ended up reconnecting.'

'That's lovely,' Suzanne said. 'Have you got a picture of her?'

Jo smiles, feeling more relaxed, even though every part of her mind screams not to let her guard down. She pulls out her phone, quickly reading the message from Louise.

Just come home, Jo. I'm worried about you. Enough is
enough x

She shakes her head, switching screens, scrolling back through
her photos. 'This is us a couple of weekends ago. Louise is always
having me over to hers. She's been an absolute gem since...' Jo
trails off, clears her throat. 'Archie, her husband, cooked for us.
We'd had a couple of drinks so excuse the silly faces.' Jo laughs
at the picture – the pair of them with their arms slung around
each other, Jo blowing a pout in Louise's direction, Louise staring
straight at the camera, making a slightly demented-looking face.

'She seems...' Suzanne takes hold of Jo's phone, almost to the
point of pulling it from her when Jo grips onto it a beat too long.
A brief tug of war. She studies it, pushing her glasses onto her nose,
zooming in on the pair of them in Louise's kitchen.

Jo holds out her hand. 'Let me show you another,' she says,
just wanting her phone back. If another text alert comes in from
Louise, she doesn't want Suzanne to read it. 'Here, this is us
having lunch. We always try to meet for a sandwich once a week.'
Jo flashes her a quick look at the selfie she took of them in their
regular café the other week. 'There's a lovely little place just—'

'I *know* you,' Suzanne says suddenly, still staring at the screen,
that strange look in her eyes again.

Jo retracts her phone quickly, sliding it under her leg.

'I *know* you...' she repeats, staring at the ceiling, her face
contorting into a strange expression. She pulls a cushion from
the sofa, hugging it tightly to her chest. Her fingers sink into it,
clawing and digging at the fabric and her shoulders rise and fall
in time with her quickening breaths. It's as if her eyes are coated
with a film, as if she's not seeing real life any more.

'Suze?' Simon says. He's immediately beside her, kneeling
down, hands on her wrists. 'It's OK. You're at home. You're safe.

Can you hear me? Look at me, Suze, it's Si. It's OK…' His voice is calm and comforting. 'Ground yourself… you know the drill.'

But Suzanne suddenly convulses, her back arching and her head thrown back against the back of the sofa. A wail erupts from somewhere deep inside her as if she's possessed.

'Nooo… *oooo*…' she cries, flinching and putting her hands up in front of her face as if to shield herself from something.

It's almost as if she's reliving something, Jo thinks. Something neither she nor Simon are privy to.

'What's happening?' Jo whispers, though he's more preoccupied with calming Suzanne. She's curled up into a ball now, writhing as if she's in pain. Her hands are over her face and she's twisted sideways on the sofa.

'It'll pass, don't worry,' he says, putting a cushion under her head. He strokes her hair. 'Suze, take it steady now. Have a sip of your drink when you're ready, it'll help you relax.'

Suzanne gradually calms, her breathing steadily slowing. After ten minutes or so, when it seems as though she's fallen asleep, Simon stands up and hoists her into his arms, as if he's done it many times before. He carries her out and Jo hears him going upstairs, the floorboards above creaking, the muffled sound of his soothing voice in the bedroom.

*

'She's fine,' he says a while later, coming back down. Jo has hardly dared move, her mind racing to find a link between what happened and the photographs she showed Suzanne.

'She's sleeping.' Simon picks up his drink and takes a long sip.

'I feel terrible, as though it was my fault. Thank goodness you were here,' Jo says quietly. 'Does she have epilepsy? It seemed… so scary. Like she was fitting.'

'It's not that. Believe me, she's had so many tests since her accident.'

'You'd know, I guess,' Jo says. 'In your line of work.'

Simon looks puzzled for a moment, but then shrugs. 'I certainly see a lot of trauma similar to what she's been through,' he says. 'And believe me, a lot of people with emotional issues subsequently.'

'Therapist extraordinaire,' Jo says, trying to make light of it.

'Well, I suppose, in a way,' he replies. 'You wouldn't believe how often, actually.' He gives a sarcastic laugh then. 'But I can't always be on duty. And when I am, I worry about Suzanne being alone. I wish she'd stayed on at the facility for treatment, but something powered her home.'

'I think it was me,' Jo says. 'I think I set her off in some way. You'd know all about triggers, I guess,' she adds, hoping he'll explain.

'In more ways than one,' Simon replies, laughing at a joke Jo doesn't quite understand. 'But she'll be OK. She's a survivor. Physically and emotionally. The accident may have damaged her body, and I also think her relationship break-up hit her harder than she realised. It's been a tough time.'

'Tell me more,' Jo says, not meaning to sound quite so pushy. *Thin ice again, Jo.*

'To be honest, she's been a bit of a dark horse about it. I think she feels ashamed as she found out the man she'd been seeing for several years had a wife. He didn't live around here so it was easy for him to hide it. And with Suzanne travelling for work a lot, her often being in London, and him having a similar lifestyle but further away, it was easy for him to go underground. Suze didn't realise a pattern until… until it was too late. It broke her. She'd put her trust in him.'

'Did she love him?' Jo can hardly get the words out.

'Oh yes,' he says. 'When Suzanne falls for someone, she really falls hard. It nearly killed her, finding out the truth.'

'And how *did* she find out?'

'There were a few signs but social media confirmed it, I think. A mix of Suzanne's suspicion and obsession, him slipping up on

Facebook and probably a fake account thrown in too, knowing her. She went into stealth mode. But you didn't hear that from me,' he adds, tapping the side of his nose.

Social media… obsession… photos… triggers… Suzanne had met Louise, too, at the party that night…

Jo lets out a little whimper, barely audible. 'Tell me, if someone's lost some of their memories because of a physical trauma, are they… are they still in there – somewhere?' She pauses, thinking. 'So if they're ignited by something – say, a photo – it can have an adverse effect on them?'

'I'm no expert,' Simon says. 'It's certainly not my field.'

'You mean amnesia?'

He shakes his head, frowning. 'No, definitely not,' leaving Jo wondering what his field of speciality actually is. Now isn't the time to digress into various forms of psychology, though. She wants answers about Suzanne.

'What I'm asking is, if Suzanne sees something that's linked to a painful memory that's seemingly lost, would she react like she did? Would she have one of her episodes?'

'From what I know, most definitely yes. PTSD is a cruel and unrelenting beast,' he says. 'I have many colleagues with experience of it.'

'I see,' Jo says, sipping her drink again, wanting to ask so many questions. But all she can think about now is creating a timeline of Will's movements over the year or two before he went missing, to see if she can piece together chunks of missing time when he would have been meeting Suzanne – seized opportunities, snatched moments. She supposes that rehearsals for the play they did together and the subsequent performances would have been a hotbed of activity for them. But outside of that, she couldn't recall Will being absent suspiciously or… or…

A couple of coincidences to get the result you want to see… She remembers Louise's words earlier on the phone.

'So it's a girls' weekend away now, is it?' Will had said. 'And a work trip to London with Margot for Fashion Week, more nights out by yourself this month than I've had in the last year… Well, Jo, my darling, it's no wonder we're not pregnant.' He'd been quite calm about it, even injecting a little humour, but equally, Jo knew he was upset. And she still felt guilty. He wasn't happy that they'd not been spending as much time together lately and it was almost as if he was turning it into a competition. A competition he *wanted* to have – as though he was almost challenging Jo to give him space.

'I can't help it, love. It's just the way it's worked out. Margot and I really want to network more. Our bridal range is getting so popular locally and we want to get it out there, get noticed in London. And surely you don't begrudge me a girls' weekend away in Louise's parents' holiday cottage? It's not exactly living the high life. Apparently it's out in the sticks and very basic. We'll be bedding in with a dozen chick flicks and a crate of Sauvignon, that's all. And as for nights out, really, I can't think of any…'

He'd turned it right round, hadn't he? Jo thinks now. *The few times you did go anywhere, even if it was just Pilates or a duty visit to your parents, as time went on, he made out as though* you *were the bad guy for not spending time with* him. *And while the cat was away…* She covers her face, making a pained sound.

'Bonnie's right here, Jo. The cat's not gone away.' Simon laughs, touches Jo's thigh. She startles, her nerves raw and on fire. Simon wipes his thumb across her brow. 'Why the deep frown?'

'Nothing,' Jo replies, gathering herself quickly. 'Nothing at all.'

CHAPTER THIRTY-SEVEN

Then

'Hardly the Ritz,' Will joked as we pulled up, squinting out of the windscreen. The light was fading as we arrived at the little stone cottage, its gingery hues muted by the sour light that threatened rain. It looked more an acid grey than the usual honey tones of the Vale of Evesham, an hour or so's drive south-west of home. 'Does it even have running water?'

'Oh, *Will*,' I said, rolling my eyes. My heart skipped with excitement. A whole week, just the two of us. 'You know what it reminds me of?' I said as Will parked, pulling on the handbrake and cutting the engine.

'A derelict hovel in the middle of nowhere?'

I poked him. 'No, silly. Don't you think it looks just like the cottage in the film *The Holiday*?'

'No idea,' Will said, sighing and getting out of the car. It hadn't been a long drive but he stretched then rubbed his face, looking exhausted. I knew he'd had a tough time of it at work lately – school and his acting. And everything else. Which is why I'd arranged this break for the Easter holidays. We both needed it.

'Well I think it's incredibly kind of Louise's parents to let us use it for free. We'd not have had a break until next year otherwise. I mean, look at the view, Will.' I pointed across the lane to the rolling fields in front of the house. To the west, the sun bowed down in a yellow-grey fizz, glinting on the tops of the lightly frosted trees.

'It had better be warm in there, is all I can say,' Will said, opening the boot. But I saw the flicker of a smile on his face, knew how he loved long, bracing walks, pub lunches, movies in front of the fire.

'Well, if it's not, just think how much time we can spend in bed *making* each other warm, eh?' I hugged him around the waist from behind as he reached in for our bags. 'And making a baby,' I whispered, squeezing him tighter.

*

'I'm sorry for being miserable earlier,' Will said later, glass of red wine to hand. 'I think it's pretty perfect here, actually,' he admitted, ducking his head under a low beam as he crossed the tiny, flagstoned living room to put another log on the open fire. 'And it's already toasty warm.'

'See?' I replied, my legs curled up on the sofa as I snuggled beneath a knitted throw. 'I shan't say "I told you so".'

'So this is where you girls hung out that time, eh? When you had that long weekend away.'

'Indeed,' I said, smiling fondly at the memory. It had been Louise, Margot and me – later joined by Louise's cousin, Fran. 'It's where I got the idea for us to come. It's romantic, right?' I'd lit a cluster of scented candles and set them on a little wooden table beside us. There was one sofa, albeit old and saggy, but the many cushions made it comfortable.

'Where's the router?' Will asked, phone to hand after he'd stoked the fire. 'I need to keep comms open in case my agent emails.'

'There's no Wi-Fi,' I said, feeling a little flat that Will couldn't leave real life behind even for an evening.

Will looked up, his face blank. 'None?' He tossed his phone onto the table and dropped down into the cushions.

I felt a twinge in my stomach. 'But I actually have good 4G and lots of data, so don't worry. We can still watch Netflix.'

'And chill,' Will said, turning to me, his blank face now spread with a wicked smile.

'I like the sound of *that*,' I said, shifting closer to him, wrapping my arms around his neck and delivering the long, lingering kiss I'd been wanting to give him since we'd set off from home.

'Do you ever feel that you just need to… to get away? And never come back?'

Will's question had taken me by surprise several months before our getaway to Louise's parents' cottage, but then, I'd also been half expecting it. I knew how Will's mind worked, how, when he was stressed, he began by testing me – to gauge if I felt the same way, or at least understood. I knew better than to shut him down. It was Will's way of wanting to talk, unload. And those last few days, he'd been restless.

'Sometimes,' I said, flinching suddenly and sucking my finger. I'd brought some work home – a delicate bridesmaid's dress that required much hand-stitching – and had accidentally stuck the needle in my forefinger. I went to fetch a plaster, not wanting to get blood on the cream fabric. 'You're feeling like a change, then?' We'd already eaten, were winding down for the evening. I loved nothing more than to be sewing while Will and I chatted, discussed plans, talked about our days.

Will had stood then, I remembered, paced about. 'I'm feeling edgy, Jo. Can't lie about it.'

I'd looked up then. 'In what way?'

'School's getting me down. Too much red tape and drama in the staffroom. Not enough hands-on time with the pupils. Though I'd like my hands round a few of their necks. It's crowd control most of the time. It's not what I went to drama school for.'

I swallowed, somehow feeling guilty for Will's career taking a trajectory he'd never envisaged. While his teaching was bread-and-butter money, going full-time had never been in his grand plan. I often wondered whether, without a wife – a wife who was desperate for a family – he'd have been quite content living a more bohemian lifestyle, winging his way around the country, possibly the world, taking whatever paid acting work he could get. And if he couldn't, then he'd be working bars, or even cruise ships, somehow scraping by. Being Will. Being alone. Having adventures. He'd never said anything, but I often wondered if, in his discontented moments, he felt it was all my fault. That he was stuck.

'I know you feel like that, love,' I'd said, not knowing what the answer was. 'And I know you find the teaching frustrating, but you've got that big production coming up soon. Do you think that will help your mood?'

'What, burning the candle at both ends?'

'I didn't mean—'

'No, of course you didn't. You're quite content with your little job in your little business with your little friends. Easy as. And how perfect will everything be for you once we have a baby? Maybe I should take on a third job.'

'That's unfair, Will,' I'd said, laying down the dress. I remembered the cold feeling sweeping through me. Numb. That was it – I'd felt numb at how he could turn his discontent around onto what he thought was my contentment. It smelt a lot like jealousy to me, but of course I said nothing. I knew he was just going through a bad patch and it wasn't worth causing a major row over. I wanted to help him, to hear him, to lift him out of the ever-increasing lows that he seemed to be experiencing lately.

'Look, I know I've said it before, but do you think it's time for a visit to the GP? There might be some medications that can help your mood.'

'Don't you think we've been spending enough time at the GP and hospital clinics lately?'

I knew he was referring to the IVF we'd been investigating. I also knew that, to Will, it seemed a whole lot of bother and expense if our allotted NHS treatments failed and we had to go private, especially when he seemed convinced that nature should be allowed to take its course. The upshot was, I wasn't sure he really wanted a baby at all.

'Mmm,' I said, responding to Will's touch as we held each other on the cottage sofa. The logs popped and crackled on the fire, while the smell of chicken roasting in a white wine and tarragon sauce filtered through from the tiny kitchen. Will had scoffed when he'd first seen the kitchen space, wondering how we were going to even make a bowl of cereal in there, but I assured him that with the ingredients I'd brought and a few utensils, I could still whip up a one-pot feast each night. And sometimes we could eat at the local pub.

I wrapped a leg over his as he pulled me close, trying not to think of the cooking time left – probably around forty-five minutes, maybe an hour if we wanted it really well done. Plenty of time to get close. Frankly, at that moment I didn't care if we ate at all. I just wanted my husband – *all* of him – and I wanted him to want me, too.

'You're so beautiful,' Will said, sliding his hands over my breasts. I manoeuvred myself into a sitting position astride him, looking down into his big dark eyes as he held me. The way he looked, the way he made me feel… no one else had ever come close. I only hoped he felt the same as he unbuttoned my blouse…

Stop! I heard myself scream. It had come out of nowhere. I jolted, gasping.

When I looked up, Will was suddenly across the other side of the room – almost as if I'd flung him there – standing beside the fireplace, arms folded, glaring at me although I could still feel his touch on me, still felt the effect he had on my body. I was confused, didn't know where I was. Where *he* was. I screwed up my eyes, only wanting to live for the moment, to enjoy the sensation, to enjoy my husband, praying that this would be the month we conceived. Not live for the nightmares I – and Will too – had been having. Since *that* night.

The party – at Annabel's apartment, Will on his phone the whole time, seeming detached, not wanting me with him in the first place, grabbing me by the arm, leaving abruptly, the journey home...

I sucked in a lungful of air – unsure if it was because of what Will was doing to me beneath me on the sofa, or because of the memories of that night. His hands were all over me, mine all over him – our mouths searching each other out, our bodies responding and eager.

Curtains. I remembered the curtains at the front window that night after we'd got back home, shaken. Once inside, I'd pulled them back an inch or two, peeking out as Will tapped at the front wing of the car with the mallet, getting beneath the wheel arch, carefully knocking out the dent before wiping it down with a cloth after he'd liberally sprayed most of it with whatever he'd found in the understairs cupboard. But the dent wasn't gone. I could see that from my watching place. And neither were the scratches and scrapes. Far from it. I could see it would take far more than a rag.

It must have been a huge deer, I remembered thinking as I looked on. And while our house was near the edge of town, close to a wooded area, I'd never once encountered a deer. Of course, I hadn't been able to look at its remains.

'Oh my *God!*' I said – unsure if I was saying it now, on the sofa, or in the passenger seat of the car that night as I was flung forward, my head almost hitting the dashboard.

At the time, on the way back from the party, I'd been fast asleep and, for some reason, the airbag hadn't gone off, though my seat belt had done its job, leaving me with a pain in my shoulder and weeks of stiffness in my neck afterwards. I had no idea where I was or what had happened. It was dark. It was cold. It was silent, yet the sound of a thousand screams filled my mind. Had I been asleep for hours? Was I in bed? Why was I freezing, completely blindsided by whatever had just happened?

'Oh *Will…*' I heard myself saying, still unsure where I was.

In the car?

Or on the sofa?

Either way, it didn't matter. The man I loved most was beside me, making everything better. As he always had done.

CHAPTER THIRTY-EIGHT

Now

'I heard you up and about,' Jo says as Suzanne comes into the kitchen. 'I have no idea what you like for breakfast, but I thought I'd take a guess.' Jo turns to check the grill. 'There's toast, eggs, bacon... tea, or coffee if you prefer.'

Suzanne stands there a moment, wearing a brightly patterned kimono loosely tied around her waist. 'All of that,' she says, smiling while still looking not quite there. 'You're an angel,' she adds. 'Not sure what I did to deserve a house-sitter like you, but while you're here, I'll run with it.' She laughs, greeting Spangle as he runs up to her, stomping about at her feet.

'I walked him earlier,' Jo says. 'A good run. And he and Bonnie are fed. I found a brush and, much to Bonnie's disgust, took to her coat with it. I hope that's OK.'

Suzanne looks at her. 'Jo, right now anything is OK. I feel as though all my hangovers from time immemorial have conspired against me to gather on this day. So walks, eggs, brushing and coffee...' she raises an appreciative hand, makes a face, 'are all absolutely fine with me.'

Jo serves what she's cooked onto two warmed plates. She pours coffee and they both sit down at the table.

'I was worried about you last night,' Jo says. 'You've had quite a few of your episodes since you arrived home.' She passes Suzanne the butter dish. 'I can't help wondering if I'm responsible, if my presence is triggering something in you. You said several times that you felt you knew me, and when I showed you pictures of my best friend, it kicked off again.'

Suzanne holds up her hands in a halt sign. 'Let's just enjoy this, shall we? And thank you.'

Jo nods, frustrated. 'Simon was concerned about you, too,' Jo says, cutting up her food.

Suzanne glances up. 'Simon doesn't know everything.' She keeps hold of Jo's gaze as she sips her coffee.

She's more confident today, Jo thinks. *The sleep has done her good. Is she on to you? Does she know why you're here?*

'I'm sorry if I bored you yesterday,' Suzanne says, buttering her toast. 'With all my acting memorabilia. It's the only thing I've got to hold onto these days, a reminder of when my life was whole.'

'I understand,' Jo says, feeling quite the opposite.

'There's more I wanted to show you,' she says, making an approving face at her breakfast. 'If you can stand it,' she adds with an embarrassed laugh. 'It does me good, believe it or not.'

Bring it on, Jo thinks. *Let's have it all. Let's see pictures of you and Will together, laughing, being happy, making a future together. Laughing at me…*

Then Jo's mind switches back to that last break she and Will took together in the tiny cottage – the pair of them on the sofa, entwined and oblivious. But it was what had happened *after* they'd made love that first night that had stuck with Jo the most. Never mind that their week of focusing on each other, on hoping and praying that they'd somehow make another life – a *new* life – had failed. No, it was some hours after they'd finished, each of them glowing, throwing on whatever clothes were to hand, stoking the fire again before stumbling, warm and content, into the tiny kitchen to retrieve and eat the chicken Jo had put on earlier – that the nightmare had begun properly.

Neither of them had slept well that night – with Will tossing and turning, sweating and thrashing in his sleep. And he'd been sleep-talking, too – entire conversations, which to begin with meant nothing to Jo. Despite her gently trying to wake him – he was so deeply asleep, so deeply immersed in whatever was playing out in his mind – it was as if she wasn't there at all.

She tried to sleep but every time she dropped off, Will would stiffen, reaching out and ripping the sheets off her, twisting them around his body as the terrified noises in his throat burst out of him. Each time, his distress grew worse, his head turning from side to side, his eyes screwing up, forming a deep frown just visible in the darkness. The cottage was so remote that there were no street lights or light pollution, so Jo had left the landing light on in case they'd needed the bathroom in the night.

Will's legs rose up then dropped down onto the mattress, pulling Jo back from the brink of sleep yet again.

'Noo-*ooo*…' he moaned. 'No, get away…'

'Will?' Jo said, holding his arm. But he whipped it away from her.

'I said get away, don't come near me… *Leave us alone… Don't hurt*…' His jaw was tight and tense, his teeth clamped together as he gulped in air.

'Who mustn't come near, Will?' Jo asked in a soothing voice, hoping to elicit some kind of clue as to what was tormenting him.

'She… she mustn't. Keep away… Noo-*oo*…' His words were broken and slurred, but Jo could make them out well enough.

'Is she going to hurt you, Will?'

Will shook his head, made a low noise that sounded like 'No'.

'Who is she going to hurt, Will?'

More thrashing and tossing as Jo caught sight of the sweat pouring from his body.

'Who, Will? Who is going to hurt who?'

Will moaned, almost on the brink of crying. Jo had never heard him like this before.

'My wife. She's going to hurt my *wife*…'

Jo shivered, suddenly chilled to the bone. He was talking as if she wasn't there, as if he was in a different place entirely.

'Well, that doesn't sound good,' she said, cajoling him. 'Tell me, who's going to hurt your wife, Will?' Jo clutched her arms around her body.

He made some unintelligible noises then and, for a moment, Jo thought he'd gone back to sleep and was about to give up questioning him, thinking it was just some random nightmare that he wouldn't even remember in the morning.

But Will suddenly sat bolt upright, staring straight ahead, the white cotton sheet a start contrast against his dark skin in the half-light as he knotted it in his fists.

'I thought I'd killed her,' he whispered, his voice quivering. And it was then that Jo saw the tears streaming down his face.

CHAPTER THIRTY-NINE

Jo clears the breakfast things away while Suzanne finishes her coffee.

'I've got this whole stash of things upstairs,' Suzanne says, her eyes tracking Jo around the kitchen. 'One thing I learnt from the clinic is that after injuries like mine, facing our past by looking over things such as old photos can really help – even if we don't realise it consciously. It's so hard to describe, but it feels as if all the missing pieces of my life – and I'm talking about the time around the accident – are so close yet so far. Every time I reach out to take back the memories, they slide a little further away. It makes me think I'm going mad.'

'I'm sure you're not,' Jo says, shutting the dishwasher door after adding a tablet. Her heart thumps. *I've got this whole stash of things upstairs...* 'But I think it's probably time for me to leave you in peace now. For me to go home. Let you go over the old times by yourself.'

'No, don't go,' Suzanne quickly replies. She grips the edge of the table, her eyes intense. 'Please. I… I like your company. Let me go and dig out these other photos. I don't know why, but I just have a feeling you'd be interested. They're up in the spare room. I keep all my private stuff locked in there. Being away so much and having sitters in, I need a secure place.'

'Of course,' Jo says, swallowing. 'How about we walk Spangle first, though? Like, right now?' Jo suggests, hoping at least that Suzanne will forget the photos and anything else in the locked room if she's distracted.

'But he's already had a walk, you said?' Suzanne laughs, giving the dog a rub on his back as he trots past. 'I'll give you a shout when I've found it all,' she says, pulling her robe around her, heading off upstairs.

OK, you need a plan, Jo… and fast. She'll see things are out of place and notice Simon's keys on the bed. Just deny, deny, deny… She has no proof…

'Jo…' she hears Suzanne call out a few minutes later. 'Come up here.'

'I'm just finishing clearing up, then I'd better get organised and head off,' Jo replies, her voice croaking.

She paces about. The last thing she wants is to be in the spare room with photos of Will everywhere.

'Come on, it'll only take a moment,' Suzanne calls out again, but sounding closer this time. She's leaning over the bannisters. '*Please?*' Her tone is begging.

'OK,' Jo says, knowing she has no choice.

Just get it over with, she thinks, heading up. *Then get out, get home.*

'Get what over with?' Suzanne says, standing in the bedroom doorway, clutching a shoebox with photos spilling out from under the lid.

'I – I… oh, nothing…' Jo trails off, knowing she's making everything worse.

'Come and look,' Suzanne says, beckoning her into the bedroom and sitting on the bed. She grabs a batch of pictures from the top of the box. 'Spangle as a baby. Wasn't he the cutest?'

Jo tentatively steps inside, her eyes drawn to the keys half hidden in the bedding behind Suzanne. 'Oh, he certainly was,' she says as Suzanne flicks through a pile of photos of him gambolling along the beach. Then she can't help but glance over at the dressing table by the window, bracing herself for being faced with

Will – his face staring out at her, praying she'd put them back in approximately the right place after swiping them all off.

But the pictures are gone. The dressing table looks like… any normal dressing table, albeit minus the broken perfume bottle.

Jo touches her head, frowning. *Will… where are you?* She looks around the room. No sign of him.

'All these were taken before my accident,' Suzanne says. 'I remember them all. Happy times.' She grabs another handful of photos, all mixed up with newspaper clippings and theatre programmes and professional headshots of herself. 'I always get the best of my digital photos printed out from my phone, but I really must sort them into albums.'

'They're lovely,' Jo says, feigning interest in a couple of the pictures. She just wants to go. 'I'd better pack my stuff up now.'

'Wait, there are more over here…' Suzanne says, standing and walking across the carpet. 'Ouch,' she says suddenly, bending down. She lifts her foot, inspecting the sole. 'Glass?' she says, wincing as she pulls out the shard. 'That's odd,' she says, holding up the piece. She rubs her hand lightly over the carpet, picking out other small fragments.

'Would you like me to fetch the vacuum cleaner?' Jo asks. 'I can give it a quick going-over.'

'No… it's OK,' Suzanne says, trailing off, looking puzzled. She puts the glass in the bin, frowning, and sits down again, spreading more pictures out on the bed. 'Come and look,' she says, patting the bed.

Nervously, Jo does as she's told, knowing that right now, there's no way out without appearing suspicious.

'I don't really remember these ones. I have a vague memory of a couple, but it could be my imagination,' Suzanne says, tossing photo after photo onto the bed between them – almost as if Jo's not there.

Jo picks a couple of them up. 'Looks like a party,' she whispers, wishing she could zoom in, like on a phone screen.

'I can't for the life of me remember which party, though. Do you know how frustrating that is? All my brain tells me is that I can date this batch close to the time of my accident.'

But Jo is silent, doesn't know what to say as she flicks through the rest of the shots. Wherever they were taken is dark and the quality isn't good, but it's enough for her to recognise the party as the same one that she and Will went to at that city apartment in Birmingham. There's a woman in several of the photos whose dress she distinctly remembers – it was stunning and she'd made a mental note of the design for her own reference. Of course, anything to do with the actual event was overshadowed by what happened later, on the way home.

'Annabel...' Jo barely whispers. 'It was Annabel's party.'

Suzanne whips the photo out of her hand, glares at Jo. 'Annabel?' she says. 'Who's Annabel?' Her voice is suddenly demanding and sharp. 'Tell me!'

'I... I don't know, to be honest. Someone I... someone I used to know was invited and I went along. But we left early.'

Suzanne flips frantically from one photo to the next as if the answers to all her missing memories will be found in there. When she comes across one in particular, she stops, touching her head, her breath quickening. Jo lets out a little gasp when she sees the picture of Will, her hand going over her mouth.

'Suzanne... are you OK? Can you hear me?' While she's not passed out or hyperventilating, it's as though she's completely left her body, just the shell of her remaining. Nothing inside.

Get out, get home...

'Speak to me, Suzanne,' Jo says, taking her by the shoulders. The photo of Will lies between them, staring up as though one eye is on her, the other on his *other woman*.

Jo feels sick, but she can hardly leave Suzanne in this state. As much as she might feel like clawing her eyes out, if Will had been deceiving her all that time, pretending he was single, then it's hardly Suzanne's fault. She's as much a victim as she is.

'Suzanne, please say something or I'll have to get Simon.'

Nothing. She's stiff and unmoving, her eyes glassy and vacant. She stares straight ahead. Jo feels that if she gently nudged her, she'd topple over.

'Let me get you safe and lying down, then,' Jo says, easing her down onto the bed. Once her head is on the pillow, she lifts her legs onto the mattress, feeling something rustle and crinkle beneath the duvet at the end. When she pulls it back, she sees all the pictures of Will that were on the dressing table. Suzanne must have hidden them just before she came in.

She knows who you are, Jo. Get help from Simon then get out… go home…

Jo turns to leave but stops in the doorway, going back and grabbing the spare keys off the bed. She shoves them in her pocket and heads downstairs.

CHAPTER FORTY

Hurriedly, Jo goes into the rear bedroom and grabs her suitcase, laying it on the bed. She opens the wardrobe and pulls the few things she'd hung up off the hangers, shoving them in the bag, not bothering to fold them. Then she whips several items from an empty drawer she'd used, dumping them on top of the other stuff. She has a few bits of make-up and some toiletries in the bathroom which she collects up as fast as she can, stuffing them into her washbag, not caring that it won't zip up properly. Her hands shake as she unplugs her phone charger, throws that in too, along with the book she was reading, her hairbrush, a couple of pairs of shoes on the floor. She shuts the lid, cramming everything in, squashing it down as she forces the zip on the suitcase closed.

'Coat and trainers,' she whispers, knowing they're downstairs, along with her handbag and scarf. She doesn't really care if she's forgotten anything, as long as she has her phone, purse and keys. *Herself.*

She quickly checks in on Suzanne, who is lying in exactly the same position, staring at the ceiling, her chest rising and falling slowly with her steady breaths. Jo lugs the bag downstairs, bumping it down each step, leaving it in the hallway as she retrieves her other belongings and laces up her trainers.

She shuts Spangle in the kitchen so he doesn't try to follow her out, knowing that both he and Bonnie have been fed and have water. Then she gathers her keys, phone and bag and heads out to the car, dragging her suitcase awkwardly across the gravel.

It's as she's heaving it in the boot that her phone rings.

'Hi, Lou,' she says breathily, scratching the back of her car as she tries to get the case in with one hand. Her heart is thumping. 'Thank God it's you. Look, I don't know what's going on here but I'm getting the hell out. Suzanne's gone all weird. She's been showing me pictures of Will as if I'm supposed to say something or react. And she gets these crazy episodes where her character changes entirely. It feels… *dangerous*. She's upstairs right now, refusing to speak. Just lying on her back staring at the ceiling. And there's the shrine and the keys and all the broken glass on the carpet I missed and it's not right, and I'm getting Simon to look after her then I'm…' Jo stops, slowing herself. 'Christ, I'm sorry Lou. I'm so self-absorbed right now. Are you OK? How's the baby, and the blood pressure? I'll come and see you tomorrow when I'm back.'

Silence down the line.

Jo shuts the boot then heads out onto the lane to go next door, praying that Simon is home. She jumps back onto the narrow pavement as a car speeds round the corner only a foot or so from her.

'Lou?' She goes onto Simon's property, up his drive. Thankfully, his car is there.

'Not great, to be honest,' Louise says. 'Archie and I have had another fight.'

'Oh *Lou*…' Jo replies, going up to Simon's door and ringing the bell. 'I'm so sorry to hear that. Have you been working still? Did he find out?' Jo's almost glad, hopes he has. If anyone can get Louise to slow down in her last couple of weeks of pregnancy, it's him.

'Found out?' she says. 'Oh… yes. He did. And he's not pleased. He ordered strict bed rest and took my laptop from me. I was in the middle of a crucial case and he wouldn't even let me hand over to my colleague. Hence… hence the row,' she adds. 'I'm so relieved you're coming back. That woman sounds unhinged, if you ask me. And I need my bestie beside me these next couple of weeks.'

'Well, you'll have me right beside you when the baby comes,' Jo says. When Simon doesn't answer the door, she knocks hard, ringing the bell again. 'Damn, doesn't look like the neighbour's home, Lou. I can hardly leave Suzanne like she is. She's in a state. I'll have to call a doctor or something.'

Feeling torn, Jo turns to go back to Suzanne's just as a car pulls into the drive.

At first, she doesn't realise what it means, doesn't take it on board fully, her mind caught up somewhere between babies, finding Simon and getting help for Suzanne – as well as getting on the road home. Getting out of here.

She knows something's wrong with what she's seeing – something *very* wrong – but, for a few seconds, her brain doesn't register the implications, perhaps protecting her a few moments longer.

But then it *does* sink in. As though a thousand pieces of a jigsaw puzzle have fallen from the sky, landing at her feet and all fitting perfectly together.

Simon gets out of the yellow and blue chequered police car, wearing full uniform. He grins when he sees Jo.

'Good timing,' he says. 'I've just got off shift. Got time for a cuppa?'

Jo sits at Simon's kitchen table, barely able to speak. She may as well be wearing handcuffs. So far, she's only uttered a 'yes' and managed a couple of nods. She feels tiny, stupid, terrified and has never wanted to go home to her empty house more than she does now. When she gets back, she vows to shut the door and never open it to a single soul as long as she lives. She doesn't even care what happened to Will any more, doesn't care if he's dead or alive or if he's with another woman or not. All she knows is that he didn't want her. And she just wants to be alone. Forever.

'You look as white as a sheet, Jo. Everything OK?'

Jo thinks she nods. She's not quite sure.

'How's it going with Suzanne? I know she can be a bit full on.'

'That's… that's why I came round, actually.' She knows she needs to get the words out, just go home – but… he's a *cop*. A police officer. Why would he lie to her about his job, make her believe he was a counsellor? Why the *hell* did she say the things she did?

Or did you just hear what you wanted *to hear, Jo? As ever, you added two and two together and made three hundred and twenty-seven.*

'Suzanne's not very well, actually. That's why I'm here. I'm going home now, so I thought maybe you could check in on her?' She stares at Simon, watching him intently, almost as if he's now a different person to the man she met only a few days ago. The man she *kissed*. 'And… and you're a police officer?' she says, feeling stupid for stating the obvious as he stands there, in his uniform, dunking teabags in mugs.

'Thanks for letting me know about Suzanne,' he says, shaking his head and sighing. 'She should never have come home from the treatment facility. She's been hanging her hopes on it for a long while now. I wish she'd stayed.'

There's so much Jo wants to say – no, *blurt out* – but with Simon standing there dressed like that, she keeps a tight check on what comes out of her mouth. Already her mind is working overtime, trying to recall what details she revealed. But she'd had too much to drink that night and everything is fuzzy in her mind.

'And yes, I am,' Simon laughs. 'Who'd have guessed?' He looks down at himself, tapping the 'police' badge on the front of his jacket. 'Surely you remember that? From when we chatted the other night?'

'Chatted?' Jo says, wanting to say 'confessed, more like'. But she puts the mug of tea to her mouth instead, willing her hand to stop shaking. She must have missed something, been too wrapped up in her own problems. 'Yes, oh yes, of course I remember. For a moment, silly me thought you were…' She shakes her head, trails off.

'Thought I was…? Apart from devilishly handsome and charming, of course.' He laughs, sitting down next to her, unfazed.

'Actually, I thought you were some kind of therapist. As in mental health. I probably poured my heart out to you too much and…' Jo thinks, wondering how to take back everything she said. She shakes her head. 'Which is why I was probably talking a load of gibberish the other night. Alcohol makes me… well, it makes me tell thunderous lies. I can't help it. So don't believe anything I told you.' Jo throws up her palms in the biggest nonchalant shrug she can muster. 'OK?'

Simon's hand is suddenly on Jo's, his fingers gently gripping her wrist, mug still in her hand.

'You're shaking,' he says. 'Just because I'm a cop, it doesn't change anything. I like you. I know you live what seems like a million miles away, but if there's any chance we can still somehow see each other once you've gone, I'd be willing to make the effort.'

Jo makes a whimpering sound.

'You've brought a little bit of sunshine to East Wincombe these last few days, you know. Do you really have to go so soon?'

Jo turns away, wondering what would happen if she just ran for the door, leapt in her car, started the engine and drove off. But between her and freedom, she sees Will – his arms firmly clamped across his chest, his body blocking the doorway, his head slowly shaking from side to side.

CHAPTER FORTY-ONE

Then

The croissants were warming in the tiny oven. Will was relighting the living room fire from the still-glowing embers of the night before. The fabric of the little cottage had retained its warmth, heated from the blaze we'd had going all last night. And Will and I were still toasty from our lie-in, having woken up in each other's arms.

It was perfect.

But I couldn't erase Will's nightmare from my mind.

And, because of that, the temperature in the cottage may as well have been sub-zero.

I shivered in the tiny kitchen, hugging my robe around me.

Just ask him…

'Hey,' I said gently, putting a pot of coffee on the little table that separated the kitchen space from the living area. 'Come and have some food.'

Will turned, looking blank before a smile spread over his face. 'Thank you,' he said, though I still thought he looked drained and exhausted. 'I'm glad we came away.' He glanced at me a couple of times, almost as if he was expecting me to say something.

He took a croissant, ripping it open, the steam rising from its middle. He pushed his knife into the butter, spreading it liberally, then took some strawberry jam, dolloping it on top.

'You didn't sleep so well last night,' I said. 'You were restless. Tossing and turning. And… and talking.'

Will immediately rolled his eyes. 'Probably rehearsing my new lines. You know what I'm like,' he said, taking a long sip of coffee, smile lines around his eyes as he looked at me over the rim of the mug.

'Is your latest play a murder mystery, then?' I said without thinking. I knew it wasn't, but couldn't let it lie. Last night had been distressing.

'Just some audition pieces,' Will said, sounding more guarded. 'Why?'

I couldn't help noticing the quiver in his voice, the look in his eye. We'd known each other too long. Knew all the gestures. The signs.

'Last night, Will, in your sleep…' I took a deep breath, jabbing the knife into the cold butter, hacking off a piece far too big for the chunk of broken croissant. 'You were saying some strange things. Some scary things.'

'I'm sorry,' he came back immediately. Unsatisfying, like a text message that was read and replied to without much thought. A placeholder. A thoughtless emoji. Something to delay the inevitable. 'For keeping you awake,' he added, a quick glance up as he indulged in his breakfast. 'This is delicious, by the way. Thank you.'

'Will, no, listen to me. In your sleep you said that someone was going to hurt me. And you said that you thought you'd… that you'd *killed* her,' I added, feeling my stomach churn. 'What were you talking about?'

I put my croissant down again, not hungry. I didn't think I could eat anything ever again, not until Will had told me what was going on inside his head. Since Annabel's party several weeks ago, he'd been acting completely out of character – more than could be attributed to the stress of his teaching job.

'Something's troubling you, Will,' I continued. 'And if you don't tell me, if you can't talk to me about what's on your mind, then however perfect and romantic this break is, you're going to ruin it for us. Christ, we don't get away often and I just want to enjoy it. Not have to worry that someone wants to hurt me, or about what you may or may not have done. At least try to put my mind at rest.'

Will stared at me. 'Like I said, it was just a bad dream.'

I stared back, watched as he bit into his croissant, not letting go of my gaze.

A moment later, I slammed down my knife, chipping the corner of the plate. 'Bollocks to that, Will. It was *not* just a bad dream.' I stood up, my hands leaning on the edge of the table as I bent forward, got up close in his face. 'You damn well tell me what's going on, William Carter, *now*, or I'm going home. Alone. You have five minutes to spill.'

Will dropped his croissant, his mouth gaping open. I had to sit down again, I was shaking so much.

'It's nothing,' he said. 'Really. And everything's fine now.'

'I know you inside out and upside down. I know you better than you know yourself, for God's sake,' I said, forcing myself not to shout again. 'I also know you're prone to anxiety and low mood sometimes, and I understand that. Haven't I always helped you through the darker times?'

Will gave a small nod, staring down at the table.

'But this is different. This isn't you. Something – or some*one* – has got to you and… and now I'm hearing that someone wants to hurt me, that you thought you'd killed them. You were having a conversation with me in your sleep.' I clutched my head for a second. 'I mean, what the hell am I supposed to think, Will? At least *try* to convince me everything's OK.' I sighed. 'I just don't know what's got into you… since that night a few weeks back at Annabel's, you've just been… not Will. Not the man I married.'

'OK,' Will said, standing up. He wiped his big hands down his face then shoved them in his pockets, sighing. He walked over to the front window of the cottage, staring out across the vale, turning his head back to me briefly. I saw the pain in his eyes. 'If I tell you, Jo, it will change everything between us. Forever. Are you prepared for that?' He was shaking.

I took a breath. 'Everything's changed anyway, Will.' I turned in my chair slightly to face him, holding onto the wooden back. 'You're not the same. *We're* not the same.'

Will gave a brief nod. 'You remember when I hit something when we were driving home from the party that night?'

I nodded. 'Yes, you killed a deer, the poor thing. I know you didn't mean to, and—'

'It wasn't a deer, Jo.'

I stiffened, said nothing.

'It was a person. A… a woman. She… she came out of nowhere. I couldn't stop in time. I didn't mean to hit her.' He stared at me, unblinking, waiting for a reaction.

I said nothing for a moment. Wasn't sure I could move, let alone speak. I wasn't even sure I'd heard him correctly. I felt sick.

'A woman? You hit a *woman*?'

I felt my eyes narrow to disbelieving slits, my jaw tightening as my teeth pressed together. My fists balled so that my nails dug into my palms, and it seemed as if the floor fell away from beneath me.

In my mind, I replayed the moment I was startled awake in the car that night – a loud thump, my head lurching forward, the seat belt cutting into my left shoulder and across my chest. I didn't know what had happened. Then Will was cursing, telling me to stay put, fumbling with his seat belt, leaping out of the car.

It had taken me a while to realise where I was – I'd been exhausted when we'd left Birmingham and the couple of drinks had gone to my head so I couldn't help nodding off, despite fighting it, despite wanting to stay awake and keep Will company.

But I'd known I was in safe hands with him at the wheel, that he wouldn't have risked having a drink; that, bad mood aside, he'd drive us the forty-five minutes home without a hitch.

'Don't worry, I... I think I just clipped something. Probably the kerb,' he'd said breathlessly, poking his head back into the car before slamming the door closed behind him. It was a quiet road, at least – I recognised it as the edge of our town, very close to home but still not yet quite under the street lights. I didn't think there were kerbs out here, though. It was more soft verges.

I'd seen Will go round the front of the car then, his face impassive in the headlights, frozen still for a moment. Then he'd walked around the back, staring at the ground, frowning, his face not giving much away. I'd thought he was checking the tyres, making sure he'd not blown one. But I hadn't paid much attention, just wanted him to get back in the car so we could go home and get to bed.

I'd pulled my coat around me then, twisted onto my side trying to get comfortable, rubbing at my sore shoulder before closing my eyes again. With the engine off, the temperature was falling but I couldn't help drifting into a light sleep, feeling guilty for not getting out too. Whatever it was, I knew Will would sort it.

Then I'd jolted awake again, even though I'd not been deeply asleep.

'Everything OK?' I'd said, stretching as Will got back in and buckled up again. His hands were shaking.

'Yeah, though it wasn't pretty,' he'd said, pulling a face – a mix of sadness and disgust. 'I hit a deer. I'm afraid it—'

'A *deer*?' I remember being incredulous and turned in my seat to look at the road behind us.

'Jo, don't. It's not nice...'

Will had made a retching sound then, fumbling with the keys to start the engine again. 'I dragged it off the road. It wasn't huge, but... *oh*...'

'It's dead?' I remembered asking, just catching the tight nod Will gave as he drove off, juddering through the gears, forgetting to change up from third until we reached home – the engine straining as much as Will seemed to be until we pulled up in front of our house.

'I'm sorry you had to deal with that, love,' I'd said as we went inside. I noticed how his hands were shaking as he unlocked the door, recalled him coming in to get the cleaning materials and the mallet before going back outside and then, when he came in again, going straight upstairs for a shower, putting his clothes in the washing machine afterwards. He loved animals. It had clearly got to him. Countless times that night, before we'd gone to bed, I'd told him that it wasn't his fault. That if it was a young creature, it would have been skittish and terrified and, aside from putting us in danger by swerving to avoid it, there was nothing he could have done. That these things sometimes happen. But I knew he hadn't slept, that he'd been tossing and turning all night long.

And nothing more had been said about it. Until now, I'd pretty much forgotten the whole incident.

'Who?' I whispered, sitting at the breakfast table, barely able to speak. 'Who did you hit?'

Will shook his head. Looked away.

'You *lied*,' I said, still whispering. 'You lied to me about something so very serious.'

Silence. Will leant on the windowsill, head down.

'Was she… is she…?' I couldn't get the words out. Too many thoughts were tumbling through my mind. How we should have called an ambulance, called the police, made statements, taken a breathalyser… 'Did she *die*, Will?' I let out a whimpering sound, curling up, head down. I couldn't stand it.

When I dared look up, Will gave a barely perceptible nod. His eyes were closed. 'At the time, I thought so, yes. That's why I panicked. That's why I drove off. That's why I *lied* to you, Jo,' he said, swinging round, his fists balled at his sides. His jaw was clenched and his shoulders were quickly heaving in time with his short breaths. 'To protect you. It would have been the end of us. The end of everything.'

'*Protect* me?' I whispered, unable to take in what he was telling me. 'What about the poor woman? Her family?'

'There was nothing to be done for her. No pulse. No breath. I couldn't rouse her.' Will came over, dragged the chair up close to mine. He sat down and took my hands in his. I wanted to pull away but couldn't move. 'I know it was wrong. So very, *very* wrong. And I deserve to pay for it, but at the time, nothing was going to bring her back to life, Jo. And that's why I ran. I pulled her off the road and... and she rolled into the ditch. I was weak and terrified and deserve to—'

'Shut up!' I yelled, yanking my hands from him. 'Don't touch me.'

I choked out an angry sob, not even able to cry properly. Then I screamed – a deep and dark sound rising up from the pit of my belly. Pure rage coming out.

'What do you fucking suggest we do now, Will?' I stood, upturning the breakfast table, the plates and mugs smashing onto the quarry-tiled floor. Will flinched. 'Everything is ruined. Our entire lives are ruined. You *killed* a woman. You've *lied* to me for weeks. There's nothing left between us, Will. What you did is unforgivable.'

I sobbed – starting slowly, disbelievingly, until thunderous cries bellowed out of me, unstoppably. I dropped onto the sofa, burying my face in the cushion, howling until there was nothing left to come out. I looked up at Will, glaring at him over the back of the sofa, my face streaked and red. He was still sitting beside the upturned table, leaning forward, forearms on his thighs, head down.

'So you've just been waiting for a knock at the door from the police these last few weeks?' I wiped my face on my dressing gown sleeve, tears and snot mixed up. 'What were you going to tell *me*, exactly, when they arrested you for murder?'

'It wasn't murder,' Will said quietly, staring at the floor.

'Oh, I'm so sorry. Hoping to get off with manslaughter, were you? Jesus fucking Christ, Will.' I shook my head.

'No, I mean it wasn't murder or manslaughter. The woman… the woman isn't dead.'

Jo half growled, half screamed in frustration. 'Can't you just tell me the truth for once?'

'I found out later that she survived. That's all. There's nothing more to say.'

'Nothing more to say? What, so we just carry on with our normal lives while some poor woman faces the aftermath of a hit and run? What if she's in a wheelchair for the rest of her life, Will? What if she's lost a limb or has brain damage or… or, I don't know. Any number of horrific things.'

'She's fine,' Will said, refusing to look at me. 'Her injuries weren't life-changing.'

'Well, I'm not fine!' I said, lunging at him, my face right in his. Will flinched.

Then he took me by the wrists, standing up, towering over me.

'Jo, you're going to have to trust me on this. The woman survived. She's getting on with her life, as we now need to do.'

'I don't know what to think any more…' I trailed off, wanting everything to be how it was half an hour ago. I'd even have tolerated Will's sour mood these last few weeks rather than know what I'd just found out. I relaxed my arms, stopped pulling away from him, dropping my shoulders. Will's grip around my wrists loosened, pulling me gently into an embrace. I was exhausted. Spent – from being awake most of the night, but also from shock.

'Just think about it, Jo – from my side. From *our* side. What's the thing you – *we* – want most in the world right now?'

I looked up at him, recognising the old Will underneath the shame, the fear. 'A baby,' I whispered without hesitation.

'Me too, my love. Me too. But if I'm arrested, if I'm put away for an innocent accident that wasn't my fault, then we're never going to be able to conceive, are we? Or be able to try IVF, if that's the route you want to go down.'

At that moment, I knew Will was right. However much I despised him for lying to me, for not doing what seemed like the right thing at the time, I saw his logic. I knew he'd never harm anyone on purpose, but then if the only man I wanted to have a child with was in prison, I'd never be a mother. *Ever.*

Nothing could change what had happened, and the woman hadn't died, after all.

'I don't like it, Will. Not one bit,' I said, falling against his chest, burying my face. He stroked my hair and we stood there together for what seemed like hours, the morning sun creeping through the front window, casting a corridor of light around us.

CHAPTER FORTY-TWO

Now

It's just as Jo turns the key in the ignition after she's left Simon's house that she notices her handbag isn't on the passenger seat. Puzzled, she feels around underneath the seat, swinging round to look in the back. Turning off the engine, she gets out and goes to the boot, opening it – only seeing her suitcase and her dirty boots in there. She swears she put it in the car.

'Maybe I left it inside,' she thinks, looking at Suzanne's house. She had everything in the hall ready to go, had put the animals in the kitchen safely before loading up the car. It's possible she could have left it on the hallway floor or at the bottom of the stairs. Her mind was frazzled, after all.

Sighing, not wanting to go back inside, she heads towards the house, patting her coat pocket to check she has her phone. She does. But something else jangles in there – and it's not her car keys because they're in her hand. 'Oh great,' she mutters. She was so shocked to see Simon in police uniform that she forgot to leave the stolen keys to Hawthorn Lodge at his place. She'd intended to hide them somewhere, make it look as though he'd lost them himself. 'Damn, damn, damn…'

But then, when she realises that she's left her own keys to Suzanne's house on the kitchen table, along with a note saying goodbye, she's grateful she still has this set. She'll go back in quietly, retrieve her bag and then leave. As an afterthought, she decides she'll hide the stolen keys down the side of Suzanne's sofa, so that when they're eventually found, it'll look as if they fell out of Simon's pocket. And then she'll get out. Get home.

Jo puts the key in the lock, turns it and goes into the hallway. She hears Spangle's claws on the tiles as he trots to the other side of the kitchen door as he lets out an excited bark. *Please be quiet*, she thinks, looking around for her bag. But it's not in the hallway. Jo curses under her breath, glances up the stairs to where she left Suzanne resting. All seems quiet up there.

'It must still be in the kitchen,' she whispers, exasperated with herself. She just wants to leave now. It has been the opposite of a relaxing break. She wants her own little home back, her friends to confide in, her job, her sewing – everything familiar. She doesn't even want to find out what's happened to Will now. Her mind is veering down routes she doesn't want to contemplate and, after everything, it's safer not knowing. It's time to move on.

Slowly, Jo opens the kitchen door, not wanting to let Spangle out as his nose pushes through the gap. 'Go back, boy,' she says quietly, reaching her hand through to take hold of his collar. His tail wags furiously as she goes in.

'Hello, Jo,' Suzanne says, looking up. She's sitting down with Jo's bag in front of her on the kitchen table, the entire contents spilt out.

Jo jumps, taking a moment to register what's going on. At first, she's just relieved to see that Suzanne seems normal again, that her episode has passed. But then her eyes narrow – trying to absorb what else she's seeing – especially when she spots the contents of her purse spread out, everything including her debit and store cards, her driving licence, her donor card, a few notes and coins. And the small photograph of Will she keeps in there – which is directly in front of Suzanne on the table, her forefinger resting on top of it. Tapping lightly.

'What are you doing – *again*?' Jo says. 'That's… that's my handbag. My personal stuff.'

'I know,' Suzanne says. 'I took it from your car. You shouldn't leave it unlocked, you know.'

'*What?*' Jo can hardly speak, barely breathe. She takes a step towards Suzanne, wondering if it's some kind of joke. While she knows that now probably isn't the time to think the best of people, she can't help it. It's her nature. The poor woman isn't well. 'Thank you… thank you for keeping it safe, Suzanne. Anyone could have stolen it. I'm sorry everything seems to have fallen out, though. Let me tidy up.'

She reaches out to gather up her items. 'I was just next door letting Simon know that you'd—'

'No!' Suzanne says, sweeping all Jo's belongings onto the floor. She hurls the empty bag across the room. The only item she doesn't discard is the photograph of Will. It's just a small passport picture, but it's recent and clear and the one Jo kept on her at all times to show people if she was out searching for him. Plus she liked to have it there, just for her to look at from time to time.

'Wait… *what?*' Jo goes to retrieve her stuff, dropping to her knees to gather it up. But, as she's on the floor, she feels a hand on her back, then a vice-like grip around her upper arm. She stops, turns, looking up at Suzanne. Her hair is across her face, in her eyes, getting in her mouth as she tries to speak. But no words come out – she's too shocked. She tries to pull out of her grip, but Suzanne holds on tight. Jo hears Spangle whining across the other side of the room.

'No need for that,' Suzanne says, kicking away some of Jo's stuff. 'It's this I want you to tell me about.' She shoves the picture of Will in front of her face, hauling Jo up by the arm.

'Oww, you're hurting me. Suzanne, what's got into you? If this is another of your strange turns, then it's too weird for me. You need medical help. You're scaring me now.' Jo frees herself and backs away, not caring if she has her belongings any more. She just wants to get in her car and go. 'I'm going home, Suzanne. Now please, give me that back.' While she's reluctant to leave her personal possessions strewn on the floor, she really doesn't want to leave the picture of Will here.

'Why do you have his picture in your purse?' Suzanne says, getting in between her and the kitchen door. 'Tell me!'

'Surely I should be asking *you* the same question,' Jo says, anger brewing inside her. 'I've seen what's in your… your…' Jo's shoulders heave, her breaths coming in and out faster than she can keep up with. She forces herself to stay calm. 'Your *shrine* to my husband. You're obsessed. You're crazy.'

Jo can't believe she's saying these things. This is not her, who she is, how she behaves, how she treats people. Especially other women who have been hurt. But she's scared, and Suzanne is still blocking her route to the hallway.

'Your *husband*…' Suzanne says flatly, almost as if she knew all along. Her eyes turn glassy, as if she's seeing something that isn't in the room – as Jo has done herself many times. Jo catches hold of the back of the chair to steady herself, not wanting to face the truth – the truth that she's put to the back of her mind since Suzanne told her about her accident when they'd had lunch in the pub.

'A hit and run,' she'd said, so matter-of-factly as they were eating soup, after describing her many operations, the broken bones, the mental trauma, the PTSD, the long recovery which still wasn't over. Jo hadn't wanted to acknowledge it at the time – marrying up what Will had confessed with Suzanne's story. But what she didn't know was *why* or *how* – or the answers to a million other questions she had bottled up. And, right now, with Suzanne's mood volatile, she didn't *want* to know.

'Yes, Will is my husband,' Jo says, reaching out to snatch his picture back. But Suzanne is too quick and whips it away, shaking her head, that look in her eyes still. 'And I want to know how you know him.'

Suzanne stares beyond Jo, a faraway look in her eyes, something softer in there now. 'Me too,' she whispers, shaking her head and shrugging, looking over Jo's shoulder as if she's talking to someone else. 'There's so much hidden in here, yet…' She pulls a pained face as if something is actually hurting inside her brain. 'Yet it's like looking through a thick fog.'

Jo wants nothing more than to sit her down, tell her the truth, what she suspects. She feels certain the fog would lift for Suzanne. But even if Will never returns, by admitting what she knows, what he did, that she didn't go to the police to report the accident – even weeks after it happened – then she'd also be incriminating *herself*. It's too late for that now. She's the one left to clean up the mess Will left behind, and she's not about to turn herself in for something she didn't do.

And then he's there, standing right beside Suzanne, looking frightened and concerned. Wringing his hands. His mouth moves, opening and closing, but this time nothing comes out.

What were *you bloody thinking?* Jo snaps, knowing it's futile. *And where* are *you when I need you?*

'What?' Suzanne says, almost as if she's perfectly coherent again. 'Where's who?'

'Nothing,' Jo says, just wanting to keep things calm. She has her keys, her phone – that's all she really needs. 'Suzanne, I'm going now. I only came back in to get my bag, but that doesn't matter—'

'No, wait!' Suzanne says, a panicked look in her eyes. 'You don't know how much I need you here. How close you are to unlocking my mind, clearing the fog. Please… please don't go. There's something I want to show you.' She takes Jo's forearms in her hands, gripping them lightly but with purpose. Her expression is pleading.

'Show me what?' Jo says, wary. From the corner of her eye, she sees Will thumping the side of his head with the heel of his hand, bowing his head as he turns away.

'Just come upstairs with me.' She reaches out for Jo's hand, her fingers splayed, her arm shaking. 'Then you can go. Please?'

Jo closes her eyes for a second, hangs her head. She remembers the moment at the cottage when Will confessed what he'd done – the guilt exploding out of him. And what, innocently, Jo discovered she'd been a part of – abandoning an injured woman who was as much in the dark as she was. It's clear that Suzanne had no idea Will was married. That he'd been conning them both.

'OK,' Jo says, sighing. 'But just for a minute. Let me pick up my stuff first though. Please…'

Suzanne nods, doing something at the worktop by the sink as Jo scoops up all her stuff from the floor, shoving it back in her bag. Then she follows Suzanne through the hallway, leaving her bag at the bottom of the stairs ready to go. Halfway up, Jo pauses, catching sight of Will in the hallway below, his hand cupping his mouth in a gesture of silence.

CHAPTER FORTY-THREE

'In here,' Suzanne says, leading the way upstairs to the locked spare bedroom. Jo hasn't bothered to take off her coat or shoes. She's not planning on staying much longer. 'There's something… something you should see.' Her voice is quiet, resigned and filled with sadness.

Suzanne holds the door open for Jo, her other arm pulling her cardigan tightly around her, fingers clenched around her waist as if she has a pain.

Once inside, Jo turns round. 'Look, I don't know what this is all about but—'

She stops when she sees the knife, shaking and glinting in Suzanne's unsteady hand – the knife from the breadboard in the kitchen. She must have hidden it underneath her cardigan before they came upstairs, when Jo was gathering up her stuff.

'What the *hell*?' Jo recoils, stepping back and stumbling over a box of papers on the carpet. 'What are you *doing*, Suzanne? Just no… please. Stop and think about this.'

Suzanne is in the doorway, one hand gripping the frame, the other pointing the blade directly at Jo.

'I know you can help me,' she says, spit spraying from her lips. 'I just don't know how yet. I don't know who you are or why you're here, but as soon as I saw you on Simon's phone when I face-timed him, I knew I had to come home. You were in my head somehow. Buried. Stuck.' She takes a step closer, the knife held out. 'See? It's him…' Suzanne points the knife towards the photographs of

Will scattered on the bed – the ones that had been hidden under the duvet. 'They're the same as him, the man in your wallet. And in that box, there are newspaper clippings. Read them. Look at all the photographs. When you're ready to tell me who he is, who you are, I'll let you out.' She begins to back away.

'What do you mean, you'll "let me out"?' Jo says, her voice squeaking. 'You can't do this!' She heads towards the door, following Suzanne, but the other woman raises the knife at her.

'Stay here!' she yells, tears welling in her eyes. 'I… I don't want you to go. You know things. You can help me. If you cause a fuss, I swear to God I'll…' She raises the knife again.

Jo nods, her mouth dry. She presses her hand against her coat pocket, knowing her phone is in there, and also Simon's spare keys. She'll wait for Suzanne to be preoccupied and then unlock the door and get out – but not before calling the police. She doesn't care about the consequences any more, will face whatever comes her way. She should have turned them both in when Will confessed to what he'd done back at the cottage. But, selfishly, she'd had her hopes set on a baby and if Will had gone to prison, that would never have happened. She was thirty-nine, after all.

'OK, OK,' Jo says, raising her hands and backing away. 'Just take it easy with that, Suzanne. I'll stay in here and I'll have a look at your pictures. Don't worry, I'm not going anywhere.'

Suzanne nods, pushing the fingers of her free hand through her hair. She doesn't look well, as though she's in pain and on the edge of another of her episodes. That's the last thing Jo wants with that knife in her grasp. 'Yes, yes, good…' she says, backing away, stepping out onto the landing and slamming the door closed behind her. The last thing Jo sees is the sadness in her eyes before she hears the key in the lock turn from the outside.

'Oh my *God*,' Jo whispers, dropping down onto the bed. She cradles her head in her hands, but whips up again, knowing she must stay calm and get help. The woman is very unwell – and clearly dangerous. Jo's hand shakes as she pulls out her phone and switches it onto silent mode. She doesn't want Suzanne hearing any alerts and taking her phone away. But then she sees her battery is only at two per cent. She was going to charge it up in the car on the drive home. She's just about to call the police when her screen lights up with Louise's name displayed. She answers immediately.

'Lou, hi,' she whispers, cupping her hand round her mouth.

'Hey, I just needed to hear your voice. How's—'

'Lou, listen to me… shush a moment. Crazy stuff is happening. Suzanne has flipped and she's locked me in a room with all these photos of Will and newspaper clippings and… and… well, Christ, she has a knife, Lou, and this mad look in her eyes. I was stupid and should never have come back, but I was looking for my bag after I went to leave the stolen keys in Simon's house, except I forgot. It turns out he's a bloody cop! So I went back into Suzanne's house to find my bag and guess what? She'd taken it, and all my stuff was spread out on the table. She was super-weird about the photo of Will she'd found and then she got a knife and now I'm locked up in a bedroom. I'm going to call the police, Lou. It's all crazy and…' Jo feels the tears welling up, fights them back. She needs to stay strong.

'What the *hell*? Oh, Jo… listen to me. Firstly, Archie and I…' Jo hears a choked-back sob. 'He's… well, he's left me.'

'What? Oh my God, Lou… no, I don't believe—'

'Listen, don't worry about that now. It sounds as though you're in danger. Can you—'

Then the line goes dead.

Jo stares at her blank screen, presses the home button repeatedly. Tries to turn her phone off then on again – but it is already off. It's dead. The battery has finally run out.

She lets out a little whimper.

Archie has left Louise? At thirty-eight weeks pregnant? Surely that's not true, not on top of everything else.

'Christ…' Her heart kicks up, thumping in her chest as though it's about to burst out. *Why the hell didn't I put my phone on charge?* she thinks, pacing about. She goes up to the door, one ear against it, listening out for noises. She hears Suzanne downstairs, clattering about in the kitchen, talking to Spangle as if nothing is wrong. It sounds as though she's loading the dishwasher.

Jo fishes in her pocket for the spare keys, her hand shaking as she slots the key in the mortice lock. At first she thinks it's because she's trembling so much that it won't go in, but even when she steadies herself, uses two hands to guide it in, it won't fully insert. She bends down, peering into the keyhole. She can't see through – but she can see the end of the key in the outside of the lock, preventing her from opening the door this side. She tries to push it out from the inside, but it won't budge.

She stands up, staring at the door, not knowing what the hell to do.

Then, without thinking, she draws her leg back and kicks it hard, beating it with her fists and screaming.

'Suzanne, Suz-*anne*! Let me out of here, for Christ's sake! Suzanne – let me *out*!'

The noises in the kitchen stop for a moment and then Jo hears the door downstairs slam and everything goes quiet. Jo feels faint, light-headed and sick. She turns, drops down onto the bed. And that's when she spots Will, standing over by the window.

'This is *your* fault,' she says to him. 'Even when you're not here, even when you're as lost and missing as possible, you're still—'

Jo, stop, he says, holding up his hands. *You need to think straight and, right now, you're not.* His voice is soothing and calm. Just what Jo needs to hear as the tears finally come.

'I know, I know,' she says, sniffing and wiping her face with the back of her hand. 'But my phone's dead and I can't bloody get out of here.' She sits up suddenly, rummaging through the box of photographs and papers on the floor. She pulls out a newspaper cutting, scanning through it. It's what Suzanne wanted her to see, as though she's forming links, putting two and two together. Though how she knows about Jo's involvement in the accident, she has no idea. She supposes the picture of Will in her wallet sealed it. Triggered something inside her, even if she doesn't quite know what yet.

'I don't understand. If she knows who you are, why she didn't report you?' Jo says to Will. He just stares at her as she thinks back to what Will had told her about that night when they were in the cottage. It was all such a shock, all such a blur, that she tried to forget it over the coming weeks. And then Will had disappeared.

'I lied for you,' Jo whispers to him, waving the newspaper cutting in his face. 'I sat with the police after you disappeared, telling them there was no reason for you to take off or run away. That there was nothing wrong with you or our life together, that we were happy, that nothing unusual had happened.' She snorts then. 'If only I'd not been so blind. Not been so fixated on having your baby. We were never going to get pregnant anyway – there's something wrong with me. There must be.'

She sees Will staring at the news clipping. Holds it up for him.

Woman Left for Dead Survives Brutal Hit and Run

'But you've already seen this, haven't you? That's how you knew she was OK. But you didn't think to tell me the truth when the rest of the world bloody well knew.' Jo fights to keep her voice down but the anger inside her is building. 'The whole world except Suzanne and me, that is,' she adds. 'She lost her memory from the time of the accident. She must have had the pictures of you from before, when you were seeing her... I don't understand. And I don't really want to. I just want to get out!'

Jo goes to the window, pushing past where Will is standing. She pulls back the net curtains and twists the handle, but the window is firmly locked. She bangs on the glass, but there's no one in sight – the front of the house shielded from the lane by thick bushes and trees anyway. She takes another swipe at the dressing table, sending all the things she'd rearranged onto the carpet again. Then she hurls herself onto the bed, curled up into a ball, her face buried in the pillow, unable to cry now even if she wanted to.

She doesn't know how long she lies there for, doesn't know if she properly falls asleep or not – just that she forces herself to switch off from the world, from reality, praying that Louise has the good sense to call someone to help her. Though she doesn't know how, as she has no idea where Suzanne's house is.

All she knows is that she can hear her own heartbeat pulsing in her ears, pounding in time with the fear running through her veins. And, when Will sits down on the bed beside her, when his soothing words calm and lull her, she doesn't fight him off. Doesn't scream at him like she wants to. Instead, she closes her eyes and waits…

CHAPTER FORTY-FOUR

It's the noise that wakes her. A doorbell. Banging. Voices. *Raised* voices. It's coming from downstairs. Beneath her.

Jo sits up, not quite sure where she is until she sees the photos of Will crumpled and creased on the end of the bed from where she's had her feet on them, the box of papers on the floor, her dead mobile phone and useless set of keys lying beside her on the duvet. And then she remembers that she's locked in.

'Christ…' She holds her head, takes a deep breath to steady herself. She has no idea how long she's been asleep.

Jo hears women's voices below. It sounds as though they're in the hall. As if there's a visitor and Suzanne is trying to get rid of her. She swings her legs over the side of the bed and stands, feeling dizzy and disorientated in the now-dark room. She pushes her hair off her face and goes to the window, spotting the roof of another car parked in the drive, but it's impossible to tell what kind because it's dark outside. It's not Simon's car – there's no need for him to drive here anyway. And it's certainly not a police car, which, despite her better instincts, is what she longs to see right now.

Just as she turns away, she thinks she sees movement inside the car, but can't be sure.

She goes to the door again and bangs hard on it. 'Hello?' she calls out. 'Anyone there? I'm up here, will you let me out?' She tries to keep her tone calm, but loud enough for someone to hear. She doesn't want to rile Suzanne, but equally she wants to be heard, to get out. 'Hel-*lo?*' she calls even louder, hearing shouting below.

She listens, straining at the door but it's hard to hear much with Spangle barking. And not his usual friendly barks either, when he greets someone. They're underpinned by a growl.

'No!' she hears someone cry out. It sounds like Suzanne. Then there are footsteps thumping up the stairs, more shouting – another woman's voice. Getting closer all the time.

'Get *off* me!' the other person shouts. Then the sound of someone tripping, a thud, a cry of pain.

'Hello? Who's there?' Jo yells through the door. 'Can you help me? I'm locked in!' She glances around the bedroom, looking for some kind of weapon in case Suzanne still has the knife. There's nothing much, apart from the small dressing table stool, so she grabs that, bracing herself behind the door, holding it in front of her, the legs facing out as if she's about to tame a lion.

There's a bang from the other side of the door, as if someone has been shoved into it, followed by a shriek.

'Just get out,' Suzanne shouts. 'You've no right to be in here. I'll call the police.'

Then Jo hears what sounds like the keys being taken from the lock on the other side of the door, then a scuffle – grunting and more shrieks and the jangling of keys as they're dropped. Jo takes her chance and swipes Simon's set of keys off the bed, wrestling with the stool while fumbling to get the correct key in the door while she has the chance. It feels as though every cell of her body is shaking.

And then the key is in. Quickly, Jo turns it, the noise of two women shouting at each other on the landing growing louder as she clicks the Yale lock too, opens the door, not knowing what to expect.

At first, it's not clear – just a mass of limbs and bodies scrapping in the doorway as she sees Suzanne's hands tearing at someone's long hair, her face twisted and contorted from effort.

'*Stop* it!' Jo says, unable to get past them, stunned by what she's seeing.

Suzanne grabs a handful of the other woman's hair, making her scream. Then Suzanne plants her palm over her face, shoving her backwards so she stumbles into the room, knocking into Jo. Both women stagger backwards as Jo tries to grab onto something to stop them falling – the door, the wall, the corner of a chest of drawers, anything. But the other woman is too heavy and sends them both stumbling backwards until Jo's legs give way and she goes down – the other woman landing on top of her.

Everything falls silent. Just the sound of their breathing as they lie on the floor, entwined, stunned, Jo trapped underneath. It seems like an age until someone moves.

*

'Jo… oh my *God*…' The woman says, rolling onto her side while pulling a face. 'What has she *done* to you? Why are you even *in* here?'

Jo can hardly breathe or speak – partly because she's been winded and partly because she's just seen Suzanne slam the door closed and heard her lock it again.

But mainly because of who the woman is.

'*Louise*…' she whispers, rolling out from underneath her. 'Are you OK? How dare she attack a pregnant woman. And what are you *doing* here, anyway? Bloody hell, Lou, you should be home, resting. Did Archie bring you? How did you even know where I was?' Jo hoists herself to her feet, part of her grateful that her best friend is here… but mostly she feels dreadful that she's been drawn into this – her mess – and now desperately worried about the baby.

'Wait… whoa,' Louise says, catching her breath, holding her bulging belly as she turns round and onto all fours. 'Too many questions. Let me steady myself.'

Jo slides her arms beneath her armpits and helps her up slowly, conscious of the huge bump hanging down beneath her. Briefly, Louise grabs hold of her belly again, making a pained face.

'Are you in pain?'

Louise makes a grunting sound as Jo helps her up.

'How did you get here?' Jo asks. 'Are you with Archie?'

'I drove,' Louise says, finally standing, sweeping the hair off her face and adjusting her maternity top. 'Just because I'm pregnant, it doesn't mean I'm pathetic.' She grimaces again, holding her stomach, taking short, sharp breaths and blowing out through her mouth. Jo suspects she's in more pain than she's letting on.

'I know you're not pathetic, Lou, but it's... well, frankly, it's not safe here. Suzanne has turned out to be... unhinged. I mean, look!' She sweeps her hands around the room then points at the door. 'And we're *both* locked in now. When we were talking earlier, I was about to phone the police but then my battery ran out. The shock must have made me fall asleep for what must be hours, and I had these wild dreams about Will and deer and cars and pub quizzes and a dog on the beach and... and...'

Jo stops when the hand goes over her mouth.

'Shhh, it's OK now. I'm here. God knows what's been going on, who this crazy woman is, but I don't like it and I've come to get you out.'

'She *is* crazy,' Jo says, feeling a sweat break out. 'And that's why you shouldn't be here. I love you for coming, but I don't like that you're at risk. It's *my* job to get *you* out, Lou.' She desperately wants to tell her the truth: how Will left Suzanne – his lover – for dead on the roadside, and how she suspects this is some kind of sick revenge by Suzanne. And how calling the police will likely end up with her being arrested for conspiracy or perverting the course of justice or whatever it's called – but she knows she can't. 'Here, give me your phone, Lou. Let me call for help.' She holds out her hand. 'Please, I'm going to call the police.'

Louise's mouth drops open and both women stare at each other. It takes a moment for Jo to realise what Louise is about to say – and a moment for Louise to work out how to say it.

'My phone… it's in the car,' she says, hanging her head.

Jo is about to speak but Louise halts her, holding up her hands.

'I'm sorry. I didn't know this was going to happen, did I? I thought you'd maybe blown things out of proportion when we spoke, but knew I wouldn't have had a wink of sleep without knowing that you were OK. I tried to call you back but couldn't get through. Archie's buggered off in a strop, so I thought I may as well make the drive down. He'd have stopped me otherwise. I got the address from the House Angels website. I set up the login details, remember?' Louise speaks quickly, as if to get everything out before catching her breath again, sucking in air sharply, her hands wrapping round her huge belly.

'Oh, *Lou*… I can't tell you how good it is to see you and how grateful I am for you caring, but you don't look well. It really was madness you driving all this way. Here, sit on the bed.' Jo glances at the door again, wondering how the hell they're going to get out.

Louise lowers herself, making a little noise as she sits down. 'Oh God…' she says again, breathless, making a pained face as her palms splay out over her baby.

'Shit, Lou, you don't think you're…?' Jo drops to her knees in front of Louise, looking up at her. 'Are these proper contractions, do you think? Are you in labour?'

'I've… I've been trying to ignore them,' Louise says, panting again. 'They started on the motorway, when I was halfway here. I pulled over at the services to get some water, hoping they'd subside if I moved about. If anything, that's just made them worse.' She moans again – a long, low sound coming from deep inside her. 'I thought they were just Braxton Hicks this morning, but I must have been mistaken. I reckon I've been in labour for a few hours. I'm pretty sure the baby's coming.'

CHAPTER FORTY-FIVE

'That's it, I've had enough,' Jo says, leaping to her feet. She goes to the door and bangs loudly on it with her fists. She doesn't care if Suzanne has a knife or not. She just needs to get help for Louise. 'Suzanne, let us *out* of here! My friend is in labour. Her contractions are getting closer together.'

Silence the other side of the door. Just the sound of Louise's intermittent moans behind her.

'Suzanne, for God's sake, can you hear me? If nothing else, then please call an ambulance for her. She needs medical help. And soon!' Jo frantically looks around, lunges for the dressing table stool, picking it up and slamming it against the door. But the legs splinter off like matchsticks and she hurls it down onto the carpet, banging the door with her fists again.

'Ow-*ww...*' Louise says, rocking back and forth on the bed. 'Oh, my back,' she wails, trying to rub it herself.

Jo sits down beside her, pressing the heel of her hand at the locus of the pain, circling it round as Louise half rises, swaying her hips from side to side. 'It's OK, it's OK, I'm here...' She pulls her close as Louise tips back her head, wailing again, before panting through the contraction, remembering what she learnt in antenatal classes.

'Shit,' she says when it subsides, her face damp with sweat. 'Oh Jo, it really hurts and I'm probably not even halfway dilated.' She pants again, sweating. 'I don't want to have my baby in this room…' She lets out a few sobs, gripping Jo's hands. 'I want Archie, and to be in the hospital I chose, with my obstetrician and my midwife and my birth plan. How the hell is this… ah-*hhh*…' She heaves herself up, waddling over to the wall, her legs apart, hands spread out on the floral wallpaper as she rocks from side to side, wailing and moaning as another contraction surges through her.

'They're getting closer together,' Jo says, desperately worried. 'And there's not even any water in here,' she mutters under her breath, furious that Suzanne has done this. She takes to the door with her fists again, yelling, almost resigned to delivering Louise's baby herself. But what if there's a problem – with Louise or the baby? She has no medical training, wouldn't know what to do in an emergency. She wants to be angry at Louise for being so stupid coming here at this late stage in her pregnancy, but she knows she was only trying to help. Under the circumstances, she'd have done the same.

'Turn your face away,' Jo says when there's a lull in Louise's groaning. She picks up one of the stool legs and brings it down, end on, repeatedly on the door handle, trying to break the lock. But after a dozen attempts at smashing it, she realises it's futile. The door is way stronger than the now-splintered stool leg. '*Christ*,' she mutters under her breath, not wanting to scare Louise. But their situation doesn't look good. She scans around the room, searching for something that she could use as a lever, something stronger than wood and narrow enough to slip between the door and its frame.

She pulls open all the drawers, flinging stuff out – clothes, pillowcases, old cosmetics, more papers. There's simply nothing she can use. Not even a pair of nail scissors. Jo's panicked breathing is almost as frantic as Louise's as she wonders if the only way out is to smash a window. She goes up to the window, splays her hands on the glass, her heart sinking when she sees that all the panes are double-glazed. She quickly searches around behind the curtains, on the windowsill, in case there's a hidden key… anything to get them open. But there's nothing. She scans the room again, looking for something weighty to smash the glass with, but apart from the useless stool legs, there's nothing heavy enough. She can hardly hurl an entire dressing table at the window.

Taking a moment to think, Jo stands there, her shoulders rising and falling as she suppresses the huge scream that wants to burst from her, the anger – about *everything*. It all wants to come out – the rage she's been harbouring, the hope she's been clinging to. It's all futile, has kept her on hold all these months as if she's barely been alive herself. It's been no way to live – seeing Will around every corner, talking to him, smelling him, hearing him.

He's not real. He's gone. He's never coming back… she yells inside her head. She just wants Will to go away, to stop haunting her, to let her live her life.

But now her best friend is caught up in it. Her *pregnant* best friend.

Jo stands rigid, her eyes screwed up, not having a clue what to do. She hears her mother's words in her head, flooding through her. She was most likely right about Will, but she's not been able to face it, just wants everything to be back to how it was a year ago. But equally she knows that what she must do right now is focus on Louise. And the baby she's about to give birth to. The baby *she's* going to have to deliver.

Jo slides her hands down her face. *You've got this, Jo*, she tells herself. *For Louise, for her baby.*

She takes a deep breath, resigned to the fact that the only way out is going to be through the window – even if she has to jump. Louise wails again, panting through another contraction – the sound of her discomfort even stronger this time, more intense.

'Breathe through it,' Jo says, holding her again, feeling completely helpless, not knowing whether to focus on getting out or tending to her friend. 'You're doing great. Everything's going to be OK. I'll make sure of it.' She rubs her back, the other hand tucking her hair behind her ear, getting it off her face, out of her mouth, as she wails. Louise mustn't know how terrified she is.

'It's OK, Lou. I'm here. You're going to be fine, and your baby is going to be fine too,' she says slowly, clearly. 'I'm so proud to be here with you right now, do you know that?' Jo feels the tears welling. She laughs and sniffs at the same time, trying to stay strong. 'We're going to be OK, you and I...'

Louise nods, grabbing hold of Jo's hand, squeezing it. 'I'm... I'm so sorry,' she pants breathlessly. 'I never meant... oh God... ow-*ww*, I never meant any of this to happen, Jo.' She sways her hips from side to side as she battles through another contraction. Gritting her teeth, head bowed down, focusing.

Once the contraction subsides, Jo knows she needs to take control. She needs medical help, and *now*.

She swipes up two of the broken stool legs and strides to the window, cupping her hand against the glass, peering out just in case anyone is passing by and she can get their attention. But there's no one there. Then she wields the legs above her head, about to bring them down on the double glazing as hard as she can, when she hears the door handle to the bedroom rattling behind her – as well as what sounds like the lock turning.

She freezes, arms above her head.

Thank Christ, Jo thinks, catching her breath, turning, praying Suzanne has changed her mind and come to help. But still, she stays alert, knowing she may have to defend Louise.

And then, as she briefly glances out of the window again, lowering her arms, she doesn't know which way to look – towards the door as she hears Suzanne's voice, or down at the gravel where she catches sight of Will standing on the drive below.

She stares at him for a moment – her eyes narrowing in disgust at the sight of him yet again. She wants him gone from her life – to stop herself imagining him, talking to him, longing for him. His presence is doing her no good. She quickly turns back to the door again, to see it opening, to see Suzanne coming in carrying several knitted blankets and some towels. She breathes out a sigh of relief. *She's come to help.* Louise is still panting and moaning, legs splayed as she rocks her hips back and forth, her face glowing with sweat.

And when Jo looks back down to the drive again, mouthing *Why, why, why...?* at Will, wishing he would just go away, finally disappear from her life, she sees he's still there, still pacing back and forth along the gravel, looking for all the world as though he's absolutely real.

CHAPTER FORTY-SIX

Then

He might as well be in prison, I thought as I lay in bed beside Will, each of us on our backs, neither of us asleep. I could tell he was awake by the sound of his breathing. *His eyes are probably open*, I thought. Staring at the ceiling in the darkness, just like I am, wondering where the hell we go from here.

We'd not had sex since he'd told me, since we'd returned from the cottage break. And I hadn't fallen pregnant from when we'd made love there – before he'd dropped the bombshell. I'd spent the rest of that day crying, asking question after question, replaying the night of the party over and over in my mind, trying to recall the faces of everyone who was there, Will's bad mood that night – as well as the days leading up to the party. I'd sensed he'd had something on his mind, that something was troubling him, but had no idea what. And I wasn't certain if any of that was related to the accident on the way home or if it was simply coincidence.

From the moment Will had told me the truth that morning, I could do nothing else except overanalyse and overthink everything that had gone before. Desperate for answers. For reasons. Because Will wasn't giving me any. It was a sum of fragments, and every time I tried to add them up, I came up with a different answer.

'Will,' I whispered as we lay there. I could almost hear his mind whirring and racing at the same pace as mine. It was as if we'd become two very separate and different people these last few weeks, with the cliché 'drifting apart' not even coming close to describing the pain I felt from watching my husband – my beautiful, kind, creative and talented husband – gradually go missing in front of my eyes. As if he was fading away. There but not there.

'What?' he replied, unmoving.

'Please tell me…' I was trying to think of a different way to phrase the question that I'd already asked a thousand times. Since that night at the cottage, when he'd had the nightmare and been sleep-talking, I couldn't get what he'd said out of my mind. 'When you said that someone was trying to… to hurt me—'

'Oh, not again. You're making things up, Jo. Imagining things. Let it lie.'

'No, no, I'm not, Will. In your sleep, you said that someone was trying to hurt me. That they were trying to hurt your wife. And that…' I stopped, swallowed. 'And that you thought you'd killed her. It was the woman you hit, wasn't it? You knew she was going to hurt me, so you hurt her first. It wasn't an accident, was it?'

But why? was the question I most wanted to ask, yet I couldn't get it out.

Suddenly the bed rocked as Will hurled himself onto his side, propped up on one arm, looming over me in the half-light.

'If I say you are making things up, then you are making things up, OK?' He stared at me, our eyes locking onto each other despite the dim light. 'I don't have any control over what I'm saying when I'm asleep. I didn't even know I was sleep-talking. I can't even remember the dream now. It was weeks ago. Just let it go, Jo. It's over. A bad thing happened and I panicked. I shouldn't have done it, I admit that. But it turns out it's not as bad as I thought. Or as you're now making out. Let's just be bloody grateful for that, at least, and move on. I'm sick of hearing about it. Can't a man make mistakes?'

'But Will…' I knew I was pushing it, would probably have forgotten the strange dream, the sleep-talking, if he'd not confessed to the hit and run when we were staying at the cottage. It was as though he'd wanted to get it off his chest, as if he *needed* to tell someone for his own sanity. 'You committed a crime, Will. And like it or not, you've now made me a part of that. I deserve to know the full story.'

Will swung his legs over the side of the bed, sitting up. 'I've had enough, Jo. What else do I need to do to make you drop this? Are you going to spend the rest of our lives going over and over the minutiae? Would you rather see me arrested, dragged through the courts for God knows what… dangerous driving, a hit and run, grievous bodily harm and probably countless other offences? I'd had a drink. I'd end up serving time, Jo. My career as a teacher would be finished. You know we can't survive on your income alone. All I've wanted to do is protect you and it's as though you're… as though you're trying to unravel everything, picking at the knot until it comes undone.' He stood up. 'Well, *I* am coming undone, Jo. And I can't take much more.'

'Will…'

He stood there in the semi-darkness, his bare back facing me as he peeled the curtains back a few inches and leant on the windowsill, staring out. The accident had happened only a short distance from our house, right on the edge of town. I hadn't been able to drive past the spot since I'd been told the truth. *Most* of the truth, as I was certain there was more. I knew Will. And I knew when he was lying.

I got out of bed, went up to him. Put my hand on his shoulder, sliding it down his back. I felt him tense.

'Will, we've not made love in ages. It's been weeks now. Since we were away. I want a baby and I want it with you. But I also miss the closeness. I don't want you to go to prison, of course I don't – that would be the end of our world, all our dreams. I may as well get put away too if that's what happens. I couldn't stand it.'

He turned slightly and I caught sight of the hard angle of his jaw – but I also saw how his tight face had relaxed a little.

'What I'm saying is that I *understand*. Really, I get why you did what you did. I don't like it, but I get it. You acted in panic. And if you say I'm making things up about someone wanting to hurt me, then I believe you. I trust you, Will. More than anyone in my entire life. If I'd been in the same situation, me driving, I have no idea what I would have done. Panicked, too, probably. So I have no right to judge you. I love you.'

Will turned then, wrapping his big arms around me, pulling me close to his chest, my face against his bare skin. I breathed in the scent of him, closing my eyes. It was the safest place in the whole world. And I couldn't stand to lose it.

But still it was playing on my mind.

'How did you know the woman was OK? You mentioned that she was fine, that her injuries hadn't been bad. I don't understand.'

Will held me at arm's length then, looking at me in a way I'd not seen in months. It was a blend of love and lust – his eyes deep and warm, speaking only to me. At that moment, I felt like the only person in the world. The only *woman* in the world. He put a finger over my lips briefly before lowering his head to kiss me, holding me around the back as he laid me down on the bed, pulling off my T-shirt as I prayed that this would be the night.

CHAPTER FORTY-SEVEN

Now

Jo doesn't know which way to turn – to press her face against the glass, hating that she has just told Will to leave her alone, to get out of her life and stop appearing when she least expects it, or to rush to Louise, to Suzanne, to help birth this baby.

I don't really *want you to go…*

'We need to call an ambulance,' Jo says, praying that Suzanne's finally seen sense, that she's going to help them. Or at least help Louise. It's not her fault she's got caught up in this. Then, afterwards, Suzanne can have out with her whatever grudge it is she's got against her. Though she suspects it's Will she should be having that conversation with.

'I already have,' Suzanne says calmly, as if she's a different person. 'They're on their way.' She looks between the two women – her eyes fixed on Jo for a moment, squinting, that look in them again. Then she stares at Louise, as if it's for the first time. She touches her head, screws up her eyes, clearly fighting something inside her. Jo prays she isn't about to have one of her episodes again.

'Thank you,' Jo says, meaning it. She needs to placate her, keep her calm. While she wants to get out of this room, Louise is in no fit state to be going anywhere right now. She watches on, almost frozen, as Suzanne guides her back towards the bed – her arms supporting her round the back as she makes encouraging and soothing sounds. She doesn't seem like the crazy woman who was fighting, screaming and locking them up.

'It's OK, Lou, help is coming,' Jo says.

Louise glances up, giving Jo a brief but pained smile as the last contraction eases and her moans die down again. 'This baby is coming too,' she says, looking exhausted as she lies back on the bed.

'We need to get these off you, love,' Suzanne says as she makes her comfortable with the pillows. She slips off Louise's shoes before gently tugging on her elasticated trousers. Louise nods, helping before the next contraction comes.

Do something, please, Jo thinks, but she's completely frozen, still standing by the window. Instinctively, she senses it'll be the last time she'll see Will, that he is slipping further and further away from her, that her mind won't be playing tricks on her or engaging with him again. She knows it's time to let him go.

She takes one last look out of the window.

'What the hell?' she whispers, going closer, not believing what she just saw. Below on the drive, Will is still there, pacing about, looking agitated. He kicks at the gravel several times, bowing his head and, even in the dark, she sees that he looks annoyed. He's not spotted her yet, doesn't know she's watching. Not even bothered talking to her like he usually does.

But the gravel has moved.

Jo sees a long scuff mark in the stones where he just dragged his foot through.

Figments of my imagination don't do that…

'He scuffed stones. He actually scuffed stones.' Jo brings her hand over her mouth, feeling dizzy and unreal as if *she's* the made-up, imagined person, not Will.

'Sorry?' Suzanne says, glancing up with a puzzled look on her face. She shakes her head. 'Come and help me, will you?'

'Yes, yes, sorry,' Jo says, still staring out of the window, straining to see Will as he approaches the house directly below. It looks as if he's going towards the front door.

Go away!

As she turns back to the bed, Louise lets out the biggest cry yet – her cheeks red, her face screwed up from pain, her eyes tiny slits as she expends all her energy and focuses on getting through the next contraction.

'That's it, you're doing great. Breathe steadily now. Breathe through it.' Suzanne takes Jo's hand, guiding it to Louise's as she tears at her own hair. 'Here, squeeze Jo's hand. The ambulance will be here soon.'

Jo doesn't know what to do. Every fibre of her wants to go back to the window, to tell Will she's sorry, that she doesn't really want him to go away, that she doesn't think she'll be able to get through the rest of her life without him. But she knows she has to help Louise.

'It's OK, Lou,' she says calmly, stroking some hair off her sweaty face. 'Just think, you'll soon have a little baby boy or girl in your arms. And the paramedics will be here and you'll be looked after and—'

'I'm no expert,' Suzanne says, crouching down beside Louise's legs. 'But that looks an awful lot like a baby's head to me.'

Louise is lying on her back, knees bent up, feet wide apart. Jo takes a quick look, exchanges glances at Suzanne before nodding. She mouths *What about the cord?* but Suzanne shrugs. It's clear neither of them knows what to do, though Jo knows it's bad news if it's wrapped around the baby's neck. Jo fights the urge to yell at her, to tell her that if anything happens to Louise or the baby it'll be her fault for locking them in.

'Oh God, I want to push…' Louise says, panting and howling again. 'I can't stop, I need to push… *now*…' Her face turns purple as she strains and grunts.

'Just pant through it if you can,' Suzanne says. 'Little short breaths, and try not to push too hard yet. You're doing fine, and I can see the baby's head getting closer. Keep going, Louise.'

Then the contraction subsides again and Louise's head flops back onto the pillow. She closes her eyes, waiting for the next onslaught. Suzanne arranges towels under Louise's legs and bottom, preparing for the baby coming.

And it's just as everything falls silent between contractions that they hear the banging on the door downstairs, followed by the doorbell sounding over and over.

'Oh thank *goodness*,' Jo says, looking at Suzanne, both women awash with relief. She grabs Louise's hand. 'Lou, it's OK. The ambulance has arrived. You're going to be fine.'

'Go and let them in,' Suzanne says. 'I'll stay here.'

Jo nods, giving an encouraging smile to Louise who manages one back, mouthing a little *thank you* as Jo turns to dash downstairs. Though for the life of her, Jo thought she mouthed *sorry*, too.

As Jo rushes down to the hallway, she's met by Spangle, barking and jumping about at the door – a combination of wagging tail and protective barks. She knows she should shut him in the kitchen but she wants to let the paramedics in as quickly as possible, show them where Louise is.

Jo undoes the chain, fumbling with the key that's been left in the lock, seeing the shape of someone through the stained glass. She pulls back the door, forcing herself to stay calm so she can brief them about what she knows of Louise's medical history. Time is of the essence.

She takes a deep breath and, when she sees who's standing there, it escapes as a scream.

Will.

She covers her mouth, glancing behind his presence, looking for the paramedics, but there's no one else there.

Just Will. Looking for all the world as though he's real.

But he *can't* be. Can he? Surely it's her mind playing tricks again.

'Hello, Jo,' he says, staring directly at her, his eyes heavy, his expression filled with something she doesn't recognise. 'I… I—'

'*Will?*' Jo whispers, her heart thumping so fast she thinks she'll need an ambulance herself. 'I… what… I don't…' He seems more real than ever.

Jo feels dizzy and sick and so unsure of her own mind, her own sense of reality, that she slams the door shut, then counts to five before opening it again.

Will is still there.

'You're not real,' Jo says, trying to convince herself. The stubble on his chin as if he hasn't shaved in several days, the thread pulled on the sleeve of his navy sweater, the ripple of his throat as he swallows, the glisten in his eyes that makes him look as though he's about to cry. And she can *smell* him, she thinks, catching his familiar scent as she stands only two feet from him.

She raises her arm, reaches out and dares to touch him. Whenever she's done this before, he's always vanished – one blink and he'd be gone. Jo sees her hand shaking as her fingers draw close to his sweater. She sees the rise and fall of his chest, hears him breathing.

Feels the warmth of him as she connects with his body.

She recoils suddenly, as if she's just had an electric shock.

'Will…' she whispers, not understanding. Then it dawns on her. *He's not come to see* you. *He's come to see Suzanne…*

Another shriek comes from upstairs, snapping her back to reality. Then Suzanne calling out for her to hurry up with the paramedics, that the baby's coming.

'Jo…' Will says, his voice deep and so very real. Nothing like the voice she's heard in her head so many times this last year.

'Is it really you?' She reaches out and touches him again. This time, he takes her hand, circling her fingers with his. He feels so warm. So alive.

'Yes,' he says. 'Can I come in?'

She's played out this situation a thousand times in her mind, their reunion different each time. None of her rehearsals were like this, though – not with her best friend giving birth upstairs.

'I… I don't know. I don't know what to say. I want to thump you and hug you… I don't know what to do. I don't know what to say…'

Stay strong, Jo. Deal with this later. Louise is your main priority…

'Where have you *been*?'

'I've missed you,' he says, just as Jo finds the strength to turn on her heels and go back upstairs. She doesn't want to hear it. She needs to help Louise. But then, with her back to him, she hesitates – part of her wanting him to follow her, part of her wanting him to leave again and never return.

She hates what he's done to her. Hates what he's done to Suzanne.

Keep your pride… she thinks, spinning round and putting up the latch on the door. 'Leave it open,' she orders. 'So the ambulance crew can get in.' Then she turns again and runs up the stairs, hearing his footsteps following behind.

'Jo, wait,' he calls out. 'I can explain… I *want* to explain. Just listen to me. Hear me out.'

But Jo keeps on going, reaching the top of the landing, hating how pathetic he sounds – begging, pleading, almost as if he's close to tears.

She stands at the top of the stairs, looking back down at him, freezing him in his tracks as he's halfway up. His expression pleads with her – his mouth bent into a shape that has words inside yet they don't know how to come out. He looks older, she thinks. Tired and unhappy.

He takes a few more steps up, making Jo want to push him back down. But when she hears the biggest cry yet from Louise, with Suzanne encouraging her, telling her the baby is coming, she turns and dashes into the bedroom, halting just inside the doorway.

Suzanne is kneeling down at the end of the bed, focusing on Louise. 'One last push now,' she says, her hands cradling a baby's head. Jo can't see much from where she's standing. She goes up to Louise, dropping to her knees beside her.

'Squeeze my hand,' she says, gripping onto her friend. She sees Louise's naked belly contract, clamping down on the baby's body as the final contraction comes.

'Push hard,' Suzanne says. 'That's it, that's it…'

'Well done, Lou, you're doing great,' Jo says, forcing herself not to look behind her. But she knows he's followed her in, senses him standing right behind her as he witnesses the birth.

How dare you, she wants to yell. *Get out and leave us all alone!* But she doesn't.

Instead, all she can do is stare at the blue-grey bundle in Suzanne's hands as she lays it on a towel. Louise strains to sit up, to staring at her baby.

'It's a little boy,' Suzanne says, looking up at Louise with tears in her eyes as if she doesn't know whether to laugh or cry. Jo feels the same. He's beautiful.

'Is he OK?' Louise asks, her voice hoarse. She sounds exhausted.

'Yes, yes, I think so,' Suzanne says, seeming to know exactly what to do. She gently rubs the baby with the soft towel, smiling as the first cries come – shrill-sounding and healthy, his clenched fist bumping against his mouth. 'He's got good lungs,' Suzanne adds, lifting him up a little for Louise to see. The baby instantly spreads all his limbs wide, the startle reflex kicking in. 'He'll pink up in a minute, I think,' she says. 'Once the oxygen gets flowing.'

Jo stares at the baby, frowning. Beautiful and wriggling, his dark eyes searching around, looking for his mother.

Suzanne lifts him carefully onto Louise's deflated belly, sliding him gently up to her breast so their bare skin is touching.

'Oh, I love him,' Louise whispers, stroking his little cheek. 'How precious are you, my little one.'

Jo can't take her eyes off the baby. But for quite different reasons to Louise, who's crooning over him, bonding, drinking in her new son.

She's aware that Suzanne is watching Louise intently – then sees her flick her gaze behind her, to where she knows Will is standing, frozen by the scene he has stumbled in on. And finally, she looks back at Louise again.

Slowly, Suzanne stands up, cupping her face with her slightly bloody hands, her eyes alight with confusion – as if she's about to have one of her episodes; as if there's been some kind of emotional eclipse from seeing the three of them together. The *four* of them together.

Jo stands up too, barely aware of what she's doing. She steps back from Louise – *needs* to get away from her before she does or says something she can't take back. She shakes her head, the words *No, no, no…* flooding her mind until they tumble out.

'No,' she says abruptly. 'Dear God, no. No, no, *no…*' She glares at Will, who's also transfixed by the infant, before staring at the baby again. Back and forth, back and forth – her eyes flashing between the two of them.

'That baby is not going to pink up, is he?' Jo whispers to them both. She shakes her head, her breath barely reaching her lungs, making her feel as though she's about to pass out. 'Louise?' she says, slightly louder.

There's no mistaking the baby has a black father. That it can't possibly be Archie's son.

But Louise is engrossed with her little boy, making noises at him, staring into his eyes, before being consumed by another contraction, her face crumpling as she tries to stifle a moan. The placenta is coming.

'You bastard,' Jo says quietly to Will so as not to startle the baby. 'He's yours, isn't he? *Isn't he?*' she yells, grabbing him by the collar.

CHAPTER FORTY-EIGHT

Jo doesn't fully understand what's going on – yet, somehow, she understands completely. The jigsaw pieces just need to settle, to take form in her mind. But she's had a glimpse of the full picture.

'Jo, wait,' Will says, backing away, holding his hands up like a shield. 'It's not what you think, OK?'

'I think it's exactly what I bloody think,' Jo hisses, locking eyes with Louise just as she moans again, pushing out the placenta. She wants to hit her, to scratch out her eyes and pull her hair, but she can't possibly – not with a baby in her arms. Not when she's vulnerable from childbirth. She hates her for what she's done – Will has been gone nearly a whole year, after all. Which means... Jo doesn't need to count the months to know that Louise has obviously been with him since he went missing. She's known where he's been all this time, yet watched her go through the agony of not knowing what has happened to her husband. It couldn't be anyone else.

'You complete shits,' she says to Will in a voice far more controlled than is warranted. 'The pair of you. This is *your* baby, isn't it? You abandoned me and you've been seeing Louise all this time, haven't you?'

Will looks at Louise, their eyes meeting for the briefest of moments before Louise turns back to the little boy, helping him latch onto her breast. He's the centre of her universe now. Then Will gazes at the baby, a longing look in his eyes, as if he wants nothing more than to be by her side, holding them both, keeping them safe. A little family of three.

Jo wants to throw up.

Everything I've ever loved or wanted in life is all here, in this room. And yet none of it can ever be mine…

She stands still for what seems like forever, the last year of her life replaying in fast forward.

'Maybe I should tell Suzanne what you did, Will?' she says, reality sinking in. Though she's unsure of Suzanne's involvement with Will now. Was he stringing both of them along? 'Would that help you answer my question?'

Will's expression remains blank and he says nothing. He's emotionless, as if he has no feelings for her, or anyone else, whatsoever.

It's as if she never even knew him.

Then, quite calmly, Will goes to Louise, bends down and kisses her on the head, then does the same to the baby. He looks at them for a moment before turning on his heels and walking out of the bedroom.

Jo follows him.

'Don't you bloody walk out on me again without explanation, Will Carter,' she calls after him. His pace kicks up to a run as he heads down the stairs. She sees him stumble, catching the bannister rail, not looking back. 'You don't get off that lightly. You don't get to walk out on me twice.'

She follows, also running to keep up with him.

'Will, get back here and explain to me what the *hell* has been going on. Louise has just given birth to your baby, hasn't she?' Jo's voice breaks as the tears come. She can hardly believe she's hearing those words coming out of her mouth. 'At least have the decency to tell me the truth. How long has it been going on? Will, wait. Come back. Talk to me.'

He's at the open front door now, about to head out into the darkness. But he stops, turns, making Jo freeze in her tracks in the hallway. He stares right at her, the cold look still set deep in his eyes.

'It just happened, Jo. One of those things. We were spending a lot of time with Louise and Archie as couples and… and I guess Louise was just there when you weren't. And she felt the same about me. And she… she wasn't obsessed like you.'

'Weren't *there*?' Jo says, shaking her head. 'But I was always there, Will.'

'No, Jo. You weren't. It was as though you were constantly living in the future and the only thing in your line of sight was a baby. I may as well not have existed. You were looking so far ahead that you forgot to see me. You forgot to see *us*.'

Jo feels as though he's kicked her in the teeth. She reels, taking in what he just said.

'So you're saying I drove you into Louise's arms, that it's *my* fault?' She shakes her head.

'Kind of, yes,' Will says, shrugging. 'Though it's not quite that simple.' Then a look on his face that Jo doesn't recognise. 'I need to go. I need to think. I'm sorry, Jo.'

Jo hears Louise call from upstairs, begging him not to leave, telling him to come up to her and his baby.

'Sorry?' Jo says, taking a step closer to him. 'You're sorry? And that's *it*? Well, guess what? I'm sorry too, Will. Sorry that I ever met you. Sorry that I gave you the best years of my life in the hope we would have a family together, and a long and happy marriage.' She takes a deep breath, letting out a half-laugh. 'And sorry that you're now trying to make it my fault that you and my best friend have been complete shits to me for Christ knows how long.

'I've been doing everything in my power to find you this last year, not knowing if you were dead or alive. In fact, it was only my hope of finding you alive that kept me going, making you so real in my head that it actually felt like you'd never even gone. I've seen you everywhere, Will. At work, at home when

I'm cooking, when I'm in bed, hell – even when I'm using the bathroom. You'd appear to me and I'd talk to you. We'd have conversations about the past, the future. Your presence kept me going through the darkest times.' She shakes her head, laughs at her own stupidity. 'But all this time you were fine, screwing Louise. And her pretending to support me is the biggest betrayal of all.' She takes a step closer. 'And to think, the moment I told you to go, that I wanted you gone from my head forever, that I'd had enough, that's when you actually step back into my life for real. But it wasn't even because of me, rather because you were concerned about Louise.'

Jo pauses, trying to get stuff straight in her head. It doesn't quite all add up.

'Who is Suzanne to you? I think it's about time I went to the police and told them what you—'

'Shut it, Jo. You don't know what you're talking about. As ever, you're living in your head, making things real that aren't. Seeing what you want to see.'

Jo can't contain her anger any longer and takes a swipe at him, all the rage and sadness and hurt and hope and fear bubbling out of her as she breaks down in tears. 'I hate you, and I hate what you've done to me. I wish I'd never met you…' She thumps at his chest with her fists but he dodges out of the way, looking at her as though she's gone mad.

He runs out of the door and into the night, but Jo isn't giving up. She needs to get it all out so she charges after him, stumbling and losing her balance as she hurtles across the gravel drive towards the road. But she's losing ground as he disappears out into the darkness, onto the lane, knowing he's slipping away from her again before she's had her say.

And then the terrible noise.

She isn't sure what she hears first – the sound of the siren as the ambulance speeds around the sharp bend just outside the drive.

Or the sound of screeching brakes, the brief yell followed by the loud thud.

Then silence.

Just the ominous tick-tick of flashing blue lights.

Followed by shouting, by cursing. The sound of terror in her own head.

It seems as though she doesn't have control over her limbs, that she's sinking neck-deep in the gravel, but somehow Jo runs to the road, forces herself to look at the ambulance, squinting at the flashing blue strobe as she sees how the vehicle has come to a sudden stop, slewed diagonally across the lane.

Will is lying on the road in front of it. His legs crushed. Blood pouring from his head. He stares, open-eyed, at the night sky.

Jo wants to scream but it won't come out. Instead, she feels it burn up her gullet, before she doubles up and vomits into the gutter, her eyes refusing to let go of the mess that barely resembles her husband lying on the road.

The paramedics gather around him, furiously checking him over, loosening his clothing, placing an oxygen mask over his face, while the other pumps his heart with his clamped hands.

Jo can't stop staring, sick dribbling from her mouth as her stomach keeps convulsing. She slumps down onto the kerb, too exhausted to even cry.

The paramedics look at each other, frowning, one with his fingers set firm beneath Will's jaw. He shakes his head and they both start up with the resuscitation again but the same thing happens. A moment later and they're shocking him with paddles placed on his chest, making him look for a split second as if he's sparked back to life.

But after several attempts one of the paramedics glances at his watch and covers Will's head and chest with a blanket. They both stand up, scuffing at the ground, calling on their radios as one goes for a clipboard from the cab.

Jo manages to stand too, to walk over to them from where she's been watching. They had no idea she was there. 'Is he…?' she hears herself asking, as if it's someone else. 'Is he dead?'

'I… I'm afraid so,' the man says, his face ashen. 'We were on a call-out and… and Christ, the bend came out of nowhere, caught us out at the speed we were going, but… but he came out of nowhere too, and then… There was no chance for us to stop. Jesus Christ,' he says, clutching his head before regaining his composure. 'We've called for backup, but we're on an emergency call-out. Are you local? Do you know where Hawthorn Lodge is?'

It's all Jo can do to point up the driveway of Suzanne's house. Her arm shakes. 'For the baby?' she says, her voice also shaking.

Dead. Will is *dead*.

The paramedic nods.

'She's had the baby,' she adds, unable to take her eyes off Will's body on the road. He suddenly seems so small. 'They're both doing fine.'

The paramedic nods again, waiting with the ambulance and Will's body for the backup to arrive, while the other one gathers up various bits of equipment and marches off up the drive.

'He's… he's my husband,' Jo hears herself saying weakly, pointing to Will. 'I thought he was dead before, and now… now I know he really is.' She lets out a hysterical laugh. 'And he's never coming back.' She clutches her head, staggering back to sit down on the front wall of the house, dizzy from shock.

It seems like hours – Jo and the paramedic waiting side by side on the wall, him wrapping a blanket around her because she can't stop shaking – though in reality it's only about ten minutes until a police car arrives, its lights flashing in the night. It's shortly followed by another ambulance, but a car this time. A fine drizzle is falling, making Jo blink more than she needs, making her unsure if the wetness on her face is because she's crying or from the rain.

The paramedic goes over to the police officer, leaving Jo on the wall, staring at the ground, only managing brief looks at Will and the pool of blood he's lying in now as the realisation sinks in.

He's gone, gone forever...

She hears the crackle of radios, calm voices talking, the paramedic explaining what happened. Then someone approaches her, stands over her for a second before sitting down.

'Jo,' says a familiar voice. When she looks up, Simon is sitting on the wall beside her, his hand on her arm. He's wearing full uniform. 'I was just on my way home when I got the emergency call. How are you? This man is your...' he trails off, unable to find the right word.

'This is Will, Simon. My husband. I... I can't even...' She breaks down then, the tears coming hot and fast. She feels Simon's arm around her, cradling her. 'He's... he's gone. I had him back for such a short time, and... and Louise had a baby and Suzanne locked us in the bedroom but then she came and helped and then the baby is black and clearly Will's, because Louise's husband is white and I just don't understand. My best friend has been lying to me for the last year, and a long while before that, I imagine, and... Oh God, I can't stand it.'

More tears, the rain soaking through the blanket, chilling her to the core.

'Let's get you inside,' Simon says calmly, as Jo hiccups through the sobs, trying to fight them back.

She nods, allowing him to help her stand and lead her into the house. There'll be statements to be made – and not just about what she witnessed tonight. It's time to tell the police everything. Time to confess what Will did.

Jo glances back over her shoulder at the scene as another police car arrives, the officer talking to the paramedic as the area is cordoned off with yellow tape. She pauses, bringing Simon to a halt too.

Will? she says, seeing him standing beside his own body, not a drop of blood on him.

I never meant to hurt you, Jo-jo… he replies, a blank, unfamiliar look on his face. In fact, she doesn't recognise anything about him any more.

But you did *mean to hurt Suzanne, didn't you?*

Will looks away, his shoulders dropping forward.

Didn't you? Jo demands, the voice in her head choked and snotty.

Jo feels a gentle hand on her arm. 'Come on, Jo, you're in shock. Let's get you inside.' Simon guides her up the drive, Jo's gaze still fixed on where Will is standing. But, as she gets further away, he gives her one last glance before shaking his head, turning and walking off in the opposite direction, disappearing into the darkness.

CHAPTER FORTY-NINE

Five Weeks Later

Jo pulls back her hair in her hand, securing a band around it – her smile broad as she heads down onto the expanse of beach, Spangle racing ahead. His barks are carried away on the warm breeze. She's come in only a T-shirt and jeans, her feet in flip-flops, which she'll kick off when they get down to the shore.

'Come on, you,' she calls back over her shoulder. Simon runs, catching up with her as he pulls his sweater off over his head.

'Yes, ma'am,' he says, looping his arm through hers as they continue walking.

'I'm so glad you were able to take today off,' she says.

'Shame I can't take all the days off,' he says, winking. 'I enjoy spending my time with you. While I can,' he adds.

'I never saw this coming, you know.' For the first time in what seems like ages, Jo laughs. Of course, it feels unnatural, as if she shouldn't, but she's put her life on hold for far too long not to at least enjoy simple moments like this. A walk on the beach with Spangle and Simon – the two males who have made the biggest impression on her life lately. 'And I never expected to stay on here. Just so you know.'

Jo knows that much of her grieving has already been done this last year – even if it was without knowing the full facts. All that time, she'd hung onto a shred of hope that Will would return. Now, a fresh round of devastation and grief has been triggered by his death – denial, disbelief, anger – made all the more painful in light of the betrayal. And it had been going on right under her nose. Hope had been her drug for so long; kept her going. These last few weeks, when she wakes up in the morning – those few blissful moments of numbness before her mind remembers, before it all comes flooding back – is when she wishes she *didn't* know he was dead. That she still had that hope. She's tried to explain to Simon that the not knowing where Will was now somehow seems preferable by comparison, even though she'd have once sworn the opposite.

'You're doing Suzanne a massive favour by staying on and house-sitting for a couple of months,' Simon tells her.

'It's a favour for me, too,' Jo adds. 'I couldn't go back home. Not yet.'

'I know. And I'm enjoying you being here too,' he adds, glancing at her as they walk on.

Jo smiles up at him. 'Mum's been at my place again to sort a few things, send some more stuff down that I'll need. And she's been amazing with…' Jo trails off. It doesn't feel right to divulge too much yet about her financial situation, that her parents were only too happy to support her through a sabbatical from Sew Perfect. Margot was completely understanding, even when Jo couldn't bring herself to divulge too much about what had happened. They'd been discussing taking on another apprentice from Beth's college anyway, so it seemed the ideal time to do that. Work was steady and Jo was still a partner in the business, promising to manage the online marketing side of things until she came home, work on some designs, too. Stepping straight back into real life after what she'd been through was the last thing she wanted. She didn't think she could do it. Not yet. Her mother and father had come down to the South Coast several days after Will died, rallying round and taking care of practical issues – as well as helping financially.

'It's a loan, Dad,' she'd said, staring at the amount received on her banking app. 'I insist.'

'Nonsense,' her mother had chipped in. 'Our girl is getting back on her feet. I've always told you that I'd be here for you, that we'd support you if...' Elizabeth had thought better of airing her thoughts, had actually managed to bite her tongue on several occasions. And for that, Jo was grateful.

'Now Will's death is official...' Jo's eyes had stung with tears, as they did at every mention of his name. 'Now it's official, his insurance policy will pay out. I'll be able to pay you back.'

'Race you,' Jo hears, snapping back to the present.

'What? Wait... that's not fair!' She squeals, kicking off her flip-flops after a few paces of trying to run in them, charging after Simon who's already nearly down by the shoreline, a stick in his hand that he lobs high in the air for Spangle. Jo catches up beside him, breathless and laughing, splashing through the foamy breakers as the tide creeps up the ridged sand. 'Crazy man,' she says, pulling on his T-shirt sleeve.

She stares up at him – and he gazes down at her. Their lips draw close for a kiss, each of them aware of Spangle yapping nearby as he chases the stick.

Jo suddenly squeals again, jumping backwards, her face flushed as she laughs. 'I'm soaked,' she says, looking down at her wet jeans. Simon is the same.

'We'll just have to strip off when we get back, then, won't we?' he says, grabbing hold of her again as they carry on walking, his arm slung around her waist.

It's nearly an hour later, as they turn to head back towards the car park, Simon whistling for an exhausted Spangle to follow them, when Jo stops dead in her tracks. Her skin prickles with goosebumps, her eyes growing wide and blinking furiously, trying to focus, trying to make what she saw go away.

'You OK?' Simon asks, urging Jo to veer inland a little as the tide creeps up on them again.

Jo's mouth opens though nothing comes out as she forces herself to see only the sand rising up to the dune, the sprouts of marram grass dotted about like a green fringe on the skyline. A couple of other dog walkers, two women, are the only other people in sight. She swears that's the case. Blinks again just to make sure.

'Yeah, yeah, I'm fine thanks. Just thought I saw… something,' she says, smiling. 'But I was mistaken. *Very* much mistaken,' she adds, convincing herself there's nothing but the sky and the sand stretching before her.

'Suzanne,' Jo says, answering her phone later. The animals are settled and the house is clean. She even managed to cut the grass today, though she was tired from the long walk. 'How's it going?'

'Surely I should be asking you the same question?'

If Jo could see Suzanne's face, she knows she would see a twinkle in her eye. Even though she's only been at the clinic a few weeks, the change in her mood and demeanour is noticeable. And Suzanne has said as much; that the few sessions she's had of EMDR therapy have already made a difference to her mood, her PTSD.

'All is well here, so fear not. Spangle and Bonnie are fine. To be honest, I don't know what I'd do without them right now.' Jo laughs. 'The painter came to do the front windows the other day. They look great. And I've forwarded some quotes for the plumbing jobs you want doing.'

'Thanks, Jo. I really appreciate it. Though you know that's not what I meant.'

Jo makes a noise down the phone. It's as much as she can manage right now to show how she feels. 'Honestly, everything's good,' she says, wanting to add 'all things considered'. Since Suzanne asked her to stay on and house-sit for several months, she's naturally become closer to Simon. 'I'm just taking things slowly – in all respects. It's all too… all too raw,' she says, knowing she'll understand. It's almost as if Suzanne has stepped into the shoes that Louise left behind when she had her baby, when Suzanne's mind flooded with memories that changed everything. The three of them in the room together. Bringing it all back. 'But it's good to spend more time with Simon,' Jo adds, hearing a little sound of approval from Suzanne.

The night that Will was killed, Simon had walked her back up to the house, made her sweet tea and calmed her down. Jo's lasting memory was of shaking – not simply her hands, arms and legs quivering, rather the very core of her trembling, as though her soul had been rocked.

The truth was, it had.

And all she could hear at the time was the baby upstairs crying – as if its screams were inside her head, taunting her, getting louder and louder.

The baby that should have been hers and Will's.

'OK, Jo,' Simon had said in the kitchen. 'I want you to tell me exactly what happened. I'll need to build a picture of what's gone on here, and you're a big part of that. You're a key witness.'

Witness, Jo had thought, wondering how much of her life she'd actually witnessed lately or, as it currently felt, how much of it had been outside of her control, passing her by, how much she'd been blind to. She was still so confused.

'Will,' she began. 'He went missing. My lovely husband. Gone. Can you imagine that?' She'd drunk some tea then, taken time to compress all her feelings into a knot of despair, something no one could unpick. She sat staring blankly across the room. 'But before that everything had already gone bad, worse than you can imagine, except neither of us wanted to admit it and still there was no baby, and then he disappeared and... and... and then I needed a holiday and Louise wasn't well and I felt like such a bad friend and... I've not seen him in nearly a year, and now he's dead.'

Through her teary eyes as she sobbed, she saw how confused Simon looked, but he allowed her to spew it out, to release what was clogged up in her head. Begin to make sense of it. He didn't interrupt, waiting patiently for her, even though none of it was relevant to what had just happened – when Will had run out into the road as the ambulance came tearing around the blind bend. He needed to take a statement.

As Jo continued, she barely managed a few words about Louise before covering her face again, holding back the rage, leaving Simon to carve it out of her, piece by piece. A jumbled mess of emotions and facts that made no sense.

'It's so ironic,' Jo remembers saying, wondering if the sweet tea he'd made for her contained whiskey. She felt herself relaxing slightly, loosening, as if her mind, thoughts and actions were betraying her. As though she was free-falling. 'It's so ironic that he was run over. After everything.'

She managed to bite her tongue then, not reveal anything to Simon about the hit and run. She'd done enough of that the other night. But it came out the next morning when she was alone with Suzanne, just as Jo was about to leave to go home. Her belongings were already packed up. Her coat was on.

'It's true,' Suzanne had said yet again, sitting quietly on the sofa as Jo stood in the doorway. She seemed different today – calmer, the worry lines on her face more relaxed. At peace with herself, Jo had thought. 'I *do* know you.'

After she'd given her statement last night, after all the officers had gone, Jo went next door and curled up on Simon's sofa, not sleeping, simply staring at the ceiling unable to get the image of

Will lying dead on the road out of her mind. Occasionally, Simon had checked in on her, brought her a glass of water, tea, whatever she wanted. She was waiting for it to get light before she faced the long drive home, even though she was dreading going back, seeing Will's belongings and all the reminders of their life together in an entirely different light.

'I *know* you,' Suzanne said again, staring at her.

The previous night, a police liaison officer had stayed with them for several hours after statements had been made, after Louise had been taken away to hospital with her baby, Jo pinning herself back against the hallway wall, saying nothing as she was taken out in a wheelchair by the paramedics, her baby swaddled in her arms. And Louise hadn't looked up or said anything to Jo as she'd passed. Kept her eyes down. She'd not heard from her since.

'And I know I keep saying it,' Suzanne continued. 'But I'm really sure of that now. It's all so clear. As though my brain has been in a permanent eclipse, but now that's passed and the light has come back.'

'And I know you too,' Jo had replied quietly, not feeling real. She wanted to stall the truth coming out, freeze things as they stood, process the pain of the last twenty-four hours alone, in private. She thought, in time, she might just be able to cope with everything. Not ever get over it, but at least cope. Learning the details about Suzanne and Will's relationship, on top of finding out about Will and Louise – that he must have been having *two* affairs – well, she wasn't certain she could deal with that as well. Not yet.

'I recognise you from a party,' Jo found herself saying. She wanted Suzanne to know her side, but didn't want the truth in return. 'It was after the play you were in with Will last year, and I was there.' She cleared her throat. 'Though you still had your thick white make-up and wig on so until I saw you in the programme here, I didn't realise it was you.' She remembers how the queen,

Suzanne, had shunned her that night, turned her back on her at the party, and also how Will had barely acknowledged her presence. What a fool she'd been. How they must have been laughing at her.

'I know your friend, Louise, too,' Suzanne had continued, as if she'd not even heard Jo. As if, by stating these things, she was simply putting her own mind in order, wanting to clear her own conscience. 'And, of course, I know your *husband*…' She'd taken a deep breath then, whereas Jo had held hers, bracing herself in the doorway.

'I have his pictures everywhere, as you've seen. After the accident, after I'd lost certain memories surrounding that time, I knew Will meant something to me, but I had no idea what. So I printed out all the pictures I could find of him online in the hope they'd trigger memories if I left them around the house. But all it did was make me have these weird turns, these *episodes*. I had the first one when he came to visit me in hospital.'

CHAPTER FIFTY

'Will came to *see* you in hospital...?' Jo asked, incredulous. She had no idea how he'd found the time to conduct not one but *two* affairs, let alone take the risk of visiting Suzanne after the hit and run. It was going back to the scene of the crime. What was he *thinking*? Why hadn't he mentioned this?

'Yes, he visited me after the accident to see how I was,' Suzanne said. 'Quite a few of the theatre company came to wish me well, though none had the same effect on me as Will. As soon as I set eyes on him, I was... I was flooded with strange feelings, flashbacks, shards of terrifying memories. And I didn't remember him at all, you see, whereas I did all the others. I felt quite bad that he had to tell me his name, explain how we knew each other, especially when he said we'd worked together recently.' Suzanne paused, took a deep breath. 'But do you want to know the very first thing he said to me, before he even knew I had amnesia?'

Jo gave a tentative nod.

'He said, "Suzanne, I beg you, please don't tell my wife. *Please*, I'll do anything". I remember it all so clearly now.'

'*What?*' Jo said, walking slowly to the sofa. She sat down next to Suzanne. 'You mean, he was begging you not to tell me about your affair with him, when you were in hospital?'

Suzanne shook her head, frowning. 'What affair? You think... you think Will and I were having an *affair?*'

'Well, yes. It's obvious.' Jo folded her arms, not quite able to believe how calm she was being with Suzanne. She wanted to scratch her eyes out but didn't have the energy.

'No, no, *no*... you've got that completely wrong, Jo. Hand on heart, there was nothing between me and your husband. I'm one hundred per cent certain of that.' She paused, locking eyes with Jo, waiting for her to process the information. 'That's not to say he didn't give me the opportunity, because he did. He had a bit of a reputation, you see. And he didn't like being turned down, either. No, Will was begging me not to tell you about him and *Louise*, though I had no idea that's what he meant when I was in hospital. I didn't remember what I knew about them. As soon as I explained that I'd got amnesia – dissociative amnesia around a certain time, to be precise – then Will backtracked, kept quiet.

'He asked me a few questions about my accident, what had happened, who had done such a thing to me. When I explained it was a hit and run, that I had no idea who had been driving the car, he... well, I remember how his shoulders dropped, how he was almost trying to suppress a smile. After he'd gone, I wrote down his name, how we knew each other and later made a point of finding him online.

'He set something off inside me during that visit, and I wanted to know what it was. I suspected it was a key to something, yet I didn't know what. When I came home, I printed out the photos I'd found and, whenever I looked at them, I'd have another of my episodes, although they waned as time went on. As if I was desensitising myself to him. And then, when I saw you on Simon's phone, when we face-timed and... and exactly the same thing happened, I knew I had to come home to meet you, to find out who you were. I felt it was my only chance of knowing the truth, of getting my mind back.'

Jo remained silent, taking it in, shuffling and reshuffling the jigsaw pieces in her own mind, still not seeing the full picture.

There was so much she wanted to say, but she couldn't find it in herself to even form a sentence.

'I've sat here all night, you know, Jo, mulling things over. Since I saw you, Will and your friend, Louise, all in the same room together, well, it did something to me. It was the moment that the fog began to lift, as if my brain had suddenly allowed me access to memories that it had locked away. It feels as if I've been glued back together. And, when I followed the paramedics out of the house last night, when they were taking Louise to hospital, that's when I saw the front of your car. You'd had it parked a different way round before. And I *knew*. I knew everything… all of it filtering back throughout the night, as if my mind was a cinema screen playing out missing time.' Suzanne raises her hand, gesturing. 'My consultant warned me that could happen, that a certain thread might suddenly be pulled that untied the knot of memories. Releasing everything. Putting me back to how I was. The trauma of the accident, the emotion of everything surrounding it – I'd blocked it all out. Bundled it all up together and packed it away. My brain trying to protect me but getting it wrong in the process. That's the only way I can describe it.'

'Oh my *God*,' Jo said, dipping her head forward. She had so many questions, she didn't know where to begin. 'How did you know that Will and Louise were… having an affair?' She can hardly bring herself to say the words.

Suzanne looked down at the floor, where Spangle was lying in front of the hearth, asleep. Bonnie was curled up on the sofa beside her. She rested a hand gently on her back. 'I walked in on them, Jo. They were alone in Will's dressing room.'

Jo closed her eyes, turned away for a moment. She wanted details – *all* the details – but then she didn't want to know anything at all.

'The first time was during the Shakespeare run, when I played the queen opposite him. I'd had my suspicions that he was seeing someone for a while, and at first I thought the woman who kept visiting and calling must have been you, his wife. But rumours were going around. I saw someone a couple of times, outside the stage door, picking him up after rehearsals, that kind of thing. An attractive woman. And then when I went into his dressing room during the interval in the last show. He was... they were...'

Jo held up her hand, stopping Suzanne. She could imagine well enough what they were doing, without hearing it word for word. And it explained why Louise had been gone so long during the interval that night, telling her there was a long queue for the toilet.

'They both looked round and saw me, of course,' Suzanne went on. 'I literally had to force myself to move, couldn't believe what I was seeing. And in the *interval*, can you believe? By this time, I knew the woman wasn't you, his wife. I'd already asked around and, at the after-show party, I saw her there with you and the penny dropped. She was so *brazen* about it, Jo, and when she introduced herself, told me that she was your best friend... honestly, I was speechless. I didn't know what to do. I felt so bad, I couldn't even bring myself to talk to you.'

'I'm so sorry you had to witness all that, Suzanne,' Jo said. 'That you became caught up in it all.'

'After you'd left the party, Will had words with me. He went from begging to angry and everything in between. He demanded that I shouldn't tell you, that it would kill you. He told me that you were pregnant and unstable – which clearly wasn't true – and that you'd likely have a miscarriage from the shock. Then he said you wouldn't believe me anyway, that he would just deny it and tell you that I'd made a pass at him and I was annoyed for being rejected. He was so full of himself, and tried every trick in the book. He was very convincing and I almost believed he was right, that maybe I *had* hit on him, that it *was* all my fault.' Suzanne laughed incredulously, shook her head. 'He was a master. Thing is, Jo, I was really hurting at the time. I'd been betrayed by a man who I thought really loved me. But it turned out I was wrong – he didn't love me at all. It cut me up hard. I couldn't sit back and watch another woman go through the same.'

'Bill?' Jo asked.

'Yes, yes, that was Bill.' She looks away for a second, closes her eyes and juts her chin forward. 'So I was in no mind or mood to cover up for some other cheating man at that point. Quite simply, I told him you deserved to know the truth about him *and* your so-called best friend so you could make your own decision whether to kick him out or not. And if he didn't confess to you himself, *I'd* tell you.'

'Oh, Suzanne,' Jo whispered, wondering how Will had managed to keep all this from her. At that moment, her mind was too raw, too fragmented to process all the information, but she knew in time that she would piece it all back together, make sense of Will's moods that she'd accommodated, put up with, cajoled him through, believing it was work making him depressed, or the pressure of them trying to conceive that was stressing him out.

'I meant business, Jo. We women need to stand up for each other, not stab each other in the back. Bill's wife had the good sense to contact me when she found out what he was up to. It wasn't easy to hear, but I'm glad she did. I'd have forever been the "other woman" otherwise, and that's simply not me.'

'You've been through so much,' Jo said quietly. 'We both have.'

Suzanne nodded and the two women sat in silence for a while, each of them processing their own side of the story, matching everything up.

'So you know it was Will who—'

'Who hit me in the car? Yes, I realise that now. But only because of you.'

'Because of *me*?'

'I heard the car coming behind me,' Suzanne says, her eyes momentarily getting that look in them again – something between fear and rage. 'It was dark but I sensed it was coming fast, could hear the engine roaring. I stepped onto the verge to get out of the way, turning round at the last minute to let it pass. And that's when I saw it was heading straight at me – so close, but by then it was too late to get out of the way. And your face, asleep in the passenger seat, was the last thing I saw before the car hit me.'

'Oh Suzanne, how dreadful. How utterly...' Jo shook her head. She barely had the words. 'I'm so very sorry. But what were you... what were you doing there? We were at Annabel's party.'

'On my way to see you, of course. I wanted to tell you the truth. I knew Will would be at the party that night and I'd hoped you would be, too. But when I saw him there, only very briefly, he told me you hadn't come. That you weren't well. I'd already found out where you lived, so I decided to get in my car and tell you in person. I hadn't banked on him leaving the party so soon. I didn't want to park right outside your house in case someone saw me. So I found a gateway a little way out and decided to walk the last bit. It wasn't too far and it somehow felt safer.' Suzanne thinks a moment. 'So you *were* there? At the party?'

Jo nodded. 'But not for long. And it explains why Will wasn't keen for me to come in the first place. And also why he suddenly insisted that we leave, almost dragging me out. He knew you were on your way to tell me and, when he saw you on the roadside he purposefully drove into you, to stop you. Suzanne, Will tried to *kill* you.'

'I know, you're right,' she said, nodding, her eyes staring at the floor. 'He did. He veered off the road to hit me. And he risked your life, too.'

'Christ, I've been such a fool,' Jo said. 'And to think we were trying for a baby all that time when he and Louise were...' She shuddered, hating that Louise had got pregnant by him when she didn't. 'So it was you who mentioned this area to Will, about how a weekend away in Hastings would be good for a break?'

Suzanne nodded. 'Yes, yes, I did suggest it to him once. But that was before I knew anything about his affair. He was asking a few people for seaside recommendations.'

'I wouldn't have found you if you hadn't mentioned it,' Jo said. 'We'd been planning on coming down for a romantic weekend but never quite made it. Then, after he'd been missing nearly a year, I thought it would be a healing thing for me to do, to come here. So that's why I looked at house-sits in this area. Did you realise you'd left photos of Will on the mantelpiece when you took the room shots?'

Suzanne half laughs. 'No, I had no idea. I probably took them in a hurry. I'd not long had some decorating done and wanted to get some new shots up online to make it look appealing. I knew I'd be away a fair bit and wanted to secure sitters for these two.' She pats the animals again. 'Look, Jo, I was wondering…'

Jo raises her eyebrows as Suzanne tilts her head to one side. 'I know it's all been horrific, but… but is there any chance you'd consider staying on here a while longer? I want to go back to the clinic, give the EMDR therapy a proper go. Plus I've a couple of voice-over jobs to do in London and one in Edinburgh. And I'd like to take a holiday, too. Visit my cousin in the States. I could be away for a couple of months at least.'

Jo didn't need to think for long. The words fell out of her mouth. 'Yes, yes, I'd like that,' she said, knowing the last place she wanted to go right now was home.

CHAPTER FIFTY-ONE

Seven Weeks Later

'Why is it always raining at funerals?' I ask Simon. We're sitting in the crematorium car park, watching through the drizzle as a couple of other vehicles arrive. I can't be sure they're not for another service – I'd not bothered telling anyone about Will's cremation in person or, indeed, arranged anything other than the few words the vicar would read out. I'd put a simple notice in a couple of papers local to where we'd lived, and had chosen a generic funeral poem from a quick search online. There would be no hymns, no readings by grieving relatives, no stories of a life well lived, and I'd ordered the cheapest wooden coffin available with no embellishments or flowers. And certainly no memorial plaque. I'd instructed the funeral parlour to scatter the ashes in the garden of remembrance.

'I'd prefer the garden of forgetfulness,' I'd said to Simon after hanging up from making arrangements a couple of weeks earlier, after his body had been released. Mum had already been into the house and got rid of all Will's belongings. Either taken them to charity shops or the local recycling centre.

'We'd better get in,' Simon says.

'Thanks for being with me,' I say, reaching out and taking his hand. 'I couldn't have faced the long drive up here alone. Nor the few who'll be here. His parents are dead and he's an only child.'

'You mean your mum and dad?'

'Them, but a couple of others too. Mum's actually been quite helpful and understanding these past weeks, but it's only because she's been proved right. Our relationship is improving, though. I'd like to think that in time, it will be stronger.'

'We'll get in and then we'll get out. You don't have to speak to anyone. Hell, if you like, we can leave now. There's no need for you to even be here.'

'I know, and you're right. But it feels like some kind of closure for me. As if I'm finally signing off and checking out.'

'I get that. Come on, then,' he says, unfastening his seat belt and getting out. I do the same. It's as we're just stepping inside the low, brick-built eighties building that I become aware of another car pulling into the car park, the hiss of tyres on the wet tarmac. I've already spotted my parents, a couple of Will's cousins, one or two colleagues from school, but no one else. Between us, we'll barely make up a single row of seats.

In the chapel, we sit down – not at the front, but a few rows back. Simon is wearing a dark suit, a plain black tie, and I'm wearing a grey dress that I made years ago. I take off the silk scarf I'd tied around my neck when we left East Wincombe early this morning. Despite the rain, it's warm inside, the overhead heaters making me perspire. I notice Simon loosen his collar.

And then Will is carried in, four of the funeral directors' men taking the place of any fond relatives. I look down, tune out of whatever the vicar recites, picking at my nails, wishing it would all hurry up and be over.

'That wasn't so bad, was it?' Simon says as we walk back to the car. 'As these things go.'

I look up at him, giving him one of my stern stares that he says he's grown so fond of over the last few weeks; usually we end up laughing about it. But not today. He pulls me close, his arm around my waist. Somehow, I've managed to fight back the tears.

'I meant meeting your parents,' he continues. 'They seem OK, though your mother is maybe a little intense.'

'That's because Mum *is* intense. And she clearly likes you,' I say. 'Especially when you told her you're a chief inspector.'

'Not because of my good looks, charm and wit, then?' he says. 'Come on, I'll buy you a coffee. Or something stronger. You look as though you could use something before we head back.'

'Sure, thanks—'

And that's when I see her. I stop, frozen in my tracks.

Louise is standing beside the car that pulled in earlier, the one I spotted before the service.

I take hold of Simon's arm, putting my head down as we continue walking to his car. 'Let's get out of here,' I whisper, breaking into a semi-run.

'Jo, wait,' I hear Louise call out.

I freeze again, squeezing Simon's arm. 'What the hell is *she* doing here?'

'What do you want to do?' Simon asks.

'I… I don't know,' I say, glancing up at him. I look over and see Louise's wan face. She's lost weight. Looks pale, gaunt and unkempt. Nothing like the vibrant, successful friend I thought I knew. 'Let's just go. I've nothing to say to her.'

I carry on towards Simon's estate car, hearing footsteps behind me, following us, getting closer.

'Please, Jo. I need to talk to you. Just for a moment. Will you listen?' Her voice is getting louder, nearer. When we reach Simon's car, I spin round.

'What the hell do you want?' I snap, scowling, my eyes glaring. 'What have you possibly got to say to me that—' I stop, speechless when I see Louise standing there, holding a baby carrier. With a baby in it.

Will's baby.

And then she's holding him out to me, both hands taking his weight, her arms trembling with the strain.

'What are you *doing*?' I whisper, sidling closer to Simon, looking up at him again. He's about to speak, but Louise beats him to it.

'I'm going to the police, Jo. I can't live like this any longer.'

'What?' I say, my eyes flicking from the baby back to Louise.

'I can't live a lie any more. It's destroying me, but worst of all, it's destroying Jack. I'm not the mother he needs.'

Jack… I think. *Will's middle name. William Jack Michael Carter…*

I stare at the baby, watching his roving eyes, his constantly mobile face and changing expression. He's grown these last few weeks, as if he's sucked the life from his mother and, while he is thriving, looking so very like Will, I see that his mother is not. She's a husk, a shell. Less than ten per cent of the woman I remember.

'Please, take him,' Louise says, her voice thin and brittle – like the rest of her. She steps closer, holding out the baby carrier.

'So, wait, what? You, my so-called best friend, who stole my husband away to God knows where, had his baby, lied constantly to me for what, at least two years, and was the cause of his death… now you want me to look after the baby I helped you give birth to when I didn't know what a back-stabbing bitch you are?'

'Jo, wait, it's not like that. I mean, yes, it is. It's exactly like that, but…' She bends down, putting the baby carrier on the tarmac between us, holding her back and wincing as she hitches up her grubby tracksuit pants. She sweeps her hair off her face and I notice the roots showing through, how her nails are chipped and broken.

'Indulge me, then, Louise. Tell me what it is like. You have exactly one minute before I'm leaving.' My arm tightens around Simon's.

'Firstly, I know you won't believe me, but I'm sorry. It... it was wrong. So *very* wrong how things turned out, and I know that, but it just happened. And once it started, it didn't feel as though there was a way back—'

I raise my hand. 'Stop. I don't want to hear that. Fifty seconds left.'

'Will was struggling, emotionally, and he turned to me for support, for advice. I'm a lawyer after all, and a family friend. He trusted me.'

I wince at the word *family*.

'I didn't know details to start with, but I offered him a... a shoulder to cry on as well as, eventually, a place to stay.'

'A place to stay?'

'My parents' cottage. It's where he's been all this time.'

'But I thought they were letting it out?'

Louise shakes her head. 'I visited him there whenever I could. Took him things. He'd left with nothing, after all. Just walked out of his job. And he fully planned on coming home after a couple of days. He just needed some time out, he said. To clear his head. To think. And eventually he told me why he was in such a state – or rather I had to prise it out of him, after all the nightmares.' Louise hangs her head. 'I'd stopped over at the cottage for a few nights, telling Archie I was away on business. Will was in a terrible state. He couldn't sleep, tossing and turning, talking to himself. Then, when I asked him, *begged* him to tell me what was wrong, he told me what had happened... He confessed to everything about the accident. About him running over a woman. He needed to get it out, off his chest.

'At first, I thought he just wanted me to help him legally, to get advice. But by then, our emotions had got in the way. Or rather, *my* emotions had got in the way. I was falling in love with him, Jo. He gave me things Archie couldn't—'

'Oh please, spare me the fucking violins,' I say, raising my hand. 'So he confessed to the hit and run, right? It wasn't an accident, just so you're clear about that.'

Louise nods. Sighs and takes a breath. 'I bought him things. Everything he could possibly want – a new phone, clothes, food, a laptop. That's where my money was going, why Archie got mad at me.' Louise hangs her head. 'Then, when he wanted to come home to you, I said no. Jo, I wouldn't let him leave. I pretty much kept him prisoner.'

'*What?*' I shake my head, not understanding. 'And what, you expect me to feel sorry for you?'

Louise closes her eyes briefly. 'When he confessed to what he'd done, I... I... and I'm not proud of this, Jo, but I was in way over my head by then. Things weren't good at home with Archie, despite appearances, and my feelings for Will had taken over. I was in love with him. When he told me he wanted to come home to you, that he wanted to be with you, that he missed you... I flipped. I told him that if he left the cottage, left *me*, I'd turn him in to the police and tell them what he'd done. I had his confession recorded and backed up. I even played it back to him to prove I was serious.

'I *wanted* him, Jo. And I wanted him to be with me forever, just the two of us. I'd got it all planned out, our new lives together. I visited as often as I could but Archie was getting suspicious, sensing something was up. And Will was getting... *difficult* about it.'

I clamp my teeth together, glancing at my watch again. I know the minute is up, but I want to hear Louise out. Want to feel the full pain of the betrayal in order to finally let go.

'And then... then I found out I was pregnant. It was about three months after he'd left you. I swear he'd only intended on going away for a weekend at first, to clear his head. But then that turned into a week, which turned into longer when I found out his story. And then the baby... I *blackmailed* him, Jo. Me, a solicitor. A fucking *family* solicitor.'

I swallow, allowing her to carry on. I couldn't speak if I wanted to.

'When I told Will I was pregnant, he went mental. And of course, Archie thought it was his. We'd been trying, after all.'

So had we... I think, saying nothing.

'Truth is, I didn't know whose baby it was. It was fifty-fifty. But it was going to be pretty obvious if it was Will's. And when I realised where you were, Jo, when I told Will everything about Suzanne, what was going on down here, it all fell into place. I'd had enough and couldn't live with myself any longer. I had to tell you everything, do the right thing.'

'Do the right thing?' I say, almost laughing as I take a step closer to Louise. 'Bit late for that by then, wasn't it?' I slip my arm out of Simon's, balling my fists.

'That's why Will was in the car with me. He wanted to see you, to explain everything from his side. I told him I'd go in first, see how things were, talk it over with you and then he would come in too. We'd got it all planned out, how we were going to tell you. I never expected that I'd give birth while I was inside. I had two weeks left to go.'

'Whether he *or* you wanted to "do the right thing", Will is now dead because of your selfishness and...' I look down at the baby. 'And this little boy doesn't have a father any more.' I fight the tears. Refuse to allow them, digging my nails into my palms.

'Which is why I want you to take him,' Louise says. 'I'm not fit to be a mother. I'm broken. I can't work, Archie's left me and I can barely make up a bottle for Jack, let alone look after myself. Which is why I'm here. I saw the funeral notice in the paper. I knew where you'd be.'

Louise picks up the baby carrier again and holds it out to me, her forearms tensing under the weight.

We stare at each other for what seems like forever.

Finally, I look down at the baby – his dark eyes gazing up at me, his fist pushing against his lips as though he's hungry.

He's beautiful, Will, I say to myself. *I'll give you that – you make good babies. But what do I do? Tell me...*

I turn away, partly to hide the tears that are welling and partly because I don't trust myself to look at the baby for a moment longer.

And then I see him. Walking around the side of the crematorium building towards the garden of remembrance. He stops, turns my way and looks directly at me – his shoulders broad within his dark suit, his black tie lying flat against his crisp white shirt, his face cleanly shaven.

Our eyes lock for what seems like eternity, yet it's only a few seconds. In my head, I beg him to say something – *anything* – but Will remains silent.

Instead, he smiles – just a small one but enough for the corners of his eyes to crease, for the dimple to appear in his left cheek. And then he nods. I swear I see him give me a little nod before he finally walks away, disappearing around the corner.

I take a deep breath, turning back to Louise. And, in turn, I give her a small nod too, so small I wonder if she's even noticed.

Then my hands reach out, my fingers spreading to take hold of the handle, my skin brushing against Louise's for just a moment as she grips on, the baby making a snuffling sound between us as I pull the carrier towards me.

A LETTER FROM SAMANTHA

Dear Reader,

Thank you so much for reading *The Happy Couple* – I do hope you enjoyed it as much as I loved writing it! I'm already busy working away on my next book and would love to share my news about upcoming titles with you, so please do sign up at the link below to get all the up-to-date info sent directly to your inbox.

www.bookouture.com/samantha-hayes

The idea for *The Happy Couple* came to me in several parts, as is often the way when I'm starting out with a new book. I have so many ideas filling my mind at any one time (often in the middle of the night!) and I always jot them down in case they come in handy.

In recent months, apart from writing, I've been preoccupied with finding a new home. Suffice it to say, I'm very familiar with Rightmove and other property websites. Of course, being a writer, I'm instinctively 'nosy' (although I prefer 'fascinated'!) and, aside from the house-hunting, I find it intriguing to glimpse inside other people's homes. I can't help imagining who lives there, what their jobs are, why they are moving, what family, friends and interests they have. What their *story* is.

Occasionally, I've seen furniture or decor similar to my own, and on a couple of occasions, I've spotted family photographs on the wall or in the background. And this has set my mind whirring! What if someone saw a picture of someone they knew on a property listing – but, more than that, someone who shouldn't *be* there in the first place… perhaps a missing person. You can probably guess the path my mind then took.

At the time of planning *The Happy Couple*, I'd also been searching for a last-minute holiday. I'd not had one in a long while and really needed a break. Not only that, but around that time I'd been chatting to a group of lovely crime writers and we got on to the subject of house-sitting and how taking care of someone's property while they were away could be a cheap alternative to a holiday. That was the spark that lit the touchpaper.

I did a little investigating and my mind went into overdrive, marrying up the two ideas. I already had my main character, Jo, fleshed out in my mind, along with her story: that her beloved husband had seemingly vanished into thin air – leaving his life behind and no clue to his whereabouts. Fast-forward a year on and Jo is in need of a holiday, convinced by her best friend to try house-sitting. And you know the rest – especially her shock when she sees Will's photos in Suzanne's house online. It was the perfect way to bring Jo's story to life through unrelated things that had happened to me.

For me, that's the best part of writing, and I suppose it's a little like knitting. One length of wool, made up of several different strands, weaves together to make a whole garment. Combine various colours, textures, patterns and shapes and the wool becomes a three-dimensional entity. Character, story, tension, setting, background, subplots, narrative arc… these are some of the knitting pattern equivalents to writing a book.

So that's the essence of how *The Happy Couple* came about. If you enjoyed reading it, it would mean the world to me if you left a quick online review. Reader feedback is so very much appreciated and I love reading your comments – and it also helps other readers when they're looking for their next book.

And if you want to keep in touch, please do join me over on Facebook, Twitter or Instagram – the links are below. Plus I have a website with a bit about me and details of all my other books.

Thanks so much again for reading *The Happy Couple*, and I can't wait to share my next book with you.

Sam x

 samanthahayesauthor

 @samhayes

 @samanthahayes.author

www.samanthahayes.co.uk

ACKNOWLEDGEMENTS

I say it every time, but only because it's one hundred per cent true – my huge thanks and gratitude to my wonderful editor Jessie Botterill for all her hard work and sparkling input. An editor makes a book shine, seeing things the author can't, and Jessie's passion for making my books the very best they can be is like a secret ingredient! The same goes for the entire team at Bookouture – it's a delight to work with such a lovely, talented group of people. And of course, huge thanks to Noelle Holten, Kim Nash and Sarah Hardy for all your hard work getting my books 'out there' – it's so very much appreciated. As is the hard work of Seán, my eagle-eyed copyeditor, who sees things I can't, and likewise Jenny my proof reader, and Lauren for keeping the process running so smoothly! Thank you, all.

Again, big love and thanks to Oli Munson, my agent extraordinaire, and likewise everyone at A. M. Heath… the dream team!

To all the bloggers and reviewers who take the time to read, review, comment and spread the word about my (and many other) books – thank you, thank you, thank you. I love hearing what you think – and I especially love the very creative pictures I'm often tagged in on Instagram! I really appreciate every social media shout-out.

And of course, thanks to you, lovely readers, for taking the time to read this book. I couldn't do what I do without you. I hope you enjoy my work and that my next one will keep you entertained too.

A special thank you to Colin Smith for all your support and laughs. As ever, much love to my dear family, Ben, Polly and Lucy, Avril and Paul, Graham and Marina, and Joe, who have all been such a great support – and are no doubt sick of my house-hunting by now! And last but not least, love and thanks to my dear friend, Deb – maybe it's time we *didn't* 'stop it' after all!

Sam xx